GODSQUAD

HEIDE GOODY

IAIN GRANT

Paperback ISBN: 978-0-9930607-2-4

Ebook ISBN: 978-0-9930607-3-1

www.pigeonparkpress.com
info@pigeonparkpress.com

For Joan.

THE CELESTIAL CITY

T *hwack!*

The laws of physics do not apply to the Celestial City. Nor do the laws of mathematics, logic, reason or common sense. The heavenly home of the blessed dead is a square city, with walls that are forty eight thousand stadia long and yet simultaneously of infinite length. In the physical world its total mass would make it fold in on itself but here in the realm of Heaven, it enjoys a pleasant Earth-like gravity and an endless succession of bright sunny days, even though there was no sun.

Thwack!

In such a place of impossible wonders and infinite variety, the blessed dead can find any scene, setting or arena to suit their tastes. An individual might discover the perfect spot in which to spend their personal eternity or, alternatively, take up an endless quest to find new and strange vistas. Whatever wholesome delights are sought, Heaven is certain to possess them.

Thwack!

Joan of Arc, the Maid of Orleans, peasant girl turned armour-plated military leader turned religious martyr had explored much of the Celestial City. However, if she was said to have a favourite place it would be a certain small garden, where rose bushes thrived in the borders and classical statues of eye-watering beauty dotted the lawn. Enclosed and sheltered from the business of the city behind a tall stone wall and a battered little door so innocuous most people would hardly have registered it, it was possible that no one else even knew of this fragrant corner's existence let alone ever entered it.

That suited Joan's needs perfectly. The last thing she wanted was someone disturbing her.

Thwack!

Joan removed a nymph's pretty head with a backhanded swipe of her broadsword and then turned the blade's motion inward and ran the marble statue through, shattering its torso. Breathing hard, she lowered her blade and looked upon her handiwork. The fragments of statuary on the floor were already rocking and rolling back together.

In Heaven, even this low level desecration of beauty was only temporary. Elsewhere in the city every broken mirror was instantly mended, each spilled cup instantly refilled, each scraped knee instantly healed. The holy restorative powers of the statues in this garden formed part of a particularly vicious circle. The fact that the statues repaired themselves meant that Joan never ran out of targets to practise on. The fact that they refused to stay destroyed only fuelled the discontent and irritation that coursed through her.

Some days, she ran riot around the lawn trying to cut down every statue before any of them were restored. Other days she focussed on just one and continually pounded it into dust, keeping it down for as long as possible. And yet on other days, she gave up the statues and turned her ire on the roses, hacking them apart only to see them grow anew in moments.

Right now, the smug carefree nymph was whole once more. All signs of the damage Joan had wrought here were gone.

"I hate you," Joan told the nymph emphatically.

There was a low, savage growl behind Joan. She turned.

The door to the garden was open. A huge shaggy wolf with a patina of drool across its massive jaws glared at her hungrily.

"Did you escape again?" she said.

The Wolf of Gubbio advanced on her, fangs bared and lips quivering. Joan raised the tip of her sword until it was millimetres from the wolf's nose.

"Really?" she said, one eyebrow raised.

The Wolf of Gubbio gave its position a rethink, sat back on its haunches and scratched itself.

"Better," said Joan.

The Wolf of Gubbio whined.

"No, I understand," she said. "I really do."

Joan lashed out, decapitating a beautiful marble youth before sheathing her sword.

"I think I've got anger management issues too."

The wolf went to have a sniff at the severed marble head.

"I foolishly shared my sense of annoyance at the last committee meeting," said Joan. "Do you know what that monstrous prig St Paul said to me?"

The Wolf of Gubbio tried to take the head in his jaws and slobbered noisily as he failed to gain purchase on its smooth surfaces. Joan took that to be a beastly equivalent of, "No, do tell."

"He suggested that maybe it was my 'time of the month.' Which not only shows that he's a retarded and insensitive chauvinist, but that he fails to grasp the whole point. Besides, if this were a less male-ordained Heaven, there would be no time of the month."

The Wolf of Gubbio gave up on biting the head and settled for licking it to death.

"There's no time in Heaven," said Joan. "I don't have a time of the month. There are no months. Look!" The plates of her gleaming armour rang against one another as she flung a hand out to point at the large sack deposited by the wall. "I've just come back from the annual Heaven/Hell Christmas gift exchange. It's not even really Christmas, wolf. There is no Christmas here."

The marble head began to roll across the grass, back towards the base of its statue. The Wolf of Gubbio pounced on it at once and pinned it to the ground with his wide paws.

"I'm nineteen years old," said Joan. "I've been nineteen years old for centuries. Well, not centuries. There are no centuries. But I've been nineteen for flipping ages. Frozen. Neither one thing or another."

She gazed at the headless youth, the curved outlines of his legs, the smooth undulations of his torso.

"I think I'm missing out on something," she said.

These words sparked a response from the wolf who sat bolt upright and stared at her.

"I'm serious," she said. "Take a look at this."

Joan produced from beneath her steel plackart that most unlikely of items: a computer tablet.

"You've seen *The Breakfast Club*, right?"

The Wolf of Gubbio licked its own nose. Joan flicked through to her movie collection.

"*Pretty in Pink*? *Sixteen Candles*?"

She angled the screen for the wolf to see.

"I mean, you must have seen *Ferris Bueller's Day Off*, right?"

The wolf looked nonplussed but Joan was undeterred.

"All these great films, all about teenagers. They're going out and doing this ... stuff. They're breaking rules, finding their place in the world, falling in love for the first time, leaving their mark and –"

Joan stopped. On the tablet screen, above the image of Ferris Bueller dancing on top of a parade float, a little bell icon was flashing.

She frowned.

"Did Francis send you to fetch me, wolf?" she asked.

The wolf whined. She tapped the icon and a calendar window opened up.

"Oh, cheese and crackers!" she gasped, grabbed the sack of hellish Christmas presents and sprinted out of the garden.

There might be no such thing as time in Heaven but Joan was late nonetheless.

ST FRANCIS, formerly of Assisi, shuffled uneasily in his seat.

"This pwoject is the physical expwession of a most vital piece of scwipture."

"It's insane," said the Venerable Pope Pius XII. "Even more insane than your last attempt, wolves-living-with-lambs insane."

"I beg to differ," said Francis. "We had sevewal successful twials."

"Not before your wolf ate twelve sheep, Francis! Twelve!"

"'The wolf and the lamb will eat together,'" quoted St Paul solemnly from the end of the table.

"See?" said Francis

"Enlighten me," said Pius. "In which verse did Isaiah say the wolf would swallow the lambs whole?"

"Dear fwiend," said Francis, "I understand your concerns. That is why we have moved onto the next phase of the pwoject."

"And how," said the Italian pope, removing his spectacles to massage the bridge of his nose, "how will leopards lying down with goats fare any better?"

"We don't know until we twy, do we?" said Francis.

"Oh, I think we do," fumed Pius.

"Gentlemen," Archangel Gabriel raised his hands to call for calm, "I'm certain we can all see St Francis is attempting to do good work here."

"Are you joking?" said Pius. "He's forcing animals to act against their nature in order to prove the literalness of divine scripture."

"Are you suggesting that the word of the Almighty is not literal truth?" St Paul tapped his fingers warningly.

"I do know that Francis is on a fool's mission," said Pius. "He's even trying to get the lions to eat straw and the serpents to eat dust. You wouldn't think serpents could cry but I've seen them. Miserable things."

"I think we can all see the benefit of a vegetawian diet," said Francis.

"Carnivores eating straw and dust!" snapped Pius. "It's an oxymoron."

On a low stool beside Gabriel's seat, Mother Teresa of Calcutta stopped writing, her quill frozen on the parchment.

Gabriel leaned over to her.

"O – X – Y – M – "

The door to the committee room slammed open and Joan of Arc staggered in, breathless, a bulky sack over her shoulder and the Wolf of Gubbio at her heels.

"I am so sorry," she panted, as she slung the sack under the table and fell into her seat with an audible clang of armour.

"Joan," said Gabriel sternly, "if you wish to maintain your place on Heaven's administrative committee, may I suggest you take your duties a little more seriously."

"Perhaps the role isn't suited to this woman," said St Paul.

"I said, I'm sorry," she said, not at all sorry.

"'I suffer not a woman to teach, nor to usurp authority over the man,'" said St Paul.

"Only a complete narcissist quotes his own letters," snarled Joan.

Mother Teresa gave a little whimper.

"If you can't spell 'narcissist', Teresa," said Joan, "you could just write selfish, arrogant cripple."

"Cripple?" said St Paul.

"Keep talking, buddy," said Joan, resting a meaningful hand on the pommel of her sword.

"Please, please," said Gabriel. "Stop your quarrels. We are now all here and we can return to the items on the agenda."

St Francis, glad that the focus of the committee's scrutiny had moved away from him, regarded the agenda.

"How went the Christmas gift exchange?" asked Gabriel.

"As well as always," said Joan. "We sent gifts of consolation and words of succour to Hell and they have sent us their..." She paused and looked down at the sack beside her. "...their response. I merely need to find members of the faithful to accept them."

St Paul clicked his fingers for Joan to pass him a parcel.

"'Let us not grow weary of doing good,'" he quoted.

Pius shook his head.

"I am uncomfortable with these deals with Hell."

"I'm trying to do something good here. Like Paul says."

"Heaven *is* goodness," said Pius. "We sing our praises to the Almighty and bask in the glory of his boundless love."

"Yes, but I also want to *do* something," said Joan.

"I do think this restlessness is unbecoming," said the archangel.

"What is this thing?"

St Paul had opened the package Joan had given him and now held up a plastic box covered in coloured squares.

"It's called a Rubik's Cube," said Joan.

"And this is one of the tortures Hell has sent us?"

Joan shrugged.

"Apparently. It's a puzzle. You've got to get the little squares to match up so that each side is just one colour."

"A child's toy," said St Paul and began disdainfully twisting the thing.

"Point is," said Joan to Gabriel, "if we're not doing something we're just... waiting. Killing time until Armageddon."

"Ooh," said St Francis, trying to keep up with matters despite the fact that the Wolf of Gubbio had its nose planted firmly in his habit, trying to sniff out his stash of dog treats. "We've got an Armageddon dwill on the agenda. I do like Armageddon dwills."

He saw Joan roll her eyes.

"What?"

"Practising for something that's never going to happen. I just..."

"'But about that day or hour no one knows,'" said St Paul, his attention now more on completing the red side of the cube.

"Quite, do you know which wapture squad you are in, Joan? Do you know where your muster point is? Do you know what you'll do when the end comes?"

"Plant beans." The words escaped before she could trap them in her mouth.

"What?" said Francis, who had finally relented and given the wolf every biscuit in his pocket.

"Nothing," she said. "Now, what's this on the agenda? NSPAU incident?"

"Perhaps the main item for our discussion today," said Gabriel. He waved his arm and the door opened. "Come in, gentlemen."

Both of the saints who entered the room had a little trouble with the door. St Christopher was a burly giant of a man, a full head higher than any normal man, with shoulders and arms so muscly it looked as if his tunic was stuffed with pillows. St Thomas Aquinas was a squat, tonsured monk who had clearly enjoyed too many monastic feasts in his lifetime. If Christopher had pillows up his sleeves then Thomas had a whole duvet wrapped around his waist.

"Christopher is one of our operators in the NSPAU," said Gabriel.

"Enspow?" said Joan.

"The Non-Specific Prayer Assessment Unit," said Gabriel.

Francis clicked his fingers in understanding.

"The 'ohgodohgodhelpme' helpline," he said.

"We don't call it that," corrected Gabriel.

"Yes, we do," said St Christopher, sitting down on a chair that creaked under his bulk.

"I don't think I've seen you around in a while, Chris," said Joan.

"Aye. That'll be on account of me no longer existing," said Christopher.

"Weally?" said Francis.

"Pope Paul VI – the bastard – declared there was no historical evidence for my existence."

"Pope Paul VI," said Francis. "I've not seen him in a long time either."

"That may be on account of him being too frightened to leave his apartments these days," said Pius.

"Hey," said Christopher. "I just want a quiet word with the feller. That's all."

Gabriel made an unhappy noise.

"You spend all your spare time standing in the street outside his house, crushing rocks with your hands."

"Man's got to have a hobby," Christopher grinned broadly. The former patron saint of traveller's smile was like a wedge of sunshine in his brutish monolithic face.

"As I'm sure you all know, NSPAU handles any prayers from Earth not directed at any particular intercessionary figure," said Gabriel. "Our team of operators, which includes many deleted saints like Christopher here, handles those prayers, responds appropriately according to our in-house scripts and either closes the call or passes it onto a higher authority."

"Sterling work," said Francis.

"Bloody boring," said Christopher.

"Anyway," said Gabriel, "Christopher took a rather unsettling call recently."

"Aye," said Christopher. "It came from this feller, Simon.

Right panicky he was. Told me he was going to kill some people, kill lots of people."

"Trust me, we get a lot of those," said Gabriel. "Killers with a conscience, the mentally deranged, the 'I am the angel of vengeance' crowd."

"I talked him through the script," said Christopher.

"So you actually speak to those who pway?" asked Francis.

"They hear it in their subconscious mind, the voice of their conscience. I talked him through. He seemed to calm down and the call ended. Nothing unusual there. Only problem came when I went to sort Simon's paperwork."

"What problem was that?" asked Joan.

Christopher gave her an uncomfortable look.

"Simon doesn't exist, flower," he said. "There's no such person. We had a location for the prayer – Toulon in southern France, if I recall – but no actual person there."

There was a reflective silence, eventually broken by Pope Pius.

"You are going to have to explain that to me again. You spoke to an individual who does not exist?"

"To be specific," said Gabriel, "Christopher engaged with a person who either does not exist or does not have a soul. Heaven trades in souls, not crude physical bodies. Our soul-tracker system is aware of every soul in creation. Whoever Christopher spoke to, this 'Simon' figure is not, or does not have, a soul."

"Is such a thing possible?" said Francis.

"I believe this is where I come in," announced St Thomas

Aquinas sonorously. "I was invited here to offer my opinions on all things animated and pneumatic."

Francis gave Joan a puzzled glance.

"I think he's into cartoons and inflatables," she whispered across the table.

"I am an expert on souls," St Thomas corrected her loudly. "And I can tell you all that the situation described by our mythical saint here is impossible. The soul or *anima* exists in all living things, be it plant, animal or human, but only humans possess an immortal soul. Ensoulment takes place within the womb, at the fortieth day of pregnancy in boys, on the eightieth day in girls."

"Really?" frowned Joan. "Why do girls get theirs later?"

St Paul sat forward to speak, although his eyes were fixed firmly on the Rubik's Cube in his hands.

"And if you're going to say anything sexist," said Joan quickly, "I will stick this sword where the sun doesn't shine."

"Scotland?" said Francis.

St Paul humphed.

"All I was going to say – fiddlesticks! Now the blue one's gone round to the other side! – was: 'the Lord formed a man from the dust of the ground and breathed into him the breath of life'—"

"The *pneuma*, the spirit, the soul," agreed St Thomas.

"—'and the man *became* a living being.'"

"Indeed," said St Thomas. "To have a soul is to be alive. To be alive is to have a soul. One without the other is impossible."

"I think we can all see the serious problem we're facing," said Gabriel. "Either—" He paused and looked down at the meeting minutes. "No, Teresa, it's a silent 'p'. P – N – as in... well, as in 'pneuma'. I don't make the rules, do I?" The archangel struggled to remember where he was up to.

"Either?" said Joan.

"Yes, either there is a person called Simon who has no soul which then contradicts Heaven's understanding of all reality, or Simon *does* have a soul and Heaven cannot see it."

"Or Simon doesn't exist at all," suggested Francis.

"Which means Heaven has gone crazy and is inventing people to talk to."

"Whatever the case, Heaven's infallibility is at stake," agreed Pius solemnly.

"There is one more thing," said Christopher. "Simon's prayer was actually directed to a specific individual."

"Who?" asked Francis.

"Mary. The Blessed Virgin."

"For crying out loud!" shouted St Paul.

Everyone looked at him. St Paul held up the puzzle cube.

"Look! I've just got the red side sorted and I'm putting the green one together and now this one's right over here! How am I going to get it back?"

"Where is the Holy Mother?" asked Joan.

Gabriel dragged his stony stare away from St Paul.

"We don't know," he said. "She's refusing to respond to our calls. She's hiding."

"Refusing? Hiding?"

The look on Gabriel's face was one of embarrassment, coupled with annoyance and overshadowed by worry.

"Mary is a law unto herself."

"But no one is above Heaven's control."

"She is the Mother of God, Joan. Only the Almighty stands above her. Do you think we give her dispensation to do all those visitations and apparitions? She's all over the shop."

There were general murmurs of agreement around the table.

"That time she appeared on a slice of toast," said St Francis disapprovingly.

"Or in that bush in Philadelphia," agreed Pius.

"What about that image in the oil spill in Milan?" said St Thomas.

The others nodded in good natured condemnation.

"Very silly," said Pius.

"So where was the Divine Mother the last time we looked?" asked Francis.

"Northern Europe," said Gabriel. "Holland, we think. Possibly Amsterdam."

"Never heard of it," said Francis.

"A city of canals and florists," said Pius with a dismissive wave of his hand. "An insignificant backwater. Nonetheless, it is clear that someone must go there."

"Is it?" said Francis.

"Whether she holds any answers to this mystery or not, it is high time that the Holy Mother be made aware of her responsibilities. Someone should go to Amsterdam, find Mary, and either bring her back here or take her directly to Toulon to resolve this issue with this impossible Simon character."

Several people started speaking at once.

"Twavel across the Earth like mortals?"

"We cannot act on this without consulting the Almighty."

"Two sides! I've got two sides!"

Mother Teresa's minutes became, for a moment, a frenzied spasm of incomprehensible squiggles.

"Please," said Gabriel, waving his hands for calm. "Please. First of all, I have already taken this matter before the Throne of the Almighty and, as is his wont, He has kept his counsel to Himself."

"He said nothing at all?" said St Francis.

"Silence itself is an answer," said St Thomas.

"Secondly," said the archangel, "I think Pius's suggestion is a good one."

"Thank you."

"And I think Joan should be the one to find Mary and bring her back."

Joan sat bolt upright with a dull clank.

"What?"

Gabriel smiled at her. The smile of an angel could be a beautiful and terrible thing.

"You did say you wanted to get out and 'do' something," he said, slinging air quotes around the significant verb.

Francis watched the teenage saint's mouth work silently for a moment or two.

"I did," she said slowly.

"Sadly, we'd have to manage without you while you were away," Gabriel's voice appeared tinged with regret. "Someone else might have to manage your vital projects in your absence."

"I mean, I could go," said Joan, warming to the idea. "But Amsterdam? Toulon? I've never been to these place and I was never a well travelled person. Will there be wildernesses to cross? Forests and mountains and such? Wild beasts to contend with?"

"Wild beasts?" said Francis, his interest piqued.

"Then perhaps some suitably qualified individual should go with you."

St Christopher coughed gently and smiled.

"I could go," said Francis.

"Really?" said Gabriel. "This mission appeals to you?"

"As some members of this committee are so dispawaging about my Heavenly work with the Lord's cweatures" – he fixed Pius with a hard stare as he said this – "then perhaps I should weturn to Earth to observe animals in the wild once more. Wefwesh my perspectives, or whatever it is people say these days."

Christopher coughed again, louder this time.

"It is clear that our Joan needs a most experienced traveller with her —"

"I went on a pilgwimage to Jewusalem in 1212," said Francis.

"Your boat sank," said Christopher.

"But I made a journey to Mowocco the following year," Francis countered.

"Which you called off because the Spanish food disagreed with your delicate constitution."

"But I later went to spwead my gospel in Fwance."

"But the pope refused to let you leave Italy."

"I've still twavelled more than you!"

"I'm the bloody patron saint of travel!"

"You were! And a fat lot of good you did me when I needed you!"

"Enough!" shouted Gabriel.

Francis and Christopher fell silent. Gabriel looked to Mother Teresa.

"I think it's one 'r' and two 'c's. We should really invest in a dictionary for you."

The committee waited patiently for Teresa's pen to catch up. Apart from the scritch-scratch of her quill, the only sounds were the furious clicking of St Paul's Rubik's Cube and the quieter sound of the Wolf of Gubbio shredding St Francis's pockets in search of biscuit crumbs.

"So, I think it's decided then," said Gabriel finally.

"It is?" said Joan.

"Yes. You are to go as soon as is practicable and both St Francis and St Christopher are to accompany you."

The three saints looked at one another.

"Any objections?" said Gabriel.

St Paul screamed in fury and flung the Rubik's Cube far away, and then got up almost instantly afterwards to retrieve it.

"Good," said Gabriel. "That's settled then."

St Christopher did his best to contain his excitement, fearing that if he let anyone see his joy at escaping the NSPAU call centre and treading the good honest Earth once more, they would somehow snatch it away from him. During the days of preparation, he forcibly maintained a blunt and surly demeanour and only burst into a toothy grin and heavy-footed tap dance when no one was looking.

He was so buoyant that he even managed to enjoy much of St Thomas Aquinas's seminar on what to expect of Earth in the twenty-first century.

St Thomas had brought the three saints to one of Heaven's many public theatres. This particular one was small with plush red velvet seats and a screen in front of the stage for showing moving picture shows. Joan had brought with her a blonde-haired woman he did not recognise. Christopher assumed it was a woman, although she appeared to be wearing the dog collar of an Anglican priest, which made no sense at all.

St Thomas, wobbled out onto the stage and pointed at the blonde woman.

"Who is this?"

"Evelyn Steed."

St Thomas pulled a face and shrugged.

"She is my friend," said Joan. "And she is one of the recently deceased."

"But she's not going with you," said St Thomas.

"But, as one of the recently deceased, she might have some insights to offer at this discussion," said Joan.

St Thomas frowned.

"This is not a discussion, mademoiselle. This is a seminar. As in seminary. I am going to plant the seeds of knowledge in your minds. I shall inseminate you and you will be grateful that I have."

The woman, Evelyn, sniggered and immediately apologised.

"I'm sorry. Mind in the gutter. Do go on."

St Thomas scowled at her for a moment and then waved to the projection booth at the back of the theatre. A colourful map of Europe appeared on the screen.

"This is Holland," said Thomas, pointing with a long cane. "Mary's last known location."

"A war-torn region in my lifetime," said Joan. "The Hooks and the Cods and then that nasty business with the Burgundians and the Habsburgs."

"Holland is now ruled by a vast empire known as the European Union or EU," said Thomas.

"Not an empire as such," said Evelyn.

"An *empire*," said St Thomas firmly, "with its capital in Brussels."

"And who is their emperor?"

"It is hard to tell for certain," said St Thomas as a picture of various men and women in tight-fitting suits appeared on the screen. "It might be this Belgian. Or this Spaniard. Frankly, it could be any of the people in this picture."

"How can people not know?" asked Francis.

"Because Europe is a democracy," said Evelyn. "It changes."

"Democwacy?" said Francis with a sour look on his face. "Like the ancient Gweeks?"

"Democracy or not," said St Thomas, "many regard *this* Hamburg woman as the de facto empress of Europe."

Joan snorted.

"The Germanic peoples have always had a thirst for power," she said.

"That's not true," said Evelyn.

A fresh picture appeared on the screen. Evelyn sighed.

"Well, yes, Hitler. Of course, Hitler. You'd have to bring him up, wouldn't you? But not all Germans are like him."

"Holland, France and all of Western Europe have been at peace for over half a century," said St Thomas. "The last war was started by this man."

"Ooh! Ooh!" said Joan excitedly. "I know this one! That was the one when all the Jews hid inside wardrobes."

Evelyn glared at her friend.

"I loaned you that book, about possibly the darkest moment in all human history and *that's* what you took away from it? I despair."

"*However*," said St Thomas, loudly, "despite the peace, the weapons of war that these countries possess grow ever more powerful."

"Spears with extra spiky bits?" suggested Christopher.

"Bigger bows?" offered Francis.

"Cannons," said St Thomas. "Guns."

"Guns?"

The saints recoiled as a cacophony of noise and violence exploded across the screen. Christopher could not even comprehend what was happening to the helmeted men and the fiery metal amulets in their hands. Francis squealed and covered his ears.

"Weapons that cause disease," continued St Thomas. "Alchemical poisons. And, most terrible of all, explosives of devastating force."

The roars and bangs were gone, the screen now displaying scenes of a city, utterly destroyed.

"You've just segued from *The Matrix* to the aftermath of Hiroshima," muttered Evelyn.

"Is there a problem with that?" said Joan.

"I couldn't even begin to explain."

"The great powers of Earth possess enough of these nuclear weapons to kill every living thing on the planet," said St Thomas.

"Impossible," said Christopher.

"They must all be sick with wowwy," said Francis.

"There's more to worry about than that," said Evelyn. "The Earth is heating up. The ice in the far north and south are melting. The sea is rising up and drowning the low lying regions of the world."

"What is causing this?" asked Joan.

"Sin, I'd reckon," said Christopher.

St Thomas nodded.

"I concur. The unnatural heat of human sinning."

"No, you great pillock," said Evelyn. "It's caused by the increase of carbon dioxide in the atmosphere."

"What is 'carbony upside'?" asked Joan.

"It's a kind of pasta," said Francis.

"Not a sin?" said Christopher.

Evelyn got to her feet and turned to address them all.

"Carbon dioxide is a gas. It's causing the Earth to heat up. The planet is now continually wracked by freak weather events. Storms. Droughts. Floods."

"Are the storms caused by sin?" asked Christopher.

"No."

"Are you sure? I hear there's a lot of nudity on Earth these days. That generally causes people to feel hot and tempestuous."

"No."

"So, they're all wowwying about the floods and the storms and that," said Francis.

"Well, no, most of them are worrying about guarding what little they have," said Evelyn. "There are over seven billion people on Earth and not enough resources to satisfy them all."

Christopher laughed along with Francis.

"Now, dear woman," said St Thomas, "we can all tell when you're pulling our legs. Seven billion. That's impossible."

"Continual population growth. And, yes, that is possibly caused by sin. Some of it."

"But there are natural forces to keep the population in check," said St Thomas. "Disease. Plague."

"Man has medicines to deal with most of those. Bubonic plague is no more. No one's contracted small pox in decades."

"So, there is no more disease?" asked Joan.

"Well, no. We still have some old favourites and a few new ones. Oh, and before anyone even says it, I will beat to a bloody pulp anyone who says *they* are caused by sin."

"Wasn't going to say anything," said Christopher hurriedly.

"If there's any root cause to the suffering and poverty on Earth," said Evelyn, "it's the inequality between the haves and the have-nots. Fortunately for you, Holland and France are in the technologically advanced and generally safe land of the haves."

"Ah, yes," said St Thomas. "If you'll take a seat, woman, I was going to say a few words about the advances in engineering and the natural sciences."

Christopher tried extraordinarily hard to follow St Thomas's explanation of the great inventions and leaps in understanding that mankind had made in recent centuries. Laszlo Biro's never-ending writing stick was astounding. The Breville sandwich toaster seemed both an obvious idea and yet simultaneously magical. He got a little lost when St Thomas talked about the slinky and an argument erupted when Evelyn contested that the slinky was not invented by Barnes Wallis to blow up German dams in World War Two. Following that, Christopher was utterly lost, and had no idea what the purpose of the pogo stick was or whether the Dustbuster was a weapon or an essential item for the maintenance of Furbies (whatever they were).

"And, of course, modern man can no longer survive without the aid of the internet," said St Thomas.

"What's that?" said Francis.

"It's the repository of all human knowledge. It's where I acquired the images for this presentation."

"So it's like a libwawy? Or a picture gallewy?"

"Yes, but one that is simultaneously in all places at all times."

"I can get in on my tablet," said Joan, waving her magic moving mirror at Christopher.

"It looks like witchcraft to me," said Christopher.

"And what is this internet thing made of?" asked Francis.

"Cats," said St Thomas, "Mostly cats. And naked women."

"Earth is insane!" Christopher declared, his confusion close to tipping over into terror. "Show us something we can comprehend. What of transport in the third millennium?"

"Most people drive horseless carriages or 'cars.'" St Thomas clicked one on the screen.

"Right," said Christopher, slowly regaining his calm. "I know about these."

"Everyone has one," said St Thomas. "They are very fast but can be dangerous."

"And produce a lot of harmful carbon dioxide," added Evelyn.

"That's the sinful pasta that's causing all the storms?" said Christopher.

"Yes," said Evelyn tiredly. "Why not?"

"And then there's trains, right?" said Christopher.

"Very good," said St Thomas.

"What are they?" asked Francis.

"They're like very big cars that run on rails for when lots of people all want to go to the same place."

"Like on a cwusade to the Holy Land?"

"That sort of thing, yes."

"By the way, which of the faithful controls the Holy Land now?" asked Christopher.

"The Jews," said St Thomas.

Francis pulled a surprised face.

"Wouldn't have been my first guess. Or my second."

"The religious situation on Earth is a complex one these

days," said St Thomas. "There's this thing they call 'diversity.'"

"What's that?"

"It means people can believe what they want," said Evelyn. "And that's a good thing."

"In your travels," said St Thomas, "you may encounter Christians, Muslims, Jews but also Hindus, Buddhists, Pastafarians and Jedis."

"What's that man holding?" asked Christopher, pointing at the screen.

"It's a lightsaber," said Evelyn.

"Is that one of the nuclear weapons?" asked Joan.

"No. It's not really real. There aren't any real Jedis."

St Thomas made a loud humphing noise.

"That's simply enough, madam. You're not only willing to argue with the evidence of your own eyes but dare to contradict my authority on matters religious and spiritual?"

"Listen, Tom," said Evelyn hotly. "Your five proofs for God's existence were inspired and we all appreciate your work on Just War theory but this is my world we're talking about and, as a Church of England rector, I think I am just as qualified as you to —"

"Wait a minute," said Christopher. "You weally are a pwiest?"

"And you're a woman?" said Francis.

Evelyn seized her dog collar.

"I'm not wearing this for a bet, boys. It's the twenty-first century. Sisters are doing it for themselves."

"Doing what for themselves?" asked Christopher.

"Everything. Thinking for themselves. Making decisions for themselves. Earning a living for themselves."

"Like pwostitutes?"

"Not like prostitutes, Francis. Women can be anything they want to be."

"Well, not anything," said Christopher, failing to keep a note of ridicule out of his voice. "Not soldiers or teachers or doctors or—"

"Anything!" Evelyn poked at her own lower torso. "Just because I've got a uterus, doesn't mean I'm some hysterical and helpless creature."

"Isn't that exactly what it means?" said St Thomas with a frown. "Hippocrates showed that the female hysteria is caused by the uterus moving through different parts of the body."

"What? Like some alien parasite? Jeez!" Evelyn had started to turn an interesting shade of red. "I can't believe you're so backward. Wandering womb theory is as stupid as bleeding the sick, the healing powers of kings and the idea that disease is caused by bad smells."

"Isn't it?" said Francis.

"You men are going down to Earth," said Evelyn. "And Joan is leading you. If there's one thing you need to get into your tiny Neanderthal brains, it's that women are every bit the equal of men and that you'd better get your sexist attitudes up to date, pronto!"

The silence that followed was long and profound. Evelyn, clearly buzzing with passion, stiffly sat down next to Joan.

"No, no, she's right," said St Thomas, eventually, quietly. "Women are generally regarded as equal to men in the modern world. And, since the Rosa Parks incident in 1955, they're also allowed to ride on buses."

"That's not quite right..." Evelyn began but she was too spent to argue further.

"What is a bus?" asked Francis.

"It's a vehicle," said Christopher. "Bigger than a car but smaller than a train."

"For when you want to go on a small cwusade, perhaps?"

"To the shops and such."

"And what are shops?"

"Right. Shops," said St Thomas as a fresh set of pictures appeared on the screen.

When the knock came on her apartment door, Joan was pleased to see that it was Evelyn, not least because it gave her the chance to thank her for her supportive (if occasionally incoherently angry) words at St Thomas's briefing.

Evelyn shrugged.

"Just looking out for a mate," she said. "Now, are you all prepared?"

"Gabriel is organising the money and equipment we might need."

"As long as he's not sending you down there with horses and a baggage train."

"I'm sure we'll be thoroughly modern and inconspicuous," said Joan. "I suggested that he give us a car. I would dearly love to have a Ferrari, like in *Ferris Bueller's Day Off*. Have you seen that film?"

"Not as often as you, no. Besides, you can't drive and a Ferrari is far from inconspicuous. You've got maps. Good. And you're taking your tablet."

"I assume it will work on Earth."

"Yes, although you will actually need to charge it from time to time. On Earth, stuff runs on electricity, not prayers and wishes."

Joan could see Evelyn shifting uncomfortably from foot to foot.

"Is something wrong?" she asked.

Evelyn grimaced.

"You and I have talked about Earth, the Earth of the present day."

"It fascinates me," smiled Joan.

Evelyn took a deep breath.

"I'm worried for you. Earth, even Holland or France or wherever, has its dangers. It's not... it's not Heaven."

Joan gave little shake of her head as though to cast off Evelyn's concerns.

"I did spend nineteen years down there. Nineteen years of mud and illness and injury and, in the end, excruciating pain. I think I can handle Holland."

"But that's it," said Evelyn, placing a hand on Joan's arm greave. "The dangers of the modern world are subtler, more insidious. It's a cynical world. There's not a lot of faith or honesty going round."

"Are you telling me that everyone on Earth is wicked?"

"No. Of course not. Most people are wonderful, flawed human beings. But the bad ones will be drawn to you. And, yes, it's because you are young, pretty and far too naïve for your own good."

"Is this about men, Evelyn? I have met men."

"No, it's not just men. Okay, it's mostly men. It's just, I've got some words of advice for you, that's all."

"Go for it."

"One: If someone says something to you, they probably don't mean it."

"They're lying?"

"No. Not necessarily. Not always. There's this thing called sarcasm. It's like sort of making a point by saying the exact opposite of what you mean."

"That's ridiculous."

"Well, be glad you're not going to Britain because their sarcasm switch is jammed in the on position."

"Are you being sarcastic now?"

"Who can say? Two: Just because you're right, doesn't mean you're right. Truth and goodness do not prevail."

"But they should."

"Doesn't matter. Three: Do not argue with anyone wearing a badge or carrying a gun. And definitely do not argue with anyone who has both."

"Got it."

"And look." Evelyn passed Joan two pieces of folded notepaper. "I've written down some phrases. If anyone says any on this first list to you, walk away. Do not stop to think, do not wait to see what happens. Walk away and don't look back."

"Sure," said Joan. "And what if anyone says any off the second list?"

Evelyn gave her a sad smile.

"Punch them in the face and *run*."

"Sure thing," said Joan.

"We need to get you to the gate. You're going to be late."

Joan looked out of the apartment window, at a city of white stone basking in sunless sunlight.

"There's no time in Heaven," she said. "And there's someone I need to speak to first."

THE ALMIGHTY IS EVERYWHERE. He is both transcendent and immanent. He is omnipresent, in all places and at all times.

Nonetheless, Joan went to visit Him.

At the heart of the Celestial City was the Empyrium, the seat of the Holy Throne room. And in the Holy Throne room, on a dais of a hundred marble steps, was the Holy Throne. And atop the Throne sat the Almighty, his glory so bright that Joan could barely raise her eyes to gaze upon Him.

"Lord," she said, on bended knee, "I have been entrusted with this mission to Earth. I have been told it could be dangerous and I am ready to face those dangers." She licked her lips nervously. "But, in all your wisdom and power, you could find the answers you seek in but a moment. Is there a need for this... this charade?"

The brilliance of the Almighty's glory shifted, expanding and receding.

"I understand, Lord," said Joan. "But Mary... Maybe if she doesn't want to be found, we should leave her alone. She is..."

puissant. If anyone is to bring her home, perhaps it should be yourself."

Light flared and curled, making fresh shadows around Joan.

"Of course," she said. "But am I the right person? Am I doing this to satisfy my own need for purpose and action? I have been self-centred and put my own desires above what is right. Is there no one more suited to this task than I?"

The glory of the Almighty pulsed and flickered, a spectrum of colours washing over the teenage saint.

"Thank you, Lord," said Joan, rising slowly. "That was all I needed to know."

THEY MET at the wall of the city before a simple wooden door that had not been there the day before. The Archangel Gabriel watched approvingly as angels of a lower order gave each of the three travellers a cloth bag containing such riches and supplies as they would need.

"The last address we have for Mary," Gabriel handed a slip of paper to Joan, "a street called Bastenakenstraat in Amsterdam. You might pick up some clues if you go there."

Joan nodded.

"We shall be watching. When your mission is completed, you shall be brought back."

"And if we don't succeed?" said France.

"Heaven is patient. We will of course be able to hear your prayers but, apart from that, you will be alone."

"And we will have real bodies on Earth?" asked

Christopher. "Real human bodies. We won't just be wandering shades?"

"Real bodies. This is an incarnation, not a visitation."

An angel stood on tiptoes to whisper something in the archangel's ear.

"So what happens if we're killed on Earth?" asked Joan.

"What happens if we sin?" asked Francis.

"Were you planning on sinning?" said Joan.

"Just a little concerned that some of us" – and Francis's tone made it clear that he didn't include himself in that group – "might jeopardise our place in Heaven."

"Just look after yourselves," said Gabriel. "And be good. I think our only real concern is with Christopher."

"What?" said the giant saint.

The whispering angel gave him a cheerful smile.

"You see, you're a non-historical figure. The only reason you exist in Heaven is because the faithful have previously asserted your existence. And as it is on Earth—"

"—so shall it be in Heaven," said Christopher. "Yes, yes. So?"

"Well," said the angel, "you're going back to Earth now."

"Yes."

"And you didn't ever truly exist there and so..."

"So?"

"You might vanish from existence the moment you step through the gate."

Christopher waved his arms around in apoplectic annoyance.

"And you couldn't have mentioned this earlier?"

"This is Heaven, time doesn't exist. There was no earlier."

Joan shrugged, stepped forward and opened the wooden door. A white luminous mist swirled in the emptiness beyond.

"It's not too late to back out."

"It might be," Christopher whined. "The folks at NSPAU gave me a leaving party. There was cake and everything."

"Then we're set," said Joan and walked through.

The brightness of the mist forced Joan to shield her eyes for a moment or two. When she opened them again and her vision had cleared, she found herself in a stall with gaily-painted wooden walls. Directly behind her was an uncomfortable looking stool fashioned from white china. The stall was tiny and she was alone.

"Hello?" she called out.

"Hello?" came Francis's equally confused voice from somewhere off to one side.

Joan undid the bolt on the door in front of her and squeezed out into a larger room. The cubicle she had emerged from was one of four along one wall of the room. Opposite was a row of washing basins and mirrors. There was a faintly unsavoury whiff in the air.

"Shhh, stay boy," whispered Francis from one of the other stalls and then there was the click of the door unlocking and Francis emerged.

The two of them looked at their surroundings and at each other.

"I suspect this might be some form of lavatorium," ventured Francis.

"Ah," nodded Joan. "Where is Christopher?"

They looked at the two remaining stalls. There was no

sound from within either. Joan carefully rapped on the doors.

"Christopher?"

"Go away," snapped a gravelly voice.

"That doesn't sound like Chwistopher."

"What's happened to him?"

Joan's mind was flooded with dreadful images. What if Christopher hadn't come through from Heaven unscathed? What if he had only *half* come through? And which half? The top half? The left half? Or had he become a horrifically reduced perversion of his former self?

Joan raised an iron-shod foot and kicked the door in, shattering the flimsy lock.

The bearded man squatting on the china seat with his trousers round his ankles gave a throttled gasp of surprise and tried to use the newspaper he was reading to cover his indignity.

"What are you doing?" he wailed. "Can't a man crap in peace? And you!" He waved his newspaper momentarily at Joan. "This is the gents! Take your fancy dress party somewhere else!"

The man, quite skilfully, swung the door shut with his foot whilst still hiding his embarrassment.

Joan and Francis looked at one another.

"So..."

The door of the final cubicle clicked open and Christopher stepped through, punching the air with his two meaty fists.

"I. Am. Alive!" he crowed joyfully.

"Wight," said Francis, "so does anybody know where we are?"

Joan shrugged.

"Let's go find out."

She led the way out of the lavatorium or 'gents' and into a wide low-ceiling room, dotted with plush chairs and tables and filled with dozens of men, women and children. Joan felt a strange feeling in her stomach, a soup of excitement, fear and wonder. The three of them stood huddled slightly together, gazing in something akin to reverence.

"So, this is Earth," said Joan, her voice barely above a whisper.

"Look at them," said Christopher. "Their clothes. The colours."

"And they're all so *clean*," said Francis.

"And there's carpet," said Joan, treading up and down on the vibrant, abstract pattern.

"You had carpet in your day, surely?" said Francis.

"But it's *everywhere*."

"It's beautiful."

"But what is this place?" said Christopher.

Joan pouted in thought, taking in the uniformed people behind a counter and the range of drinks and packaged foods the people were eating.

"It's some kind of tavern," she said.

"Some of these women aren't wearing very much," said Christopher. "What is that one wearing?"

"I think it's called a rude tube," said Joan and immediately felt that she had it a little wrong.

"It certainly looks quite rude. Perhaps this is a bawdyhouse."

Francis had his arms out at his sides and his head tilted to one side.

"Is it me, fwiends, or are we moving?"

Joan was about to admonish his foolishness but stopped. There did seem to be a thrumming sensation beneath her feet and the feeling that the world was gently tilting.

"A castle built on shifting sands?" said Christopher.

Joan frowned and walked slowly over to one of the many broad windows in the room.

"Oh, criminey!" she gasped.

"It's the sea!" said Francis.

"And we're so high!" said Christopher. "A castle in the sea."

"The wising sea levels," nodded Francis.

"Sinful pasta," agreed Joan.

"Or..." said Christopher slowly, uncertainly, "we could be on a ship."

Francis blew out his lips.

"A ship this big?"

"Don't you remember the Titanic?"

"No. What's that?"

Christopher pulled a face.

"Probably not the best time to mention it, not one of my finest moments."

～

FRANCIS WAS SURPRISED to discover that Christopher was correct. A little bit of exploration and reading of signs informed them that they were on *The Pride of Yorkshire*, a North Sea ferry taking passengers from Kingston-Upon-Hull in England to the port of Zeebrugge in somewhere called Belgium. The statistics were either bald-faced lies or so mind-boggling as to be beyond comprehension.

"Twelve decks?" Francis wasn't convinced.

"Weighs sixty thousand tons?" said Joan, equally incredulous.

"Over a thousand passengers," Christopher tried not to worry.

"This world..." said Joan. "Maybe there are seven billion people on Earth now..."

"...if wondwous floating cities like this are commonplace," nodded Francis.

They came upon an external door and stepped out onto the outer deck. The cold wind slapped Francis in the face with a startling freshness he had not experienced in centuries.

"Blimey!" he said, as the stiff breeze whipped around, through and under his habit. "That is bwacing!"

They stepped to the railing and over the steely blue sea. Joan shuddered and grinned.

"That's sharp," she said. "So chill it almost.."

"...hurts," said Francis.

Joan nodded.

"Not in a bad way but it..."

"...hurts."

Francis looked at Joan's reddening cheeks and could see the wind had brought tears to her eyes.

"I'd forgotten what pain was," she said.

"We forget," he replied.

"Oh, cheese and crackers! What in Heaven's name is that doing here?"

Francis looked and his stomach flipped.

"I told you to wait in the cubicle," he hissed.

The Wolf of Gubbio shook itself, its shaggy fur tousled by the wind, and gave Francis a look which clearly said that this particular wolf did not hang around in toilet cubicles for any man.

"You brought the wolf!" exclaimed Christopher.

"Why?" cried Joan. "In the name of all that's holy, why?"

Francis went and stood beside his savage pet.

"He's never weally liked Heaven. We're going to be twavelling across the gweat wilds of Euwope. Wide open spaces. Dark fowests. It'll do him good."

"I can't believe you've been so reckless," said Christopher.

"You've already put our entire mission in jeopardy," Joan added.

"It's not that big a pwoblem."

Joan's furious gaze said otherwise.

"Not a problem? Not a... I'm going back to Heaven right now," she said coldly. "And I'll tell them what you've done. Your little holiday is over."

The Wolf of Gubbio whined and then Francis realised it wasn't the wolf but himself.

As Joan stomped back inside, Christopher patted Francis on the shoulder.

"You are a knuckle-brain, mate," he said kindly. "Let's go get some grub while we wait for Heaven's judgement."

With the Wolf of Gubbio at their heels, Francis let Christopher steer him back into the tavern place and to the food counter. Christopher called for the serving wench's attention but she ignored him, even when he clicked his fingers at her and whistled.

"Come on," he said. "I'm bloody starving."

"Excuse me," called Francis.

The young woman drifted over. She looked Francis up and down, clearly taken by his rough-woven Franciscan habit.

"We would like some food," said Francis.

"What can I get you?" she smiled.

"Do you have jugged venison?"

The woman frowned.

"Or some game tart?"

"I'm sorry. We only have what's on the menu."

"Not even some forced gwuel? Or sops?"

"Only what's on the menu."

Francis peered at the large printed sign behind the woman. The names of the food items were meaningless nonsense. What was a 'tuna melt'? Or a 'cottage pie'? 'Curly fries' sounded sinister and a 'kid's selection box' sounded like goat offal.

"Do you have a Breville sandwich toaster?" suggested Christopher helpfully but the woman paid him no attention.

Francis opened his purse and laid two gold florins on the counter.

"My friend and I just want something wholesome and tasty. Whatever you recommend."

The wench picked up one of the heavy gold coins and inspected it critically.

"What are these?" she said.

Francis was about to explain when there was a tap on his shoulder. A man in a white shirt, with a thin patterned cravat tied around his neck and a clipboard in his hand, pointed at the Wolf of Gubbio.

"Is this your dog, sir?"

"It is."

"You know that animals are not allowed out of the kennels during the crossing?"

"Do I?"

The man jotted something down on his clipboard.

"Could I see your ticket and passport, sir?"

"Ticket?"

"And passport."

Francis looked helplessly at Christopher.

"What's a passport?"

"I think it's some sort of papers. Is that right, mate?"

The man was not listening.

"You do have a passport, don't you, sir?"

Francis could tell from the tone of the man's voice that to not have a passport would be a very bad thing. He grinned.

"I'm sure I do. Somewhere. What do they look like?"

The man sighed.

"Don't play games, sir."

Christopher cast about.

"A passport. You need documents, Francis."

"I know," said Francis.

"You know what, sir?" said the man.

Christopher grinned. "You need *travel* documents."

He clapped his hands and something was suddenly thrust into Francis's hand. Francis looked at the small purple booklet and length of stiff card he held.

"I knew I had them somewhere," he said hopefully, holding them out to the man as an offering.

The official scrutinised the items.

"Thank you, Mr D'Assisi. Now, we might not be far from port but we must return your... what breed of dog is this?"

"A wolf... hound," said Francis. "A Gubbio Wolfhound."

"Yes, we must get it back down to the kennels. He'll be perfectly safe there. Follow me."

"How did you do that?" Francis asked Christopher as they walked down some stairs. "The little book thing..."

Christopher shrugged.

"Patron saint of travel, aren't I?"

"Do what?" asked the clipboard man, who had apparently not heard Christopher.

"My friend was just... commenting on your witing stylus," said Francis. "I believe that's one of Mr Laszlo Biro's new fangled pens you have there. Vewy modern."

"Friend?" said the man, looking past Francis and entirely ignoring Christopher.

"My fwiend..." began Francis but Christopher put a hand on his arm to stop him.

"The man's an imbecile," he whispered, a strange quality to his voice. "Just nod and smile."

Francis did as he was told and gestured for the man to lead on.

JOAN EMERGED FROM THE TOILETS, still angry and feeling more than a little lost. Of course, there had been no way back to the Celestial City through the stalls in the 'gents', although she'd given it a good go. She banged, rattled and implored the Almighty in each of the tiny chambers and had only stopped when the third successive man asked if she was feeling all right.

And now Christopher and Francis were only enhancing her anger levels by disappearing from sight. With increasing speed and armour-clanking volume, she strode around the lounge area, searching for them and drawing the attention of many.

"Oi, love!" called a man, sat on a high stool at a drinks bar. He beckoned her over with a jerk of his head.

His friends whispered and grinned. One hid his smile in his glass of frothy beer.

"Yes?" she said.

He gestured up and down at her plate armour with his pint of ale.

"What is this?" he leered. "Some kind of marketing gimmick?"

"I don't understand."

"What are you selling? Medieval banquets? Metal polish? I don't mind taking a consumer test. Happy to buff you up."

"I'm sorry, I'm busy," she said. "I'm looking for two men."

This drew uproarious laughter from the drinkers.

"Course you are," said one.

"Looking for a bit of sword action are you?" said another, nudging his mate.

"Do you have weapons?" she asked, frowning. "Perhaps a lightsaber."

"Love, the only weapon I would need is a tin-opener."

"Tin-opener?"

"Nah," said the ale-drinker. "Bet she's wearing an iron chastity belt under that lot."

With a horrible sensation, Joan realised that they were making vile suggestive comments about her and had been all along. She was appalled with herself for taking so long to realise. Men had not changed at all in the last six hundred years.

"Not to fear," said ale-drinker. "I bet I could get her to lower her drawbridge, raise her portcullis and let me storm her—"

He stopped abruptly, as one might with the tip of a broadsword at one's throat.

"Easy, love," he said. "We were just having a joke."

The sword quivered in Joan's hand. Here she was, the only modestly dressed woman in a room full of women in licentiously skimpy skirts and tops, and yet these oafs had made her feel ashamed, as though she was as naked as Eve. It would only take a moment to make an example of this lecherous brute. Perhaps it would make the world a better place...

"Joan!" called Francis, panting as he ran up to her.

"We've got problems," said Christopher, a footstep behind.

"Where have you been?" she snapped. "I was..."

Francis stared at her blade.

"What are you doing?" he asked.

"Nothing," she said and, with a flick of her sword, smashed the base of the man's glass, emptying its contents into his lap.

"Good," said Christopher. "Now about this problem..."

JOAN TRIED to make sense of what her two companions were saying as they descended the spiral stairs into the bowels of the ship.

"It's called a passport," said Francis.

"What's it for?" said Joan.

"It allows you to pass through a port, I guess, and we'll be in Zeebrugge vewy soon."

"Well, can't Christopher magic up some more?"

Christopher looked back her as he turned a corner.

"I produced something that looked like a passport. I think we'll be put under greater examination when we dock."

"I don't recall the Flemish being particularly officious people," said Joan.

"Well, it's not just that." Christopher gestured at the three of them.

"What?"

"It's clear that our appawel is dwawing some attention,"

said Francis. "We're hardly going to be able to slip ashore unchallenged."

"I think Gabriel intended us to buy local clothing when we arrived."

"But did he intend for us to appear on a ship leagues and leagues from Holland?" Christopher had a point.

"...a good point," said Francis. "Whatever the case, we need a solution."

Christopher stopped before a heavy metal door and raised the locking bar with a twist of his mighty fist.

"The man with the clipboard and the Laszlo had us bring the wolf down here."

"Where is the wolf?" asked Joan.

"He instwucted me to put him in a cage weserved for another hound. There might have been some confusion with the ticket Chwistopher pwoduced. What is a Bichon Frisé anyway?"

"'Curly bitch'?" Joan frowned at her own translation. "What was it like?"

"A big ball of yarn with legs." He shrugged. "I'm sure they'll get on perfectly well. Thwough here."

Joan stepped through into the cold hold, yet another space of astonishing dimensions.

"It's full of horseless carriages. And those... thingies, for going on a short crusade to the shops."

"Buses," said Christopher.

"That's the ones. Why, half the cars and buses in the world must be here. Why?"

"Perhaps the English are sending them as twibute to their overlords in Bwussels," suggested Francis.

Joan nodded at this sage piece of deduction.

"Regardless," said Christopher, "they will need to unload them when we dock."

Joan smiled.

"And all we need to do is hide inside one."

"Exactly."

"Smart thinking."

In their ensuing search for the ideal carriage within which to hide, most were discounted on account of their windows and the lack of places to hide. Christopher ultimately located a large square wagon with windows only in the front cabin. The metal door at the rear was held in place by a padlock, which Joan removed with a stab and a twist of her sword. Once the door had rolled magically into the roof of the wagon, the three saints climbed in among the boxes and plastic-wrapped furnishings. Christopher reached up and pulled the rolling door back down, plunging the interior into darkness.

Joan felt her way through the darkness, tripped and landed on a large and fortunately soft bag that appeared to be stuffed with beans or peas.

"Well, this is good," she said.

"All we need to do is wait until the ship is unloaded at the port," said Christopher, "then we slip out, find the wolf – I guess we have to – and be on our way."

A small bright circle of white light appeared in the wagon and bobbed around.

"It's a torch with the spiwit of light twapped inside it," said Francis. "Look. These boxes are full of twibute for the empwess."

Further torches were produced and the three of them were able to explore the hoard around them.

"They are gifts for the empress's palace," suggested Joan. "A chaise longue. A mattress. And, here, a box marked 'Kitchen' full of goods for the palace kitchens."

There were sounds of general movement beyond the walls of the wagon: chatter, footsteps and the echoing thuds of car doors.

"People are readying to leave," said Christopher and then shushed himself as they heard the doors to the wagon's front cabin open.

A muffled roar and subsequently ceaseless thrumming startled Joan so much that she dropped the dustbuster she had found.

"What is that?" she squeaked, fighting to keep her voice down.

"It is the power of horses that makes the wagon go," said Francis.

"It's the engine," tutted Christopher.

"That's what I said," snapped Francis.

"Shhh. Not so loud," said Joan.

Christopher shook his head.

"They won't be able to hear us over the engine, and look!" In his hands, Francis held a long floppy spring which shifted from one hand to the other as he moved them up and down. "It's a slinky!"

"Put that down!" said Joan firmly. "Before it explodes."

2

AMSTERDAM

Francis shifted position on the chaise longue, taking care not to dislodge the cushions that were holding the very dangerous slinky as still as possible.

"How far do you think we've twavelled now?" he asked.

Christopher considered the question.

"It's been two hours by the chimes of that clock in the box."

"We could have covered sevewal miles in that time," said Francis, wringing his hands.

"The wolf is fine, Francis," said Joan, reading his mind. "It's the rest of the world we need to worry about."

"These new-fangled contrivances can travel for many miles without stop," said Christopher.

"And I'm guessing we're moving too quickly to jump out," said Joan.

Christopher moved towards the door and rolled it upwards.

"I think I'll have a gander. Maybe it's not so — aargh!"

His hands remained gripped on the door as it rolled up. He was flung forward and swung out over the road, his sandalled feet flailing in the air. Joan leapt across and grabbed at the giant saint's shoulder.

"Can you see the wolf?" said Francis.

"Francis!" Joan yelled.

"Sorry. I was just asking—"

"Grab his other shoulder, man!"

Francis looked down in horror at the road whizzing beneath them. It was brutal and unnatural. How were the people of this modern world able to survive such stomach-churning speed? A car was travelling close behind them. The driver flicked his eyes towards the open door of the lorry but seemed unconcerned with the man hanging onto the edge.

"Francis!"

He moved forward, fearful and hesitant. He gripped the edge of a large box with one hand and tentatively gripped Christopher's sleeve with his free hand. He tugged, eyes shut tightly against the terrifying view. He kept his eyes shut until he heard the door slam back down.

Christopher lay on his back panting, and Joan stood shaking her head, throwing displeased looks at Francis from time to time.

"We do seem to be twavelling at gweat speed," said Francis.

"You think?" panted Christopher.

Joan threw herself down on the chaise longue.

"Whatever will become of the poor wolf?" said Francis.

Joan flung a cushion at his head. Francis ducked.

"Oh no!" he shouted, pointing.

The slinky rolled away from its nest among the cushions and fell, expanding, onto the floor.

Francis threw his hands over his head and waited for death.

"MILOU'S MAKING a lot of noise in there," Adelaide Chevrolet suggested to her husband, as they drove south away from the ferry terminal.

"She wants to come out," said little Anna in the back.

"She still wishes she was on holiday, like us," said Antoine Chevrolet.

"Hey, I'm sorry," said Adelaide. "The office called. This computer hiccup clearly hasn't resolved itself."

"Sure," said Antoine peevishly. "And only you can fix it. Well, we will be able to let Milou out for a proper walk at Willemspark."

A curiously loud growl came from the carrier in the back of the car, followed by a tiny whimper.

Travel sedation rarely agreed with Milou's temperamental constitution. Adelaide reflected on the fact that Milou had a digestive tract like the army's computer facility. Whatever the quality of the input, everything was magically transformed into an unholy mess that she would need to take care of. Her heart sank as she imagined the cleaning up that might be needed.

"It's unusual for her to wake up so early," she said as her husband pulled into the parking bay nearest the park entrance. Adelaide got out, went round to the boot, pulled the cover off the carrier and opened the door.

"Oh!"

Adelaide was knocked backwards by the enormous grey creature that erupted from the cage. It stood for a moment by the low wall of the park, sniffing the air.

"Big doggy!" shouted little Anna.

In a sense, Anna was right, thought Adelaide. That monster was just like a doggy, in the same way that a T-Rex was just like a chicken.

"It's a wolf!" gasped Adelaide. "Anna, back into the car!"

Anna scrambled back to her seat and peered over the parcel shelf as her father pulled her mother to her feet. The wolf walked back towards the car and Adelaide screamed but stood her ground, putting herself between the wolf and the inside of the car.

"Back, monster! Back!"

Adelaide's hand closed on the first thing that was available and she brought Milou's stainless steel dog bowl down sharply onto the wolf's head.

The wolf barely seemed to register the blow, but was drawn to the bag that she had dislodged from the boot. It was a sealed pack of beef tripe dog treats. The wolf delicately picked it up and presented it to Adelaide with a pitiful whine.

She took it from his mouth, fingers shaking and opened the packet. She tipped the contents out and the wolf caught them neatly. The hairy brute backed off, and Adelaide heard another, much smaller whine from inside the carrier.

"Shush Milou. Stay quiet and he might go away," hissed Adelaide. "I can get you some more snacks later."

She peered down at Milou and was astonished to see that the tiny dog had her eyes turned wistfully towards the wolf and appeared to be whining to see him go. The wolf had decided which direction he wanted. He loped back to the main road, sniffed the air again and began to run north, gathering pace as he disappeared from view around the bend.

THE CHIMES of the clock indicated that another hour had passed when there was a change in the tone of the engine noise. Joan got to her feet.

"I think we're stopping."

They waited for a few long moments as the movement slowed and then stopped. The rumble of the engine was shut off abruptly.

"Quickly, we must go before anyone finds us."

They opened the back door and Joan leapt out. From the front of the vehicle came two voices, chatting amiably. On either side of the road they were on were unbroken rows of tall stone buildings, more like the Celestial City than anything Joan recalled from her mortal life.

Francis scrambled down beside her but Chris was still in the lorry.

"What are you doing?" she hissed.

"I just want to fetch some things that might come in handy," he called.

"Don't touch the slinky!"

"Don't be a flaming worry-wart. It's clearly a dud," called Christopher.

"Hurry!" she hissed and drew her sword, hoping she wouldn't need to use it. But it was too late, the chatting men had reached the back of the lorry.

"Distraction time." Joan nudged Francis in the ribs.

"Ouch!"

"Oh look! A dancing monk!" yelled Joan at the top of her voice.

"Where?" Francis swivelled his head.

"Dance, you idiot," hissed Joan and booted him into the centre of the road.

"See him leap in the air!"

Francis stumbled and then awkwardly but gamely leapt up and came down on his tippy-toes.

His capering was more like an outbreak of St Vitus' dance but it worked. The two men stared at him. Joan couldn't understand how they had failed to notice Christopher, who climbed down from the lorry, almost stepping on their toes, but they were transfixed with the spectacle of Francis twirling uncomfortably.

Christopher jogged down the pavement to join Joan.

"Come on," Joan whispered loudly. "You nearly got us caught!"

Francis ran to catch up with them once they were clear of the lorry and together they walked briskly down a street of low brick buildings. Joan inspected the buildings' construction. She bashed a wall with her sword hilt to see how solid it was.

"Incredible. People must be so happy to have buildings this sturdy."

"I reckon it'd be nigh on impossible to burn a village when the houses are made like this," said Christopher.

"There are *so* many of them," said Francis, looking up and down the road at the neat terraces. The late afternoon sun slanted across the buildings. Rows and rows of them, disappearing into the distance. "So vewwy similar. Good gwief!"

"What?" said Joan.

"There's an astonishing tweasure twove in there!"

The monk was staring through a ground level window. Rows of sparkling glass figurines lined up on the window sill.

"Look, look! A tiny wolf."

"Woo hoo," said Christopher flatly.

"Oh I do miss him."

"I think that treasure like this is probably more commonplace in the modern world," said Joan. "Let's not get distracted from what we need to do. Let's ask."

Joan stepped in front of a car coming along the road and waved.

"Ho, stranger!" she called.

The car slowed down, but the man behind the wheel made an unusual yet quite graphic hand gesture that even the Maid of Orleans could translate. The car emitted a loud honking noise that made all three saints jump. Joan stepped quickly out of the way. The car whizzed past and she looked after it in surprise.

"Well, that wasn't very friendly," she said.

Francis rapped on the window with the glass animals.

"Let us seek advice from the wesidents," he said. "At least they can't wun us over."

A face appeared at the window. The woman's brow wrinkled briefly with confusion but then she smiled and pushed up the sash.

"You're from out of town," she gestured at their clothes.

"Yes, we are," said Joan, surprised. "Er, which town, exactly?"

The woman laughed.

"Hey, you're not *that* lost. You're still in Amsterdam."

Joan could not help but smile. Through no plan or design, they had appeared in the very city they were trying to reach. Luck or providence, it was good news.

"Here for the Pride?"

"Um, no. We're looking for Bastenakenstraat. Do you know where that might be?"

The woman shrugged.

"I think I've got one of those maps they hand out..." She disappeared briefly and then reappeared with a colourful pamphlet in her hand. "There you are."

"Thank you," said Joan.

"Off you go the pair of you and have fun! And be sure to get a spot early for tomorrow's parade. It gets busy."

She winked and closed the window.

"Pawade?" said Francis.

Joan opened up the pamphlet and looked at the city map at its centre, a web of whites and yellows intercut with blue lines.

"What are all these fancy rainbow symbols?" said Christopher.

"Doesn't matter," said Joan. "Look. Here. We haven't got too far to go. Come on."

Joan knocked on the door. The houses on Bastenakenstraat had a squat, modern appearance, but Francis decided that they looked rather comfortable. He peered into windows to see what other treasures might be displayed.

Joan knocked on the door again.

"It's possible that the Blessed Mother is out," ventured Francis.

"The other houses have lit their candles now it's starting to get dark," said Francis.

"They have *electric* candles now," Joan peered at the upper storey.

"Candles are candles," said Francis. "All the darkness in the world cannot extinguish the light of a single candle."

"We're not in Heaven now Francis," said Joan. "So I can cheerfully smack anyone who quotes their own work. You're right though, it looks as though nobody's here."

"We need to know where she's gone."

"Assuming she didn't leave months ago," said Christopher.

"Or Heaven has got its facts wrong. I might be able to help."

Francis hitched up his habit and knelt down by the wall.

He crouched forward and made a high-pitched squeaking noise.

"He's lost it," muttered Christopher.

"Shush!" said Francis and continued to squeak.

A movement caught his eye and he smiled as a small brown rat emerged from a nearby alley.

"You see! Local knowledge, that's what we need!"

Francis sat cross-legged on the pavement and addressed the rat.

"Evening, bwother wat. I wonder if you could help us. We're looking for the lady who lives here."

He tilted his head to listen.

"Hmmm, well, I can assure you that she *is* a lady. In fact, she is a most wevered figure."

"The rat saw her?" said Joan.

Christopher cast his eyes to the sky.

"We're paying attention to the rat now? Really? Heaven help us."

"Not for sevewal days?" said Francis to the rat. "Oh dear — what?"

Christopher muttered to himself.

"No," said Francis earnestly. "Of course he didn't say *'filthy cweature'*, he regards you vewy highly and is gwateful for your help. I think he *might* have said it's vewy nice to *meet you*. Do you know where she went? Yes, the lady who lived here? There might be some biscuit cwumbs in it for you."

The rat considered this and twitched its nose.

"You see!" said Francis, jumping up. "If people are kind to animals they can be so vewy useful... oh, where's Joan?"

"She went to ask an actual human," said Christopher. "Maybe she thinks your furry friend would tell you any old guff for a bit of cheese."

Joan approached a car parked across the street and tapped the window.

"Hello."

The man inside gripped his *Volkskrant* newspaper even more tightly. He hadn't seemed to notice her. Joan knocked harder and raised her voice.

"Hello!"

The young man reluctantly looked up from his paper and wound down the window. She indicated the house where Christopher and Francis seemed to be exchanging heated words. She'd need to sort them out in a minute.

"I see that you're watching the house over there."

"I'm not," he said. "I'm just reading this newspaper."

"I saw you looking over."

"The sight of a Franciscan monk and a woman in full plate kind of draws the eye."

"Oh, right. Do you often read your newspaper here?"

"That would be strange and suspicious behaviour, wouldn't it?"

He grinned and it was a nice smile. The man radiated an air of self-assurance, a kind of easy and charming Ferris Bueller-style confidence.

"We're just really really keen to find the woman who lives there," she said.

"Friend of yours?"

"Sort of. She's the mother of our... our boss."

"Boss?"

"You know, the man upstairs."

The man folded his newspaper and straightened his crumpled tie.

"Look, I'm really not watching the house," he said, "but I do look up from time to time, and from what I've noticed, the lady hasn't been back for several days."

Christopher and Francis walked over to the car.

"She hasn't been here for sevewal days," said Francis.

"Well, so his new little buddy says," mocked Christopher.

"She's gone to the city centre," said Francis. "We should go there now."

"Let's see how far that is." Joan unfolded the map onto the bonnet of the man's car. The three saints huddled round as Joan stabbed a finger on their current location and traced a route towards the centre.

"Sorry. What are you doing?" the man asked, stepping out of his car.

"We're looking for our friend. She's moved on to the city centre, so we're going there now."

"How do you know?" he asked.

"Someone told us." Joan was suddenly very conscious that it would be a bad idea to mention that a rat was the source of the information.

"I was watching the whole time and you haven't spoken to anyone except me."

"I thought you weren't watching," said Joan, eyebrows raised.

The young man sighed heavily.

"Look," he said. "Why don't I give you a lift there? I was heading that way anyway."

"You've finished reading your newspaper now?"

"Yes, I have. Where do you need to go, Miss....?"

"I'm Joan. This is Francis and Christopher."

The man frowned at Francis, seemingly confused.

"Well, I'm Matt."

Matt, thought Joan. Like Matthew Broderick. Although there was little physical similarity. This Matt was taller, his hairstyle less *fluffy* than the eighties movie star.

"I just need to text my mother and then we can skedaddle," said Matt.

Joan did not understand what Matt had just said but, after stabbing at a little handheld device for a few seconds he seemed satisfied.

"Thank you," she said, as Matt opened the door for her. "This will speed things up, even though it's not a Ferrari."

She paused and peered down at the badge on the front.

"It's not a Ferrari, is it?" she asked.

"No, it's a Fiat 500," said Matt.

"I like Ferraris."

"Well, you can pretend it's a Ferrari if it makes you happy."

Joan indicated that Francis and Christopher should get into the back of the car. She got into the passenger seat and wrestled with the seatbelt until Matt suggested that she might want to unbuckle her scabbard. Joan placed it into the footwell with a small scowl. It left her feeling quite exposed.

It was a short drive into the city centre. Joan decided that motorised transport was far less scary if one had an actual seat and a window. Despite the car's monstrous speed, the journey was more comfortable than any cart ride she had taken in life. Evening was descending upon the city; lights glittered all around them.

They pulled up at a junction, allowing a small group of

Roman gladiators to cross the road. Joan had met some gladiators in Heaven, and had never noticed that a bare behind was part of the uniform.

"So you're here for the Pride then." Matt changed down the gears almost gracefully.

"The woman mentioned a 'pride' earlier," said Christopher.

"Pride?" asked Joan. "What is that?"

"You know, the Gay Pride weekend."

Joan understood each of the individual words Matt said but together they were meaningless.

"Gay Pride weekend?"

Matt waved vaguely at Joan's armour.

"Surely, that's why you're dressed up. I mean, it looks nice — really suits you — but it's a strange outfit otherwise. No? Not into Gay Pride?"

Joan thought on it deeply.

"I don't think I could take part in something as sinful as that," she said.

"Sinful?" said Matt. "Wow. That's a bit harsh."

"I'm all for being gay. I think I'm not gay enough, most of the time."

"Right?"

"But pride is one of the seven deadly sins and must be avoided by all right-minded people. No, gay modesty. That's me."

"I see," said Matt, clearly nonplussed.

"And are you here for the 'pwide'?" asked Francis from the back seat.

"It's a lot of fun. Is it Francis or Christopher?"

"I'm Fwancis. He's Chwistopher."

"Who is?" said Matt.

"Ignore him," said Christopher to Francis.

"No, the Gay Pride is a lot of fun. Really good atmosphere," said Matt. "But, sadly, I'm working."

"Reading the newspaper's not work," said Joan.

"Well, not usually. I'm over here doing some liaison work. Normally I'm based in the UK."

"UK?"

"Britain. England."

"Oh, you're British," said Joan, suddenly re-evaluating the entire conversation.

"Don't tell me I've picked up a Dutch accent in less than a month," Matt joked.

"Speaking of accents, you're obviously French."

"You recognised my accent."

"That and the way that you go 'pff' to punctuate your sentences. I'm right aren't I?"

Joan considered his answer in light of Evelyn's warning about British sarcasm. Everything they said was opposite to its true meaning. If a British person said that they were British, did it mean that they really weren't? She knew that she was French, so that part wasn't sarcasm. She found that the whole concept made her head hurt. She was saddened by the realisation that Matt's previous comments about her outfit looking nice were not to be believed. In fact, he must surely think that she *didn't* look nice. She sighed with exasperation.

"They've closed the roads ahead in preparation for

tomorrow's parade," said Matt. "Where exactly am I dropping you off?"

"Here is fine," said Francis.

"Really?" said Joan.

"I'll need to find somewhere to park the car," said Matt. "Maybe I'll come and find you later."

"That would be nice," said Joan honestly and suddenly worried whether, to sarcastic British ears, that comment had been an insult.

She got out, clanking, and struggling once more with her sword.

"Where will you be?" asked Matt leaning across to look at her. "Exactly."

Joan looked to Francis. Francis shrugged.

"Not sure," she said.

"I'll give you a call then," said Matt. "What's your number?"

"Nineteen."

"Nineteen?"

"Yes."

"Are you sure?"

Joan nodded grimly.

"It's been nineteen for a long, long time."

Wim looked up from his chair and gazed across the water. The views of the Westerschelde estuary were one of the most admirable features of this rather bland apartment. He'd moved here from his beloved smallholding at the insistence of his surviving daughter, Clara, after Laila's disappearance the year before. That was all very well and kept the remains of the grieving family together in one place, but being twelve floors above the land only added to his depression.

He saw a dark shape in the water that he couldn't make out. He stepped over to the telescope that had been the most exciting birthday gift he'd received in years. There was always something to look at with its powerful lens. He focussed the telescope at the shape, maybe a hundred and fifty yards out from the edge. It appeared to be a dog, a huge one at that. He followed its progress until it emerged at the small beach. It trotted out of the water and gave itself a vigorous shake. Wim gasped as he saw it on land.

"Wolf."

His hand hovered over the phone. Should he call Clara? But did he really want to give her any more to worry about? He pushed the phone back onto the side table and watched the wolf run purposefully onwards. Moments later it was out of his sight.

THE THREE SAINTS walked through narrow streets hung with striped rainbow bunting until they came to a railing overlooking an expanse of water. Christopher spotted several boats moored at the side. They had many seats, and curved glass roofs. Useful for a small crusade where you could get there by water and you wanted a really good view, perhaps.

"Is this a river?" asked Francis.

Joan gazed at the still water. "It's a canal."

"I've taken many a prayer from people travelling on canals," said Christopher. "Mostly they pray for an inn to be close by."

The buildings were much taller round here, shoulder to shoulder in a chaotic and colourful jumble. There were indeed inns, shops and other businesses housed within them.

"Where did the rat say we'd find Mary?" said Joan to Francis.

"He didn't know exactly where she went," said Francis, reddening slightly. "Only that she came to the centre. We'd better look awound."

"What about a drink first?" said Christopher. "We can start our search in an inn, perhaps?"

"We won't find the Blessed Mother in an inn, I'm sure."

"The Holy Mother frequented inns at least once in her life," Christopher countered.

"The stables, you mean," said Francis.

"Fine," said Christopher. "Let's go into an inn and ask if we can poke around their stables."

"No," said Joan. "There's a coffeehouse over there. That's much more our scene. It's not as if we want beer, is it?"

"Oh no, course not," said Christopher and his shoulders sagged as he followed his teenage commander into the coffeehouse.

"These people don't look very alert for people who've been drinking coffee," said Joan, as they passed a roomful of young men lolling on sofas. "In fact they look as if they're half asleep, which can't be easy for that man with the butterfly wings."

"Or those ones with the mermaid tails," said Francis. "Did you notice they have scales all over their faces? Nobody seems to find this sort of thing wemarkable."

"Evelyn says that we should be tolerant of people whose appearance is different to our own. She must have been trying to tell us how many modern people are afflicted with this sort of abnormality. Just pretend we didn't see it. That's what people do, apparently."

"So I can't see that man with green hair?"

"No."

"Nor the one with lumps of metal stuck in his face?"

"Who?"

They settled at a table.

They ordered some drinks from the polite coffeehouse wench, and Christopher ordered a large piece of square cake that was displayed under a glass dome. He had to ask Joan to order it for him; his two self-obsessed companions had still failed to notice what was happening to him.

"We'll need to find somewhere to sleep."

"Quite," said Francis. "It might take us a while to find Mawy."

"Of course, an inn would have beds," muttered Christopher. "But, no, we have to come to a coffeehouse..."

The wench brought their order over.

"We didn't have coffee in my day."

"Nor mine," said Joan. "But all the cool people drink coffee in the movies."

Francis sipped at his black coffee and pulled a tight-lipped face.

"Wefweshingly... bitter," he said, shuddering. "And yet..."

He sipped it again.

"There's something inexpwessably... Mmmm."

He drained the cup.

"Good?" said Joan, who had ordered a skinny frappuccino, principally because she could.

"I'm uncertain," said Francis. "I will need to consume two or thwee more to form an opinion."

Christopher was ignoring his coffee but scoffing down the cake.

"'m starving," he mumbled.

"It's strange," said Joan. "These mortal bodies can feel hunger. I don't remember the last time I felt hunger."

Francis paused mid-sip. "Oh, I do. The turnip blight of 1223. There wasn't a single root vegetable to be found in all Italy."

"Is that all?" said Joan. "In the June of 1429 on the roads to Riems, my armies had to march for five days without so much as a crumb of bread to eat. It was only when we reached Troyes and found Brother Richard's crop of beans that—"

"Five days? That's nothing," said Francis. "In 1199, volcanic eruptions caused crop failure across the land..."

The two of them fell to good natured argument over which of them had endured the greatest hardship, Francis becoming more animated after waving the wench over to bring further coffee. It was a conversation in which Christopher couldn't participate. If he so much as mentioned any of the trials or deprivations he had suffered, the others would simply point out that his own memories – realistic though they might have been – were the alleged invention of early church fathers.

The cake Christopher had eaten sat pleasantly in his belly – that felt real! – and he could feel a warm contentment expand through his muscles, clearing out the troubles of his mind like a broom sweeping through a cluttered room. Clarity of thought. That was what he needed.

"Historically inaccurate, am I, eh?" he said, at least he thought he'd said it.

With clarity came lethargy and a sense that he was drifting away from himself. For the first time, Christopher could grasp that being technically imaginary was not enough and that it might be preferable to disappear from reality entirely...

A hand slapped him on the knee. Christopher sat up with a start.

"Dozed off for a while there, fwiend," said Francis.

"Where's Joan?" said Christopher, dazedly rubbing his eyes.

"She's gone to pay the barkeep. Maybe, if we're lucky, they know where Mawy is."

At the counter, Joan put a gold florin down and the wench shook her head and said something to her. Joan picked up the florin and bit down on it, to demonstrate that it was real gold, but the woman shook her head again.

Christopher giggled, although wasn't at all sure why.

"Think I need another cake," he said.

A woman approached Joan, said something and put a hand on her arm. She handed some coins to the man at the counter and followed Joan back to the table.

"Hey, everybody, this is Brandy," said Joan. "She helped me out with the local coinage just now."

Christopher mumbled hello, wondering how Brandy's hair could be so outlandishly tall. There was her face, which was brightly painted, but then her coppery hair was piled up like a tall cottage loaf, with no visible means of support. He fought the overwhelming urge to give it an exploratory prod.

"Joan tells me you need a place to stay for the night," said Brandy, smiling widely.

"We do, we do," said Christopher.

"Brandy has a friend who rents out rooms."

"Weally?" said Francis. "That's wonderful."

Outside the coffeeshop, Christopher suffered a moment's giddiness. He decided it was just as well they would soon have somewhere to rest. It had been a long day. However, something caught his eye, something that couldn't be ignored.

"Heeeyy," he said. "You know what you two are going to need?"

"What?" said Joan.

"You need to know how to ride a bicycle. This place has loads of them."

Christopher wheeled one away from a nearby rack.

"Looks a bit dangerous to me." Joan rocked one back and forth, seeing how it wobbled.

"How does it work?" asked Francis.

"Are you sure you know how to ride one?"

"The place is not too far," said Brandy. "We can easily walk. Follow me."

Brandy walked ahead.

"Do I know how to ride a bicycle?" crowed Christopher. "Do I ever! Patron saint of bloody bicycles, me!"

Christopher swung his leg over the crossbar and spent some time searching for the pedals.

"Watch and learn," he said.

He launched forward, whooping and cheering as he managed to move the bicycle. He wobbled for a few feet and then moved more smoothly.

"Look at me!" he called as he turned back to wave at the others. "I told you I could ride —"

There was a lurching sensation and he looked forward again, just in time to see the front wheel go over the side into the canal.

JOAN FOLLOWED Brandy through dark and crowded streets, glancing at Christopher who trailed soggily behind. Francis kept his distance, complaining about the smell, which Joan decided was somewhere between a stagnant pond and an overflowing cess pit.

The area they were in seemed to be home to the poorer people of Amsterdam. Joan noticed several women whose clothing was so worn and flimsy, it was possible to see right through it. Some of the houses were lit by presumably cheaper, red electric candles.

"Here's your place for the night, luvvies," said Brandy.

Joan looked up at the narrow building. It looked shabbier than some of the other buildings in the city, there were large chunks of masonry missing from the front, and it was no longer possible to tell what colour it might once have been painted. However, wasn't it entirely appropriate that three saints should dwell among the poorer people?

"The owner's a friend of mine," continued Brandy, "and he'll be very happy to take your, ah, unusual coins as payment."

Joan smiled.

"That is good news. We've got lots of those coins."

"Lots?"

"Absolutely, and I'd hate to think that they were useless."

"Not useless at all. We can certainly help you there, luvvie."

Brandy led the way up the stairs, past closed doors and muffled voices, right to the top of the building to an attic room.

"I'll go and have words with the owner," said Brandy. "Make yourselves comfy!"

Brandy shut the door and they looked round the tiny space.

"Look at this!" said Joan, running a finger across a grimy dressing table. "Dust! I'd almost forgotten what it looked like. You don't get dust in Heaven. Not proper dust."

"No," said Francis, regarding the floor. "Not so many cockwoaches, either."

"Aren't they all God's creatures?" asked Christopher.

"Even God makes exceptions," said Francis.

Joan picked up the corner of a bedspread.

"I'm sure it will be comfortable enough for our needs. We –urgh!"

"What?" said Christopher.

"Bed bug," said Francis with warm recognition. "A gwossly maligned cweature in my view."

"I'm all for humble lodgings, but I won't be sharing them with parasites," said Joan firmly, shaking out the sheets. She paused for a moment. "Wait a second, why are there only two beds here? Do we have another room?"

Christopher coughed lightly.

"You really haven't noticed, have you?" he asked.

"Noticed what?" Joan asked.

"The man with the never-ending Laszlo on the boat refused to talk to me."

"So?"

"No one noticed me jumping out of the back of the lorry."

"Because of my embawwassing but effective distwaction," said Francis.

"Really? What about the fact that Joan's friend with the car thought you were called Francis—and—Christopher?"

"I truly don't understand what point you're making," said Joan.

"Fine. Let me be blunt," said Christopher. "People here can't see me."

"I'm sorry?"

"They don't notice me, whatever I do."

"That can't be true," said Joan.

"I fell in the bloody canal right in front of crowds of people, for crying out loud! Don't you think that someone might have said something? No. They all act as if I'm not here."

"You can't be the centre of attention *all* the time you know," said Joan. "I think you're overreacting a bit just because people have been talking to me and not listening to you."

"Because most of the time you only talk about one thing," said Francis.

"I don't."

"You do. 'Did you know, I cawwied the baby Chwist acwoss a waging wiver. Ooh, aye, dead 'ard it were.'"

"Was that seriously meant to be an impression of me? Now you're just being mean. You need to open your eyes."

"No," said Joan. "You need to think straight. What you're saying doesn't make sense. Why can't they see you?"

Christopher sighed angrily.

"Because I don't exist on earth. I *never* existed on earth. Francis, don't tell me you haven't noticed?"

"To be honest, I've been distwacted, thinking about the poor wolf," said Francis.

Joan rolled her eyes and counted to ten. She'd asked for this. She wanted to get out and do something. She was the leader, but they'd been on earth for less than a day and the other two were so wrapped up in their own problems that it seemed as though they had forgotten their mission.

"How about this?" she said, after taking a deep breath. "Christopher, we'll try and make sure you take more of a proactive role."

"Proactive? Is that like active?"

"Yeah, just more so — make sure you're in the thick of it so people notice you more. Francis, we'll keep a careful eye out for the wolf. I'm not sure we can do much more than that at this stage."

Christopher opened his mouth to speak, but was interrupted by a knock at the door.

"Little pigs," sang a deep voice outside the door, "little pigs. Let me come in."

The door swung open and a tall, heavy-set man with wavy black hair and huge sideburns stood in the doorway.

"It's only me," he grinned.

He was flanked by Brandy and an even larger man with crudely inked bone tattoos on his arms and a fearsome scowl on his face.

"You," the man continued, "must be Brandy's new friends from out of town. You can call me Wolfie. Cos it's my name, right?"

"Watch this, I'll prove that they can't see me. Christopher stepped right up to Wolfie and stuck out his tongue in front of his face.

"Hello, Mr Wolfie," said Joan. "Ignore my friend."

But Wolfie had not responded in any way.

"Let's cut to the chase, little pigs," said Wolfie. "You have my gold."

"Your gold?" said Joan, distracted by the realisation that other people really couldn't see Christopher.

"Look!" said Christopher and tugged sharply on Wolfie's sideburns. Wolfie slapped at his face, with a fleeting look of mild puzzlement.

"My gold." Wolfie rubbed his cheek. "Hand it over and there will be no need for huffing and puffing and blowing down of houses."

"Good grief," said Joan. "I can't believe it. They really don't see you. Francis, what do you make of it?"

"As Chwistopher suggests, it is clearly a phenomenon that welates to his deleted status. Most intewesting," said Francis.

"You're ignoring me. Mad people. Give me the gold right now!" said Wolfie.

"Yet you can touch and influence the physical world," continued Joan. "That bicycle really did go into the canal. That tweak just then really did hurt. It's just that nobody sees what happens. Hey, you're showing off now."

Christopher was capering around behind Wolfie, pinching the other man's ears. He pulled Brandy's hair as well. His victims exchanged glances and looked in disgust at the room as if the fleas had turned unusually aggressive.

"Enough of this. Bonio, grab the tin-plated bitch."

Wolfie grabbed at Francis. The huge and tattooed Bonio pulled out a four-inch blade from his waistband.

Joan looked at his knife.

"Are you kidding?" she asked and she unsheathed her sword, relishing the protracted *sch-ting* sound that it made. Bonio looked mildly uncomfortable.

"Hey Joan, you've given him something to think about," said Christopher, watching with interest. "Do we think he's got a plan?"

Bonio's plan appeared to amount to snarling. He thrust the knife forward in the direction of Joan's face, while snarling some more. Joan didn't want to kill him so she brought up the flat of her sword to whack the underside of his hand. The knife flew into the air where Christopher caught it.

Joan then hit Bonio on the side of his head with the flat of the blade and he dropped to the floor, unconscious.

She turned to see how Francis was getting on. He wasn't as bulky as Wolfie, so he was currently pinned against the wall, while Wolfie thrust his hands into the pocket of Francis's habit. Joan stepped forward to assist, but at that moment Wolfie let out a howl of pain. He drew his hand free and tried to shake loose the rat that hung onto the end of it, but the rodent's teeth were firmly embedded into his finger.

"Who'd have thought your ratty friend would be actually useful?" said Christopher.

Francis took advantage of Wolfie's distraction to bring a brisk knee up into his groin, and then clubbed him with a nearby table lamp. Wolfie joined Bonio on the floor.

"Watch the girl," called Christopher. "She's got a, um, what would you call that, Francis? An ornamental cat?"

"Looks more like a weally ugly wabbit to me."

Brandy had picked up the heavy ornament and now she grunted with the effort as she sliced it through the air towards Joan's head. Joan raised her sword and met it in mid air. The shattered remains dropped harmlessly to either side. Joan slammed her fist into Brandy's face. The woman fell and joined the clutter of villains on the floor of the room.

"Yeah, that showed them!" Christopher jigged with excitement.

Joan sheathed her sword. "Some friend Brandy turned out to be."

"We'd better leave," said Francis.

"Yes, I don't want to be here when they wake up."

"There may be a solution to our cuwwency pwoblem,"

said Francis, stooping down to Wolfie's side. "We could take some of these."

He held up a wallet that was stuffed with banknotes.

"Hm, I'm not sure it's ethical," said Joan. "But we can leave some of our gold in exchange. How much is fair, I wonder?"

"I say we leave them a couple of coins," said Christopher. "They did attack us."

"There's a gweat many of these notes, perhaps we should leave a little more. Do you think a gold florin for each of these five euro things?"

"Let's just leave them one of the bags," said Joan. "I'm a bit fed up with carrying it anyway. The notes will be lighter. Hopefully they won't mind."

"WAKE UP, MIRIAM," said Agnes and jabbed her elbow in her companion's ribs.

Miriam, who in Agnes' opinion might have been an actual farmer's wife but really let the side down by actually looking like one, snorted and sat up, the imprint of velour on her face from where she'd been slumped on the coach seat.

"Are we there?" she said.

"No, you daft mare," said Agnes. "We only left The Hague two hours ago."

Miriam peered out of the window.

"There's water everywhere."

"It's called the North Sea. I don't know why the Dutch

had to build a road over it instead of around but there you go."

Miriam nodded and then looked at Agnes.

"Why did you wake me up?"

"I wanted to point out the wolf to you."

"What wolf?"

"The one that just ran by in the opposite direction."

Miriam looked back and forth along the dual carriageway and the sea that bordered it on both sides.

"Where is it then?"

"It's gone now," scowled Agnes. "Honestly, with reactions like that I'm not surprised you've written off so many tractors."

Miriam shrugged and went back to sleep.

FRANCIS HAD a surreptitious rummage through another drift of litter. In the nighttime hours they'd spent wandering the streets, all three of them had expressed surprise at the amount of waste there was in the centre of Amsterdam. As dawn broke, teams of men wearing fluorescent jackets emerged to sweep up and throw bags of rubbish into the back of a lorry, but they hadn't yet started to make much of a dent in it.

They spent some time puzzling over Christopher's invisibility. Joan declared that it wasn't really helpful to have someone who was entirely unable to interact with the population of earth.

"Interact? You mean talking to them, don't you?" said

Christopher. "Talking's all very well, but I can wallop someone on the nose and they'll *stay* walloped, so don't go telling me I can't interact."

"Whoa, steady," she replied, knowing that a sleepless night added a crabby note to her voice. "It wasn't a personal criticism, just another thing we need to deal with. I mean, just look at us. We've got no idea where to look for Mary, Christopher can't be seen by anyone but us, and our outfits clearly don't fit in. We've no way of fixing the Christopher thing, but Francis and I do need to find some clothes that blend in."

Francis bridled at this.

"My outfit is as good in the modern world as it's always been. A Franciscan monk pwides himself on the timeless design of his habit," he said. "Well he would do if pwide were allowed, of course."

"What is this Gay Pride thing everyone keeps talking about?" said Christopher.

Joan sighed.

"I've no idea. I'm sorry, Francis. I guess there just aren't too many Franciscan monks in the busy capitals of modern-day Europe."

Francis went back to kicking through the piles of litter with a scowl. He sifted through the rainbow-coloured flyers and spotted some more half-eaten food. It was similar to others that he'd found. There was a thin layer of something that he'd assumed was packaging, but the rat had told him was bread. It was unlike any bread that Francis had ever known in his lifetime, but the rat had been happy to eat it. Apparently these discarded burgers were considered a delicacy by modern city rats. Francis was pleased that the residents took such care of the rodent population. He extracted the meat and added it to the small stash that he was accumulating as a treat for the wolf. The wolf would not turn his nose up at the strange orange deposits on top, although Francis suspected it was candle wax. He refused to entertain the thought that he wouldn't see the wolf again, so he wanted to be prepared with some delicious tidbits. The rat sat on his palm and nibbled the bread delicately. Christopher and Joan had grudgingly agreed that the rat was a worthy travelling companion.

"That rat's making me really hungry," said Christopher. "Tell me if you spot any more of those burgers, I might try one."

There was a squeak, and the rat raised its head, whiskers quivering. He leapt from Francis's hand and scampered to the door of a nearby eatery. He turned and looked at them expectantly.

Francis and Christopher approached the Teefkoningin Cafe.

"Are those pancakes? They smell so good," said Christopher.

"No, it's coffee, I can smell coffee," said Francis.

Joan shook her head.

"Have you two just been manipulated by an opportunistic, greedy rodent?"

"I'm thirsty," said Francis.

"And hungry," said Christopher.

"Fine. Why don't you go and have something to eat. I'm

going to see if I can find some clothes, so I'll come and meet you back here. Try not to get into too much trouble."

Christopher scoffed.

"What trouble can we get into in a restaurant?"

THE WOLF of Gubbio circled the interior of the empty truck, sniffing at the dusty floor. He had the scent of his master in his nostrils.

"Oi! Get out of there!"

The wolf looked up at the man on the road and bared its teeth.

"Jesus," the man said to his mate, backing off. "Mad, dancing priests. The customer claiming we've been messing with their stuff. And now this."

The wolf sniffed at a long, loose spring on the floor. Yes, his master's scent was strong. He was close.

The wolf turned and leapt over the removal men's heads and onward towards his goal.

JOAN CROSSED THE CANAL, enjoying the warmth of the morning sun as the city became more active.

She stopped for a moment to look at the buses that had started to appear on the larger roads. No not buses, trains. They looked like the pictures of buses but ran on rails with a power source from above. Her brow wrinkled. She could consult her tablet about this curious hybrid, but she was mindful of the limited battery life that was available on earth, so she decided she'd ask Christopher about it later.

She walked along the river bank and then turned into a smaller street which was crowded with shops. She examined the windows as she walked and dismissed most of them, as they were concerned with bicycles, colourful rugs and a strange pointed leaf that seemed to feature widely. She came at last to a clothes shop in a narrow street. It was called *Smart Fetish en Fantasy*. Joan had a vague idea that a fetish was something to do with idolatry, but it was clear that, in this age, the names of things and their actual meaning and function rarely coincided.

The assistant behind the counter was drinking coffee and reading a magazine as she entered. His head was shaven, putting Joan in mind of a monk, but the rest of his appearance was most curious. There were so many rips and tears in the trousers and top that he wore that Joan nearly turned and left. If you sold clothes, why would you continue to wear damaged ones like that?

"Morning," he said. "Love the hair. And the outfit. Very Joan of Arc."

"Oh," said Joan, momentarily startled.

"Hope you're not going on a boat in that," he smiled. "Straight to the bottom. Glug. Glug. Here for the Gay Pride?"

"I haven't been feeling too gay at all," said Joan. "I need some new clothes to help with that."

"Something to wear for today's festivities? You've come to just the right place, sweetie."

"Have I? Oh, good."

"We have one of the biggest stocks of leather and fetish gear in the city."

"I'm very fond of leather," said Joan. "It's very practical."

"That's exactly right! Wipes clean in a jiffy. So, what's your style? Are we talking playful, slutty, dominant? I'm sure you've got a lovely petite figure under there, that kind of demure thing going on, but that armour says butch no-nonsense."

"I want to be dominant," said Joan. "Definitely."

"Ooh, I bet you've broken a few hearts. A couple of spines too, eh?"

"I just need people to take me seriously."

"Totally understand. We have outfits here that will shut them right up. Pop into that cubicle there and take your things off."

"Disrobe? In here?"

"I'm harmless, sweetie. Listen, I'll bring you something in studded leather to start off with. How would that be?"

"That sounds great."

Joan went inside the curtained-off area and removed her plate armour with a series of loud clanking sounds. Once out of her chainmail hauberk she was left in only her cotton chemise.

"Here, try this."

A hanger came through the curtain, displaying a tunic that was made entirely of leather. The upper and lower halves were connected with a series of elasticated strips. Joan stepped into the garment and fastened up the elaborate buckles at the side. It was light and flexible but had the comforting feel and security of armour.

"How's the fit?" came the man's voice

"Good, I think," said Joan.

"I'm never wrong on size, I've got the eye! Come on out, let's take a look."

Joan stepped through the curtain and the man waved her over to a full-length mirror. She eyed herself critically.

"It's beautifully crafted," she said, checking out the quality of the stitching and the rivets.

"Hand made in Spain, and you won't find that design anywhere else in town. Looks fabulous on, I must say."

"Really?"

"You were born to wear this, sweetie. I'd take off the cotton shirt though, to show it at its best."

"Oh? I don't know about this big gap round the middle," she said. "It's a bit immodest, isn't it?"

"Immodest? Not a word we hear often in this place."

"And I think the skirt's too short as well. Too much of me is, well, on show."

"Well, I see you as a long boot kinda girl. Am I right? Let's layer it up without going to complete gimp, shall we? And you know what, I have a special something that I know you're going to love!"

He dived into a stock cupboard and came out with a huge, studded belt.

"Look at this. It comes with a scabbard, completely functional. You'll need somewhere to put your sword, yes?"

Joan put it over the dress, and slipped on the thigh-length boots that he handed to her.

She looked again in the mirror and smiled broadly.

"I had no idea I could fit in here so easily," she said happily. "Can I try those please?"

She pointed to a pair of studded wrist straps.

"I'll throw those in," said the assistant, totting up the bill. "And a whip as well — you can't *possibly* leave without one of those."

Joan grinned and admired herself in the mirror once more.

"And you think men will take me seriously in this?"

"Sweetie, I'm as queer as they come and even I want to throw myself at your feet. You'll have them falling over themselves to do your wicked bidding."

CHRISTOPHER STARTED on his third plateful of tiny pancakes, while Francis looked on in disapproval.

"These are great! Here, watch this!" He tossed one into the air and caught it in his mouth.

"Weally, Christopher! You're an embawwassment."

"Well, nobody can see me," said Christopher. "I can do what I flaming well want and, besides, I'm right famished."

"*I* can see you," said Francis, "and wemember I've had to order that stuff. The waitwess thinks I'm an absolute glutton."

But Christopher wasn't listening and had already put six of the pancakes into his mouth at once and was waggling his hamster cheeks in Francis's face.

"She probably thinks I have tapeworms," said Francis. "I had a tapeworm once."

"I know a cure for tapeworms."

"Cure?" said Francis. "I tell you, I cwied when little Walter died."

"Why does that not surprise me?"

Christopher finished the pancakes, swilled them down with coffee and leaned back in his chair.

Francis picked up a crumb from the plate and moved his hand to his pocket.

"Oh."

"What?"

"My little fwiend has gone," he said.

"I assume that's not a euphemism."

"The rat, Chwistopher."

"He's a rat," said Christopher. "He's probably found the midden."

"No, he's a fwiendly and sociable cweature. We have to look for him."

Francis dropped to the floor and began scurrying around, making friendly squeaking sounds.

"And you think *I'm* an embarrassment?" said Christopher.

JOAN WALKED BACK to the cafe, savouring the rich smell and soft creak of the new leather. A posse of pink cowboys in leather chaps whistled and waved at her. She waved back to them. The bare-bummed gladiators were out in force and the streets were beginning to throng with all manner of painted dolls, bare-chested angels and close knots of grinning, partying men. Things were certainly starting to look pretty gay.

"Hello, little pig," came that unmistakeable and deep voice from behind her.

"Wolfie," she said, and started to turn to face him, a hand on her sword hilt.

"No. Face that way. I have a gun," he said.

Evelyn had been clear on the subject of guns. Guns and badges. Joan complied. Wolfie drew her into the doorway of a closed business.

"Where's Brandy?" she asked.

"You embarrassed us, little pig. That was Brandy's fault. I'm not particularly pleased with her. Bonio, get the sword."

Meaty hands reached to Joan's waist and wrestled with the scabbard.

Joan grunted as he failed to loosen it.

"There's a little buckle," she said.

"Shut up," said Bonio.

"Look. Here. Yep. Through the little hole."

Bonio huffed as he finally pulled her blade away.

"Now, we talk," said Wolfie.

"About what?" said Joan. "Why can't you leave us alone? We left you some of our gold."

"Ah, so there is some more? Good."

He kicked at the plastic bag in Joan's hand. It clanked.

"Give it to me."

"That's not it. That's my armour."

"Metal armour, this dominatrix shit... You're some kind of kinky bitch."

"This outfit is meant to make men obey me. Throw

themselves at my feet, the shopkeeper said. I think I might ask for my money back. I mean, your money..."

"Where is the gold?" Wolfie growled.

"My friends have it."

"No problem," said Wolfie. "Let's go see them. Lead the way."

CHRISTOPHER AND FRANCIS scanned the floor of the cafe for the rat. They were the only customers, so they soon checked every corner of the room. There was an arched doorway that led into another area. It was sectioned off with a beaded curtain, no barrier at all to a curious rat or his worried owner.

Christopher followed Francis into a large room with bright white walls. It was a display space, a gallery of sorts. But all thoughts of rats went from their heads when they saw the exhibits, which were all huge, improbable, and indefinably *rude*.

The one that faced the door was ostensibly a car, but it was a heavily stylised car that leaned back on its back wheels and pointed at the ceiling as though climbing a steep, invisible hill. Huge, bulbous wheel arches at the back, and a bonnet that extended upwards put Christopher in mind of something but he couldn't place it.

He read the placard to the side. It was called 'Road Rage'.

"Francis, what do you make of —"

"Urgh, it's a penis!" squeaked Francis.

"Oh, aye — *that's* what it looks like!" said Christopher,

but then as he turned, he saw that Francis actually meant another exhibit. This one looked like a leather bag filled with marbles, but the card declared that the bag was made from an elephant's penis. It was entitled 'Boys and their Toys'.

"Elephant's penis," said Christopher. "That's..."

"Tewwible. The poor thing. Wandering awound without his member."

"Hang on, is this stuff meant to be *art*?"

"Is it?"

"Whatever happened to the kind of art where painters made pictures of things? I don't hold with this modern faffing about," said Christopher, as he recoiled from something that looked like a chair with penis shapes sprouting from every surface.

"Just the sort of comment I've come to expect," came a gravelly voice.

Christopher and Francis swivelled their heads to see that one of the exhibits was not fixed in place, but was wedged halfway through a door, while a woman with her back to them was trying to push it through.

"Care to give me a hand?" she asked, turning to look at them.

She had black hair, cut in a severe Cleopatra style. From the back she had a boyish figure, but they saw that her face was lined. Heavy eye make-up dared them to cast her as old though. She gave them a challenging glare, an unlit cigarette hanging from the corner of her mouth.

"Er, yes, of course," said Francis, knowing that she must be addressing him. He leant his weight against the large pink structure, only to find that it folded inwards and enveloped him. He gave a shout and backed out rapidly.

"It's latex," explained the woman. "It'll fit through all right, it's just a bit of a handful. It's a fetish dragon costume for the parade."

Francis looked at it critically.

"Is this thing a penis too? I mean, secwetly, metaphowically."

"Isn't everything?" said the woman.

Francis tried to gather folds of the quivering latex while Christopher stood by and laughed.

"It's true, you know," said the woman. "It's all penises. The world is ruled by penises. Politicians, bankers, priests. The people we're supposed to trust to run things. They're all knobs."

Francis had become trapped in the latex again, so Christopher came and gathered the entire thing in his bulky arms and heaved it through the doorway. The pink dragon popped through like a cork, disgorging Francis onto a footpath that ran alongside the canal.

"Great, thanks," said the woman, stepping back inside. "Now, who are you two and what are you doing in my gallery?"

"I'm Fwancis. This is Chwistopher."

"Figures," said the woman, taking out a little flame-making device to light her cigarette and then thinking better of it. "I'm Em. And I guess you're not here just for a weekend of tolerance-themed partying and some heavy man-on-man action."

Christopher was about to answer but was interrupted by the arrival of three people.

"Hi, guys," said Joan as Wolfie and his henchman, Bonio, shepherded her through the curtain. Bonio had a livid bruise on the side of his head from where Joan had clonked him the night before.

"This place is closed," said Em. "No visitors today."

"He's got a gun," announced Joan.

"I don't care if he's got a Turner Prize for me. We're closed."

Wolfie roughly shoved Joan forward past the penis car, the penis chair and an upright plastic contraption of pipes and concertina tubing.

"Is that a penis too?" said Christopher.

"No, that's a vacuum cleaner," said Em. "Although, given the whole witch/broomstick thing is a phallic metaphor, maybe it's just an electric penis."

"Enough of the mad talk," said Wolfie.

"He says he wants more gold," said Joan.

"Didn't we leave him enough?" said Francis.

"I think we left him more than enough. Greed has worked its devilry upon his heart."

"Really?," said Em, shaking her head. "Are you really going to talk like a bad Shakespearean actor in a porn version of a Midsummer's Wet Dream?"

"Who is this woman?" said Joan to Francis.

"Enough!" shouted Wolfie.

"No, it's a good question."

Matt, the newspaper-reading young man who had given them a lift the day before, casually entered the gallery.

"Knock knock," he said. "Hi Joan. Francis. Interesting outfit, Joan. Kind of sexy."

"Yes, what are you wearing?" said Francis.

"The man in the shop said it suited me," said Joan.

"I bet he did," said Matt. "But what you and Francis get up to in your spare time is none of my business."

"See?" said Christopher. "He can't see me. Never could."

"But you, Mrs Van Jochem," he said to Em. "What you get up to in your spare time is of the greatest interest to me."

"You're just an idiot who sticks his nose in where it's not welcome," said Em, with a roll of her eyes.

Wolfie turned and aimed his heavy pistol at Matt.

"I did *not* see that when I entered," said Matt, his swaggering bravado instantly dented.

"I don't give a damn who any of you are," said Wolfie. "You in the dress!"

"Me?" said Francis. "This is a habit."

"We all have habits friend, kinky or otherwise. Now give me my gold before I blow your house down."

"Best do what he says," said Joan. "Evelyn told me. Never argue with people with guns. Or badges."

"Well, this is my badge," said Matt, holding up his wallet to display a card embossed with a crest. "And there's a dozen Dutch police officers outside with their shiny metal badges."

"Well, this is my badge," said Em, pointing to a coloured disc on her lapel that declared her to be a 'Tofu Champion.'

Christopher could see that Joan was trying to calculate the relative importance of a Tofu Champion against a villain, so he decided to change the balance of things a bit. He hefted his weight against the 'Road Rage' installation.

"No!" yelled Em.

The tall structure crashed downward in the space between Matt and Wolfie, nearly crushing Bonio and knocking the gun from Wolfie's hand.

"Patron saint of penis-shaped cars, that's me!" bellowed Christopher as the obscene sculpture smashed apart.

"Run!" yelled Francis, although Em had already done that, fleeing out of the canalside door.

Wolfie and Matt had both leapt for the pistol and rolled on the floor, wrestling among the fragments of the penis car. Joan turned on the stunned Bonio, drew her sword from the scabbard in his hand and laid him out with a flat-bladed blow to the other side of his head. Christopher could see that she was contemplating intervening in the scrap on the floor and barged her towards the rear exit before she could do the right thing.

The canal was packed with colourful boats laden with outlandishly dressed passengers. More people walked along the footpaths, sporting rainbow colours, painted faces and all manner of bizarre accessories.

"Aw crap," said Em.

"What?"

Em pointed out three men in blue uniforms walking up the footpath in their direction.

"Police?" said Christopher.

"Do they have badges?" asked Joan.

Em held up the side of the pink latex sculpture.

"Enter the dragon!"

"What?"

"In! Now!"

Joan went behind Em, Christopher took the middle position and Francis went at the back. They had little handles to hold onto and Christopher found that they could animate the dragon somewhat by moving them around.

He took up the rhythm of some music from a boat that travelled alongside them in the canal. It was loud and joyous, so Christopher made the central part of the dragon leap in time.

"There are so many costumes," said Joan. "So colourful! How lovely to spend time celebrating gayness."

"You do know that 'gay' means 'homosexual' in modern parlance?" said Em from the front.

"Homosexual?" said Joan surprised. "As in..."

"Not straight," said Em.

"What?" said Francis. "Men and, er, men?"

"That's the one."

"And the empress of Europe doesn't punish them for their sinfulness?"

"Careful now," said Em in a darkly warning tone.

"No, that can't be right," Christopher chipped in. "I've seen lots of women joining in the party too."

"Women can be homosexual too," said Em.

Christopher roared with laughter at that.

"Oh, you are funny. Imagine that! How, I mean *how* would that even work?"

Em turned and fixed him with steely look, which wasn't easy when she was threading a path through the crowd for them.

"If I had the time, I'd draw you some diagrams, but right now we have more pressing problems."

Christopher shut up, but giggled every few minutes at the absurdity of the suggestion.

"Chwistopher!" came a loud whisper from behind.

"Yes Francis?"

"Someone else has joined us. He's holding onto my, er, my postewior!"

"Is it a policeman?" Christopher asked.

"No."

"Well ask him what he's doing then."

"Excuse me," said Francis, slightly louder, and turning to the balding man behind him. "Who are you and what are you doing?"

"Hey, I'm Heinz from Helsinki," drawled the man.

"Yes and..?"

"I saw your super-funky dragon and thought I'd insert myself."

"That's, um..."

"Peace and love, man."

"If you say so."

Francis turned back to the front and Christopher caught a glimpse of his tight-lipped expression. He shrugged and continued to make the dragon dance along to the music and tried to avoid staring at Joan's leather-clad fundament jiggling in front of him.

It was a shame that the translucent material prevented them clearly seeing much of the festivities outside. Christopher wondered what their dragon costume looked like from the outside. He hoped it looked like a massive, undulating caterpillar but feared it was just another penis.

"I'm going to have dreams about penises for a month," he muttered.

"I know," said Heinz from the back. "Magical, isn't it?"

"We're going to have to ditch the dragon in a minute," said Em up front.

"So soon?" said Heinz, disappointed.

"Round this corner and then I'm going one way and you lot are not to follow me."

"We understand," said Joan. "So that man, Matt, he's like a thief-taker?"

"He's British police. He could make a lot of trouble for me. And you've clearly met him before."

"Only yesterday. So, does that mean you're some sort of..."

"Criminal? I live on the edges. I do my own thing. Laws are made by cocks for cocks and you've got no right to judge me."

"We all face judgement one day," said Joan.

"Jeez," sighed Em. "*Definitely* not to follow me. Now, three, two, one!"

The dragon collapsed into a rubbery heap at the side of the footpath with Heinz still happily entangled in its rear end. Christopher looked round to get his bearings. Em was already walking briskly up a side street, through the partying masses of men and women.

"We should head this way," he said, pointing.

"Why?" said Joan.

"Travel's my thing. Trust my instincts."

In the direction he was pointing, Christopher saw Wolfie

and a groggy-looking Bonio push through a group of men in grassy hula-skirts.

"Or not," said Christopher.

"This way!" declared Joan.

They hurried down a narrow street through a flock of angels. Some had wings of traditional white, while others had shades of pink and baby blue. All of them had well-oiled six packs and muscly legs. Christopher squeezed through after Joan.

"Homosexuals!" he heard Francis squeak behind him. "They're evewywhere!"

"Just think of them as angels," said Christopher. "Imagine you're back in the Celestial City. There's Gabriel and Uriel and—"

"Whoa!" said Joan. "That one's the spitting image of the Archangel Michael!"

They all paused for a moment to stare.

"Little pigs!" shouted Wolfie from somewhere not too distant, certainly not distant enough.

"Run!" yelled Joan.

"There!" said Christopher.

Down another street, Em stood by a motor vehicle. The door was open and there was a key in her hand.

"VW camper van," said Christopher.

"What?"

"Our quick exit."

Joan nodded tersely and ran to catch up with the woman.

"Em!"

Em looked at them and swore.

"I told you *not* to follow me! You followed me! That's the exact opposite of not following me!"

"We don't know where to go," said Joan.

"Not my problem," snarled the older woman, finally lighting the cigarette clenched between her lips.

Christopher grinned broadly and he ran his hand over the chassis of the vintage vehicle. The paintwork was blotchy in places and there were spots of rust, although it appeared that Em had attempted to cover most up with stickers and badges.

"I've had more prayers and curses directed my way about this beauty than any other vehicle," he said to Francis. He tugged open the side door.

"Oh no you don't!" said Em, smacking his hand.

"But those men keep chasing us," said Joan.

"What men?"

"Bad men."

Em gritted her teeth and then her expression softened.

"I'm running you to the city limits and then you're to leave me the hell alone. I've got enough problems."

"Thank you!" said Joan.

The saints filed in through the side door while Em slid into the driver's seat and started the engine.

"Let's go!" said Christopher.

"Problem," said Em.

Christopher looked up. Wolfie was stood at the driver's window, gun aimed squarely at Em's head.

"See? This is what happens when you're nice to people," said Em to herself.

"Gold," panted Wolfie, breathless from running.

Christopher looked to Francis. Francis dug into his pockets.

"Oh."

"What?"

"There's good news and there's bad news."

"Now!" said Wolfie.

"The bad news is that, in all the kerfuffle, I've mislaid our gold."

"Hand it over," said Wolfie. "Or I'll huff..." – he pulled back the hammer on his pistol – "and I'll puff..."

At that instant, a large grey shape clattered round the corner and launched itself at Wolfie. The villain went down with a scream. There was a loud bang from the pistol and the distant tinkle of breaking glass.

The Wolf of Gubbio stood over Wolfie snarling and drooling into his face. Francis pressed his nose to the window, delight on his face. And then Em floored the accelerator and the three saints tumbled as one to the back of the van.

"Stop! Stop!" howled Francis. "We have to go back for him!"

"Keep going! Keep going!" yelled Joan and Christopher in unison.

Em took corners at terrifying speed, flinging the three of them from side to side. Only when they were passing the city's outskirts did she slow down to a merely alarming speed.

"Let's find a good place to drop you off," said Em. "I can't take you with me."

"We appreciate your help," said Joan. "Although our mission seems to have failed before it's begun."

Francis gazed gloomily out of the back window.

"Hey, buddy," said Christopher. "At least you know he's alive now."

"I suppose so."

"Anyway, you said there was good news and bad news. What's the good news?"

Francis gave him a tiny smile and held aloft a fat brown rat.

"He was in my other pocket all along," said Francis.

"Champion," said Christopher sourly. "We lost all our gold and gained a pet rat."

"Rat? What rat?" said Em from the front.

"Actually, I have a question," said Joan.

"Just the one?" said Em.

"Yes. How come you can see and hear Christopher?"

3

SINT-JAN-IN-EREMO

"**S**till not worked it out?" said Em.

"It's because you're an artist and trained to see what's *really* there," suggested Joan.

"You've ignored church teachings about my deletion perhaps," said Christopher.

"You'd like a little bit, wouldn't you? Wouldn't you?" cooed Francis.

The others looked at him.

Francis was feeding pieces of his hotdog to the rat. The delightful rodent – Always interested! Always sniffing! – gladly took the bread but turned its nose up at the sausage.

"Are you wasting good food on that thing?" said Christopher, stuffing the remainder of his hotdog into his giant gob.

The back roads leading south had, in the late afternoon, brought them back over the border into Belgium. Although Em had explained that country borders in the European Empire were no barrier to the imperial police officers, it seemed as good a time and place as any to stop in order to stretch legs, refuel the camper van and celebrate their freedom with a 'hot dog', a modern delicacy that Francis had been assured did not contain real dog. However, neither he nor the rat could identify exactly what meat it did contain. Francis was in half a mind to go back into the garage café and ask the man what it was.

"Okay," said Em, sighing. "A clue."

She ducked back in the open door of the camper van, came out with a blue and white tea towel and draped it over her head.

"Well, you're no Mother Teresa," said Christopher.

"Seriously? That's your first guess?"

Em adjusted the tea towel, put her hands together and gazed upward in soppy doe-eyed devotion.

"Holy Mary, Mother of God!" gasped Joan.

"Bingo!" shouted Em, one index finger on her nose, the other pointed at Joan.

Francis looked at the woman narrowly.

"No," he said. "The Blessed Mother looks... well, she doesn't look like that."

Em flung the tea towel back in the van, mussed up her hair and lit a cigarette.

"I'll manifest how I damn well please, Franky-Boy. Black, white, Hispanic. Never done Aborigine, but I'm sure I will one day."

"But that policeman called you Mrs van – what was it?"

"What? Mary van Jochem? I've had hundreds of names.

Our Lady of the Gate of Dawn. Star of the Sea. Untier of fucking Knots. Names are nothing."

"But this is great news!" said Joan. "I thought we'd failed but we've found you now and that's fantastic."

Em – Mary – shook her head.

"I don't know what the Big Guy Upstairs wants but the answer's no. I'm not going back just yet. I've got my own plans."

"We don't want you to go back," said Joan. "We want you to come with us to Toulon."

"Toulon? South of France, Toulon?"

"To help us answer a prayer from someone called Simon."

"Never heard of him," said Em.

"That's the problem," said Christopher. "Neither has Heaven. I took the call, listened to him rant about death and killing and the end of the world. I spoke to the bloody feller. And then, then we discover that he doesn't exist."

"What?"

"No such soul," said Christopher.

Em pushed herself out of her slouch against the side of the camper van, cracked her knuckles and opened the driver's door.

"Sorry, kids," she said. "Firstly, what you're saying is gibberish. Secondly, I've got no desire to go to Toulon. That's hundreds of miles from where I need to be."

Joan climbed into the passenger seat. Francis scrambled into the back with Christopher and managed to get the door shut just before Em pulled away from the garage forecourt.

"Besides," said Em, accelerating hard through the flat,

green countryside, "Heaven's got that unit for prayer handling."

"The NSPAU, yes," said Christopher. "I've been rotting away there for over forty years Earth-time. The Almighty says this prayer requires your personal touch."

Em made a disagreeable retching noise.

"What? And just because the High and Mighty says jump, we have to jump?"

"Er, yes," said Joan. "He's God. You know, *the* God."

"Shall I tell you something?"

"Please do."

"God is a man."

"I'm not sure we can impose a gender on the supreme —"

"He's a man," insisted Em, "and like all men, His head is full of dreams and ideas. Lofty thoughts and absolute rules. Black and white. Right and wrong. He's all theory, nothing practical."

"He is the creator of the Heavens and the Earth," said Joan. "You can't get more practical than that."

"Oh, sure. He says, 'let there be light,' and there is light. Grand sweeping bloody gestures. Point is, He can dictate from on high but He doesn't have to live with the reality. He is the creator of all life, but has He ever had to give birth? Or raise a child? Has He ever had to tend a fever or bury a loved one?"

"God is omniscient. He's the gaffer," said Christopher a little uncertainly. "He knows all, doesn't He?"

Em shook her head viciously.

"He can sit on his sodding throne and pass His decrees. Meanwhile, I'm down here on Earth, doing good with my own hands. You ever felt that, eh? The need to actually get out there and *do* something?"

"All the time," said Joan. "That's why I'm here."

Em threw her a split-second smile.

"And yet the Almighty still sends Zippy and Bungle with you to make sure that the little woman doesn't mess it up," she said wryly.

"Who are Zippy and Bungle?" said Francis, looking up.

"Christopher and Francis were not sent to watch over me," said Joan. "I am a proudly independent woman and perfectly capable of handling everything that the world can throw at me."

"Are you sure?" said Em as she threaded the steering wheel loosely through her hands. "Most people would say you're about as much of a feminist icon as the Spice Girls."

"Who?" said Christopher.

"Nobody move!" shouted Francis, arms wide and scouring about.

"What?" said Em, veering across the road in surprise.

"I've lost him," said Francis and got down on his hands and knees.

"I've told you," said Joan. "The wolf can look after himself."

"Not the wolf. Weggie."

"Wedgie?"

"Weginald."

"The rat," sighed Christopher. "Can't have gone far."

"Jeez," said Em. "Look, you guys clearly are a crack squad on a really important mission. I will swing past Brussels Airport and you can fly to your final destination."

"That's not going to be possible," said Christopher.

"Oh?"

"French air traffic controllers are on strike this week."

"How do you know that?" said Joan.

"What's an air twaffic contwoller?" said Francis.

"I just know," said Christopher. "Patron saint of travel and all that. And they're always on strike anyway."

"Well, that's just swell," said Em. "Fine. I've got to go to Paris. That's on your way. I'll take you that far but no further."

"Very kind of you," said Joan.

"There!" shouted Francis, seeing Reggie round by Em's feet.

He shoved forward into the front of the van, hands outstretched. Perhaps the sudden movement had been unwise. Jostled, Em swerved and tried to stamp on the brakes. Francis grabbed her foot and the pedal before either could crush the cowering rat.

Em swore loudly. Joan gripped the dashboard. Christopher apparently offered a prayer up to himself. Francis, down in the foot-well didn't see the grassy verge, the hedge or the beet field beyond but felt every jolt and judder as the van ploughed through them.

Joan stepped out on the soft loamy soil and inspected the campervan. Much of the front was bent and buckled. One of the little round lights had exploded. The front wheels, each pointing in different directions were half buried in the mud.

"It doesn't look too bad," she said. "Perhaps, we could get some ropes and..."

"Too bad?" shrieked Em, slamming the driver's door and stomping round in white-soled exercise shoes that were perhaps not well suited to a muddy Belgian field. Joan was glad that her thigh-length dominatrix boots were made of sturdier stuff. "We've snapped a cocking axle!" yelled Em. "And as for the bodywork..."

Francis slipped and stumbled out the side door, clutching his head. He had clearly bashed it in the final impact. Em went up to him and grabbed him by the temples.

"Not bleeding," she said. "Can you see straight?"

Francis breathed deeply.

"Think so."

Em tilted his head back and peered in his eyes, one at a time.

"No wooziness or vomiting?"

He shook his head.

"Good," she said, took a step back and laid a vicious punch on his jaw that laid him out on the ground.

"What did I do?" he moaned, clutching his face.

"What did you...?" Em's words slipped away into an inarticulate roar.

She patted her pockets aggressively for her cigarettes and, failing to find them, swore again. She looked past the campervan, at the long muddy grooves in the field and the ragged hole in the hedge.

"Right," she declared loudly. "Travel-boy, get out here."

Christopher stepped from the campervan.

"That town we just passed, Sint-Jan..."

"Sint-Jan-in-Eremo."

"There was a tow truck behind that garage, wasn't there?"

"Bruggeman Sleepdiensten."

"Right. You and me. It can't be more than a four mile walk," she said and began to make her way back to the road.

"And what should we do?" asked Joan.

"Think for yourself, woman," shouted Em without looking back. And then she stopped and turned briefly. "It's going to be night soon. We need accommodation, unless you want us to camp out in this bloody field. Mr Invisible! This way!"

Joan watched them go and then went to help Francis up.

"She hurt me," said Francis. "Weally hurt me."

"I think she considers us a burden," said Joan.

Reggie scrabbled up Francis' leg and inside his habit.

"Us?" he said.

"Let's do our best to help out. Maybe we can find rooms at that place over there," she said, looking at a square brick-built house further up the road. "Or at least get some directions to the nearest inn."

THE SQUARE HOUSE, it transpired, was a farmhouse. Beneath a carved pig's head, were the words, 'De Wilde Zwijnen - Kosthuis.' Francis knocked at the front door but there was no response and so the two saints, one in leather bondage gear, the other in a mud-spattered habit, went round the back of the building to where a low wire fence separated the house from an array of animal pens and the fields beyond.

The woman scooping food into a rabbit cage looked up at them, not with surprise but with great interest.

"I imagine you have quite a story to tell," she said.

"I'm sorry," said Joan. "We tried knocking. Our vehicle has broken down and we're looking for rooms to rent."

The woman tossed the scoop into a bucket and called out to the man tending to some larger animals.

"Hey, Martijn! Visitors!"

The man waved and began to make his way up towards them. The woman wiped her hands on her apron and shook hands with the pair of saints across the wire fence.

"Ida Couckuyt. Let me guess," she said, looking them up and down. "You've come from Amsterdam. Had a crazy time of it too, I should think."

"How did you know?" said Francis.

"Spooky, huh? Martijn, this is..."

"Joan," said Joan. "This is Francis."

Martijn gave them a wave of greeting. Like the woman – who Francis guessed was his wife or maybe sister – he was dressed in a shabby jumper and jeans. Both had lined faces and ruddy cheeks, offset by intelligent eyes and an almost constant smile.

"They want rooms," said Ida.

"And a bit of a warm up and some food," added Martijn. "And some fresh clothes for the lady?"

"But these are new."

"I'm sure we can find you something a little more... comfortable."

The woman stepped over the little fence and led them through the side door into a large, clean kitchen.

"Martijn, take Joan through to the good room, get them checked in and then let her have her pick of the women's clothes upstairs. Francis, put yourself down there. Tea?"

"Thank you," said Francis, grateful for a simple seat in a warm house.

As Joan and the man left the room, the woman Ida filled a kettle from a tap and placed it on the top of the wide cooking range. At the flick of a button a ring of blue flame appeared beneath the kettle.

"Do you mind me asking," she said. "Are you really a man of the cloth or is this some sort of fancy dress thing?"

"I am a lesser bwother of the church."

"But you travel with...?"

"Joan is also of the faith."

"Really?"

Ida opened a tall cupboard that was some form of ingenious ice-box and inspected the plastic tubs within. All were marked with names. Laila, Hans, Yasmine, Henri.

"Would sausages for dinner be acceptable?" asked Ida, taking down a box marked 'Arnaud'.

"We ate hotdog sausages in the last town," said Francis.

"At old Bruggeman's place? Then you've already tried our produce. We supply meat products to a lot of the local places."

"You keep animals for food?" said Francis, attempting to keep any note of condemnation out of his voice.

"That too," said Ida. "Do you like animals?"

Francis smiled.

"I love animals."

Ida smiled.

"Then tea and sausages can wait. I'll give you the tour of

the menagerie."

MARTIJN SAT Joan down on a lumpy settee covered with a crocheted throw and took a sheaf of printed forms and a pencil from a sideboard.

He licked the pencil and smiled.

"So. Name?"

"Joan."

"Surname?"

"D'Arc."

"Joan Dark. And where are you from?"

"Domrémy. In Lorraine."

"France. You live there with your family?"

"Er, no. I don't have any family. Not alive I mean."

"No parents?" said Martijn.

"No. They died a long... long time ago."

"So no one knows that you and Francis are out this way?"

Joan shrugged.

"Heaven knows."

Martijn smiled at that and made a note on the form.

Martijn produced a device from the side of his seat and held it up in front of his face. There was a click, a temporarily blinding flash and a shiny square of card rolled out of the base of the device.

"Right," he smiled brightly. "I'm sure that will be lovely. Now, health. Do you drink?"

"Doesn't everyone?"

"Alcohol."

"Oh. Only communion wine."

"Smoke?"

Joan shook her head. She could honestly say she had only smoked once and that was when they burned her at the stake.

"I have to ask," said Martijn, "do you use drugs?"

"My body is a temple," said Joan.

"Glad to hear it. No history of STIs."

"STIs?" said Joan.

"I'll put that as a no. Any incidence of Creutzfeldt-Jakob Disease in your family?"

"Do you ask all your guests this many questions?" she said, curious despite not wishing to appear naïve and unworldly.

"Nearly done," Martijn said cheerily. "Do you know your Body Mass Index?"

"Does it?" she said.

"So, what's in Paris?"

"Sorry?"

Christopher gazed at the road ahead. It might be only four miles back to the garage but on a road so straight and featureless – field, field, wooden post, field – boredom had settled on him very quickly. Belgium, he guessed, was one of those places that the Almighty had created as an afterthought to fill a hole in the map.

"You said you had to go to Paris," he said. "Or did I mishear?"

"I have friends in Paris," said Em.

"Oh, right. Who?"

"Well, not friends as such. Contacts."

Christopher shrugged.

"What does that mean?"

"You wouldn't understand." Em patted herself down for cigarettes for the tenth time in as many minutes. "I'm something of a player in the anti-capitalist movement."

"You're right. I don't understand. You're against capitalism?"

"Yes."

"The idea of... capital."

"If you wish."

"So people shouldn't own stuff."

"Exactly."

Christopher considered this.

"So... if you had your way, these wouldn't be *my* sandals?"

"I think you can have your own sandals."

"This tunic?"

Em grimaced and sped up a little. Christopher had no problems keeping pace with her.

"It's not about the little things," said Em. "It's about the big things."

"Like houses?"

"Perhaps."

"So, my house shouldn't belong to me?"

"No."

"Who should it belong to?"

"Everyone."

"But it's not a big house. I don't think there'd be room for everyone."

"You're missing the point," she said.

"I hope so."

"It's about entitlement. It's about breaking down the plutocratic oligarchies."

"Ah..." said Christopher, none the wiser.

"For example, have you heard of Anonymous?" said Em.

"Heard of him," said Christopher. "Never met him. But I know he's written lots of stuff."

For the next two miles, Christopher was subjected to a lecture on Anonymous, the anti-capitalist movement and the reasons why a thing called 'globalisation' was bad. Apparently, globalisation was something that people did naturally, but Christopher got the distinct impression that Em regarded it as the fault of men generally and the Almighty in particular. Christopher listened patiently. It wasn't interesting but, as far as boring stuff went, it was better than just staring at Belgium.

By the time they arrived back at the garage, Christopher was convinced he'd be an ideal recruit for Anonymous and told Em as much.

"Why?" she said.

"I'm invisible," he said. "I'd be ideal for all that 'anti-establishment' stuff. Below the radar. Off the grid. Whatever that means."

"It's closed," said Em.

"Have they got too many members already?"

"Not Anonymous, you fool. The garage."

She was right. The shop door was shut. The lights were off. Even in the evening gloom, Christopher could see the tow truck had gone. Christopher followed Em as she strolled over to a pair of cars at the edge of the forecourt.

"Anyone can join the fight against the dicks and dictators," said Em. "Whether it's part of an organisation or alone. Just get out there and stand up for the rights of the common people. Stand up for freedom of information, for the freedom to be who we want to be, for the freedom to choose our own destinies."

Em peered into the windows of the first car. It was a dusty old saloon. Christopher knew, without knowing how he knew, that despite its appalling fuel consumption, the car was a relatively sound vehicle.

"Freedom of information?" he asked.

"Sure. Knowledge is power," she said, moving on to look at the second car, a Volvo estate with a leaky carburettor and a dodgy gearbox. "If we are to have equality for all people then everyone is entitled to know everything."

"Everything? What, even like my own personal secrets?"

"Well, no. The individual's right to privacy and personal security is very important," said Em and, gathering her coat sleeve up around her fist, punched in the Volvo's passenger window.

"What are you doing?" said Christopher, astonished.

"We need a ride. Our need is greater."

"Yes, but..."

"But what?" said Em, giving him a challenging glare. "Still clinging to notions of property and privilege?"

"Yes, but, I mean... I could have done that." Christopher clicked his fingers and the door locks all sprung open. "Patron saint of cars, me."

Em gave him a withering look.

"You know, you can't fight an army of dicks if you're going to be one yourself."

At the local Carrefour, Antoine Chevrolet bought several packs of luxury dog food.

"These are the ones mummy buys, aren't they?" he asked of little Anna as they loaded up the car.

"Mummy's gone," said little Anna.

"Just back to work. Important stuff. Computer stuff." Antoine inspected one of the tins. The dog on the label looked very happy. At those prices, it ought to. "Let's see if this helps dear Milou get back to her usual perky self," he said.

Dear little Milou had been off her food for more than a day. Antoine Chevrolet was certain her encounter with that horrible shaggy beast was to blame.

"Big doggy," said little Anna.

"Yes, it was," said Antoine. "But it was a wolf."

"Big doggy!"

"No, a wolf."

"Big doggy!"

Before Antoine could open his mouth to correct his daughter once more, the beast bounded onto the bonnet of the car, over the other side and sprinted off towards the south.

FRANCIS FOUND the Couckuyt gardens and menagerie a thorough delight. Francis, though an advocate of vegetarianism and love towards all living things, respected the natural order of the Almighty's world. And although Ida and Martijn were, to be blunt, butchers, he regarded their attempts to live close to nature to be quite inspirational.

Behind the rabbit pens and guinea pig hutches, was Ida's small but crowded herb garden.

"It's not only the meat and vegetables we produce ourselves," she said. "We have a pair of goats for milk and cheese and here we have all the herbs I use in our cooking."

She plucked a sprig of fennel and thrust it under Francis' nose.

"The right seasoning transforms food," she said.

"Absolutely," said Francis.

"And I think matching scents and tastes is really important. It's like finding the right perfume for a person."

She took hold of Francis' wrist and bent her head to smell it.

"You see, you're not a fennel person."

"No?"

She picked a leaf and rubbed it against his wrist.

"Mmm, yes," she said. "You're a rosemary person. Maybe with a touch of mint."

"Weally?" said Francis and sniffed at his wrist. "Indeed. Well, best pop me in the pot and serve with potatoes and gween beans," he laughed.

Ida led him on.

"And here is our prize stock," she said, gesturing to a square enclosure of squat, bristle-covered boars.

"Wild boar," said Francis. "Beautiful things."

He crouched down and snorted at the one nearest the fence. It trotted over to him and stuck its snout through between the fence slats. Francis got his nose right down to the boar's and they snuffled at each other, talking and listening.

"You really do love animals," said Ida.

"All my best fwiends are animals," he replied, thinking about the rat inside his habit and the Wolf of Gubbio, many miles distant and all alone. "You eat these animals?"

"Yes."

"But they don't know that?"

Ida frowned at him.

Francis gave the boar one last snort and, with a squeal, it ran off.

"I never lie to animals," he said, standing up. "Animals are honest cweatures. We should be nothing less."

"Something we've learned," said Ida, "is that the emotional state of the, er, animal has an effect on the flavour of the meat."

"Weally?"

"Sadness and depression ruins the taste of the meat. And yet..." Ida smiled to herself.

"Yes?" said Francis.

"Let me show you," she said and beckoned him towards a shed with a corrugated iron roof.

Ida threw the stiff bolt across on the door.

"My grandfather lived in Mol over to the east, the other side of Antwerp. He used to hunt boar in the woods there." She opened the door and reached into the shadowed interior for a long bundle in a greased cloth. She unwrapped it to reveal a narrow-barrelled rifle. "He was a great hunter."

"That's a gun, isn't it?"

"What else? My grandfather believed that wild boar tasted better when it had died knowing it was being hunted, as though fear were the most vital seasoning."

"I see," said Francis uncomfortably.

"And then came 1940 and the Nazi invasion and my grandfather hunted a wholly different kind of animal in those woods." Ida stroked the rifle thoughtfully. "But," she said with sudden brightness, "if it wasn't for him, Martijn and I wouldn't be the people we are today."

"My," said Joan. "There are a lot of clothes here."

She sifted quickly but politely through the tops, trousers and skirts on the low shelves in the upstairs room. They were all different sizes and styles but were clean and precisely folded.

"Ida can't bear to throw anything away," said Martijn from the other side of the closed door. "But take what you like."

Joan called out her thanks but she could already hear his footsteps tramping down the wooden stairs.

It was apparent, despite the shopkeeper's enthusiasm, that she wasn't going to be taken particularly seriously dressed all in leather. Joan swiftly selected a black top emblazoned with the words, 'The Clash', a pair of lace-up boots — she hoped calf length wasn't as scandalous as thigh length — a pair of lightweight trousers and a cotton jacket with a hood and zipper. As she shrugged into this last item, she felt the weight of objects in the jacket pocket.

The first item was a small plastic toy, a soft-bodied goblin figure with an enormous shock of pink hair. The weird troll-like thing had large eyes, an idiotic grin on its face and made a squeaky sound when squeezed. The second item was a black rectangle, which she recognised as a phone.

As she looked at the phone, it began to vibrate in her hand and the screen lit up. Automatically, she lifted it to her ear.

"Hello?"

"Mother Mary, is that you?"

It was a man's voice, quiet but earnest.

"Who is this?" said Joan.

"It is done."

"What is? Who are you?"

"It is Simon. Mother Mary, I have done it."

"What have you done?"

"The first angel sounded his trumpet, and there came hail and fire mixed with blood, and it was hurled down upon the earth. A third of the earth was burned up, a third of the trees were burned up, and all the green grass was burned up."

Joan recognised the quotation.

"Simon, what have you done?"

There was no reply.

"Simon? Simon?"

She looked at the phone. The screen was covered in little pictures, like tiny religious icons. She tapped at them experimentally. The screen changed and something began to flash. She held the phone up again.

"Simon?" she said.

"Laila?" said the man's voice on the other end. This was a different voice. Tired and old and strained.

"I'm sorry," said Joan. "I think I..."

"Is that you? Where are you?"

"Where am I?" she asked.

"Please," said the man, a whine of desperation in his voice.

Joan wasn't sure what he wanted.

"Er, I'm at the Wild Boar Guesthouse near Sint-Jan-something-or-other. In Belgium."

"Are you safe? Are you well?"

Confused and a tad disturbed by the man's demanding tone, Joan held the phone away and pressed the icons again until his voice stopped.

Joan put the phone and the troll toy back in her pocket and went downstairs. Maybe Martijn could explain about the man with all the questions, although she imagined she would need to go to a higher authority for answers about the call from Simon.

Martijn was neither in the kitchen or the 'good room'. There was no sign of Ida or Francis either. Joan was on the verge of going outside to search for them, when she saw a line of light outlining a previously unopened door off from the kitchen. The door had a heavy clasp and padlock on it, but the padlock was undone and the clasp thrown back. Joan tried the door. It opened to reveal a flight of concrete steps leading down into a brightly lit cellar. There was the hum of electricity in the air.

Joan stepped down, slowly, with a trill of guilt at the possible incursion into the Couckuyt's privacy. At a half turn in the stairs, there was a side door. Joan looked in. Stacked neatly in one corner of the storeroom was a pile of rucksacks, next to them a smaller pile of suitcases and pull-along bags. In another corner was a collection of sleeping bags, blankets and items of camping equipment. Joan might have paid them closer attention had she not then been drawn to a collection of pictures pinned to the wall just inside the door.

Twenty or more square photographs of individual men and women, of all ages although most of them quite young, were arranged in a neat grid on the wall, held in place with brass pins. In fat black pen, names had been written underneath each of them. Arnaud, David, Eva...

"Laila," said Joan, touching the picture of a young, fair-haired woman.

And then she understood.

"So obvious," she chided herself.

Laila had been one of the guests. The Couckuyt's took photographs of all their guests and Laila must have accidentally left her phone behind, or perhaps the jacket containing her phone, when she moved on.

Joan looked at the pile of bags and belongings. And maybe these were items other guests had forgotten to take with them.

"There are a lot of forgetful people in Belgium," she said.

~

FRANCIS PETTED THE ALPACA.

"Twuly beautiful cweatures," he said to Ida. "Fwiendly. Hard-working. The softest wool."

"And they have a rich taste and texture," said Ida.

"You eat these too?" said Francis.

"Absolutely," said Ida. "All the breeds and species we keep have ended up on our plates at one time or another."

"Guinea pigs?"

"Everything."

"The hedgehogs?"

"Everything."

"Even the little fewwets with the cute little noses?" said Francis, moving over to the wire-fronted shed in which the weasel creatures scampered.

"We are subsistence farmers," said Ida. "We are pragmatists. But Martijn and I also like to consider ourselves to be culinary explorers."

Francis made clicking noises at the ferrets through the wire. Several of them ran over to him.

"Such intelligent cweatures," he said.

"Almost any living thing can be food for us," said Ida, behind him. "What matters is that, whatever we eat, we source the finest ingredients available. Good eating costs. Look at the scandal there was a few years back when they discovered that all the big supermarkets put illegal horsemeat in their 'economy' meals. Martijn and I have eaten horse in our time but at least we know it was the finest grass-fed horse."

The ferrets chattered to one another and Francis chattered with them.

"We are what we eat," said Ida.

"Oh, that we are," Francis agreed.

"But most people don't understand that. They feed animals on things that we wouldn't even contemplate touching and yet those people, in turn, eat those very same animals."

The ferrets had become agitated and were bouncing back and forth across their cage.

"I mean, it's true," said Ida philosophically, "that, if we should only feed animals on foodstuffs we would be prepared to eat ourselves, we could argue that we should all become vegetarian, eat those foodstuffs ourselves and cut out the middle man as it were."

"A wise position to take," said Francis.

"But the thing is," said Ida, "we just love the taste of meat."

There was a metallic click. Francis turned.

Ida had the rifle pointed at his face and, although he knew very little about the modern ways of earth, he knew he was looking directly into the dangerous end.

"I imagine you've been a clean-living man all your life," said Ida. "Lots of fruit and vegetables."

In fear, Francis clutched at the wire barrier behind him.

"You eat people?!" he choked.

Ida took a deep, satisfied breath.

"Are you surprised? Wasn't it *your* lord who said, 'This is my body. Eat it in memory of me'?"

In a single moment, Francis found a knot of defiance in his belly, born of the woman's blasphemy, and also found the latch to the ferret cage beneath his hand. Francis twisted the latch, pulled and threw himself to one side as Ida fired.

WIM SAW that the wolf was back, this time swimming south back across the Westerschelde. Not that he cared. His attention, his whole heart, was focused on getting the detective to listen.

"I know," he said, wearily. "I know, I know. But I spoke to her or someone who sounded very much like her. It was her phone."

"And what did she say?" asked the detective.

"Not much," said Wim. "But she said she was at a place called the Wild Boar Guesthouse. It's in Belgium. Some nowhere place called Sint-Jan-in-Eremo."

"I understand," said the detective. "We can look into it."

Wim recognised that tone of voice.

"No," he insisted. "You must do something. Find Laila for me."

"I'm just going to put you on hold for a minute," said the detective.

Wim sighed as the line went silent. He gazed out of the window but the wolf had gone from sight.

"IDA?" called a voice from downstairs.

"No, it's me, Mr Couckuyt," said Joan.

The final steps, with no support banister at the side,

overlooked a clean, tiled room. The manacles and chains against one wall reminded Joan of the dungeons at Rouen but she was certain this was no dungeon. This was a workshop of some variety. There was a steel device of sliding blades over there and, above a long bench, various cleavers, skewers and hooks. Martijn stood by a table-shaped machine directly below the stairs. Interlocking lines of sharp-edged screws within covered a funnel beneath that then fed out into a steel pan.

"You shouldn't be here," he said. "Not yet."

"I'm sorry," said Joan. "I didn't mean to intrude."

"You're here now though."

Martijn flicked a switch on the machine and it came to life, the long screws rolling against one another in a continuous slicing action. Joan stared down into its maw from her position on the stairs.

"The Haarstek Crusher 30. We use this one for doing a whole carcass at once. Sometimes we need to process one in a hurry. It's a sight to behold, I can tell you. Ida has certain theories regarding the effect that fear has on the taste of the meat." Martijn held his hands over the grinding screws. "The look in their eyes when they're fed into it feet first..."

Joan wasn't sure she understood. Like most of the conversations she'd had since coming back to Earth, Joan had understood perhaps one word in three. She realised that her hand in her pocket was clutching the phone.

"I came down to ask you about something," she said.

"I imagine that you have plenty of questions right now," said Martijn and stepped towards her, his rubber-soled boots creaking on the tiles.

"It's about these clothes," she said.

"Which you won't be needing any longer."

"Sorry? Look." She pulled the phone from her pocket. The little plastic troll fell out from her pocket as she did so, landing on the edge of the steps.

"There's no reception down here," said Martijn, one foot on the stairs. "Ida will be back any minute and then we can begin."

IDA COUCKUYT SCREAMED and staggered round in the garden, arms outstretched, trying to dislodge the half dozen blonde ferrets that clung to her, their sharp teeth embedded in her flesh. She scraped a pair of them off with the rifle she still clutched in her hand. She bashed another off against the guinea pig hutch. She threw herself into a high-speed spin, an uncoordinated pirouette which sent two more flying off her, wheeling end over end and squeaking into the night. She stopped and stumbled dizzily. Her thighs caught the edge of a fence and she tumbled over into the mud on the other side.

One ferret — the usually placid Erica, she noted with anger and surprise — sat on her face, claws and teeth biting at her cheek. Ida roared, grabbed Erica's furry little body and ripped her away, crying through the pain as Erica's teeth pulled apart the flesh of her cheek. She flung the ferret away, back over the fence, and lay on the ground panting and groaning.

She was bewildered. She hurt but, more than that, she

was bewildered. The ferrets had never shown aggressive behaviour like that before.

What had that weird monk done to them? And where was he now? Had he stirred them up in some way? He had been squeaking and clicking at them just before it happened. But he had also been speaking in his strange little way to the alpaca and the rabbits and the boars...

There was a snort from the darkness behind her head. Ida rolled over. There were several snorts and snuffles from the darkness, short, sharp sounds of disagreement. She got to her feet with difficulty and peered into the murk.

Eight squat, hairy boars charged at her from the shadows, snouts glistening, teeth bared. Ida instinctively brought the rifle up to shoot and then saw the barrel was bent out of true.

"Oh, hell," she muttered and then it was too late.

By torchlight, Christopher helped Em transfer the essentials from the crashed campervan to the stolen Volvo. Most of the stuff was Em's. He and Francis had no personal belongings and Joan's amounted to a heavy duty plastic bag that contained her armour. He removed her computer tablet as Joan had complained earlier about the battery being dead.

"You sure you can manage that lot?" said Em, watching him take the armour, a duffel bag of Em's things and several blankets in one go.

"I've carried much heavier in my time," said Christopher.

"Really?" Em gathered up the few remaining items.

"Oh, aye. As I'm sure you know, I once carried the infant

Christ across a raging river."

"Is that so?"

The Virgin Mother had relaxed considerably since finding her spare cigarettes and lighter in the campervan.

"Right heavy he were," said Christopher. "His weight bore down on me more and more with every step."

"He was a skinny whelp," said Em.

"Not in my recollection, but he was as bonny as the sun itself. Radiant and beautiful."

"Really?" said Em and then grunted to herself. "Let me show you something."

She pulled a flat silver box from her inner pocket, flicked a switch on the side and a picture appeared on the grey screen.

"It's a piece of burned toast," said Christopher.

"Ah, but look at the burnt bits. There, the eyes, the shape of the jaw..."

Em pressed a button and the image changed.

"A cloud," said Christopher.

"But if you imagine that these are his legs and this his robe and this..."

"Sorry?"

Another image.

"What is that?" said Christopher.

"A patch of damp I found in a hotel in Warsaw."

"You made this picture of it?"

"Took it, yes. It's a camera."

"Why?"

"Can't you see?" she said. "The nose, the mouth, the beard. It's him. It looks just like him."

Christopher frowned.

"Father Christmas?"

"Jesus! It's Jesus. My son."

"Oh, that Jesus," said Christopher slowly. "Oh, oh, of course. See it now. Obvious."

Em's shoulders slumped and she stuffed the picture box camera thing back in her pocket.

"Two thousand years," she said. "And I don't even have any proper pictures of him. But a mother knows her son when she sees him. Come on."

They carried their items to the car.

"You met my boy once – allegedly," said Em. "You didn't have to raise the little bugger."

"Bugger?"

Christopher stopped at the roadside and unloaded his burden into the car boot.

"He was not an easy child," said Em. "Keys."

"Front seat. I don't think you can pass that sort of judgement on Christ," said Christopher disapprovingly.

"I'm his mum. Of course I bloody can."

They got in the car. Em started the engine which, with a little patience and some additional willpower from Christopher, spluttered into action.

"Where to?" said Christopher.

"To find Franky-Boy and Girl Wonder," said Em as she pulled away. "Tell me, have you ever heard of the Infancy Gospel of Thomas?"

"The stories of your time in Egypt after you had to run away from King What's-His-Name? They're made up, aren't they?"

"I wish," said Em. "Some of the miracles he performed in the early days were harmless enough. Bringing clay birds to life, making a plank expand to fit his father's wonky table but, generally, he was insufferable as a toddler."

"I must protest," said Christopher.

"You weren't there. Imagine a three year old throwing a tantrum, a three year old with the power of God. If a kid took his toys or accidentally knocked him over, he'd blind them or worse. He turned one boy to dust, like an Egyptian mummy. You think it's hard getting a three year old to give up his nu-nu, you try getting him to restore sight or bring someone back to life."

"I simply can't believe our Lord would be such a mardy little tyke."

"He was a child. I think the worst was when he learned how to turn breastmilk into wine. I was drunk for a week before I worked out what he was doing. He was tough one to raise, all right."

"Let's try here," said Christopher, pointing at a driveway and a sign shaped like a boar's head.

Em swung into the driveway at speed.

"Yeah, that boy was wilful. Like his dad."

"Which dad?" said Christopher.

"Ha! Both. Bloody men."

A robed figure staggered into their headlights, waving his arms frantically.

"Watch out!" yelled Christopher.

Em wrenched the wheel to the right to avoid St Francis. Unfortunately, there was a house in the way.

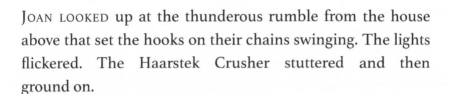

JOAN LOOKED up at the thunderous rumble from the house above that set the hooks on their chains swinging. The lights flickered. The Haarstek Crusher stuttered and then ground on.

"What the—" exclaimed Martijn.

Joan turned to go and investigate.

"No!" yelled Martijn. "You're not going anywhere."

Joan was sure that she should stay to continue to offer her apologies for trespass to Martijn, but that violent roar spoke to her of destruction and possible threat to life. She couldn't ignore such things. She ran up the stairs, Martijn close on her heels.

As she neared the top, she heard the sharp squeak of the troll toy, perhaps beneath Martijn's booted feet.

"Oh," said Martijn, his voice rising in genuine surprise. "Oh... oh..."

WITH THE PASSENGER door blocked by fallen brickwork, Christopher had to climb over the driver's seat to get out. The front end of the Volvo was at one with the wall of the house, rubble, steel and plastic strewn around.

Em stood in the muddy driveway over the fallen figure of Francis.

"We hit him?" said Christopher.

"*We* didn't," said Em. "*I* did."

There was a crunch of brickwork and Joan clambered out

through the remains of the house door.

"What happened?" she called.

"This bearded tit," spat Em, pointing a finger at Francis, "seems intent on destroying every vehicle I get into."

Francis scrambled to his feet, wide-eyed.

"They're killers..." he mumbled. "All the animals... sausages..."

"I know," said Joan, reassuringly. "They're meat farmers. Don't let it get to you."

"No." Francis, close to tears, shook his head.

"Can anyone smell anything?" said Christopher.

Em looked at the remains of the kitchen wall and then at Christopher.

"Shit. We've ruptured a gas pipe. Come on. Away. Away."

"What?" said Joan.

"Bad stuff," said Em. "We need to get some distance."

Christopher helped the incoherently upset Francis down the driveway, while Em rescued all she could from the car boot.

"Was there anyone else in the house?"

"Martijn was in the cellar," said Joan. "I think I upset him. Where's Ida, Francis?"

Francis flung his hand in the general direction of the gardens.

"Perhaps it is best if we leave now," agreed Joan.

A large coach — ideal for long crusades, thought Christopher – rumbled past as they reached the road. There was no other traffic visible on the road, no other signs of life in the darkness.

"Great," muttered Em. "Stranded in Belgium. The stuff of

nightmares."

"We need transport," said Christopher.

"Well, obviously."

Christopher looked down the road, concentrated for a second and coughed. There was a bang from the coach, a blaze of red lights and the vehicle came to a halt, with a noise like a sack of cement falling onto a set of bagpipes.

"Let's catch ourselves a lift," he said.

They hurried down the road to the coach. The driver, a portly fellow with a loose tie around his neck looked under the vehicle.

"Hello," said Joan.

The driver scratched his head.

"Could swear we'd had a blow out but they're all sound."

"Probably just a stone bouncing off the underside," suggested Christopher.

"Probably just a stone bouncing off the underside," Joan relayed to the driver.

"If you say so," he said, confused.

"Sir," said Joan, "our vehicle has crashed some distance back and we're without transport."

"Is everyone all right?" said the driver, looking at Francis.

"All the little animals..." whimpered Francis.

"He'll be fine," said Em. "Could you possibly give us a lift?"

The driver took a noisy intake of breath.

"Ooh, that would be against company policy."

"Colin!" snapped a woman's voice from aboard the coach. "Don't you dare leave those people out there in this Godforsaken country!"

The driver gave them the look of a man who had been subject to such stern treatment for a very long time and waved them onto the bus. The coach appeared to be full of old women, some asleep in their seat but most of them intent on the new passengers.

A sharp-faced and beady-eyed woman gestured to spaces beside her.

"Plenty of seats here," she said. "Sit down before that fool Colin changes his mind."

Christopher dumped Francis into a seat and tried to squeeze into the cramped space beside him. In the end, he admitted defeat and sat down with his legs in the aisle.

"Thank you," said Joan. "I'm Joan. This is Em."

"And your overwrought friend?"

"Franky-Boy is bit sensitive," said Em. "He's also a dick."

The sharp-faced woman smiled.

"I'm Agnes. Don't you worry, Em. We in the Aberdaron Women's Institute are very good at keeping our men in line. Now, I gather you've had something of an eventful evening."

IDA COUCKUYT TOTTERED up the garden to the house, weeping in pain and distress. The attack by the ferrets had been bad enough. But then the boars had turned on her and she had barely got away with her life. There were deep cuts to her arms and the ache of a hundred trotter stamps on her back and she could still hear them out there, cavorting and snorting victoriously in their field. And *now* she was presented with the sight of a car embedded in her kitchen wall and brickwork either fallen or leaning precariously out of position.

"Martijn!"

There was no response. Sniffing back tears, she stumbled inside, looking for her beloved. He had gone down to the cellar to clean the machines and make preparations for their latest 'guests'. Even in the lightless kitchen, she could see the cellar door was open and she carefully, painfully, made her way down the stairs.

Most of the lights had gone out — perhaps the car crash had tripped some of the circuits — but, as she neared the bottom, she could see something was clearly wrong. From what little light came down the stairs, it was possible to see the Haarstek Crusher and something sticking out of it. Were those things legs? Were those Martijn's rubber boots?

Ida dashed the tears from her eyes. She couldn't see clearly. She refused to *believe* what she was seeing.

Ida sniffed and reached for the light switch.

CHRISTOPHER LOOKED round to see an enormous explosion of yellow fire unfold in the fields behind them. He turned to tell Joan but it had burned itself out almost instantly and was gone.

"Eventful evening?" said Agnes.

"No," said Em hurriedly. "Not at all. It's been quite boring all told."

Agnes tutted.

"Well, that's Belgium for you."

4

ROUEN

Francis was suspicious of the bed covering.

It was so flimsy and light that he had assumed he'd need to sleep in his habit and yet so delightfully cosy that he suspected that modern bed coverings might be responsible for a lapse in morals. Loud snoring noises from the next bed told him that Christopher was more than comfortable too. The sun was well up, daylight a golden haze in the gauzy curtains of the hotel room.

"Positively encourages sloth," said Francis and, with some reluctance, flung the bed covering aside.

He padded through to the lavatorium and gazed round at the collection of porcelain that sparkled before him. He turned the taps on and off in the wash basin, certain that he had the measure of that one. There was another basin, lower down, presumably for feet. He tested the flush on the toilet with a knowing nod. Em had explained about chamberpots as she saw Francis discreetly pick up an ice bucket on the way to the rooms last night. So, that just left the puzzle of the partitioned area to the left. He approached it cautiously.

It was equipped with controls and levers similar to the automobiles that he'd seen, and he really didn't want to crash this one. He opened the door and pushed a button. He was horrified to discover that water cascaded from above.

"Oh, Heavens," he squeaked. "I've broken it."

As his hands dithered over the controls, he realised that the water washing over them was warm. Could this strange booth actually be intended for ablutions? Francis pulled his hand back and then moved it forward into the warm water.

"That *is* nice."

He wondered what would happen if he stepped inside.

CHRISTOPHER WOKE TO A CURIOUS NOISE. An anguished howling accompanied by a splashing sound emanated from the bathroom. He rolled his bulk out of the sagging bed and pressed his ear against the closed door of the bathroom. The noise was definitely coming from inside; Francis appeared to be in some distress. Christopher shouldered the door open.

"What's up, Francis? Oh."

Francis was completely naked amongst the steam behind the glass partition. He was massaging some sort of foam into his tonsure, and had his eyes closed as he continued to make the appalling noise.

"Hop, little wa-a-a-bbits, who have such playful ha-a-a-bits!"

"What on earth are you doing?" yelled Christopher. "It's soaking wet in there! Have you taken leave of your senses?"

He opened the door to haul Francis out.

"No, no!" moaned Francis. "It's some sort of washing cupboard, and it's utterly divine! Try for yourself."

"What? Get wet all over?" Christopher, pulled a face. "Only time I ever did that was when I helped the infant Christ cross a river. Did I ever tell you about that?"

"You might have done. This is for washing. You have washed before, haven't you?"

"It wasn't all that popular a concept in my day."

"Well this water is delightful," said Francis. "Twy it."

Christopher wondered if Francis was delirious after getting so wet, but he put his arm into the spray and it found that it really didn't feel so bad. Moments later he was luxuriating under the stream of water, turning around and letting it warm his shoulders.

"Mm, I see what you mean!" he said.

"Twy the bubbles, twy them!" exclaimed Francis, who was now wrapped in a fluffy white garment.

Christopher was soon awash with slippery, fragrant bubbles. He peered at the shower head.

"This is a fair impressive contrivance. Where does all the water come from?"

"No idea," said Francis. "There must be someone in the ceiling, pouring it through or something."

Christopher peered upward at the showerhead and the air vent in the ceiling above. He couldn't see anyone and, he remembered, they couldn't see him either. But that didn't mean that he should appear ungrateful.

"Thanking you, shower flunkies," he called.

"Indeed, thank you," agreed Francis, adding, "It must be a peculiar job for a serving man to spend his days pouwing water over the unclothed guests of this hostel."

"Who says it's a man up there?" said Christopher with a grin. "If only you could see me, girls! You've no idea what you're missing."

Francis suddenly paled and hurried back into the bedroom.

Christopher emerged into the room, eventually, in a waft of steam.

"Any more of those spare habits?" he asked Francis.

He picked up the bathrobe that Francis handed to him and wrapped it round his barrel chest with a grin.

"We fell on our feet here, Francis," he said. "Meal last night, transport to help us on our way and now this! If we can find some breakfast from somewhere, I'll be a very happy man."

"It says here that bweakfast is served on the first floor," said Francis, holding a little card.

Christopher's eyes lit up.

"Then what are we waiting for?" he said, rubbing his hands together in anticipation.

"Weggie," said Francis to the rat curled up on the pillow. "Stay there and daddy will bwing you back a cwoissant."

THE WOLF of Gubbio sniffed around the dented campervan. A morning mist clung to the furrows of the muddy field. He picked up the scent of his master, leading off towards some nearby buildings. He trotted across the fields to see a great deal of activity. Several people wearing fluorescent jackets were picking over the ruins of a house. Smoke drifted languorously from the rubble. A man led a nervous alpaca round to a horse box. The alpaca eyed the wolf and strained backwards. The wolf ignored it and ran to the rear of the house where his master had definitely lingered for a while amongst the interesting animal scents.

A pair of humans were conversing over something that they held in a plastic bag.

"We had a call from her father," said a tall man with a moustache. "He received a call from her mobile phone at this location. We're waiting for the DNA results, but we think we're dealing with human remains in some meat products that have been found. We've got Laila's bank card and passport in this rucksack. There are others."

The other human, who, the wolf noted with interest, had a dog biscuit in his pocket, took the plastic bag and looked at its contents.

"How many?"

"Lots."

"Where's the phone now?" asked the biscuit-man. "I don't see it with Laila's belongings."

"It's not here," said the tall man. "We have traced the phone to Rouen."

"Rouen? Interesting. Perhaps – What the hell is that?"

"What?" said the moustachioed one.

"There! Is that a wolf?"

But the wolf was already bounding away to the south west on the trail of his master.

JOAN LOOKED up as Christopher and Francis entered the dining room. They were both wrapped in white robes and looked extremely pleased with themselves. Em took a little longer to notice as she was taking a photograph of the dried scum in her bowl of hot chocolate (which apparently bore a striking resemblance to her son, Jesus Christ and was, according to Em, ripe for posting on www.thingsthatlook-likejesus.com).

"Dead chuffed with this place," said Christopher as he walked past to take his seat among the many women of the Aberdaron Women's Institute.

"What are you wearing?" said Joan, pausing in the act of tearing her pastry apart.

"Complementary habits," said Francis, giving a twirl that raised his hem far too high for Joan's liking. "They've got everything!"

"Unless you need a kettle in your room," said Agnes, who was sitting to the right of Joan and Em. "How on earth are you supposed to make yourself a hot drink, that's what I'd like to know?"

"Bring your own travel kettle, like me," said the woman next to Agnes, "I've got travel adapters and four hundred tea bags."

"Well, Miriam," Agnes replied tartly. "I'm surprised to

find you have room in your suitcase for *moeth* like that. Is that
yet *another* cable—knit cardigan you're wearing there?"

Miriam smoothed down the lumpy item, although it was
hard to make out what were creases in the garment and what
were folds in Miriam's shapeless body. The cardigan's colour
was a match for Miriam's red hair.

"Knitted it myself," said Miriam proudly.

"Then again that's the problem with making your own
clothes," said Agnes.

"What is?"

"You can't take them back to the shop if you don't like
them."

"I heard that English people are very keen on tea," cut in
Joan, certain that, back in Heaven, Evelyn had mentioned its
mystical status.

"I'm sure they are," said Agnes.

"We're Welsh, not English," added Miriam firmly.

"Oh."

"Aberdaron is in the farthest corner of Wales," said Em.
"Gwenda here was telling me. Quite far from England. In
fact, we're probably closer to London right now than these
ladies would be at home."

"Oh," said Joan. "And you chose to come to Belgium for a
mini crusade."

"Mini what?"

"Mini break," said Em.

"Oh. Just passing through on our tour," said Agnes.
"We're doing Greatest Women from History. Anne Frank was
our last stop. Have you ever been to Anne Frank's house in
Amsterdam?"

Em nodded. "It's a moving experience."

"Lovely cakes in the museum café," said Miriam.

"Exactly what you need after all that gloom and sorrow," said Agnes.

There were murmurs of agreement from the other women around the table.

"I don't think you can simply wash away the tragedy of the Holocaust with cake and tea," said Em.

"Oh, don't get me wrong," said Agnes, unfazed. "What's important is that we learn the lessons that history has to teach us. To be sure, dear, I know that the world is a ghastly place and life is filled with horror and pain. That doesn't mean we can't enjoy a nice macaroon along the way."

Em buttered some toast and raised an eyebrow. "So where is your tour taking you?" she asked.

"We end up on the south coast of France," said Miriam excitedly. "At the Monte Carlo Casino in Monaco."

"Are there many famous women associated with the casino?"

"No," said Agnes, "but Miriam does like to play *cardiau*."

"We're visiting the Palace of Versailles and the hospital where Marie Curie died on the way."

"But it's Paris next," said Agnes. "We plan to lay wreaths in the Pont de l'Alma road tunnel."

"The what?" said Francis around a mouthful of *pain au raisin*.

"Pont de l'Alma tunnel," said Agnes. "I hope I am saying it right. It's where Diana died."

"Diana?" The name meant little to Joan.

"Princess Diana," said Agnes.

"Lady Di," said Miriam.

"The Princess of Wales," said Gwenda.

"The people's princess."

"The Queen of Our Hearts."

"She was the most photographed woman in the world," said Miriam.

"All that work she did to get rid of landmines," chipped in another woman, Lynne.

"But she was a wonderful mother to her two boys too."

"Absolutely. It's no wonder the nation was heartbroken when she died in that car accident."

"I cried for three days solid," said a woman, sat alone at a distinctly separate table.

"I'm sorry," said Agnes sharply. "I'm sure I heard something then. A noise, like some sort of annoying animal."

"I didn't hear anything," declared Miriam loudly.

"I think it was that lady over there." Francis pointed with his croissant.

"That is no lady," said Agnes stiffly. "That is Gloria."

"Isn't she one of your group?" asked Joan.

"We share a coach," Agnes admitted.

"Gloria used to tell us that she'd met Diana," whispered Miriam.

"Yes?"

"Filthy liar," said Gwenda.

"Turned out it was only Princess Michael of Kent," said Lynne. "Can you believe it?"

"And that's why she has to sit apart from you?" asked Joan.

"That's not the only thing she's done, by any means."

Agnes took out a small black notebook, licked a finger and flicked through the pages, tutting at the entries.

"The business on the Eurostar train. Sure, we can all be claustrophobic but we don't have to shout about it. Then there was that matter in Amsterdam when she bought some..." Agnes quailed, leaned over the table and whispered. "Do you know what 'love eggs' are, dear?"

"No," said Joan.

"And that's just the way it should be. Filthy jezebel."

"No better than she ought to be," added Miriam.

"And don't forget the masks," said Gwenda.

"Masks?" asked Joan, not certain she wanted to hear the answer.

"Gloria," said Agnes, loudly enough to make Gloria look up sheepishly, "thought that it would be a good idea to honour Princess Diana by all wearing rubber masks of her. See, look at her face. She knows what she's done."

"So, Paris next," said Em.

"That's right."

"By chance, that's exactly where I was headed. I'd love to tag along with you ladies."

"Of course," said Agnes. "Take no notice of Colin. He will keep on about rules and policies, but sometimes he needs to be reminded of who's paying his wages."

"Sorry," said Joan. "I didn't realise. We got here so late last night and I was so tired. Are we not in Paris yet?"

Agnes smiled condescendingly.

"No, precious. Paris this evening. We're having a little stopover."

"Oh?"

"We're in Rouen."

The Maid of Orleans dropped her pastry and felt the colour drain from her face.

MATT ROSE WAS SHOWN through to the office of Brigadier-Major Baland.

He shook the hand of the rotund officer and sat down in the visitor's chair.

"Welcome to Rouen, Monsieur Rose," said Baland. "So what can I do to assist you?"

"The matter of Mary Van Jochem," said Matt. "You've seen the files, of course. She's wanted for questioning in connection with terrorism offences across Europe."

"And you believe that she is here in Rouen? Bien sûr. We will extend you every possible courtesy," said Baland, "but it will not be a simple matter to find this woman by sight in Rouen." He turned to a map on the wall, and indicated the size of the problem. "It's hardly likely that she is touring the historical sites, after all."

FRANCIS GAZED up at the tower as Agnes read from the guidebook for the edification of the women of the Aberdaron WI, the four saints, and everyone else within a hundred yards who wasn't stone deaf.

"The Joan of Arc tower is all that remains of Rouen's castle," she read loudly. "Joan of Arc was held captive in a tower like this prior to her trial and was subsequently executed by being burnt at the stake in the old market place."

"Oh, that can't have been nice," commented Miriam.

"Joan attempted several escapes from her various places of capture, including a jump of seventy feet from the window of her tower. Hmph!"

Agnes thrust the guidebook back into her handbag.

"Well, I'm not at all sure I believe that. Who could survive a jump of seventy feet?"

"It did bloody hurt," said Joan.

"I'm a bit confused about Joan of Arc," said Gwenda, a polite woman who had been kind enough to point out to Francis that the white robes provided by the hotel were not considered suitable outdoor apparel. "If she was French, and she was fighting for the French, then how come she was burned at the stake here in Rouen, which is, well, *in France*?"

Joan found herself speaking without realising it.

"Things were different then. This area wasn't controlled by the French king. It got all complicated by the Normans conquering England and then not staying loyal to France. Burgundians. Lancastrians. Armagnacs. The Hundred Years War was a mess."

"You can't have a war for a hundred years," said Gwenda. "That would be silly. How long did it really last?"

Joan looked at her narrowly, wondering if the Welsh had that British fondness for sarcasm.

"One hundwed and sixteen years," said Francis.

Joan looked at him.

"It's twue," he said.

"So whose side was Joan of Arc on?" asked Miriam. "It

sounds as though both sides were French really, and it was just a power play between a couple of pampered aristo blokes."

"The king needed a pretty face to carry the standard for him. Some might say Joan of Arc was simply a public relations figure," said Em.

"What?" said Joan between clenched teeth.

"*Some* might say," said Em coolly. "I'm sure she was simply a plucky girl trying to make her way in a man's world."

"So she really didn't get *stuck in* like Diana did then?" said Agnes. "You only had to watch the news back in the day to see that Diana actually went right into those dangerous places like Angola and Great Ormond Street Hospital."

"Great Ormond Street is dangerous?" said Miriam.

"You know what I mean. She was much more practical. Fearless, even. A real inspiration."

"Maybe it was all those corsets and chin bras and chastity belts that held them back in the old days," said Gwenda.

Francis glanced at Joan and saw her mouth agape in horror.

"Modern women just get on and change things," said Gwenda. "You know, I was at Greenham Common. My mom thought I was doing work experience in a machine shop in Chester."

"Was that when you burned your bra and told your mom that it was a stray spark from a mig welder?" asked Miriam.

"She's still sending them letters of complaint in the hopes of some Marks and Spencer vouchers."

"Small world," said Em. "I was at Greenham Common too."

"Is it an attwactive common?" asked Francis, picturing the wildlife that might frolic there.

Em fixed him with an unfriendly glare.

"It was a US military base in England, which was blockaded by women to protest about its use for nuclear weapons."

"I was with the Women for Life on Earth group," said Gwenda.

"CND," said Em.

"Oh, nuclear weapons," said Francis, filled with fear as he remembered the terrible images of destruction that they'd been shown. His face fell. "These — these weapons are to be found as close as *England*?"

Em rolled her eyes.

"They're closer than that, dimwit. The French military love their nukes, absolutely love them. Bozos, all of them. The other month, I helped some guys who hacked their army mainframe and replaced the key directives with a random text. And years ago, I took on the French Navy when I was on the Rainbow Warrior."

"The Wainbow what?" asked Francis.

"Rainbow Warrior?" said Gwenda, clearly impressed.

"Greenpeace used the ship to protest against the hunting of whales, and the testing of nuclear weapons," Em explained to Francis. "The French military trashed a good few Pacific islands with their ridiculous tests. See, they're no better now than they were in Joan of Arc's day, they just have bigger toys to show off with."

There were a few laughs around the group, but Joan's face was like granite.

"Did you see that there was a terrible forest fire in Senegal started by French Air Force weapons just yesterday?" said Miriam.

"Not at all surprised," said Em. "Buffoons. Always have been. Arrogant, pompous buffoons. When they're not being cheese-eating surrender monkeys they're blowing stuff up by mistake."

"Wait," said Francis. "Do you mean to say that people hunt *whales*? Those magnificent beasts of the oceans?"

"They're not supposed to," said Em with a sad look that Francis knew echoed his own. "I've done my fair share of facing down a whaling ship from a small boat. It's a hairy business when a giant harpoon fires over your head, I can tell you."

"Wemarkable," said Francis in a hushed tone. He decided that he might forgive Em some of her previous harshness.

Christopher nudged him in the ribs. Francis was about to respond, when he remembered that Christopher was invisible to most of the group. He looked at him questioningly.

"Think Joan's got the hump." Christopher nodded across at Joan who was marching stiffly away from the group. "I'll go after her."

Francis gazed after Joan, wondering why she looked so angry.

"Let her go," said Em.

"Surprised the dear put up with us old fuddy-duddies for so long," said Miriam.

"*Us* old fuddy-duddies?" said Em.

"Your — niece, is it? – is a delightful young woman. At university, is she? Studying history I imagine. She probably doesn't want to hang around with us all day."

Francis could see Em was about to correct Miriam's assumptions but she was interrupted by a shriek from Lynne.

"Oh, I've stepped in some dog's *business!*" she squealed. "What's the matter with these people?"

"They should clean up after their dogs!"

Gwenda stepped forward with a carrier bag and scooped up the mess with a grimace.

"Baby wipe, Lynne?" she said, thrusting a packet at her.

"I think we all need a sit down and a drink." Agnes steered everyone along the pavement to a nearby cafe. "What with no kettle in the hotel room, I'm gasping for a decent cup of tea. I'll call Colin to pick us up from here in a little while."

The ladies of the WI all stepped with exaggerated care to avoid the dog mess. They entered the cafe and allowed Agnes to organise them.

"Right, we'll take these three tables here. No, not you Gloria, you can sit over there. Right garçon. GARÇON!" Agnes shouted. "We'd like tea, please. That's T—E—A."

She mimed an exaggerated sipping motion and then sat down, satisfied that her message had got across. She fetched a stopwatch from her handbag and clicked the top.

"I heard that the average French waiter takes seventeen minutes to bring a drinks order," she explained, to no-one in particular. "Seventeen minutes! I don't see how anyone could possibly take that long, but let's see, shall we?"

CHRISTOPHER TRAILED behind Joan as she muttered to herself, striding across the Pont Jeanne d'Arc that spanned the wide river Seine. He wondered if she might be comforted by the tale of how he once carried the infant Christ across a similar river, but Joan was practising her twenty first century swearing, and Christopher found himself wondering what a 'nipple-juicing son of a biscuit' was.

"Joan, Joan!" he called as a tram rumbled past them. "Give over, it can't be all that bad."

"Can't be that bad? Are you kidding?" she fumed. "My whole life was completely pointless, apparently."

"Could be worse," said Christopher.

"Yeah? How?"

"Oh, I don't know. Say you never even existed at all?"

"Different. Completely different," said Joan and stomped on.

Christopher shrugged and followed her across a tree-lined boulevard and up past the concrete Theatre des Arts, pausing briefly to restart a stalled car with a waggle of his eyebrows. He caught up with her as she entered a large square.

She stopped and turned in a slow circle, gazing at the surrounding buildings.

"This place. Oh, Lord. This place," she said.

"What?" said Christopher, looking round. He saw a pleasant façade of medieval buildings looking out over the busy pedestrian area. There was a curious building in the centre, which appeared to be a church, but with a mish-mash of steep roofs that then continued across the square to make a low walkway. "I'll grant you the church is a bit odd. More brontosaurus than place of worship. Hey, it's named after you, look!"

Christopher pointed eagerly to the sign.

"They burned me right over there," said Joan.

"Eh?"

"It's the place where I died."

"Oh," said Christopher. "Right, um."

Christopher was out of his depth. He could deal with lost tickets, engine faults and blocked roads, but anything that involved what he thought of as 'finer feelings' was generally beyond his powers.

Joan shook her head.

"Who am I, Christopher?" she sighed despondently. "What am I?"

"You're Joan of Arc. You're a saint."

"I don't recognise this place," she said, gesturing to the square. "This city has changed beyond recognition. Admittedly, these stone roads beat wading through ordure but... According to those Welsh harpies, my place in history was without meaning and I have no place in this world. Do you know, I'd give anything to be an ordinary girl again, lead a normal life. Meet a boy and... and... other people too and just..." She groaned loudly. "I'm so tired. And angry. Tired and angry."

"Cheer up," said Christopher, indicating an alabaster figure on a nearby plinth. "They made a nice statue of you."

"Really?"

"Captures that sort of mardy look you normally have —
oh bugger!"

The statue winked at them and stuck its tongue out. The
surprise was evidently too much for Joan.

"Witchcraft!" she yelled.

"Er, no, Joan…"

"How dare you practise sorcery like that in my image!"

"Er, I think it's just someone dressed up," said
Christopher, but Joan had already lunged at the statue,
which stepped off its plinth and backed away rapidly.

Joan kicked the wooden plinth aside and charged at the
statue with a roar. The white-faced woman turned and ran,
dropping the cardboard sword that she had carried. Joan
picked up the sword and gave chase but the street performer
had fled through a surging crowd of tourists on a walking
tour and was gone.

Joan brandished the cardboard sword in her fury,
swinging it wildly. Christopher was glad that her real blade
was still on the coach, imagining the accidental amputations
that she might do in her rage.

"I'm fed up of being mocked for who I am!" Joan
bellowed. "I didn't ask for this! I didn't ask for *any* of this. I
was a simple country girl, happy enough to do the work that
was needed on the farm, praying whenever I got the chance.
Why me, eh? Why was it *me* who had to have the visions?
Saint Michael, Saint Catharine, Saint Margaret. It was
enough to make you dizzy, you never knew when some saint
or other was going to pop up! Did I complain? Did I?
Everyone thought I was some sort of nutter, but I just kept
my chin up."

"Joan, Joan!" hissed Christopher. "These people are all watching you. Are you sure you want to draw attention to yourself like this?"

The walking tour had halted and were watching Joan as she swung and hefted the broadsword against the memories of people who had slighted her over the years.

"Do you know I never even had any real friends?" she continued, ignoring them all. "Not proper friends like other people have. No. It's just not possible, with saints and angels telling you that *you're* the one who's supposed to end the war. That *you're* the one who needs to go and talk to the king and tell him how it's all going to be. Even my parents didn't want to know me by the time I went to join the army."

A few of the onlookers were nudging each other and taking photos. A ripple of applause broke out as Joan paused for breath, but she wasn't done.

"How *dare* they laugh at my place in the French Army? How DARE they mock me? I was right at the front, I *led* that army to victory FROM THE FRONT! It wasn't easy, being smaller than nearly everyone else there, but I stood my ground. I *made* them believe in me. I *made* them believe in themselves."

Christopher stood back with a sigh and let Joan get on with it. So much for keeping a low profile.

FRANCIS WATCHED the waiter set down a teapot on each of the tables, maintaining a conversation throughout the manoeuvre with a woman who was wiping down the bar. A man came in wearing the stripy apron of a butcher's shop and dropped a plastic carrier bag near to the woman, calling out that it was the steaks for the evening meals. Francis settled forward in his seat and regarded the teapot. He was looking forward to trying tea. This trip was turning out to be educational if nothing else. Agnes glared at the waiter's back as she stopped the stopwatch with a flourish.

"Twenty minutes and forty eight seconds. I can barely believe my eyes," she declared, shaking her head. "Now. Who's got the milk?"

She checked along all three tables and realised that nobody had any milk.

"Gloria?" she called.

Gloria looked up in momentary horror, wondering what new crime would be recorded against her in Agnes' book, but then she realised that she was being asked about milk. She shook her head.

"Well, this simply isn't good enough!" said Agnes. She stood up and raised her voice. "Young man, come back here!"

Francis wondered if the waiter might have been a little hard of hearing, as he watched him continue through the door into the kitchen as if he hadn't heard. Agnes seemed to be incensed by this. She stalked over to the bar where there was a bell for gaining the attention of the staff. She banged the bell heavily and repeatedly until the woman with the polishing rag called out to the kitchen.

"Jean-Paul!"

The waiter reappeared and approached Agnes.

"We need milk for our tea," she said. "You can't expect us to drink tea without milk."

The waiter shrugged, rolled his eyes and headed back to the kitchen.

"Did you see that?" hissed Agnes as she sat back down. "Just shrugged at me, as if it just doesn't matter at all. Barbarians, the lot of them."

Francis tapped his foot nervously as Agnes glared at the kitchen door for what felt like an eternity.

"Where on earth can he be?" she fumed. "He's been a good five minutes, our tea will be stone cold!"

Eventually the kitchen door swung open and the waiter emerged.

He walked to their tables and deposited a handful of longlife milk capsules casually on each, carefully avoiding eye contact with anyone.

"You can't be serious," said Agnes, rising from her seat with slow menace. The waiter ignored her. She blocked his way as he made for the kitchen.

"What is it?" he said in English.

"This milk is UHT."

"It is," he agreed.

"I don't want UHT milk in my tea."

"You said you wanted milk."

"Proper milk."

"This is the milk that we have," said the waiter, and tried to move around Agnes. She sidestepped and blocked his way again.

"It's not good enough, I'm afraid. We want proper milk from a proper cow. I know you have cows here in Brittany."

"Normandy," came a murmur from Gloria. Agnes shot her a look and Gloria dropped her gaze into her lap.

"Milk from a cow," said Agnes. "You know, cow. Cow. What's the French for 'cow'? You know what I'm on about. Moo, moo!"

"Vache," said the waiter. "And this milk is from a cow."

"A fresh cow. I mean, fresh milk from a cow. And I know that you have cows around here," said Agnes, "because of this."

She grabbed a plastic carrier bag and upended it onto the bar. Everyone recoiled from the stinking pile of dog crap. Its powerful stench quickly filled the café.

"Wrong bag," said Francis in a tiny voice to himself.

Francis decided that Agnes' mind was like a donkey on a set of stairs; stubborn and incapable of back-tracking.

"Well, er, that steak's clearly off," she said, unabashed. "But the point is still valid. If you can get steak, you can get fresh milk. That's what we want. We want a nice cup of tea with some fresh milk. Tea au lait. *Au lait,* do you hear?"

"I'm enjoying this," Em whispered to him with a smile. "France is usually so boring."

The waiter glanced at the woman who had stopped cleaning the bar. She shrugged at him helplessly.

Miriam stood up next to Agnes.

"Au *lait*, au lait—au lait—au lait!" she sang loudly. She motioned to the other women to join in with the football chant, and they took up the refrain. "Au LAIT, au LAIT!"

The waiter tried to say something to Agnes, but she had joined in with the singing and the noise drowned him out.

∾

JOAN WASN'T LISTENING to Christopher, who kept trying to interrupt her, blathering on about a crowd that was following her.

"I had to put up with all the stupid charges they made against me," she thundered, as she strode through the streets. "They accused me of everything they could think up with their tiny, stupid minds. I was a *sorceress*, I was a *heretic*. Do you know what they used against me in the end, do you know what was the only charge those idiots could actually stick on me? Cross dressing. Dressing up as a man! I only did it to protect my virtue, but they burnt me at the stake for wearing trousers. English mormons!"

"I think you mean morons," said Christopher, at her side, but Joan wasn't listening.

"It's not as if they were ever as great as they thought they were, either," she continued. "The English have always been a nation of bloated fools."

"Have they?"

"Look at their food! Nobody abuses food like the English do. Their national dish is a hunk of perfectly good meat roasted in a ton of fat with greasy potatoes. They call it Sunday lunch. I call it gluttony and heartburn."

"Everyone likes a nice roast," said Christopher reasonably.

"Their second finest dish, oh what's that? It's *fish* cooked in a ton of fat served up with greasy potatoes. No imagination. Their beer is always warm, did you know that? They love warm beer."

"I'd love a beer," said Christopher. "I don't care what temperature it—"

"The reason that they love warm beer is because they are all drunkards! They can't afford the *time* to let their beer get cold in between the pints and pints that they quaff."

There was laughter at this from the considerable crowd that now followed Joan.

"They have so much rain in England, too. They get the weather that they deserve. It rains *all* the time!" She took a vicious swipe with her sword. "That must be why they all smell like DOGS! Lord, I remember that smell. I slept in ditches for months when I led the French army, but I never smelled as bad as those mildewy Englishmen that came for me."

FRANCIS TRIED to shrink back into his seat as spectators gathered and cameras flashed at the ladies of the WI who continued to sing and hammer the tables in the cafe. The waiter had fled to the kitchen and refused to respond to the cries and taunts from Agnes and the others.

"Hey!" said Em. "I'm all for a decent protest, but I need to get out of here, I can't afford to have my face broadcast on the media."

She indicated some new arrivals, who entered the cafe with video cameras and jackets that declared they were from *Normandie TV*.

"Hold on," said Agnes. "There might be something we can do about that. Gloria!"

Gloria flinched automatically, like a kicked puppy.

"Do you have the offending items on you?" said Agnes.

Gloria frowned.

"The *masks*."

Gloria delved into her enormous handbag and produced several dozen masks, nested together like stacked bowls.

"Here, everyone," said Agnes. "Put these on."

"I like it," said Em. "An Anonymous protest."

Francis slipped the soft mask over his face. He was now one of thirty or more identical figures, all with bouffant blonde hair and a toothy rubber smile.

When Francis had time to reflect later, he wasn't sure if it was the masks that did it or the new audience. Em had started to sing along with the other women and punched the air at the same time, even though, Francis noted, she'd been happy enough to drink her tea *without* milk. The women of the Aberdaron WI became noticeably bolder and started to bang their cups on the saucers, smashing some of them in their enthusiasm. A teapot sailed through the air and shattered the plate glass window of the cafe, causing the spectators that had drifted in from the street to back up onto the pavement in alarm.

A voice broke through the crowd, and Francis saw that Joan had arrived, pushing through them, waving a cardboard sword, and shouting. Christopher was at her elbow, and he gave Francis a helpless shrug.

"You lot! I want to talk to you!" Joan yelled, recognising the group in spite of their masks. "Joan of Arc served her country in every possible way and you need to show her some more respect. The English have no respect for anyone. They've gone around for years trying to take over the world. Even when there's parts of the world they haven't taken over, they just act as if they own the place anyway. I hate the English, HATE them!"

Agnes lifted her mask to smile at Joan.

"Well, of course, my dear. Couldn't agree more. We're Welsh, remember?"

She turned to the rest of the group. A couple of them were breaking up a chair to use as weapons.

"Down with the English!" she yelled. There were cries of agreement from the group.

"Down with nuclear weapons!" called Gwenda. Em joined her chant, and thumped the table with her fists to hammer the message home.

"Save the whale!" called Francis, not wanting to be left out. He clapped his hands together, as he didn't feel comfortable destroying the property of the cafe.

"You've all gone mad," said Christopher in disbelief.

"We're pwotesting," Francis explained.

Joan swung her cardboard sword above her head in general agreement with all of the sentiments. She hadn't noticed the light fitting until she saw it hurtling from her sword towards the bar area where it smashed into a mirrored display, earning her a raucous cheer of applause from multiple Dianas, who leapt up and started to throw anything that came to hand.

"Can anyone else hear a siren?" asked Miriam.

Agnes held up a hand and the rioting Dianas all stopped what they were doing.

"You're right Miriam," Agnes said. "Let's go and see if Colin's turned up yet. We can always get a nice cup of tea from the drinks machine on the coach."

There were nods of agreement from the women, who immediately dropped their weapons and all trooped out of the café, silent but for the occasional "excuse me" and "thank you" as they stepped round and sometimes over the café's stunned staff and patrons.

MATT HELD onto the door handle as Baland threw his car into a tight corner, sirens blaring, lights flashing.

"Does this sort of thing happen a lot with tourists?" asked Matt.

"We get trouble in the bars sometimes," said Baland admitted, swerving to dodge a downtrodden living statue performer who wasn't looking where she was walking. "It seems as though the cheap alcohol can sometimes overexcite our foreign visitors. Why can't they be a bit more like the French? Drinking wine in the day should be like making love, taken slowly and savoured. Do you not agree?"

"Um. I'm not much of a..."

"Lover?"

"Wine drinker."

"Hmmm. Well, it's definitely not usual for the trouble to be during the day, though, and it's almost unheard of for it to be middle-aged women, which is what the reports are saying."

"Middle-aged women?"

They pulled up outside a cafe, where there was a crowd of people peering at the mess inside. Matt followed Baland inside and saw furniture upturned and smashed. There was the dissipating but nonetheless pervasive smell of sewage in the air. There was broken crockery everywhere, and all of the windows were shattered. There were daubs of what looked like tomato sauce on the wall.

"What do these say?" said Baland. "*UHT = MERDE*? And what on earth is *PEN PIDYN*?"

Matt shook his head and picked up a squashed rubber mask from the floor. Pummelled by footprints and rolled against the hard floor, Matt couldn't tell if it was meant to be Margaret Thatcher or Marilyn Monroe.

"It's like some sort of code?" suggested Baland. "Is this anything you do with your Mrs Van Jochem?"

Matt shrugged. "The woman thrives on chaos," he admitted.

Glass crunched under Matt's feet as he walked out.

On the far side of the carriageway, a coach pulled away from the kerbside. There was a red dragon emblem along the side.

Colin's Coaches, Pwhelli.

"Pwhelli," he said.

"What?" said Baland.

"Worst holiday of my childhood."

Baland frowned at him and then went off to direct his officers.

"Damp and grey," said Matt. "And that was just the hotel..."

A large dog trotted along the kerb where the coach had just been. Except it wasn't just any large dog. In fact, it might not be a dog at all...

Matt cautiously crossed the road, waving thanks to the cars that peeped at him.

"Hey, boy," he said in his friendliest voice.

The shaggy creature swung its large head to look at him.

"Are you some kind of giant husky or malamute?" he asked, knowing it wasn't so. The great grey beast was taller than his Aunt Judith's Irish wolfhound.

"I saw you at the Couckuyt farm, didn't I?"

The wolf eyed Matt. Matt smiled at the wolf while a little voice inside his head screamed, *It's a bloody wolf! Look at the size of its teeth! It's drooling, for God's sake!*

"Are you following the same trail as me?" he asked.

The wolf approached Matt. Matt concentrated on smiling and not soiling himself in fear.

The wolf pressed his nose to Matt's jacket pocket and sniffed. Matt gingerly slipped his hand into the pocket, past the wolf's wet nose and produced a half-eaten pack of shortbread biscuits. The wolf sat back on its haunches and licked its lips.

Matt held out one of the biscuits and prepared to wish his fingers a tearful farewell.

The wolf took the biscuit (not his fingers) and chomped it into crumbs.

Matt ruffled the wolf's ears and it lolled its tongue and looked up at him in appreciation.

"So," said Matt, "we're two amateur sleuths chasing the same quarry."

The wolf whined for another biscuit.

"I can see that you and I are going to get along just fine."

5

PARIS

At breakfast in the Hotel la Défense Centre in Paris, Christopher found Francis staring glumly into the remains of his hot chocolate.

"Still pining for that flaming rat?"

"Poor Weggie," he sighed. "I can't believe I left him behind. First, the wolf. Now, the wat. What kind of fwiend to animals am I?"

"You left that rat in one of the best hotels in Rouen," said Christopher. "I think that makes him a jammy little rat."

"I'm a tewwible man," sniffed Francis.

Agnes Thomas smiled. It was not a particularly convincing smile, more of an upside down scowl.

"*So,*" she said pointedly, "will you three be joining us on our little jolly today?"

"Laying wreaths, aren't you?" said Joan.

"That's tomorrow morning. Today, a trip to the Louvre — get our dose of culture – and then an evening cruise along the Seine. Joan, Em, you are very welcome. Perhaps your Uncle Francis needs some time *alone* to process his grief."

"I'm sorry," said Em. "Today, we need to buy Joan and Francis here tickets for their onward journey."

"Quite," agreed Christopher.

"Oh, you're not going with them?"

"I have business to attend to in Paris," she said.

Christopher saw Agnes look at Em, at her army surplus jacket, purple trousers and thick eye make-up, and could tell that she was wondering what kind of business this woman could possibly be involved in.

"Shame you're not coming," said Lynne. "I hear the Louvre's lovely. I've bought a special guide book."

"I'm going to see the Mona Lisa," said Miriam. "And the Venus de Milo."

"Tourist," said Gwenda critically.

"Oh, and what would you recommend?" asked Miriam tartly.

"Skipping the Louvre entirely and finding a pub," Christopher said, sound in the knowledge that the woman couldn't hear him.

"For me," said Gwenda, "it has to be the paintings of Titian."

"Oh, that sounds thrilling," said Christopher.

Joan kicked him under the table.

"There's the gorgeous portrait of Francis the First."

"Eh?" said Francis.

"Not you," said Em.

"The Entombment of Christ," continued Gwenda. "It's so

human. The poses. And then there's Titian's painting of St Christopher."

"What?" said Christopher.

"He's this hulky brute with the baby Christ on his shoulder," Gwenda's eyes glazed over dreamily. "The muscles..."

Christopher coughed loudly.

"Maybe *I* will join the ladies on their tour today," he said as casually as he could. "Take a gander at the paintings like."

"Narcissist," said Joan.

"I beg your pardon?" said Agnes.

"Yes, we will have to 'miss it,'" said Em. "We need to go to the Gare de Lyon today and make sure *all* my family are heading south tomorrow morning."

She glared at Christopher as she said this.

Christopher waved her concerns away.

"Look, Aunty Em, I can do the Louvre, check out some real art and catch up with you later. It's not as though I'm going to miss the train. I'm the patron saint of travel, after all."

"YES, Major Chevrolet, we have rules against workplace harassment in the UK as well, but I'm working on sound information that Mary van Joachem may be in Puteaux in Paris. We're there now, I need a new location for the phone – get your nose out of my ear, boy! – No, not you, Major. It's..."

The man, Matt, put the phone down. The Wolf of

Gubbio, hunched up in the passenger seat, looked at him. The man looked cranky and irritable.

"It looks like it's just you and me for now, partner. Well, you, me and your nose. Where are they, boy?"

The wolf sniffed the air. He leaned forward.

"That way?"

The wolf nudged the glove compartment open with his nose and sniffed the empty packet of crisps inside.

"Right, you're hungry," said the man, Matt. He pointed to a shop across the road from where they were parked.

"Salon Pluche Toilettage. Well, we need a break. A short one."

The wolf yawned loudly, his tongue rolling several inches along the tiny car's dashboard.

"Yeah, well sleeping on the back seat with you as a blanket wasn't much fun for me either."

The man, Matt, opened the door and the Wolf of Gubbio leapt out into the road. A car swerved and beeped its horn. The wolf didn't even look up. In his experience, everything, big or small, moved out of his way, not the other way round.

"Come on, boy."

The man pushed the shop door open and the wolf caught a waft of the most amazing range of smells. True, there were some strange chemical and flowery scents but there was an interweaving haze of dozens of dogs, smells new and old. It was like a library of dog scent, a digest of doggy doings and business for miles around. The wolf could have spent the entire day just smelling and discovering those smells but, rising above the dogginess, was the delicious smell of food and the wolf was very hungry. The wolf raked open a nearby paper sack and chomped on the crunchy snacks within.

"I hope you can pay for that," said the woman at the counter.

"Absolutely," said the man, Matt, getting out his wallet. "While I'm here, I wonder if you could help me with some directions."

"What kind of dog is that anyway?"

"Er, a malamute wolfhound crossbreed."

"He should be on a lead."

"We discussed it. We argued about it. He won."

The Wolf of Gubbio ignored the human conversation. He even ignored the ping of the shop door as other people came and went. He was sufficiently focussed on sating his hunger that he even let one of the humans ruffle his fur without bothering to bite their hand off at the wrist.

However, soon enough, the sack was empty and the wolf was full. The man, Matt, was still in conversation with the woman. He had his phone in his hand and they had spread a street map out on the counter.

Next to the wolf was a door with the words 'salon toilettage' written on it. He nosed his way through and found himself in a tiled room of taps and stinking bottles of soaps, and of a row of floor level pens. The wolf padded up to the first pen and sniffed.

The large poodle bitch within sniffed back and whined.

The wolf growled softly in his throat. He had eaten his fill. His master was not many miles distant. He should be on his way. And yet...

"Where's he gone?" said the man, Matt, in the other room.

"I do not know," said the woman. "I think he went out."

"Damn!" said the man, Matt.

The shop door chimed as the man ran out.

"I told you he should be on a lead."

The wolf sniffed. The bitches in the other pens crowded forward. A short Lhasa Apso yipped at him eagerly.

The wolf carefully grasped the latch on the poodle's door in his teeth and, without effort, ripped it away.

EM STABBED the touch screen of the automated ticket machine at Gare de Lyon.

"You understand that this is my precious cash I'm spending on you, Joan?" she said around the cigarette clenched in her lips.

"That's very kind of you. Are you sure you won't reconsider coming with us?"

"Oh, I'm sure. Here. A train from Paris to Toulon via Aix-en-Provence. Ten o'clock tomorrow morning."

She pressed the confirm button and the machine recited her journey selection back at her. She pressed again.

"You have selected two adult tickets," said the machine smoothly.

"Invisi—boy will have to sit in the baggage cart."

"If you need us to give you a few days here to sort out your private business, I am sure we can wait," said Joan.

"The Almighty Himself wequested we take you with us."

"Not interested," said Em.

"Insert payment," said the machine.

"One should not wefuse the Lord's orders so lightly."

"Listen, Frank. When a girl says, 'no,' it means, 'no.'"

"Insert payment," said the machine.

"All right, all right." Em pulled several grubby euro notes from her pocket.

"Mother Mary," said the machine.

"For tit's sake!" she snarled. "I'm doing it –"

Joan blinked. Em cleared her throat.

"Did that machine just...?"

"It did," said Joan.

"Mother Mary, is that you?" said the machine.

"What the fuck?" said Em.

"It's Simon," said Joan.

"That doesn't make sense," said Em. "That's not possible..."

"I have done it, Mother Mary," said the machine, calm and measured.

Em looked at the screen. She poked the touch screen experimentally.

"Is this some sort of joke?"

"The second angel sounded his trumpet," said Simon, "and something like a huge mountain, all ablaze, was thrown into the sea. A third of the sea turned into blood, a third of the living creatures in the sea died, and a third of the ships were destroyed."

"The second trumpet," said Joan.

"Wevelation," said Francis.

"I know it's the bloody book of Revelation," said Em. "But – fuck! – how?"

"Insert payment," said the machine.

"No, no," said Em. "That machine was speaking to us. I mean, to *us*."

"Like the telephone," said Joan.

"What telephone?" said Francis.

"In the house, in Belgium. It's Simon. It's him."

Em gripped Joan's arm tightly.

"You need to start talking, Joan. And you need to start making sense."

CHRISTOPHER KNEW Paris with an intimacy that no mortal man or woman could have hoped to match. As a former patron saint of travel, his knowledge of the world came from the prayers of those in dire straits. Those places that were rarely travelled or which presented no problems were blank spaces in Christopher's map of the world, whereas travel black spots were familiar to him in painfully clear detail. No one knew Beijing, London, New York or São Paulo quite like Christopher. And Paris... Paris had, for centuries, been a city of stuck vehicles, overcrowded trains and a million frustrated drivers. And if one place was the high definition centre of Paris's traffic woes it was the roundabout that circled the Arc de Triomphe.

Christopher had followed the WI tour party along the historic axis of the city, from La Grande Arche de la Defense, past Napoleon's triumphal arch, down the Champs-Élysées and on to the Louvre museum. He stayed with the party after they had paid to enter (getting in for free was small compensation for being unseen and unheard) and stayed by Lynne as she led a bunch of them round with a paperback *Guide Erotique de Louvre* in her hand.

The women quickly found their way to the Greek sculptures and, despite the signs prohibiting photography, took plenty of pictures of key parts of sculptural anatomy while Lynne read from the book.

"Ooh, look at his *pidyn*," said Miriam. "He's a bit timid, isn't he?"

"He's probably just cold," Val ventured.

"Greece is a hot country," said Julie. "He's got no excuse."

"Now, this one over here..." said Lynne.

"Is a bit more like it," said Val.

"Reminds me of my Howard," lamented Lynne. "In his younger days."

"And what's he doing with his fingers? Filthy, filthy."

Soon enough, Christopher tired of a grand tour of the willies and bums of the Louvre and, leaving the ladies in hysterics as they looked over a recumbent Hermaphrodite, went looking for *his* Titian.

The maze of multi-levelled corridors of the Louvre was no maze to Christopher and he was, within minutes, standing in a gallery of Renaissance oil paintings, gazing at himself.

"Blimey, it looks just like me," he said.

He approached, stroking his own beard as he contemplated the striding figure in the image.

"Look, look," he said to visitors passing by. "It's uncanny. I never posed for it, you know."

Few stopped to look and those that did mostly stared at the image blankly for a few second before moving on.

"Look at me. I mean, the river was deeper than that. It looks like me and the baby Jesus are just off for a paddle. He looks happy though, doesn't he?"

A man and woman stopped in front of the picture.

"St Christopher," said the man.

"That's me."

"There's a real bucolic air about this figure," said the woman.

The man nodded.

"I look bloody marvellous," said Christopher.

"A sense of raw energy," said the man.

"Aye," said Christopher. "Check me out."

He stood in front of the painting and, glancing back to correct his posture, adopted a pose identical to that in the picture.

"You have to imagine the lad Christ on my back," he said. "He were just like that too. Happy lad. That's what he was like. Em ought to take a photo of this one. Looks a darn sight more like Our Lord than that oil spill outside the hotel Em got worked up about."

"It's very good," said the woman. "Striking."

"Thank you," said Christopher. A notion occurred to him. He addressed the woman. "Tell you what, you're only small — hop on. Go on, have a go!"

The man and woman moved on. Christopher sighed and worked on perfecting the pose.

JOAN RECOUNTED her previous conversation with Simon several times as they walked across Paris and, even to Francis, who had little grasp of the limitations of modern communication technology, it sounded incredible. By the time they reached the river, Joan had repeated herself so often and been totally unable to answer Em's increasingly tough questioning that they had all become, by turn, perplexed, irritated and worn out.

"It's not my problem," said Em, apparently her final word on the matter. "We're going in here."

Francis looked at the sign of the Cafe Bouffon Aveugle and the narrow doorway. Paint peeled around the doorway and there was barely any light from within.

"I am sure we can find somewhere better for lunch," he said.

"I'm meeting some people here."

"We can leave you if you need some privacy," said Joan.

"Not a chance. I don't want you going off causing explosions, starting riots or bringing the cops to my door again."

"We've never done any of those —" Joan said and then stopped, recalling that they had done all of those things.

"I'm keeping you close until tomorrow morning. We're like glue until you're on that train and out of my hair."

Em led the way inside.

"Just keep quiet and be cool. These people respect me."

"Cool?" said Francis. "Like cold?"

"Oh, Christ, you're such dweebs. These people are important in the protest movement. Do not embarrass me."

The bar was decorated in varying shades of brown and smelled of tobacco and wood polish. Em spoke briefly to an unshaven man in an apron who pointed her towards a rear room. Em gestured for Joan and Francis to follow her. Past the kitchens was another room of dark wood tables and rattan backed chairs. There was a battered piano in one corner and, in another, the room's only occupants.

Em gave the two men the first unabashedly genuine smile Francis had ever seen on her face and kissed each firmly on the cheek.

"These are my *old* friends, Frank and Joan," said Em. "And these are my *good* friends, Claude and Michel."

"We have not met these friends of yours before," said the narrow-faced Michel. "I do not like surprises."

Claude smiled, a grin of teeth so crooked, it would be a surprise that he didn't eat his own face when he chewed.

"You don't like people, my friend. You forced me to write a risk assessment before you would come over to my apartment for dinner."

"That electrical fitting in the bathroom will prove lethal one day," said Michel.

The barman came in with a tray of bottles and glasses.

Michel inspected the glasses for dust before pouring wine for the five of them.

"We had not expected to see you again so soon, Em" said Claude.

"Amsterdam went tits up."

"Yes?"

"That British cop."

"Mateus Rosé?"

"Someone led him to my door," said Em, her gazed pinned on Francis.

"A bad business."

"I'm hoping that you might be able to find me a safe house for a month or two."

"Not Claude's then," said Michel with a wry, almost invisible smile.

Francis sipped at the red wine. It wasn't on a par with the communion wine in the Celestial City but was, nonetheless, quite palatable.

"Here," said Michel. "A toast. To old friends and good friends."

"Cheers," said Em.

"Salut," said Francis.

"And death to the oligarchs!" added Claude.

"And proportionate and democratically sanctioned retribution against the oligarchs," agreed Michel. "Em, we have plans for a protest action we aim to carry out in the next few days. I wonder if I could get your opinion on certain aspects."

"Careful," said Claude. "He'll have you doing a SWOT analysis within the hour."

IN THE SALON GROOMING ROOM, eight pens had been ripped open and eight poodles, spaniels and terriers, and one man-eating Wolf of Gubbio, lay exhausted amongst the wreckage of their love-making.

The wolf yawned and stretched. It was time to move on.

The blue-haired poodle sensed him moving and whined. The wolf looked at her, looked at them all. There could be no words between them and the wolf preferred it that way.

What was there to say? The wolf had had his fun and no bitch was going to tie him down. He had a mission to complete, a master to find.

The wolf jumped onto a counter and considered the high window in the corner of the room. It was shut, but it was only a single pane of glass. He backed up a foot or two and then leapt.

"So," said Claude, swinging round to talk to Joan and Francis. "How long have you known Em?"

"Centuries," said Joan.

Claude laughed and topped up their glasses. Francis wasn't quite sure how many drinks he'd had or how long they'd been in the café. Time and light barely seemed to impact on the place. The Parisian café was a pocket universe, totally separated from the rest of reality, and (although it might have been the wine doing his thinking) he was falling in love with the place.

"Em tells me you were involved in that protest in Rouen yesterday," said Claude.

Francis flushed. "It was sort of spontaneous."

"A flashmob. Excellent. What were you protesting against?"

"The English," said Joan.

"No," said Francis. "We were trying to save the whales."

"From the English." Joan slurred a little.

"Michel won't let us do flashmobs," said Claude.

"You fill in all the right Health and Safety evaluation forms and you can," called Michel from the other table.

Claude waved his words away.

"He's like an old lady. Too cautious. I started out in the Convergence des Luttes Anti-Capitalistes."

"You," said Michel, "started out among the true anarchists, the brawlers, pirates and guns-for-hire around the Bar Couteau Noir in Marseilles. If you hadn't been such a wimp, you'd have become a soldier of fortune in the Congo or God knows where."

"Okay," admitted Claude. "But then I did, fortunately, grow up. In the CLACs, did the *Take the Capital* protests in oh-one. Street action. Direct action."

"But that's not Michel's type of thing?" said Joan.

"He's a hacktivist mostly. Online stuff. Some say he wrote the WANK Worm."

"WANK Worm?"

"Worms Against Nuclear Killers. That's truly old school. Eighty-nine, I think. He still does some of that stuff – he and Em pulled a similar stunt here in France a while back – but these days he's mostly a Health and Safety nut."

"Just because we're anti-globalisation anarchists," said Michel, "doesn't mean we shouldn't be concerned for the health and wellbeing of our comrades. Em here shares my concerns about tomorrow's action on the financial centre. Isn't that right?"

"I think it's very... interesting," said Em diplomatically. "There are logistics to consider."

"And a lot of heavy lifting and carrying," said Michel. "And not all of our comrades remember to bend at the knees when lifting."

"I think they can carry a few coins," said Claude.

"We have a truck in the fourteenth arrondissement, laden with nine tonnes of one cent euros. Hardly a few coins."

"We're going to drive them into Paris's financial heart and dump them on the street," said Claude, "as a protest against the appalling wages offered to immigrant workers."

"Couldn't you just give the money directly to the poor immigrant workers?" suggested Francis but no one was listening.

"Em has agreed to come and look over my assessment paperwork," said Michel.

"Have I?" said Em. "Oh, sure."

She pointed at Joan and Francis in turn.

"You kids stay here. No wandering unescorted, okay?"

"Of course," said Francis.

"I need the ladies room." Joan clumsily got to her feet.

Em and Michel left. Joan knocked over a chair as she struggled past and just managed to catch it before it struck the floor.

"The world is falling apart," said Claude.

"It's not that bad," said Joan, disappearing down the corridor.

"Look," said Claude, slapping a copy of Le Monde on the

table and turning to the middle pages. "A ship graveyard on the Karachi coast ablaze. Twelve kilometres of abandoned oil tankers and cruise liners burning up and spilling their pollutants and chemicals into the sea."

"That's tewwible." Francis boggled once more at the scale of the modern world. "Twelve kilometres!"

"A coastline ruined. They say that something exploded onto one of the wrecks and started the fire. The suggestion here is that it's some downed satellite but... Think of the damage to marine wildlife."

"All the fishes," said Francis.

"And the sea turtles. It's an important nesting site for them."

"I love turtles," said Francis morosely.

Claude made a disgusted noise.

"You heard what they're doing now? Sealing up live baby turtles in plastic jewellery so women can wear them as accessories. It's sick. The pain and suffering we cause for our own vanity." He suddenly slapped the table. "And do you know what?"

"What, comrade?" said Francis.

"A few years ago, we thought the fur trade was dead, that we had educated the world. But, no, it's on a resurgence. There's a 'Coureurs de Bois' fashion show going on right now, not half a mile from here, showcasing the latest in fur fashion."

"The poor fluffy things killed for their hides," said Francis. "Something must be done about it."

"I suggested it to Michel but he said it was too risky."

Francis drained his glass and poured the last trickle from the bottle into Claude's glass.

"But Michel's not here," he said.

Francis's gaze met Claude's. Francis suspected that the pair of them were a tiny bit inebriated and not in the best state to make rash decisions.

"Where is this fashion show?" he asked.

CHRISTOPHER WASN'T QUITE sure how gratifying his day had been.

On the plus side, he had received a considerable amount of reflected praise from the admirers of Titian's work. He'd also managed to catch up with WI ladies as they left the Louvre and snaffled some of the food brought to them at a pavement restaurant. Furthermore, this meal passed without the women abusing the serving staff or causing any other form of international incident.

On the negative side, he had never felt more stymied in his inability to communicate with the people of Earth. He couldn't correct the art lovers who mistook him for Hercules, Abraham or Arnold Schwarzenegger. He couldn't inform the WI ladies that the 'tête de veau' on the restaurant menu was not beef burger. He couldn't even ask them to pass the salt or to stop passing phone images of marble genitalia to one another through his field of vision. And walking through Paris was a nightmare, wading through a sea of rude and hurrying individuals who refused to acknowledge his existence (although, to be fair, it did appear that the locals had treated the WI ladies with identical contempt).

As the party mooched over to the glass-roofed tourist boats on the Seine, Christopher wondered if this was how the Almighty felt: loved by many but frequently forgotten or misunderstood, free to do whatever he wished but unable to connect with humanity. It was a challenging thought and a slightly depressing one.

Christopher's large frame took up two of the moulded plastic seats on the boat. That was fine by him. He could do with some time alone with his thoughts. He leaned back and looked up through the glass roof at the Cathedral of Notre Dame on the Ile de la Cité.

"Frankly, Lord," he said, "I don't know how you put up with it."

JOAN LOOKED AROUND AND, knowing she had drunk perhaps one glass too many, wondered if she'd come into the wrong room. But, no, there was the chipped and scratched piano in the corner and, there, the remains of the four bottles of wine they had demolished between them.

She went through to the front bar and asked the barman if he had seen her friends.

"They are gone," he said simply.

"All of them?"

He nodded and continued to clean out the coffee machine.

"But I only went to the toilet," she said.

The barman shrugged.

"Ridiculous," Joan muttered to herself and, in search of fresh air and someone to punch, stepped out onto the street.

She was initially surprised to discover that evening was not only falling but had pretty much fallen. She was further surprised to find a familiar face having an argument with his mobile phone on the pavement.

"Yes, Major Chevrolet. Of course, I understand that you have a home to go to. Yes, we have restraining orders in England too. I just need an update on..." The man stopped when he saw Joan. "Goodnight, major," he said and turned the phone off.

"It's Matt, isn't it?" she said.

"Joan," he said. "I almost didn't recognise you in..."

"In?"

"Clothes." He gestured generally at her hoody, trousers and boots ensemble.

Joan recalled the chaos in the café gallery in Amsterdam and her all-leather outfit. Well, more holes than leather.

"Oh, that," she said. "I was just trying it out."

"It, um." He made a noise. "I like this."

Joan frowned a little. There was so much that had been confusing in their first few days on Earth that she couldn't quite work out Matt's role in it all. There had been those villains in search of gold and Matt's need to speak to Em. Joan vaguely recalled he was some sort of thief-taker...

"It's a nice surprise to see you," said Matt. "What are you doing in Paris?"

Joan pulled a wide-eyed face of consternation.

"I think I'm lost. I've certainly lost all my friends."

"You mean Mary?"

"Yes," she nodded. "And Francis and Christopher."

"Francis and Christopher. Is this one person or two?" said Matt. "In Amsterdam there was only one person but..."

"It's complicated."

"It's not a split personality thing, is it? Listen, I can help you find them."

Again, Joan felt that confusion and suspicion.

"What are *you* doing in Paris?"

"I'm looking for someone too."

"Em?"

"Mary. Yes. I'm a detective. I do need to speak to her. It's in the public interest. You understand?"

"Sure, I understand," said Joan. "What's a detective?"

FRANCIS TOOK a swig from the bottle of wine and passed it to Claude.

"So what do we do?"

Claude looked down from the bridge at the large pontoon on the Left Bank of the Seine. Bordered on three sides by the river and on the fourth by a mock-marble façade and a line of serious people in dark suits and sunglasses, the pontoon (despite being essentially nothing more than a huge raft floating on the Seine) was a crowded affair of red carpets, tiered seating, twinkling and flashing lights and more than a hundred people.

"That covered area is where the models and clothes will

be," said Claude, pointing with the bottle. "A morgue for a thousand furry souls."

"Poor things," said Francis.

"We need to get in there, make a scene, sabotage it all."

"We could sink them all into the wiver."

"I like your thinking," said Claude, "but I don't have any torpedoes on me. We need a closer look."

"Then let's go."

Claude shook his head, drank deeply and passed the bottle back.

"Those security bozos will have my picture. My face is known. If anyone's to reconnoitre the area, it's you."

Francis took a fortifying gulp of wine. "Just point me in the wight diwection."

Joan and Matt walked side by side in what she guessed was a roughly northerly direction. Paris was a city of grand soaring edifices and street-level grime. It was a city of smells, of thin electric light and of constant noise, often distant but always there.

"The world is a fragile place," explained Matt. "Our civilisation is a leaf floating on a pool of chaos and people like Mary – Em – just want to poke at it with a sharp stick."

"I'm sure that's not true," said Joan.

"Really? Think of all those things you rely on. Well-stocked supermarkets. The petrol for your car. The power that heats your home. Your phone. The internet."

"I like the internet," said Joan, who had an idea from the films she'd seen that supermarkets were places where teenagers packed bags until they were sacked by an unsympathetic boss.

"Of course. And so do the activists and hacktivists who don't realise that the very medium they use to organise their actions could fall apart if someone wasn't constantly seeing what they're up to, informing the public of the damage they do."

"But Em..."

"... is not a nice woman. She's part of a ring of European anarchists who attempted to bring down the Nuclear Operations and Military Intelligence System – the *Système Intelligent Militaire et Opérations Nucléaires* if you will — here in France. That's World War Three type stuff. Have you ever seen the film, *War Games*? Nah, you're too young. Matthew Broderick plays this young computer nerd —"

"Who hacks into the computer controlling the nuclear weapons," said Joan. "It's a good movie, although I prefer him in *Ferris Bueller*."

"Right," said Matt. "At least you didn't say you preferred him in *Godzilla*. It's that kind of Armageddon scenario one of these activist nuts is going to set off some day. And what will they do when Armageddon comes knocking at their door, eh?"

"Plant beans," said Joan.

"What?"

She waved the comment away.

"I'll tell you later. So, what, you chase thieves around the European Empire..."

"Union."

"European Union, right."

"I'm a British police officer, but we have to try and work closely with our European buddies. The bad guys won't stay in the same place, so a pan-European police presence is essential."

Joan nodded. From her time in rural France, subduing wrongdoers with a pan was something she understood.

"A knight errant then," she said.

"What?"

"You. On your noble quest in unknown lands."

Matt laughed.

"Seriously?"

She shrugged.

"Just trying to make sense of it."

"I don't know if you're mocking me, being deliberately obtuse or you're just wonderfully, unbelievably naïve."

"Maybe all three," said Joan.

"How old are you, Joan?"

"That's not an easy question to answer."

"I think it is."

"I'm nineteen."

He shook his head.

"I can't quite believe that."

"Oh?" she said. "You're saying that I look like an old woman."

"Don't put words in my mouth," he said. "I don't know. It's... You're a contradictory character."

"You mean contrary?"

"Contradictory. You've got this wide-eyed ingénue look about you, like you've spent your whole life locked up in a commune somewhere. You've not escaped from some weird cult have you? That guy you were with, Frank or Christopher, he was wearing some new age robes."

"His religious habit."

"If you like. You act as though you've been locked away half your life or stuck on some nowhere Amish farm —"

"Shockingly close to the truth."

"— and that the world around you is just one surprise after another. And yet – and yet – you seem very... mature."

"Old?"

"Wise."

Joan raised her eyebrows.

"Teenagers are, by and large, idiots," said Matt.

"Harsh," said Joan.

"Hey. I was one a few short years ago. I know I seem like a man of the world with my jet-setting lifestyle, but I clearly remember my voice breaking when I still thought that lego was more interesting than girls." He coughed, and averted his eyes. "I want to make it clear though that I don't make a habit of hanging out with unaccompanied young women."

"Only the ones you've followed across northern Europe."

Matt stopped and looked at her.

"I'm sure I was trying to make a point," he said.

"You were saying I was mature."

"Wise. You look like someone with a plan, a person who can cope with whatever the world throws at them."

"The world has thrown a lot at me so far," agreed Joan, thinking of the pink rubber dragons, angry Belgians and rude old ladies she'd had to contend with recently.

"Most of us don't get our act together until we're in our

mid-twenties at the earliest. I'm getting there. Nearly. Maybe we need to get the craziness out of our systems when we're young," Matt suggested. "I'm sure you've been known to let your hair down."

"My hair...?" Joan's hand went to her head.

"When we're young, we all want to go out and just do stuff."

"Stuff?"

"You know, break the rules, find our own place in the world, fall in love..."

Joan stopped by the crowded doorway to a place called Club Dinosaure. A muffled, distant but insistent bass beat thrummed around them.

"Have you done all those things?" asked Joan.

Matt looked up in thought.

"Pretty much. Broke a lot of rules, certainly."

"Oh?"

"Bunch of mates and I got drunk on the local scrumpy one night and decided to bungee jump off the Clifton Suspension Bridge, using my dad's roof rack straps. That was stupid."

"Well, yes," said Joan, who wasn't sure what scrumpy, bungee or roof racks were.

"And then the inevitable house party when my parents were away in Exeter."

"Inevitable?"

"Mmmm. And I think all of them end the same way. We partied all night, I thoroughly failed to make an impression on any of the girls who came. I woke up the next morning in the potting shed and discovered that there had been a massive flour and egg fight in the house in the wee small hours."

"It's terrible that your guests would abuse your parents' house so much."

"Oh no," said Matt. "I woke covered in flour and eggs myself. Apparently, even though I have no recollection at all, I stood on the dining table, declared myself the 'Pantry King' and led the charge with a bag of self-raising in one hand and a sieve in the other."

Joan considered this.

"I've never bungee jumped or partied all night or got drunk and declared myself to be the 'Panty King.'"

"Pantry King," said Matt. "Well, it's clear that you are currently a little drunk, Joan."

"A little doesn't count. I've got to tell you, Matt," she said, placing a hand on his chest. "I've not had a chance to do half the things you have."

"Not all of them good."

"Doesn't matter," she said, feeling a righteous certainty grow within her. "I came down here to do *stuff*, make a stand, make an impact. But while I'm here, I am going to do all those things I failed to do in life. By Jove, I'm going to party all night, get absolutely cotton-picking drunk and, if the mood takes me, bungee jump off a bridge."

"Well, good for you."

"Quite." Joan grabbed his hand and pulled him towards the entrance of Club Dinosaure.

"Where are we going?" he said.

"To get drunk and party all night."

"Wait a minute," said Matt. "I thought we were going to find your friends."

"That can wait."

"Okay." Matt's hand squirmed in her grip but he was unable to break free. "I'll buy you one drink and then we go find your friends."

"Five," said Joan, picking a number out of nowhere.

"Five. No, no. Two then."

"Six," she said.

"What? You're meant to come down to meet me, not go up. Where did you learn to negotiate?"

"The siege of Orleans. I'm bloody Joan of Arc, me."

Matt looked at her. The disbelief on his face was tempered by the smile he was trying to suppress.

"Three," he said. "And that's my final offer."

"Three drinks. At least. You swear?"

"All the time," said Matt.

"CAN I HELP YOU, SIR?"

Francis looked up at the black-suited and neckless man-mountain next to him. Francis's covert reconnaissance mission had lasted a full twenty seconds before he had been spotted teasing apart the panels that formed part of the street-side security barricade in front of the Coureurs de Bois fashion show.

"Erm," said Francis and looked round to see if he could see Claude among the shadows across the street.

"You need to go away now, sir," said the man. "You don't want to cause a scene."

"Cause a scene?"

"We don't want to ruin the evening for the lovely people, do we?"

Francis looked along to the entrance, the cordon ropes and the carpet, the white trellis arch through which smartly dressed men and immodestly dressed women walked without any hindrance. So close, thought Francis.

"I just wanted to look inside," said Francis.

"Of course you did, sir," said the huge man.

"If I could just..."

Francis made to move towards the entrance but, with a speed that was surprising for a man who was essentially spherical in shape, the security guard snatched Francis's wrist and twisted it in a way his wrist had never been twisted before and which he hoped never to experience again. Francis squealed and doubled up.

"Let's not do anything unwise, sir," said the man.

By the entrance, another black-clad wall of flesh and a woman with a clipboard looked over.

"That weally hurts," squeaked Francis.

There was the clack of heels on paving stones.

"What's going on here?" enquired the woman with the clipboard.

"Just a trespasser."

"No, no, no. Oh, my God. Is it you?"

Francis realised she was talking to him.

"Is it?" he said.

"Ante Dzalto?"

"Yes?" suggested Francis, hoping that that was the answer that would make the pain stop.

"Let him up! Let him up!" hissed the woman.

The pain vanished as abruptly as it had arrived and the guard helped Francis straighten up.

"Apologies, Monsieur... um."

"Dzalto," said the woman. "The famous Croatian designer. I recognised you by your delightfully ethnic kaftan, Monsieur Dzalto. I read an article about you in last month's Harper's Bazaar." She turned to address the security guard sternly. "Mr Dzalto is at the forefront of the revolutionary Ergo-Eco movement."

"Therefore the house?" translated Francis uncertainly.

"You are the most important man in the house," said the woman. "Come this way."

As the woman swept him towards the entrance, Francis waved to Claude across the street.

"My fwiend," he said, adopting what he thought might be a Croatian accent.

"Friend?"

"He's vewy shy. Come on!"

Claude ran out across the road, bottle in hand and his collar turned up to hide much of his face.

"This is Restani Krumpir," lied Francis, plumping for something that he hoped sounded sufficiently suitable for a Croat. "He's a..."

"Dadaist poet," said Claude, glancing about furtively. "Are we going in?"

"I'll put you down as Monsieur Dzalto's plus one," said the woman and ushered them through the entrance.

She grabbed the arm of a skinny young man.

"Leo. Please ensure Monsieur Dzalto and his friend are escorted directly to the VIP area."

The skinny Leo bowed sharply and gestured for them to follow.

"I don't know how you did it," whispered Claude, stopping a waiter to swap his wine bottle for a flute of champagne, "but I like your style."

MATT HANDED over a banknote at the bar and didn't seem to be impressed with the amount of change he was given. He passed a bottle to Joan and she drank deeply.

"What's this?" she shouted to be heard over the music.

"It's beer," Matt shouted back. "Or at least something that used to be beer or maybe once had a dream about being beer. It's alcohol."

Joan drank again.

"Why were people standing in a line outside?"

"They were queueing, Joan. Waiting to take their turn."

Joan pulled a face.

"Is that what people do now, on account of there being so *many* of them?"

"Most people do," said Matt, "and who knew that you could just stride to the front and demand entrance because you're Joan of Arc?"

Joan looked down at the figures on the sunken dance-floor, moving through the frenetically stuttering lights. The music was so loud it seemed to pass right through her, as though she were listening to it with her bones, not her ears.

"This is great!" she shouted.

"Is it?"

"I've never heard music like this. The beat. The drums. It's like we're inside a heart, beating. No, it's like a military drum."

She grinned and turned to Matt. In the flickering half-light of the nightclub, he appeared to be something other than just a man she had met in the street.

"When we were marching on Troyes I met this friar, Brother Richard."

"Who's doing what now?" said Matt.

"It was 1429."

"What? Today?" Matt looked at his watch.

"I was leading the French army to Riems. We passed through Troyes. Our soldiers were starving. There was nothing to eat. But we were lucky. This friar, Brother Richard, had been in the town and had been preaching to the townsfolk that the end of the world was coming. Armageddon."

"Armageddon," shouted Matt. "I heard that bit."

"So what did the townsfolk do?" shouted Joan.

"I don't know."

"They planted beans."

Matt nodded.

"Why?"

"Because beans grow quickly. The people of Troyes believed – wrongly I admit – that they had very little time left and so used it to the fullest. They grew beans and, even though they were wrong, their crop saved us from starvation."

Joan chinked her bottle against Matt's and drank the last of it. Matt grinned.

"You know before you stepped out in the big wide world, that place you escaped from..."

"What about it?"

"By any chance, did it have big high walls and strong gates and lots of people in white uniforms?"

Joan nodded, impressed.

"That's amazing. How did you guess?"

"I'm a copper," said Matt.

"Copper what?"

He gave her a look.

"So what's the meaning of it?"

"What?"

"Your bean story."

"I don't know," said Joan. "I suppose that when you've not got much time, you've just got to seize the opportunities. Plant beans. Dance."

"Dance?"

"Dance!" she said, took his bottle from his hand and dragged him towards the dance-floor.

SQUASHED in amongst the party hubbub at the periphery of the catwalk show, Francis and Claude made their plans.

"We do something dramatic," said Claude. "We make a scene."

"The big nasty man who twisted my arm said we didn't want to make a scene," said Francis. "What's a scene?"

"A bold statement. Make people take notice. Here."

Francis looked at the fresh glass of champagne in his hand.

"For courage," said Claude. "Look at that. It's sickening. What's that? A fur bikini!"

"A fukini!" said Francis drunkenly. "Disgwaceful. In my day, people took the furs of animals for essential warmth but that... thwee – what is it? Gerbils? – thwee whatevers died just to cover her thingies and doo-dah."

"Chinchilla," said Claude.

"Is that what they call it? We must act, comwade."

"Yes, yes. After a bit more fortification. Wine! We need more wine!"

A woman sidled up to Francis.

"Mr Dzalto? Can I get your opinion on tonight's offerings?"

She thrust a black electronic device with a flashing red light in front of Francis's face.

"Press," whispered Claude in his ear.

"Press what?" Francis could see nothing to press.

"Journalists," said Claude. "Like the seagulls following the trawler, hoping for sardines."

"I like seagulls," said Francis.

The woman seemed to take this as a positive sign. "So, do you approve of the clothes on show tonight?"

"No," declared Francis vehemently. "I would rather see these women naked than parading around in these obscenities."

"If everyone was naked, wouldn't that put you and your fellow clothes designers out of business?" she asked with a wry smile.

"What is your name, child?" he asked.

"Aurélie."

"Listen, Aurélie. If nakedness was good enough for Adam and Eve in the Garden, then it is more than good enough for us," he said.

Claude nudged Francis in the ribs.

"Brilliant plan, comrade."

"Eh?"

"Aurélie, if you've got a friend with a camera, get them over here now."

"Why?" said Francis. "What are we doing?"

"We're going to throw a couple of sardines their way."

"Okay," said Matt, stepping out onto the pavement and waggling his little finger in his ear. "I think I've gone completely deaf."

"Music's better when it's loud," said Joan, a grin fixed on her face.

"Yes, I'm sure I used to believe that too. I think I also used to believe dancing was fun."

"You were amazing," said Joan. "Your dancing. Like nobody else in there. Where did you learn it?"

"School disco."

"There's a school of disco? Wow." Joan stumbled for a

moment and clutched Matt's arm for support. "I think the alcohol has gone to my legs. I need a sit down."

"No," said Matt. "We need to find your friends."

Joan looked up and down the street.

"I'm too tired to walk. Where's your Ferrari?"

"Same place it always was," said Matt. "My dinky little Fiat is parked somewhere on the Left Bank."

"Is it far?"

"We can make it, I'm sure. If you managed to march all the way from – where was it? – Troyes to Riems."

Joan linked arms with Matt and leaned on him for support as they walked.

"I do wonder if you might be mad," said Matt conversationally.

"My mother said I was touched by angels."

"Well, there's a worrying statement, depending how much you want to read into it."

There was an entirely novel whirling sensation in Joan's stomach and she held onto Matt more tightly until it subsided.

"What are these?" she said and pointed to more than a hundred little padlocks attached to the railings of the bridge they were crossing.

"Love locks," said Matt. "Young couples inscribe their initials on the lock and then attach it to fences, gates, whatever. I believe this bridge is particularly popular. The lovers put their lock here and then throw the key into the river."

Joan moved from the support of Matt's arm to the sturdier

but colder support of the railings. A glass-roofed boat was emerging from directly beneath them. A distance ahead there was a party of some sort on a pontoon by the side of the river.

"This city never sleeps," she said. "Why do they do it?"

"Do what?" said Matt.

"Put the locks here."

"Oh, I don't know. It's the kind of cute, dumb thing people do. A symbol of the unbreakable bonds of love."

"That's beautiful."

"If you say so. I think the city government regards it as vandalism. As for unbreakable, give me a piece of wire and half an hour, I'm sure I could have most of these off."

"Don't you dare," said Joan, giving him a gentle slap on the shoulder. "You are a cynical man, Officer Rose. My friend, Evelyn, warned me against talking to British people."

"You know, you sound very French, when you make that dismissive little 'pff' noise when you talk. What did your friend say about British people?"

"I do not make a noise like that," said Joan, trying and failing to replay the conversation in her head. "Evelyn said that what British people say is usually the opposite of what they mean."

"I've no idea what you're talking about," he said happily.

"I bet you don't even believe in love," she said.

"Love?" Matt gave it some thought. "I believe in lust. I believe in the biological imperative to find a mate. I believe that we are controlled by a soup of hormones and chemicals that bond us together. That's love."

"That is *not* love," said Joan. "I'm talking about the union of two souls. A pure emotion. An earthly reflection of God's love for us."

Matt grimaced.

"I can't quite buy that."

"I wasn't offering it up as opinion."

"Then we'll have to disagree. I mean, yes, emotion is just another way of talking about our physiological reaction to the world around us. But souls? God?"

"What about them?"

"No offence meant, but those kinds of concepts are entirely meaningless to an atheist."

Joan was surprised. She knew there was a word 'atheist' and that it was attached to a concept and a meaning and, if she thought on it, she knew that there were, somewhere, people who didn't believe in God, but she didn't actually expect to meet one. In her heart, she hadn't really believed that they genuinely existed.

"You don't believe in God?"

"No."

"Why?"

"I don't know. I used to believe as a child but then, along with Father Christmas and the Tooth Fairy, I put God to one side. The universe doesn't need him."

"No," said Joan firmly. "Without God, we'd be nothing. He is the ultimate, the only explanation for everything. To deny God is to deny the wonder of creation."

Matt shook his head.

"Quite the opposite," he said. "The way I see it, God removes all wonder from existence. What is life? God made it. What is love? It comes from God. Why are we here?

Because God put us here. It's monotonous. Take God out of the equation and suddenly the world is more miraculous. That the laws of physics should make a universe like ours and that, in one tiny corner of that universe, on a planet that's just the right distance from its sun for life to exist, the forces of chance and evolution have led to the creation of two people, you and I, and that we should find each other here..."

"You speak as though we are lonely and insignificant specks in a loveless void," said Joan.

"No. Flip your perspective around, Joan. We're the centre. We're everything. Two conscious entities, brought together at this point in space and time against all probability. It's you and me against the universe, kiddo."

Joan realised that Matt had her hands in his at the same moment that he did.

"That is," he said, withdrawing his hand, "it's not necessarily *you* and *me*. I mean, you *and* me. I mean, it could be but I was just making a point – hang on! I know that wolf!"

He pointed at a shadow sprinting along the embankment.

"So do I," said Joan.

Christopher was seriously considering moving seat or simply leaping overboard to get away from the sound of the Aberdaron WI.

It was astonishing that the women could find such hilarity in the pictures they had taken of members at the

Louvre. It was equally astonishing that they had taken them in such numbers that it had provided entertainment for them for the entire river cruise. It was further astonishing that Christopher had not spotted exactly when their lady-like chuckles had transformed into shrieking cackles.

"Honestly, Lord," he said, "back in my day, we would have burned them as witches. I don't suppose you could see your way to shutting them up?"

At that, a sudden bang from above silenced the women. Something large and furry had landed heavily on the glass roof.

"Oh, Christ!" quailed Miriam.

"What is it?" shrieked Val, staring at the four fat feet padding along the ceiling.

"Calm, ladies!" commanded Agnes.

There was a shout from the driver ahead. Agnes began to reply but was interrupted by the smashing of glass as the roof finally gave way and a great shaggy beast fell into the passenger cabin.

"Wolf!" shouted Christopher in recognition.

The Women's Institute ladies screamed.

"I won't look at another willy again, I promise," whimpered Lynne as she cowered in her seat.

"It's okay," said Christopher, holding up invisible hands to appeal for calm.

The driver, abandoning the wheel, ran back into the cabin to see what was occurring. The Wolf of Gubbio turned on him, snarling.

"No!" shouted Christopher. "Bad dog!"

AURÉLIE, her camerawoman Marcelle, and some lady called Sabina who was all toothy smiles and brazen laughter all thought it was a brilliant idea. It required no planning and, Claude assured him, would have high impact.

"For the fuwwy animals," agreed Francis solemnly and, with only a second of prudish hesitation, flung his habit over his head, pushed his way through the seated crowd and clambered onto the catwalk.

"Ladies and gentlemen," he shouted, naked in the glare of the catwalk footlights. "This must stop."

The seated men and women looked at him. No shock or awe or disgust but simple interest, as though his appearance was a natural part of the parade of fur fashion. And, indeed, the models (such tiny slips of things even up close that Francis felt an instinctive urge to offer them alms for the poor) continued to strut up and down in complete ignorance of him.

As one tried to walk past him, Francis took hold of the woman's fur jerkin and waved both it and her at the crowd.

"Did this... this... What is it?" he asked the model.

"Mink," she spat and tried to pull away from his grip.

"Did this mink die just to decowate this woman's body?" he shouted. "What kind of stewards of God's earth are we if we engage in such senseless slaughter?"

The model jerked away from him and, slipping from Francis's hold, pitched off the runway and into the laps of the front row audience. Now, they all reacted. There were gasps and shouts and the black suited men of security came muscling through towards him.

"We were born naked," Francis shouted. "Our bodies are beautiful without such fwipperwies."

"Please, come down, Mr Dzalto!" shouted a voice from the crowd.

"Go on, Francis!" shouted another voice.

"A wighteous man cares for the needs of his animals!" quoted Francis, screaming to be heard above the noise of the crowd.

Cameras flashed, people stumbled to get to or get away from the scene and, down in the crowd, Francis could see Claude and the toothsome Sabina doing battle with the security guards.

"Come all!" shouted Francis. "Fling your furs away!"

One of the few remaining models on the catwalk strode up to him.

"Cast aside this wicked garment, my dear!" Francis implored.

The woman gave him a tight, thin-lipped smile and then punched him square in the nose.

"Prick!"

Francis clutched his nose and squeaked in pain.

"Ow! That really hurt! I was only..."

He stopped and pointed past the woman.

"Is that boat going to hit us?"

ENTRANCED by the slow inevitability of the scene, Joan and Matt watched the tourist boat veer to the side and towards the floating party pontoon. The wolf was somewhere inside that boat and, by its sudden deviation from course, Joan could imagine he was at the tiller.

"It is," said Matt. "It's going to hit it. Wait here."

He ran off, stopped and turned to face Joan.

"Seriously. Stay here. Don't go anywhere," he said and then ran across the Pont des Arts towards the Left Bank.

Joan, too drunk and weary to follow, stayed at the railings and watched the broad river cruiser ram into the floating platform. The great squares that formed the pontoon collided, pitched and folded up, turning the pontoon into a series of slopes that flung people, furnishings and fixtures into the Seine.

And now, speeding along the path, a phone in his hand, came the daring atheist, Matt Rose. Watching the man as he ran to help others, Joan felt that strange swirling sensation in the pit of her stomach again. In all her centuries in the Celestial City, she hadn't felt like this. What could it be?

She looked for Matt among the chaos on the riverside and saw his dark hair and grim expression. The feeling expanded within her. A sudden thought occurred to her. Was this it? Could this feeling be lo—

Suddenly, several glasses of wine and an unidentified quantity of something that might once have been beer, came rushing up from her stomach. Joan leaned over the railings and threw up into the Seine.

She stared down as her vomit rained onto the river, to go down among all those keys thrown by young lovers.

"Oh," she said, disappointed for a whole variety of reasons.

WITH A WRINKLE OF HIS NOSE, Christopher killed the boat's engines but, while the boat had suffered little beyond a superficially cracked prow, the damage to the pontoon was significant and already done. Among slowly sinking pot plants and bobbing plastic chairs, dozens of soggy men and women trod water in the dark river.

Christopher wrenched open a locker by the forward entrance to the boat and flung orange life vests out to the swimmers. There were squeals and shouts as models, fashionistas and the well-to-do squabbled over the floatation devices.

"Typical," he said.

He looked down at the Wolf of Gubbio beside him.

"This is your fault, you know," he said.

The wolf snorted and then leapt into the water. Christopher momentarily thought that it was a simple act of indignation but then saw that the beast was swimming purposefully towards a somewhat familiar and apparently naked figure.

"Oh, great," said Christopher and jumped in after him.

With strong strokes, Christopher quickly caught up with the wolf and, together, they approached Francis who was flailing unproductively. Francis saw the wolf, gave a shout of joy and immediately sank.

"All right, mate," said Christopher, hooking an arm

around Francis's neck and dragging him back up. "I've got you."

Francis spat out a stream of water.

"Ack! It's like my pilgwimage to Jewusalem all over again!" he moaned.

"Yeah, yeah," said Christopher as he hauled him towards the bank. "At least I'm here this time. Patron saint of travel here to get you out of shtuck."

"A decent patwon saint of twavel would have stopped the boat hitting us in the first place," said Francis.

"I could let you drown if you don't stop mithering," said Christopher.

"No, thank you. You've got to go back for my entourwage afterwards."

"Entourage?"

"Claude and Aurelie and Marcelle and Sabina. I'm a famous fashion designer, you know."

"And is that why you're naked?"

Francis frowned.

"I might have had a bit to drink."

"Is that so?" said Christopher wearily but, despite himself, smiling. "Do you know what this reminds me of?" he said.

"By any chance," said Francis, "is it something to do with cawwying the infant Chwist across a wiver?"

"That's spooky," said Christopher, impressed.

"Lucky guess," said Francis.

6

LYON

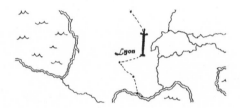

As Joan approached the Gare de Lyon on foot, her eyes scanned the morning crowd for signs of Christopher and Francis. They should have been easy to spot, a medieval monk and a muscle-bound brute with a fashion sense taken straight from the Dark Ages.

"They're not here," said a voice.

Joan looked in surprise at a table positioned near to the entrance. Em was sipping a coffee with a newspaper in front of her.

"Join me," said the Mother of God. "Pull up a pew."

Joan sat, putting her carrier bag of plate mail down beside her, and wrinkled her nose in confusion.

"I didn't expect to see you here."

"Hmph. Me neither."

"Are you just making sure we all get on the train?"

Em pulled a bitter expression that probably had nothing to do with the coffee.

"I'm coming with you."

"To Toulon?" asked Joan.

"Yes," said Em. "Something funny's going on. Those quotes."

"Quotes?"

"From Revelation, which that bloody machine spouted at us yesterday."

She gestured through the door to the bank of machines, one of which looked like it had recently taken a severe denting at knee height.

"Three days ago," said Em, "you received a phone call in which 'Simon' spoke of the earth, the trees and the green grass being burned up. And that day there was a forest fire in Africa."

"Coincidence?" suggested Joan.

"The second message, the one we all heard, was about a third of the sea being turned into blood, a third of the living creatures in the sea dying, and a third of the ships being destroyed."

"Yes?"

Em stabbed a finger at a newspaper story on the page in front of her.

"Well, a whole junkyard of ships were set ablaze off the coast of Karachi yesterday."

"Karachi?"

"That's Pakistan, dear. Nobody seems to know why these things happened but it's beyond coincidence."

Joan frowned.

"You think someone is *making* these accidents happen?"

Em gave her a shrug.

"God moves in fucking mysterious ways but he's not the only one. Quite frankly it reeks of some Satanic plot. If 'Simon' is a demon, that would explain the lack of a soul. That thought is bad enough, but I need to know why they keep mentioning me by name. I don't like it."

Joan pulled the newspaper towards her to read the story.

"So you're coming with us?"

"Yes," said Em unhappily.

"Perfect." Joan smiled despite the mystery now laid before her.

"Don't get excited," said Em. "As soon as I've satisfied myself, I'm ditching you three as fast as I can. Where are the others anyway?"

"I expect they'll be here in a moment," said Joan, glancing around hopefully. "Any... moment... now..."

"I told you lot to stay at the bar," said Em.

"And then you went off and left us," retorted Joan. "Where did you go?"

"To help Michel with a protest event."

"Did it go well?" asked Joan.

Em shook her head, her eyes hidden behind the glasses.

"Tits up," she muttered.

"I..." said Joan, looking down at her chest.

"*It* went tits up. Two hours ago, our lorry-load of coins crashed in the Pont d'Alma tunnel as it swerved to miss a party of British women who were walking up the carriageway."

"Oh no," said Joan, hand over mouth.

"Ach, it's not so bad," said Em. "Michel has decided that we can claim it as a victory. The coins were spilled across four lanes. By the time he's written-up the press release, it will be as if we planned a dramatic road block all along, a simultaneous protest against immigrant wages and the government's transport policy."

A horn sounded. Joan and Em looked round at the monstrous car that had just mounted the kerb.

The door swung open and Francis and Christopher climbed out of the zebra-print interior. Francis was wearing dark glasses, a rhinestone-studded baseball cap and several heavy-looking pendants. More disturbingly, he was wearing a blonde woman on each arm, dressed in ripped and scrappy dresses. Joan wasn't sure if they were related, but they both seemed to be suffering from a wasting disease of some sort.

"Has he been out helping the waif and strays of the city?" asked Joan.

"I doubt it's alms he's been giving them, if you know what I mean," said Em.

Joan frowned at her.

"Which of course you don't," said Em.

The Wolf of Gubbio followed Francis, and Joan saw that he sported a collar with some sort of slogan that she couldn't quite make out.

Francis stepped forward and held up his arms while he shimmied his hips. He watched with a wide grin while the two women shimmied in the same way.

"Ladies, wegwetfully, I must leave you now," he said. "Do pass on my best wegards to Mr Galliano and thank Mr Louboutin for the shoes."

Joan looked at Francis's feet and saw that his sandals had been replaced with new ones. They featured elaborate, interwoven thongs of leather, and she saw a flash of red as Francis wiggled his foot and exposed the sole. The women giggled and planted kisses on Francis's cheeks. They climbed back into the car and it pulled away.

"Why don't you both sit down?" said Em frostily. "In fact, Christopher looks as though he'd better sit down before he falls down."

Christopher winced at the scraping of the chairs on the floor as he and Francis dragged them into place. He lowered himself gently into his seat and smiled weakly.

"Fall over? Not likely," he said. "I'm used to soldiering on, me. Any coffee going?"

"You're hung over," said Em, as she pressed a coffee into his shaking hand.

"He's been at the beer!" said Joan, glad that her night of drinking with Matt had only left her with a buzzing head and a foul taste in her mouth. "For shame, Christopher! So, Francis, who were your friends?"

"Twixie and Twacey. Lovely girls. They seemed to be genuinely intewested in my views on fashion."

"You have views on fashion?" asked Joan.

"It seems I do. I'm a famous fashion designer, you see."

"What became of Claude?" asked Em, leaning forward. "Did you see where he went?"

"Yes, he's gone for a networking bwunch at one of the fashion ateliers on the Wue de Faubourg Saint-Honore. There are quite a few people who want to talk to him about the working pwactices in our workshop in Cwoatia."

"You have a workshop in Croatia?" said Joan.

"They were all fascinated to know that human uwine is used

to fix pleats in fabwic. He was forced to explain, as they seemed a little angwy at his demonstwation in the dwessing room."

Em stood up, shaking her head.

"I don't doubt that he will keep them entertained with tales of his fashion expertise," she said. "In the meantime, we have a train to catch."

"We?" said Christopher. "All of us?"

"I'll explain," said Joan.

EM LOOKED at her travelling companions from behind her sunglasses. Fifteen minutes into the train journey and she was already regretting her decision to travel with them. She certainly doubted she could take another two hours of the excited babble from Joan and Francis. They marvelled over everything from the speed of travel, to the table that was able to balance on a single leg.

"And look," said Francis. "They've got carpet in here too. Carpet *inside* a vehicle."

"These modern people will put carpet on everything," said Joan.

"I wouldn't be surpwised if they haven't carpeted the vewy fields," joked Francis.

"Astroturf," said Em.

"What's that?"

"Nothing," she said.

At least Christopher, squashed in next to Em, was trying to sleep off his hangover. Every couple of minutes he either belched or farted in his sleep. The only entertainment on the train was trying to guess from which end Christopher's next gaseous emission would come. That, and pondering if the other passengers in the carriage could smell the noxious saint, even if they couldn't see him.

Em's phone buzzed. It was a text message from Claude.

Your man Francis is a genius. Let me no when he's nxt in town, I'd love to wk with him again.

She had originally texted him to ask what on earth he'd been up to the previous evening. The reply puzzled her but she decided to drop the matter until she could have a proper conversation with him.

Joan was talking again and Em realised that she had just been asked a direct question.

"What did you say?" said Em.

"I was just saying that... if you meet someone, a man for example, and you feel that there might be... something, you know..." Joan grimaced, coughed and started over. "I have a friend and she met someone last night."

"A man," said Em.

"Yes."

"An attractive man?"

"Yes, I suppose."

"And this friend of yours has questions she needs answering?" said Em.

"Yes, she does," said Joan.

"And is this friend of yours called Joan?"

"What? No."

"Does she, by any chance, carry a stupid sword with her everywhere she goes?"

"I think you've got the wrong end of the stick, Em..."

"And is she perhaps a fifteenth century dweeb who has all the guile of a cushion and hasn't got any female friends, never had, never will?"

Joan crossed her arms angrily. Francis looked from one of them to the other.

"I'm weally confused. Has Joan got a fwiend called Joan?"

Em stretched, cracked her knuckles and put her feet up on the seat space between Francis and Joan.

"The girl wants to know about men," she said.

"I was just asking an innocent question," said Joan. "I just wanted to know *how* do you know if it means something? If it's, you know, *special*?"

"Special how?" asked Em.

"How do you know if you've met someone you can enjoy being friends with, or if it's someone you could maybe..."

"Careful!"

"Fall in love with. I don't understand how you recognise the difference," said Joan.

"Are you seriously asking me what love is?" asked Em.

"I suppose I am."

"You're hilarious, Joan."

Joan looked at her. Em recognised the look. Joan was unfazed by Em's scorn and she really wanted an answer. She groaned inwardly.

"I don't know that I'm the right person to answer questions about love. Don't forget that I had a husband who was much, much older than me. He used to say that he had piles of sawdust in his workshop that were older than me. Why don't you ask Francis?" she said, and then turned to stare out of the window to indicate that she would not be providing any further thoughts on the matter.

"Ask me what?" said Francis.

"Did you ever know love?" said Joan.

"There is no gweater love than the love I have for our Lord," he said.

"Uh-huh. If you're going to come on all pious, you might want to take off the rapper's hat," said Em, still looking out of the window. "Anyway, you know that's not what Joan wants to know. Why don't you spill the beans? I bet you put it about a bit before you got religion."

Francis shifted uncomfortably in his seat.

"I certainly wouldn't put it like that," he said. "I came from a pwivileged family, it's twue. As a member of the awistocwacy, my youth was spent in the usual manner."

"Eating, drinking and fornicating to excess, you mean?" said Em, scornfully.

"I was only doing what was expected of me," said Francis.

"And that makes it okay, apparently," said Em.

"Wait, so not all of us saints are celibate?"

"Nope," said Christopher, his eyes still closed.

"No," said Francis shamefully.

"Depends," said Em.

"I don't believe it!" exploded Joan. "No wonder you all think I'm so naive. You all *know* what it's like to be with someone else. You've all done it. How dare you have the nerve to laugh at me when I ask you what it's like. How *dare* you!"

"Turn the volume down please," said Christopher.

"Head still hurting?" asked Joan snidely.

Christopher nodded.

"Tell you what, ghost-saint, you share your wealth of romantic experiences with Joan and I'll stump up for some fresh coffees," said Em.

"Not much to say really. I found that aspect of life a bit of a drag. I used to lose patience with lasses throwing themselves at me all the time."

Em burst into raucous laughter. Joan and Francis giggled as well.

"Hey, that's enough of that malarkey," he said. "I don't know why you think that's funny."

"Throwing themselves at you?" grinned Em.

"Aye."

"Go on, tell us about these women, then. I can't wait to hear this."

Christopher cleared his throat.

"It's the oldest story in the book. Well, one of them," he said. "I was going about my saintly business. Most of the time I'd be helping people across this river. As a matter of fact, this one time —"

"We know about the time you helped the infant Christ," interjected Joan.

"Oh, have I told you that story?"

"Yes. Get back to the women throwing themselves at you."

"Right. Well one of the other things I used to do, as a loyal servant of our Lord, was to go and visit places which were a little bit, how you might say, Godless. I went to Lycia once. They were in the habit of persecuting Christians there. So, along comes I and the folks there thought they'd have a bit of sport with me, didn't they?"

"Ooh, sport," said Em. "Pray tell."

"They sent a pair of temple strumpets to try and persuade me to sacrifice to their idols. Lovely girls they were, but a bit forward. I say a bit forward. One of them was *all* forward, if you know what I mean."

He held his hands out, cupping two huge imaginary breasts.

"Gee," said Em. "Such a gift with euphemism and figurative language, I'm sure I can't imagine what you're on about."

"Anyroad," Christopher continued unabashed, "I was entertaining them with tales of my adventures, and they kept putting their hands on my thighs and what have you. I told them, look, these thighs have supported the weight of our Lord, so I can see why you're impressed at their mighty girth, but they just giggled and made suggestive comments about wanting to see the girth of my, ahem..."

He wolf-whistled and waggled his eyebrows.

"Again with the subtle symbolism," said Em.

"I know this bit!" said Francis. "You wejected their advances and converted them to the twue faith!"

"Course I did, yeah, afterwards."

"You succumbed to the pleasures of the flesh first?"

"What could I do?" asked Christopher, palms raised. "One of them, the little minx, you know what she asked me?"

"No," said Francis.

"She asked me for a *double entendre*," said Christopher. "So what did I do?"

Francis shrugged.

"I gave her one!" roared Christopher and rocked with laughter. Em rolled her eyes.

"I don't get it," said Joan.

"None of that weally happened, did it?" said Francis.

"It did, sunshine," said Christopher. "Don't go telling me otherwise."

"It's all made up," said Em.

"I remember it," said Christopher. "I was there. It's a famous legend too, so I'm sure it's real."

Em turned round in her seat to face him fully.

"I've got a theory about that," she said.

"Theory?"

"Can you remember any details?"

"I gave you the details. Lycia. Godlessness. Temple strumpets. And then there was the angry king who tortured and decapitated me afterwards."

"No," said Em, "I mean, can you remember what Lycia smelled like?"

"Smelled like?"

"Or can you remember what food you ate while you were there?"

Christopher's brow creased.

"It were a long time ago," he said. "I don't remember what I ate last week, let alone seventeen centuries ago. No one remembers that stuff."

"I disagree," said Em. "It's the tastes and smells that stay with you more than anything. I can still recall what I had for breakfast on the day my boy rose from the dead."

Everyone stared at the table for a long moment.

Em tilted her head in thought.

"Admittedly, I saw that breakfast twice. Once going down and once coming up."

Joan pulled a face.

"Hey," said Em, "*you* have an encounter with the walking dead and keep hold of *your* bread and figs. You don't have any extra detail, Chrissie, because you weren't there and it didn't happen."

"Maybe it's true," said Christopher. "Maybe I really didn't exist, but then I think there's an important lesson right there about love. There you go, Joan, I do have something to say about love."

"What's that?"

"Well I exist now, don't I?"

"Definitely," said Em, wafting her hand in front of her nose.

"I know it's all down to the 'as it is on earth so shall it be in Heaven' blah-de-blah, but I exist because people *want* me to exist. Everything I am is created by people's love for me. I'm only here because I'm needed and I'm loved."

"You are an ideal," said Francis. "Perfection."

"This is an ideal?" said Em. "There sure are some twisted believers out there."

"Thanks, Francis," said Christopher. "Now, someone mentioned coffee..."

Em dug in her pockets and produced some screwed up euro notes. Francis stood up.

"I'll get the dwinks," he said. "I want to see how the wolf's holding up."

"What did you do with him?" asked Joan.

"I hid him in a toilet," said Francis as he walked down the carriage. "Nobody will ever notice him in there."

The medieval bling-covered saint wobbled out of the carriage.

"Anyway," continued Joan, "what do you mean by 'depends'?"

"Sorry?" said Em.

"I asked if your lives had been celibate and you said, 'depends.'"

Em sighed, folding her sunglasses into her pocket. "You asked for it. I'll tell you what you want to know. I'm still not sure I'm any kind of role model though."

"Let me decide that," said Joan.

"In my earthly life, I remained a virgin. I was married to Joseph, as you know. Joseph didn't look like most people imagine him. If the filmmakers of Hollywood were to cast him in a movie he'd be played by Russell Crowe or Hugh Jackman or..."

"Who are these people?" said Joan.

"Handsome men," said Em. "Big, hairy, manly men with muscles and more muscles and torsos you'd just want to wrap your—" She stopped, her lips pursed. "Good looking men, okay? But actually, Joseph was old enough to be my granddad. He wanted someone to look after the house, really. After that whole virgin birth thing, I honestly think he suffered a little performance anxiety."

"You bore the son of God," said Christopher. "I can see that might make a lasting impression."

"He wasn't intimidated by me. No, he was intimidated by being in bed with Him upstairs. He didn't feel as if we were ever alone. You know, *God is watching*," intoned Em in a deep voice. "Joseph took it very literally, you can imagine."

"So you never, ever..." asked Joan.

"Did the bedsheet shuffle? No. Never."

"So what did you mean by 'depends' then?" asked Joan.

Em looked at her pointedly.

"Work it out, wonder-sword. I've been back to earth lots of times since then. I haven't let the grass grow under my feet."

"You came down to earth to find out about love?"

"Oh, puh-lease! You sound like an alien in a bad sci-fi movie. I came back to earth to set certain things right. I've been doing it ever since. When you have a world that's dominated by dicks, there is always *something* for a smart woman to sort out. I've been very busy. No, what I mean is that while I was here, I've made sure that I've experienced everything that earth has to offer. In my view, the best way to look after the world is to understand it very well. I don't think that most of our friends in Heaven understand that. Take it from me, there isn't a corner of this planet or an aspect of human behaviour that I haven't explored."

"Go on," said Joan.

"What do you want to know?"

"Well, you know, who have you loved? What did it feel like?"

"Not sure that I *really* loved many of them," said Em,

settling back and staring into space as she remembered. "So many were interesting in their own way. Leo da Vinci was a fascinating man. I think he captured something of me in that portrait he did, don't you?"

"What portrait?" asked Joan.

"Christopher must have seen it when he went to the Louvre. It's rather popular. Billy the Bard knew how to soften a woman up with sonnets, I rather liked that. Later on, I made a point of seeking out Casanova, when I heard of his reputation. Seriously overrated."

"Really?"

"A sexual show-off, though there was this one thing he did, with his little finger, he..."

"Wait," said Christopher, "are you saying that you were the model for —"

"Don't interrupt," said Em, "I'm trying to answer Joan's question. Now, I'll tell you who was really interesting, Papa Hemingway. He was a man who had the all-too-rare combination of a wild imagination and absolute disregard for convention. I liked him a lot. He took me on a fishing trip once. Francis would not approve of his methods."

"Really?" said Joan.

"He'd use a machine gun on sharks if they tried to interfere with the fish he was reeling in."

"Oh dear."

"We didn't see eye to eye on everything," said Em, "but he had *such* passion, and a fair-sized..."

"Aye, well, he were lucky he had me to look after him," said Christopher. "Never knew a man so careless with his travel. Had my work cut out keeping him out of trouble with all his buggering about."

"Didn't his plane crash?" asked Em.

"Well I can't be everywhere," said Christopher with a sniff.

"Didn't the rescue plane crash as well?"

"He lived, didn't he?" snapped Christopher. "That man would try the patience of a saint, honestly."

A voice came over the train's tannoy.

"Mother Mary. By the sound of the third trumpet, a great star called Wormwood falls to the Earth poisoning a third of the planet's freshwater sources. Men will die from drinking its bitter taste."

"Simon! Simon, wait!" called Mary, getting to her feet. "I'm not sure what you think you're doing but —"

"Passengers are reminded that they must keep their baggage with them at all times."

Em looked at Joan and Christopher.

"That was the third trumpet. What the Hell's going on?"

"HEEY, DON'T I KNOW YOU?"

Francis stopped in first class and turned around to see who had spoken. It was a balding man, dressed in a suit of lemon yellow velour with a large gold zipper, which bulged around his ample middle. After his brief flirtation with the world of high fashion, Francis reckoned that such a brazenly vulgar outfit was likely to have cost a lot of money.

"Do you?" said Francis.

"Yah. Your face is not so familiar but..." He peered round at Francis's behind. "Oh yes," he said waggling his fingers, "I believe we met inside a pink rubber dragon, no?"

"In Amsterdam?" asked Francis.

"In Amsterdam," the man beamed. "It's me, Heinz."

"From Helsinki, I wemember," said Francis. "What an extwaordinawy coincidence to see you here."

"If we allow the world to reveal its magic to us then it inspires constant awe."

"I couldn't agwee more."

"Please! Sit. Sit."

"I can't," said Francis. "I have to check on my wolf."

This seemed to amuse Heinz.

"How saucy you're being or maybe mystical. Or mystically saucy. But, please, join me for a moment. First class passengers are given many little treats and I can't possibly eat them all by myself."

Francis regarded the basket of pastries on the table and decided that he would eat one and perhaps take some more as a snack for the wolf.

He sat down.

"A moment then," he said. "And where are you going today?"

"Oh, I have the most *thrilling* day planned," said Heinz, putting his hand over his mouth as he squeaked with excitement. "First you must understand the history." He brushed a crumb from his lurid trousers. "Liam and I, we had a tumultuous past. Fighting and making up, always on and then off."

"Off what?" said Francis.

"Oh, you kid, funny man. He's Irish you know."

"Liam?"

"So quick tempered. The last time I saw him, two years ago, I said some things, he said some things. We *both* said some things. I can be such a bitch. Can you imagine? I can."

Francis had no idea what the man was on about. He suspected it might be something *homosexual.*

"So stupid. So very stupid," said Heinz.

"Who was?" asked Francis.

"Me. Him. Mostly me. Liam and I have not spoken since then. I don't know why we left it so long. Both too proud to say sorry. Well today's the day!"

"Today's the day you're saying sowwy?" Francis asked.

"No, today's the day I declare my feelings properly. In a way that will sweep him right off his gorgeous Irish feet and into my arms!" declared Heinz. "Take a look at this."

He handed Francis a brochure. It was entitled *'Love Balloons — write your message across the sky'.*

"I came into some money recently," said Heinz. "So I have the chance to say what I need to say."

Within the colourful printed pages were many inflated 'hot air balloons.' Alien things, the closest point of comparison Francis could think of were the inflated pig's bladders that festival clowns waved about. The balloons in the brochure ranged from the simple to the outlandish, from pear-shaped orbs to hearts, doves and even rainbows.

"I'm having a custom balloon made for Liam," said Heinz. "I just couldn't resist having a giant cock."

"Cock?"

"I can just picture his face."

"How nice," said Francis, unsure if it was common practice in the modern world to use farm animals to express love. "And will yours carry a banner message like these ones here?"

"For sure. Liam's apartment is just outside Lyon. There's a car waiting at the station after next, ready to take me to the airfield. I will be ringing him as we take off and he will see my message of love."

"And, er, what message will it carry for him?"

"I wrestled with this for many hours," said Heinz, smiling shyly. "It's so important to get it right. I wanted to make sure that Liam knows exactly how I feel." He unfolded a piece of paper from his pocket. "Here it is. You can see how many versions I crossed out before I got it right." He cleared his throat. "*Liam, I hate being without you. Your face is etched on my mind. Kiss my waiting lips if you forgive me for being such an arse.* Arse. He used to call me that all the time."

Francis smiled politely. "It sounds vewy heartfelt," he said and stood up. "Listen, I really must go check on my wolf."

"You think my message is too forward," said Heinz.

"Well..."

"God, I hope so!" grinned the delighted man.

In the café-bar carriage beyond first class, a smell struck Francis's nostrils. It was more than just a smell, more than a mere stink. It was a high-powered assault on his sense of smell, the olfactory equivalent of a stun grenade, composed of high knife-like notes that speared his brain and some funky bass stenches that almost felled him with their weight.

"Sweet Lord in Heaven help me," he choked.

Fearing the worst, Francis hurried through the café-bar

towards the toilet at the end of the carriage. The café-bar was deserted apart from a poor young serving woman behind the counter who had resorted to stuffing wads of tissue up her nose.

"I'm sorry, sir," she coughed. "I have no idea where that smell is coming from."

"Smell?" he said, having a strong idea exactly where it was coming from. "Hadn't noticed."

He shuffled past the counter to the toilet and used the edge of one of his many spangly pendants to unjam the toilet door he had artfully jammed shut earlier. He slipped inside and shut the door behind him.

"What have you done?" he croaked.

Francis's points of comparisons were few but he had previously concluded that French public toilets were not the cleanest or most inviting in the world. It seemed that all the luxury and artistry the French had poured into food preparation and the ritual of what went *into* the body had resulted in a bizarre contempt for the manner in which matter *left* the body. However, the train toilets were decently presented and pleasant or at least this one had been before the wolf had been ensconced in it.

The Wolf of Gubbio sat in the centre of the large cubicle, at the epicentre of a reeking storm of destruction. He wore an expression of deep regret on his face. Not shame, because Francis was not so blind as to think the wolf had a conscience, but regret on a much more personal level.

Behind the wolf was a large chewed hole in the partition wall that hadn't been there before. Francis saw that it led directly into the café-bar carriage and the corner of the serving counter. There was a bin on the other side of the hole and from the detritus in the toilet cubicle, it was clear that the wolf had been plundering the contents. The most puzzling thing adrift on the floor was the shredded cardboard box that according to its labelling had once held an entire wheel of Camembert cheese.

Francis held it up and sniffed it. The savaged box held some distant relation of the fetid odour that permeated the carriage, but, Francis realised with horror, this was how the cheese smelled before it passed through the digestive tract of a wolf.

A great moan, like the burblings of a drowning hippopotamus emanated from the wolf's innards.

"Oh, boy," gasped Francis.

The Wolf of Gubbio gave him a pained look and let loose a long flatulent whine, the drowning hippopotamus having apparently taken up the clarinet in its death throes.

Francis gagged and clamped his hand over his mouth and nose.

"I was going to bwing you a snack, but I think we'll leave that for now," he mumbled and backed out.

With the toilet door securely re-locked, Francis went back along to the café-bar to get drinks for everyone. The wolf's nose poked through the surprisingly discreet hole by Francis's feet.

"I really am sorry for the smell," said the serving woman.

"Barely noticeable," lied Francis. "Right, I'd like two waters, a diet coke, and er what was it? A coffee *that's so strong it will take a layer off my eyeballs just looking at it.*"

The young woman prepared the drinks and took his money.

"Now you should take care, sir. We've had some reports of minor theft this morning."

"Minor theft?" asked Francis.

"I'd hate to see someone take advantage of a man of the cloth, such as yourself," she said. "People have had their bags taken. Small items pilfered."

"That's deplorable."

"One lady lost three wheels of Camembert she'd bought for a gift, she was most upset."

"Three? There were three?" squeaked Francis.

"Sorry?"

"Er, how very upsetting for her," said Francis with a sympathetic smile, and retreated swiftly.

He walked back through the first class carriage with a tray of drinks, wondering how long the wolf could escape detection while his guts processed such vast amounts of stinky French cheese.

The train slowed into a station as Francis passed Heinz.

"One stop to go!" grinned the excited Finn. "Oh, and here come some delightful policemen too. Or 'scum pigs' as my charmingly rough Liam would say."

Francis had crouched a little to get a better look. Four uniformed officers, badges and weapons clearly visible, got on at the rear of the train before it set off once more.

"I think I'd better get back to my fwiends," said Francis.

"You tell them Uncle Heinz says hi."

Francis hurried down the train to join the others.

"Did you see the policemen?" he hissed.

"Are they here for us?" said Christopher.

"But we're not bad people," protested Joan.

"I think they're doing a sweep of the train," said Em. "They're sure to be looking for me."

"A little arrogant assumption there."

"I'm not taking any chances, Christopher. We need to move that way. Now."

She nodded in the direction of the first class carriages and the café-bar.

"We're only a few minutes from the next stop," she said over her shoulder, "we'd better get off the train there."

"And then what?" said Joan. "I thought we were going to stay on this train until Toulon."

"I have an idea," said Francis.

"Oh?" said Em. Francis squeezed past and beckoned for them all to follow.

"Heinz," said Francis.

"You've brought your friends to see me," Heinz smiled. "Do you all want a pastry?"

Francis shook his head tersely.

"You said you had a car waiting at the next station."

Heinz stared at them for a moment and then clasped a hand to his mouth.

"Oh, goodness. Are you in trouble with the scum pigs?"

"Sort of."

"Of course I'll help. Liam will be thrilled!"

Francis led them on into the café-bar.

"Cheese and crackers!" gasped Joan. "What is that terrible smell?"

"I have to release my wolf," said Francis.

"He's so rude," said Heinz happily, totally oblivious to the fact that St Christopher was retching almost uncontrollably at the stink.

Francis hurried them all forward, flung open the toilet cubicle and unleashed the Wolf of Gubbio and a fresh barrage of stench.

"Goodness!" said Heinz. "Your dog is huge. I bet people mistake him for a wolf all the time!"

"Jesus!" said Em. "What did he do? Shit out a brick of Roquefort?"

"It was Camembert," said Francis. "And I don't think it's actually made it all the way through yet."

"I love his crazy collar," said Heinz. "What does it say? *Be my bitch.* Oh, he's a ladykiller all right!"

Heinz ruffled the wolf's ears playfully. Francis dragged the wolf forward as his teeth snapped together, just missing Heinz's outstretched hand.

"What fun!" shouted Heinz, dancing a little as he trotted after Francis. "Look, we're just pulling into Gare de Saint Germain now."

"Hey, you! Stop!" came a shout from the end of the carriage.

"Go!" shouted Em. "Go now!"

The train had almost stopped. People were rising from their seats. Em stabbed repeatedly at the opening button at the nearest door.

"Stop in the name of the law!" shouted one of the three policemen battling their way down the carriage over bags and travellers.

Joan pulled a piece of paper out of her pocket, scanned

through it briefly and nodded.

"It's on the list," she said.

"What list?" said Em.

"Evelyn made us a list. If we hear someone say anything off this list, we're to run away really quickly."

Em fixed her with a look that said they would be having words later and then the door opened and Em dragged her out onto the crowded platform.

"Heinz!" growled Em. "This car of yours, how quickly can we get to it?"

"Oh don't worry about that," said Heinz. "It will be very easy to spot."

"Which way?" she asked.

"Here we go," said Heinz, heading for the exit. "We just need to get out to the short stay car park."

Francis checked that Joan and Christopher were keeping up. Joan seemed to be looking behind her a lot, trying to see where the police were, and Christopher brought up the rear, looking conspicuous and queasy as he stood head and shoulders above the rest of the crowd that milled around them.

A deafening howl reminded Francis that Christopher was probably not the most conspicuous (or queasy) member of their party. The wolf stood with his hackles raised and howled. He then crouched and snarled at the crowd, ears flattened against his head. The effect was instant. People pressed away from the terrifying spectacle, some of them stepping back onto the train, some of them shrinking against the nearest wall. A wide space appeared around the wolf, and all attention was diverted away from the retreating saints. The wolf turned full circle howled again and then, in a move that probably surprised them all, evacuated his ample bowels in a wide sloppy arc across the platform.

Francis lost sight of him as they crossed the main concourse of Gare de Saint Germain au Mont d'Or.

Out in the car park, Heinz pointed at an enormous purple limousine occupying several bays.

"I believe this is our ride," he said. "Climb aboard, kids!"

Em rolled her eyes at the sight of the car, but she piled into the back, closely followed by the others. Francis turned around in his seat, looking out the rear window for the wolf.

Heinz slapped the driver on the shoulder.

"I'm Heinz! It's me! It's now time to go."

"Drive!" shouted Em.

The limousine pulled smoothly and unhurriedly away from the kerb.

"Not again," muttered Francis.

"The wolf can take care of himself," said Joan.

"Your dog is not coming with us?" said Heinz.

"He'll start to get a complex," said Francis, "and think that no one loves him."

Heinz spread out on his seat.

"I think we lost them, eh? You will come with me to see my big balloon of love, yes?"

"Um, pardon?" said Joan.

"Yes, yes," said Francis. "Anywhere away from here is good."

Heinz nodded.

"This is surely the way to travel, don't you think?"

"Extravagant," said Em.

"For sure," said Heinz. "There should be some fizz in that little fridge there, yes?"

Em opened the fridge and inspected the bottle of champagne within.

"What are you?" she asked, ripping out the cork with a savage grip and twist. "Some sort of tech billionaire?"

"Nothing of the sort," said Heinz. "Please pour some for everyone."

Francis began to hand round the flutes of champagne as their luxurious getaway vehicle eased through the traffic of Lyon's suburbs.

"I was telling your friend earlier," said Heinz to Em. "Remember what I was saying about the world being a magical place?"

"I do," said Francis.

"Well, I had been partying hard across the Low Countries and, on that sweet day when I was dancing with my hands on your butt, I was completely down on my luck and down to my last euros and about to get down on my knees too."

"And pray," Francis nodded approvingly.

"If you like. Well, there I was, wrapped up in the remains a rubber dragon, the last of the good times slipping through my fingers and, suddenly, there, in my hand was a bag of coins. Not just any coins but big fat golden—"

"A small hessian sack?"

"Yes?"

Francis smiled.

"I wondered where that went," he said. "Things got a bit complicated when we were attacked by some local bwigands."

"Wait, the gold was *yours*?" said Heinz, his face dropping.

"I suppose," said Francis. "I mean, do we ever really own anything? Isn't everything just on loan from the Lord?"

"Oh my! Oh my, I'm so sorry," said Heinz. "I've spent most of —"

"Oh please, don't fwet," said Francis.

Heinz grasped the sleeve of Francis's robe, his eyes glistening with tears.

"If you knew how much this means to me... it's my chance to put everything right with Liam. I really believed it was pennies from Heaven. Or Krugerrands or whatever they are."

"We've managed quite well without it, and we've nearly completed our twavels," said Francis.

"Oh right," said Em. "More than a hundred miles from our destination and only shrapnel in our pockets."

"Fate," said Francis, "chose to put our money in Heinz's hands. It's God's will. God wants to be sure that Liam sees his cock."

Joan, Christopher and Em all stared at Francis with questions on their faces.

"Cheers!" said Heinz, holding up his glass. "To Liam! Now shush everyone, I must call him to make sure he's looking out."

Their expressions were no less confused as Heinz got through to Liam. He flapped his hand in an excited gesture to emphasise that they should stay quiet.

"Liam? Liam it's Heinz from Helsinki."

Heinz glanced around with wide eyes as he listened to Liam's response.

"I know, pumpkin, I know! It certainly has been a while.

It doesn't mean I haven't been thinking about you though. I wonder if you ever think about me?"

Heinz chewed a thumbnail.

"Now listen, I have some things that I need to say to you. There are so many things we never said to each other, I'm sure you'll agree."

Francis found himself straining to catch the tone of Liam's response, but he heard nothing.

"This is important so I won't say them right now. I want you to stay in your apartment – you still have that place on... good, good – stay there for the next thirty minutes and watch out over the car park. Can you do that for me, Liam? I'll phone again soon. Now remember to watch out. Ciao baby!"

Heinz ended the call and clapped his hands together.

"We're nearly there, I can see the signs for the airfield, I am *so* excited!"

"Just a couple of minutes now," said the driver.

"I don't want to worry you all, but the police seem to be following us," said Joan.

Em pulled herself across Joan's lap to look out of the window. There was a flashing light visible several cars back.

"Not the scum pigs! I can't have them spoiling it for Liam!"

"Scum pigs?" said Joan. "We might have had a few run ins with them but the police frequently do a difficult job in trying circumstances. Last night, Matt was telling that they often — "

"Wait," said Em turning on Joan. "Are you saying that this man you've been mooning over —"

"I've not been mooning over anyone."

"— was Officer bloody Rose? Are you completely nuts? He was in Paris? And you told him where we were going, didn't you?"

"No, of course I didn't," said Joan.

"Well he's tracking us somehow," said Em. "Did he give you something?"

"Like beer?"

"Probably after the beer. Something you'd be carrying. What have you got that he can be tracking?"

Joan looked at Em.

"What?"

"Empty your pockets. There must be something that you have. It's beyond coincidence that they keep turning up. Come on! Let's have a look."

"Maybe they're following the wolf," said Francis.

"We left the wolf at the station," said Em.

"Yes, but he's running along behind us," said Francis, pointing and giving a delighted wave out of the rear window.

"It's a wolf?" said Heinz, shaking his head.

"Super," said Em, flinging herself back into her seat. "Because a purple limo isn't quite eye-catching enough. What we really needed was a freakish mutt bounding down the carriageway after us, in case anyone hadn't noticed us."

"He's not fweakish, he's just big-boned."

"How about this phone?" asked Joan.

"What phone?" said Em.

"It's the one I got from that house in Belgium."

Em held out her hand and took the phone.

"Why on earth would you hold onto this?" she asked.

"I wasn't sure what I should do with it," said Joan.

"This."

She wound down the window and tossed it out.

"*La Valbonne Airfield*," read Christopher as they passed through a large chain-link gate.

Up ahead was a large metal shell of a building, a smaller hut to one side, a blue plastic closet and the strangest vehicle Christopher had laid eyes on in centuries. As the former patron saint of travel, he knew a lot about hot air balloons, had even received a couple of direct pleas from the Montgolfier brothers, but he had not seen one quite like this.

"Behold my enormous cock!" declared Heinz.

"Looking a mite flaccid at the moment," said Christopher. "The temple strumpets would have just laughed at that."

"What is it?" said Joan.

"A... member," said Francis faintly, gazing up at the pink and purple balloon as it waggled erect.

"There are enough dicks in the world without you adding more," sighed Em.

"The more dicks the better I say," said Heinz as the limo pulled up.

"The police." Christopher could see distant blue lights along the edge of the airfield as he climbed out.

"We've got to go," said Joan.

"You might have noticed the eight foot security fence around the whole place," said Em. "There's no way we're getting out of here unless we use the gate, and the police are coming through it at any moment."

"Then we hide."

"You people are too much," grinned Heinz. "You hide. I will talk to the balloon people and then I will bamboozle the French police with my Scandinavian charm and wit."

The middle-aged man practically skipped over to the overall-wearing engineers by the balloon basket.

"I've got an idea," said Joan.

"Does it involve hiding in the chemical toilet?"

"The what?"

"The Portaloo. The little blue box there."

"Exactly. We hide in there and, when Heinz's finished talking to the police, we'll sneak back over and steal the car."

"The limo?" Em shrugged. "Not a terrible idea. Christopher, they won't see you anyway. You're our eyes and ears out here. Keep an eye out for the bloody wolf."

Joan soon discovered what a Portaloo was.

"Why does it smell so horrible?" she asked. She was pressed up against Francis's armpit with Em wedged in behind her.

"They use those stinky chemicals so that we don't have to smell the human waste," said Em.

"But it smells so much *worse* than human waste," complained Joan.

"Shhhh," hissed Christopher from outside. "The police are talking to Heinz now. I can see he's giving them some long, long story that they're not really interested in. He's doing all these big arm movements up to the sky."

"I expect he's telling them about his love balloon," Francis chipped in.

"Dunno," said Christopher. "The police are splitting up now, there's a couple coming over this way. Oh no, wait. Heinz's calling them scum pigs and they're going back again. One of them was going to hit him, I think, but the other one said he's not worth it. *Now* they're coming over here. Oh. Oh, hell fire!"

"What?" hissed Em.

"Not good," said Christopher. "I need to distract them."

There was silence and then the shouts of several people.

"Tie those down!" shouted one man.

"I did!" shouted another.

"Can anyone else hear that roaring noise?" asked Joan.

Something clattered onto the roof of the Portaloo.

"This will work, trust me!" called Christopher from above them.

"What will?" asked Joan, but then her world rocked. The Portaloo threatened to topple over but righted itself, swaying vigorously so that Joan, Em and Francis were flung from side to side on top of each other.

"I'm just gonna say this," shouted Christopher's voice, with a slight tremble of uncertainty. "I'm the patron saint of travel, as you all know, so I will do my best to make sure that this ends well. You might want to keep the door shut though."

"The patron saint of drama queens, more like," said Em, and cracked open the door to the Portaloo. The three saints cried out in unison when they both saw the ground rushing away from them.

"Cwistopher, what *have* you done?" screamed Francis.

"I think," called Christopher on the ground now far

below them, "that I've invented the first hot air balloon with en-suite facilities."

"WHAT DO YOU MEAN, you can't stop it!" screamed Heinz at the balloon engineer. He tugged at his thinning hair as his balloon took off without him. That was bad enough. What made it worse was that his precious custom-made balloon was towing a chemical toilet beneath it.

"Nothing I can do," said the engineer. "Someone loosed the ropes and, er, tied one of them to the Porta – *Merde!* Is that a wolf?"

The startling appearance of Francis's pet wolf caused more than one police officer to draw his pistol. The wolf ignored them, mounted a police car and leapt for the balloon. The animal missed the balloon basket but managed to latch onto the bottom of Heinz's message banner.

"Never seen that before," said the balloon engineer. "Looks good though doesn't it? You can read your message perfectly!"

"Yes, but it's not supposed to have a wolf hanging onto it by his teeth," wailed Heinz.

"He can't stay like that," predicted the engineer. "He's sure to drop off when his jaw gets tired. Look at the balloon now it's inflated. Purple vein and everything, just like you wanted."

The engineer turned out to be half-right. The wolf did indeed plummet earthwards shortly afterwards, but it wasn't his jaw muscles that failed, it was the fabric of the banner. A long tearing sound and the right half of the banner accompanied the wolf's descent. The wolf landed heavily, but then stood up and shook himself.

Heinz looked up at the balloon.

"Oh no, no, *no*. The message!"

The engineer followed his gaze.

"Mmmm, there's quite a bit missing now, isn't there?" he said, adjusting his bifocals. "Oh. That's most unfortunate."

The message below the monstrous penis now read:

Liam, I hate
your face
kiss my
arse

Heinz made a thin, keening noise as he ran up to a policeman.

"Shoot it down! You need to shoot it down!" he yelled, pointing at the balloon.

"Sir, I'd like you to please calm down," said the policeman.

Heinz sobbed, shoulder-barged the policeman and made a grab for his gun.

"I need to stop it!" he howled, pulling the pistol from the man's grip. He ran across the airfield, waving the pistol and fumbling with the mechanism, trying to work out how to use it. He fired some shots into the sky, but then found himself rugby-tackled to the ground by strong arms. The gun was wrenched from his hand and he found himself handcuffed with several guns trained on him.

He rolled carefully to his side, to see the balloon floating into the distance, Portaloo still attached. It was likely that the love of his life would be able to see it by now. He closed his eyes and sobbed in misery just as his phone rang out with *Miss you nights* — Liam's ringtone.

7

IN THE FOREST

Christopher watched the phallic balloon and the attached chemical toilet as they headed off in a south-easterly direction. The former patron saint of travel offered it benedictions and fair winds until it was gone from sight and then looked down at the Wolf of Gubbio, which was still gnawing on a scrap of banner.

"Well, you horrible bag of teeth and fur," said Christopher, "looks like it's just you and me."

The wolf, clearly equally unimpressed with the new situation, sniffed loudly and ran off.

"Hey!" shouted Christopher. "Come on! Team Heaven sticks together."

But the wolf had not run far. A familiar Fiat 500 car had drawn up on the airfield and the wolf was vigorously snuffling at the driver's jacket pocket.

"Sure, go to the man with the treats," muttered Christopher as Officer Matt Rose tousled the wolf's fur and fed him a biscuit from his pocket. "A bloody Judas with fleas, that's what you are."

The Wolf of Gubbio gave Christopher a brief glance that told him it wouldn't take thirty pieces of silver or even thirty dog biscuits to buy his shaggy loyalty, and then went back to pestering Matt for more titbits.

Matt spoke briefly to the police and the balloon engineers and then scanned the southern skies.

"Gone beyond your reach, thief-taker," said Christopher, sauntering over.

Matt took out his phone held it to his ear.

"Ah, Major Chevrolet," he said. "Yes, it's me again. No, I can't leave you alone. Not just yet. I wondered if I could get a location on that... yes, please. And I promise I won't bother you again for at least another hour."

Matt nodded as the person on the phone spoke. The Wolf of Gubbio belched and whined unhappily.

"No," said Matt. "I'm afraid, that's simply not possible." He looked around at the closely cropped grass of the airfield. "That would be exactly where I'm standing right now. I can't see a sign of – Hello. Hello! Major?"

Matt lowered the phone and sighed.

"Impossible."

"What is?" said Christopher.

Matt tapped another number into his phone and held it to his ear once more.

There was a ringing sound which, to Christopher's ears, sounded paradoxically distant yet close by, near but muffled. Matt frowned and looked round. Christopher tilted his head to listen.

"Um," said Matt.

Christopher got down on one knee and, tentatively, put his ear to the wolf's side. Matt stared down at the wolf.

"You didn't, by any chance, eat a phone, boy?"

The wolf with the ringing innards whined once more.

"Swallowed it whole," said Christopher.

He stood up and brushed the dirt from his knee.

"That's impressive," he said. "Stupid. But really quite impressive."

SEVERAL HOURS AFTER TAKE-OFF, the blue box came to a sudden halt and, if there had perhaps been only one passenger on board, it wouldn't have been so painful an experience. As it was, Francis's head bounced off the wall on impact, was nutted savagely by Joan's on the rebound and both met with Em's as she too slammed against them.

"Cuntybollocks!"

"Fudging heck!"

"Chwist Almighty!"

Francis put a blue chemical-painted hand to his head.

"We've landed."

Joan, who took several moments to determine that the drunken swaying feeling she was getting was not entirely due to a knocked noggin, shook her head.

"I don't think so. Em, are you all right?"

"I think my fags have dropped down the bog," groaned the Holy Mother.

"I'll take that as a 'yes,'" said Joan and cautiously opened the door. It halted against a thick tangle of branches.

"Where are we?" said Francis.

"In a tree," Joan replied. "But not far from the ground."

"How far is not far?" asked Em.

"I think the rope is just tangled up."

With some contortions, Joan drew her sword and fed it through the crack in the door.

"What are you doing?" said Francis.

"I'm just trying to angle my blade," Joan grunted, slipping her whole arm out and waving her sword blindly around the space above the toilet closet. "If I can just locate the —"

As her sword did indeed locate the rope above them, the box dropped several feet, smashed into unyielding ground and tipped over onto its back.

"Lord above!"

"Cocks!"

Entangled and in pain, Joan looked up as the no longer entangled penis balloon became erect once more.

"Do all... willies look like that?"

Em huffed as she tried to free herself.

"More or less," she said. "Although not usually that big."

They watched it recede into the sky.

With difficulty, the three saints climbed out of the box. They all took a minute to stretch, check for injuries and assess their position.

"So," said Francis, as he wrung toilet chemicals from his habit, "we're in a fowest."

"And covered in blue shit and pilot's piss," said Em.

Joan looked round at the deep trackless woodland.

"And chances are no one knows that we're here."

"Wherever here is," said Francis.

"Toulon is on the coast," said Joan. "Whatever direction we've travelled in, we know we need to head south."

"I could ask a passing squiwwel," said Francis.

"Cos there's always going to be one of those, isn't there?" snorted Em.

"There is," said Francis, pointing at a red squirrel perched in a low branch. He went over to chat.

"Now we could find a bearing by the sun," said Joan, trying to find the sun in the grey, tree-cloaked sky. "If only we had Christopher here."

"I think we can manage fine without him," said Em. "And, if he's so bloody brilliant, he can find us in Toulon or en route."

"What's that?" said Joan, nodding at the plastic dial now in Em's hand.

"My compass," said the Virgin Mother. "South is that way."

"But Bwother Squiwwel says the best path is that way," said Francis.

"I'm not putting my faith in another rat."

"*Sciuwus vulgarwis* and *wattus norvegicus* are quite unalike. Completely diffewent species," protested Francis. "Aren't you, Bwother Squiwwel? Yes, you are."

Em inspected her cigarettes, half-removed one of the now blue and soggy sticks and spat in annoyance.

"Well, I'm going this way," she said firmly. "Joan. Coming?"

"Sure," said Joan and picked up her sword and carrier bag of armour.

IN THE PREFAB cabin that served as an airfield office, Christopher watched Matt, the balloon engineer and a couple of local police officers pore over maps of the local area.

"They'll have floated in this general direction," said the engineer, drawing a line to the south east with a marker. "And moving at speeds of up to twenty miles an hour." He consulted his watch. "Which might put them as far away as this."

He ringed an area on the map.

"Miles off," snorted Christopher. "I gave them a helpful push and they're going to be way over yonder if anywhere."

"Of course, it might have come to earth much sooner," said the engineer.

"We've had no reports of a downed balloon," said a police officer. "And I think one as... distinctive as this one will be noticed."

The engineer sighed.

"I'm worried that it will come down in these forests. My enormous penis balloon will be torn to shreds."

"We're losing time and daylight," said Matt. "I'm driving over there right now."

"If it lands in the forest then this search could take days," said the police officer.

"My wife's sister has a guesthouse in Longecombe, here,

if you're looking for somewhere to stay." The engineer smiled hopefully.

"Let's hope it doesn't come to that," said Matt.

"Huh," said Joan, a humourless laugh.

"What?" said Em.

"I'd never seen a Portaloo before and then I see two in one day."

"What?"

Joan gestured down the slope to where a large plastic box lay on its side at the base of a tree.

"Arse trousers!" exclaimed Em.

"Is that *our* Portaloo?"

Em gripped the compass in her hand savagely.

"How the titting hell did that happen? We've been walking south the whole time."

Joan shrugged and walked on.

"It could be a different Portaloo. I mean this forest is generally lacking in amenities and people would certainly appreci —"

"Stop!" said Em.

"What?"

"Walk back."

Joan slowly backtracked. Em turned equally slowly as Joan approached.

Em kicked Joan's bag with a clank.

"Hey!" said the Maid of Orleans.

"Your sodding metal armour's thrown off the needle,"

said Em. "We've walked in a damned circle. Two hours to walk in a damned circle."

"We should not have left Francis by himself," said Joan.

"You've said that already."

"I'm just saying it again. And I wish Christopher was here."

"You've said that too."

"I know."

CHRISTOPHER'S BULK took up all the back seat of Matt's small car and yet still he was squashed, his shoulders straining against the roof.

"Not exactly the roomiest of cars, your Fiat 500," he commented, as Matt drove away from Lyon. "I mean it has great fuel economy and it's a really neat design. However, diesel versions like this don't like doing short runs from cold and they have this nasty habit of contaminating the sump oil with fuel which can have disastrous consequences. Oh, and the transmission can make this worrying knocking sound. Yep, there it is. Can you hear it?"

Matt was concentrating on the road ahead. The Wolf of Gubbio looked back at Christopher from the front passenger seat.

"Eyes front, boy," said Matt. "If you can *magically* intuit where your friends are, I'd appreciate it."

The wolf raised its head obediently and sniffed for good measure.

"That woman, Mary, is becoming increasingly desperate," said Matt.

"Only because you're flaming well chasing her," said Christopher.

"She could really have hurt people with that balloon stunt. The sooner she's behind bars, the better."

"I'm not having that," said Christopher and clicked his fingers. The engine coughed and died and the car began to coast to a halt.

"Oh, look," he said. "I think there's that transmission problem playing up."

"No, no, no," said Matt as he tried to re-engage the engine whilst simultaneously pulling the car over towards the hard shoulder.

"Yes," said Christopher. "I can't have you arresting the Mother of God before our mission is complete. The Celestial City crowd are depending on us and I've got to demonstrate my mettle because there's no way I'm going back to the Prayer Assessment Unit."

"This is not what I need right now," huffed Matt.

"Well, I'm sorry," said Christopher. "I appreciate the lift and all, but I think this ends now."

Matt put on the handbrake and shook his head in despair.

"Seventy miles from any possible crash site."

"Seventy miles?"

"... give or take," said Matt. He looked at the wolf. "What now, eh, boy?"

"Tell you what, Matt. How about I let you drive me to the

woods where they are but I won't be able to let you proceed any further? Deal?"

Christopher grunted. In response, the engine spluttered and began to run smoothly once more.

"Okay," said Matt with a smile of relief. "Let's hope that doesn't happen again."

EM KICKED A PINE CONE SAVAGELY.

"I do not want to spend a night in the arsing woods," she said.

Joan continued to gauge the area in which their chemical toilet had crash-landed.

"As camping sites go, this is as good as any. It's elevated, dry and, if Francis comes looking for us, it might be best to be at the spot where we landed."

"We don't even have sleeping bags," said Em.

Joan nodded thoughtfully.

"We do need to sort out the basic necessities: water, shelter, food, fire."

"Okay," said Em, resigned. "I'll sort out water and fire. You go find us some dinner."

"There was a stream down the hill there," said Joan. "Any thoughts on how you'll carry the water?"

"No problem," said Em. She stamped her foot and, at once, a spring of clear water bubbled through the ground and formed a shallow pool.

"Impressive," said Joan.

"Bernadette of Lourdes near screamed in terror when I

performed that one in 1858. Miraculous springs I can do. Undoing of knots is another speciality. Healing of the sick and lame not guaranteed. Right, for dinner, I'd like an American hamburger with all the trimmings."

Joan wrinkled her nose.

"I'm sorry, Em, I'm not sure I can promise those things..."

"I'm joking, you doofus," said Em, waving her away. "Go collect nuts and berries or whatever."

"I think I can snare some rabbits or the like," said Joan. "And I might find some edible berries. Shout if there's trouble."

Em took out her lighter and stared into its small flame as Joan departed.

"I think we're already in trouble," she said to herself.

She sighed and began to gather dry pine needles and fallen branches to construct a fire.

"I'd kill for a cigarette or coffee right now," she said. "I'd maim for a cushion or a blanket," she added on reflection.

"Do you know what I want?" said Matt, unexpectedly breaking the silence of their journey. He didn't really expect a two way conversation with the wolf, but it felt better than talking to himself.

"A car with legroom?" suggested Christopher who had known ancient torture devices that offered more comfort to the larger man. Well, maybe not the ones with the spikes pointing inward but still...

"I want to go home," said Matt. "Pootling round Europe is

fine in its way, but I'd rather be back in Blighty. I miss the telly. I miss decent fish and chips. I miss the grey skies, the rain and the bloody people."

"Your balloon mate's guesthouse is down that road, by the way," said Christopher, pointing.

Matt instinctively indicated and turned.

"The Brits know how to respect a man's property. And privacy and personal space. You wouldn't catch people striking up a conversation with you on British public transport or in the street. Lord, no. Eyes averted. Everyone keeping themselves to themselves. Bliss."

"Sounds downright miserable," said Christopher.

"And, yes," said Matt, "we may be the most miserable buggers on the planet but at least there's some consistency in that." He looked across at the Wolf of Gubbio. "Your friends or owners or whatever are a funny bunch, wouldn't you say? Definitely not British."

The wolf said nothing, naturally.

"That Francis character – is he your owner, huh? – is he actually a real monk or friar or whatever it is he's dressed as? It's like he's going to a fancy dress party. Although that Joan... Every time I see her she's got some new get up. That knight in shining armour outfit, the, um, leather thing with all the straps. She's quite a character."

"No comments on me I noticed," said Christopher.

Matt frowned at himself.

"There's no doubt she's an... attractive character," he said.

"Oh, my goodness, you've taken a shine to her," said Christopher.

"She's a bit of a puzzle. She's this strange mixture of self-confidence and utter naivety. The things she said. I do wonder if she and Francis have escaped from some kind of institution."

"Institution?"

"She's not got a personality like anyone else I've ever encountered. It's... it's..." Matt suddenly laughed, the car wobbling on the road. "Bloody hell, boy, she's honest. That's all it is. She's honest. That's something you almost never see in a person. No wonder I didn't recognise it."

"Hey, I'm honest," said Christopher. "It's not our fault that you live among ne'er-do-wells, liars and charlatans."

"She's also got the cutest smile and she certainly threw some athletic shapes on the dance floor last night."

"Dance floor?" said Christopher, sitting up abruptly and squashing his head on the ceiling. "I hope you and she haven't been doing anything improper."

"Mind you, I don't think there can be anything between us," sighed Matt.

"Quite."

"Not given the company she keeps."

"Hey!"

Longecombe had shut up shop for the evening by the time Matt's car drew into the town. Shutters were down, many windows were dark and the only sign of movement came from the shifting green lights on the local pharmacy sign.

"Left here," said Christopher. "Here."

Matt didn't quite know why but he turned down the side street. A woman stood in the gateway of a large house. She watched them approach, arms crossed.

"Are you the English detective?" she asked when Matt stepped out.

"I'm a police officer."

"And what's this about you looking for my brother-in-law's penis?"

"It's a balloon," said Matt.

"I'm not sure that makes any more sense. You'll want to see the room."

"I really need to check in with the local police and begin searching those woods."

The woman cast her eyes upwards.

"It'll be dark before you know it."

"Aye," said Christopher, squeezing out the car door. "Wait until morning, Matt. Have a lie-in."

"Do you have any luggage?" asked the woman.

"Barely any," said Matt. "Just —"

"A great big dog. Is that a dog?"

Matt nodded.

"Of course. He's big, I grant you, but he's just an ordinary dog."

"So why is he ringing?"

"What?"

Christopher got down beside the wolf and listened.

"It *is* ringing again. I'm surprised the phone gets any reception in there."

Matt knelt at the wolf's other side and held his ear to the beast's chest.

"There's a voice talking."

Christopher listened harder.

"... sounded his trumpet," said a very muffled voice, "and

a third of the sun was struck, a third of the moon and a third of the star..."

"I can't quite make it out," said Matt.

"'so that a third of the day was without light and a third of the night,'" quoted Christopher. "It's our psycho soulless client, Simon, giving us chapter and verse from the Book of Revelation, the Apocalypse."

"No, I can't hear it anymore," said Matt.

"And is it normal to listen for voices coming from inside your dog?" asked the woman.

"Probably not," said Matt.

"SLOW DOWN, BWOTHER SQUIWWEL," called Francis, tripping over another low branch and snagging himself on yet more bramble. Night was falling rapidly and their trek seemed to have no end in sight.

The red squirrel sat on a tree limb a dozen yards ahead and chittered at Francis.

"Well, yes," agreed the saint. "I am a big clumsy lummox. I would dearly love to scamper from twee to twee like yourself. Is there no easier way thwough these woods?"

The squirrel squeaked.

"No, I don't know these woods at all. I defer to your expert judgement, bwother. It just seems that this path is awfully difficult and circuitous."

Francis freed his habit from the brambles and scratched his extensive nettle rash while the squirrel berated him noisily.

"No," Francis said in reasonable tones. "I am vewy gwateful and I appweciate you taking the time to – what? What did you say? Where?"

Francis hurried forward and pushed aside the undergrowth to reveal a small grey rabbit entangled in a loop made from a shoelace. The rabbit bucked frantically but was securely held.

"Are you twapped, little wabbit?" asked Francis.

The rabbit rolled over and eyed him critically.

"It was more of a whetowical question," said the saint. "Now, if you just hold still, for a second... Some people nearby you say? Well, we shall be having words with them."

Francis loosened the noose of cord around the rabbit's legs and took her into his arms.

"There. All safe now, sister," he said.

Francis stood and gestured for the squirrel to lead on.

"I do hope we will find the edge of this wood soon," said Francis. "Or at least a better path."

The rabbit wriggled in Francis's cradling arms.

"I have put my trust in Bwother Squiwwel," Francis replied. "I am welying on him to lead me twue."

Francis stepped through a screen of undergrowth and into a clearing. Em and Joan sat beside a small fire. Joan appeared to be cooking some form of nettle broth over the fire, using her armour breastplate as a makeshift pot. Em had placed her blue, chemical soaked cigarettes beside the fire to dry out.

"Well met," called Francis. "I didn't expect you two to have made such sterling pwogwess through this difficult tewwain. We must have made at least ten miles this day."

"Really?" said Em and nodded over to a tree and the blue toilet that sat beneath it.

"What?" gasped Francis and whirled round, looking for the squirrel. "Bwother!" he said. "I thought you knew this fowest well... Then how come we have come full circle?"

From a high branch, the squirrel chattered and twitched.

"Did he lose his way?" asked Joan, stirring the nettle soup.

"No," said Francis moodily. "Turns out my new fwiend is something of a pwactical joker."

"Git," said Em. "I think the word you're looking for is 'git.'"

Shortly before midnight, Christopher crept out of the guesthouse with the Wolf of Gubbio in tow.

As he tiptoed along the hallway, it occurred to him that, being invisible and all that, there was no need for tiptoeing or any other stealthy behaviour. However, he felt it set the right mood and helped convey the need for silence to the generally indifferent wolf.

He slowly opened the latch on the front door and waved the wolf through.

"Come on, you bloody rug," he hissed. "We're going to find your master."

The wolf padded out and sniffed at the overcast night.

"Best foot forward," said Christopher, "and we'll have them found before the copper even wakes up."

JOAN WOKE SLOWLY, grunting as she stretched. She sat up. A dewy dampness clung to her clothes. The air was cool but the rays of the morning sun were warm on her face.

"Best night's sleep I've had since we came to earth," she said.

"You're kidding, right?" said Em.

The older woman sat by the embers of their camp fire, a fat roll-up cigarette between her lips. She looked like she had been awake for hours, the lines in her face more deeply scored than ever before.

"There was many a time when I slept out in the open," said Joan. "You know, back when I was alive."

"Doesn't mean you have to like it."

Joan brushed the forest dirt from her clothes where she had lain. There were a couple of twigs in her hair that were soon extracted.

"Where's Francis?" said Joan.

"Gone off. He was getting on my tits."

"How?"

"Calling all his woodland 'bwothers and sisters' to him for worship. Rabbits, birds. Even a bloody deer. It was like that scene from Snow White. I told him and his cutesy backing dancers to go do it somewhere else before I turned some of his furry chums into slippers."

Joan knelt down by Em's ever-filling pool of fresh water and washed her face.

"And what are you doing?"

"Well, first up, I'm trying to work out why the hell I'm

being forced to spend my nights sleeping out in the open. Currently, I can't help but think it's all your fault but, no fear, I'm not finished thinking yet. Secondly," she said, relighting the extinguished roll-up between her lips, "I'm trying to find something to smoke that doesn't taste like shit." Em inhaled and then coughed violently. "Shredded dock leaves are not the way to go."

"I'm sure you'll find something eventually."

"And thirdly, since Francis rescued last night's barbecue banquet from your snare, I'm thinking I've got to eat something soon and I might try these berries that Francis's squirrel butler brought for us."

Joan looked at the pile of berries on the leaf next to Em.

"Poisonous," she said.

"You sure?" said Em.

Joan shrugged.

"You can eat them but you'll be squatting in the bushes within half an hour."

"At least we've got plenty of toilet paper." Em jerked her head towards the Portaloo.

Joan looked round for a suitable pine cone and then passed it to Em.

"Chew on this," she said.

"Seriously?" said Em.

"It has some value. And it fools your mouth into thinking you're eating something proper."

Em took the offering and nibbled tentatively on a corner.

"Hmm," she said. "It's not exactly the breakfast of kings, is it? Hey." She held it out for Joan to see. "Do you think this looks like my boy?"

Joan squinted at the cone.

"Did Jesus have a brown knobbly face?"

Em shrugged.

"I think it looks like him a bit. Fancy finding that here. Although, on reflection, I'd still trade it for a comfy mattress."

"You surprise me," said Joan.

"Really? How?"

"I don't mean to be rude but you give off this air of being in control, of being totally self-sufficient."

"Thank you."

"But, put you in the middle of a forest and suddenly you're pining for your creature comforts."

"You can't blame a woman for wanting a little of the good life," said Em.

"No, but..." Joan sought the most diplomatic words. "Everything you say, everything you and your friends have talked about doing, is about tearing down the structures of civilisation, removing the patriarchs from power. And yet, your life is secretly built around all those things."

"Listen," said Em, pointing with her pine cone. "Just because I want a fag and decent cup of coffee in the morning doesn't mean I'm in thrall to the cocks of this world."

Joan hummed to herself, lightly amused.

"What?" said Em.

"Nothing." Joan began to eat her own woody breakfast-substitute.

"No. Clearly you've got some thoughts on the matter."

"Well," said Joan, "it occurs to me that you do want to tear civilisation down to its roots and then rebuild it exactly the way it was before."

"What would be the point in that?"

"Because then the world would be made in your image, not His."

Em spat.

"What? God? Are you suggesting I'm..." – Em swallowed hard, although whether this was due to bitter emotions or inedible pine cone was difficult to tell – "You think I'm *jealous*?"

"I think you might have some resentment issues with..."

"With what?" Em glowered.

"Nothing. I've upset you. Forget it."

"With what?" demanded Em.

"With men."

Em shook her head.

"Such a narrow-minded, parochial and... and chauvinistic view of the complex philosophical and political beliefs I try to uphold. What? You'd cast centuries of feminist ideology aside, arguing that it's just the 'little woman' getting her knickers in a twist because she had the 'misfortune' to be born with a uterus."

"I didn't say that."

"But that's what you meant. That's just the pot calling the kettle black."

"What do you mean?" said Joan.

"It's an old saying which comes from the time when —"

"I know what the expression means," said Joan. "I meant, what do you mean?"

"Well, sweetheart," said Em, throwing her clearly

unsatisfying pine cone breakfast into the bushes, "I'm not the one who spent her short adult life trying her damnedest to become a man."

Joan turned to face Em squarely and, when she spoke, there was an icy bite to her tone.

"What did you just say?"

CAST OUT FROM THE CAMPSITE, Francis had found the perfect spot for his woodland spiritual gathering, his church of animals. He had found a clearing little more than a hundred yards away. It was grassy and vaguely bowl-shaped, a natural amphitheatre for a wilderness sermon.

"Settle down, my bwethwen," he called, with a calming wave of his hands.

The hedgehogs, voles and crows settled down on their grassy pews. However there were certainly glances exchanged between the stoats and the foxes, the falcons and the hawks, each of them hungrily eyeing the rabbits, moles and dormice. Part of Francis felt it would have been simpler if he'd deliberately seated the carnivores and herbivores apart, but that was exactly the sort of divisively negative behaviour that he wanted to undo with his forest service. Also, he wasn't sure what he would have done with the badgers. How could he place them and the other omnivores based on diet? Should they be together or ranged in the space between meat-eaters and plant-eaters?

"Vewy well, my flock," he said. "We are gathered here today to —"

He stopped as something brushed against his ankle. An adder looped over his grubby designer shoes.

"Oh," he said, suppressing a shudder. "Bwother adder, how delightful to see you. No, you're not too late at all. Perhaps you can find a pew over there with the fwogs, toads and worms."

The adder looked up at him and flicked its tongue.

"Not at all," said Francis. "I'm against segregation and I certainly have nothing against any cold-blooded animals. Besides, I do believe that our insect fwiends are entirely bloodless."

The snake licked the air questioningly.

"Ichor, I think," said Francis.

Francis maintained a beatific smile as the adder slithered over to join the other icky and slimy creatures. He reflected that the animal kingdom was like a big happy family, although there was always that creepy uncle that everyone preferred to forget.

"Vewy good," he said. "Now, today I would like to speak to you about the twin virtues of chawity —"

A seedcase bounced off Francis's shoulder.

"Chawity and tolewance," said Francis. "I want us all to weflect on how we can" – another seedcase narrowly missed him. – "be kinder to one another, give more to one another and, in the end" – a third seedcase struck Francis in the forehead – "accept the shortcomings of others without wesorting to violence."

In the branches above, a certain squirrel looked at him innocently with shiny black eyes.

"Later, there will be an opportunity for confession of

sins," said Francis gruffly, staring at the squirrel, "but now let us start with our first hymn, *All Things Bwight and Beautiful*."

"I'VE NEVER WANTED to be a man," said Joan.

"Oh, really?" said Em.

"Perhaps, unlike other women of my time, I felt the need for action and a sense of purpose, the desire to *do* something. Nonetheless, I am a woman, a maiden, and though I spent my life among soldiers and kings, I have never wanted to be anything other than what I am."

"Interesting," said Em. "Shall we look at the evidence?"

"What evidence?"

"You have a man's haircut."

"What?"

Em pointed at Joan's short bob.

"You have man's hair."

"Lots of women wear their hair like this," Joan protested.

"Nowadays they do, most inspired by fanciful pictures of you. But in your time, that was a man's haircut."

"I was a wanted woman. I had to travel incognito in my last few years. I was trying to blend in."

"Which brings me onto the men's clothing you wore."

"You try fighting a battle in a dress. I was safer from harm of all kinds in hosen and tunic."

"And more like a man. And, you reminded me, what was it you carried in battle?"

"My sword sometimes," said Joan. "And my standard. I was both leader and standard bearer for the king's armies."

"Mmm," nodded Em. "That's right. Joan of Arc, striding about with a big pole in her hand. Her fingers wrapped around the thick shaft. I bet holding your big pole brought you a lot of comfort."

"I think it brought comfort to a lot of the men," said Joan. Em sniggered.

"Next verse!"

Francis swung his arms in great circles, trying to keep the animals in time.

"The purple headed mountain, the wiver wunning by..."

The rabbits had the best sense of rhythm but, lacking powerful voices (they could produce little more than intermittent squeaks) did little to counteract the toneless squawks of the sparrowhawk and the wretched screams of the foxes.

The forest frogs added their own weird belches and pops to the ensemble, creating a complex arrhythmic syncopation which was either a deliberate work of sabotage or perhaps an attempt to inject a bit of Gallic jazz into the proceedings.

The snails and slugs had seemingly decided that the whole event was simply not for them but, fortunately, were leaving at such a slow pace that no one noticed or cared. Francis sympathised with their views. It had been centuries since he had conducted an animal choir on earth and, in the Celestial City, he'd had the finest Amazonian songbirds to carry the melody and a couple of well-practised elephants to keep the whole thing in time with foot stomps and their *basso profundo* trumpeting.

"The sunset and the morning, that bwightens up the sky... All together now!" yelled Francis. "All things bwight and beautiful, all cweatures gweat and small..."

The slugs and snails continued to flee at top speed.

"Where's my wolf?"

The landlady did not take her eyes off the eggs frying on the hob. She had a cigarette tucked in the corner of her mouth and was successfully focussed on keep cigarette ash out of the frying pan.

"Wolf?" she said. "I thought you had a dog."

Matt ran an anxious hand through his uncombed hair.

"Dog. I meant to say dog."

"He's not in your room?" said the woman.

"I think I would have noticed. He's huge."

"Almost wolf-like in his proportions."

"Wolf-*like*, yes. I think he's escaped."

"Ah," said the woman, flipping the eggs over. "That explains it."

"Explains what?"

"Someone opened the front door last night. It was ajar when I came down."

Matt frowned.

"Someone broke in?"

"No. I lock up last thing at night, keys in the lock, the door bolted."

Matt blinked and tried to clear the muzzy sleepiness from his head.

"So, someone let him out?"

"Either that or your wolf has very dextrous paws." She turned and smiled at him. "Sorry. Dog."

CHRISTOPHER STOPPED as they came up against an impenetrable tangle of bramble. He looked left and right but there was no continuation of the path, no way for them to press on.

Christopher huffed, looked up and down and back the way they had come. He caught the wolf looking at him.

"First up, we're not lost. We're not. I'm the patron saint of travel."

The wolf sat down and scratched itself.

"Ex-patron saint of travel. Point is, I know travel. I do not get lost." He spun around, utterly stumped. "And even if I were lost, it's not a problem. This is just my own way of enacting the Almighty's ineffable plan. We're clearly here for – Ha!"

The wolf flinched at the giant saint's sudden outburst.

"Up there," said Christopher, pointing up into a nearby tree. "Come on. Give me a leg up."

"I'm GOING to ignore your vile comments about my lifestyle choices," said Joan to Em. "You're simply trying to deflect attention from yourself."

"Deflect?"

"Deflect. I think I struck a nerve with you."

"Have not," said Em. "You know nothing about me."

"I know that you've been wandering the earth for nearly two thousand years, ignoring all of Heaven's edicts and generally doing what you want."

"I'm an independent woman."

"You're sulking," said Joan, hearing a harshness in her own voice she hadn't intended. "You're all big strops and grand defiant gestures. No wonder you've fallen in with the anarchists and anti-globalisation crowd. They may have noble intentions but, for the most part, it's about shouting 'No!' as loud as you can in whatever way you want. It's throwing your baby toys out of the cradle."

"Good mother-twatting God!" shouted Em. "I had no idea you were so fucking... bourgeois!"

"Bourgeois? I don't even know what that means but it sounds filthy. You're only angry because I'm right. You're striking out in whatever way you can, without thought. Mad silly stuff like – what was it you said in Rouen? – when you and your hacker friend compromised a government computer and replaced the main programme with random text. Childish."

"It was the French military mainframe. We were having a pop at the hawks of this world."

Joan froze.

"Wait."

"What?" said Em. "You've just realised that you're a complete arse and need time to rewind?"

"The military mainframe. That was you and Michel who did that?"

"Maybe."

Joan looked aside, her mind whirring, loose fragments of information struggling to fit together.

"The Système Intelligent Militaire et Opérations Nucléaires."

"That's the one. Who told you?"

"Matt."

"You see, I blame him for this attitude of yours. He's put ideas in your head and tried to turn —"

"Shut up. I'm thinking. It controls the armies, does it? The planes and the missiles?"

"And all their other phallic symbols of male dominance."

Joan clutched her head.

"What text?"

Em frowned.

"What?"

"The random text you copied over the mainframe's – what was it? – key directives."

"I don't know. Why?"

Joan held Em in her steely gaze.

"Système Intelligent Militaire et Opérations Nucléaires. S – I – M – O – N."

Colour drained from Em's worn face.

"No," she said, her voice a hoarse whisper. "That's silly. That's nonsense."

"A soulless being makes a prayer to Heaven."

"No."

"A being who has the power to launch weapons, set fires and bring destruction raining down from the skies?"

"No," whispered Em, shaking her head robotically.

Joan smiled but it was a bitter, crazy smile.

"Because you thought it would be funny, didn't you? A computer system capable of bringing about the end of the world or something very much like it. You picked the book of Revelation as a joke and fed it to the computer."

"No."

"Mother Mary, he called you. *It* called you. And that's who you are."

"No! Listen —"

"You're its mother. You made it!"

"That can't be true!"

"And it's doing what its mummy told it to do. It's taken your words as a set of instructions. There are seven trumpets, Em. It's already sounded at least three of them. What happens after the seventh trumpet, Em?"

"This is all conjecture, Joan."

Joan stepped to the tree where her belongings sat, grabbed her sword and swung it to point directly at Em.

"Damn you, Mary! Admit it. What happens when the seventh trumpet sounds?"

Em took a deep breath, her jaw clenched with emotion.

"The world ends," she said. "Everything. All of it. It ends."

Joan turned away violently and picked up her bag of armour.

"But is that such a bad thing?" said Em.

"The end of the world?" spat Joan without even looking round. "Yes, I think it might be."

"The flaming Almighty has let His creation go to ruin for too long. It's time He stepped in and took some responsibility! If it takes Armageddon to make that happen then so be it."

Joan gave Em a last backward glance.

"I've just realised something," she said.

"What?"

"You're an idiot."

Joan set off through the undergrowth in a possibly southerly direction.

"Where are you going?" Em called.

"To stop what you started!" she shouted back.

"I can help!"

Joan sneered.

"You've helped enough," she shouted and stomped on, taking out her plate arm greaves as she did.

Francis conducted the animals through the final verse with the passion and urgency of a trapped miner clawing his way towards a speck of daylight.

"He gave us eyes to see them, and lips that we might tell... Keep it together, guys!"

He stepped aside as Brother Squirrel launched yet another missile at him from his perch in the ash tree. Like it or not, decided Francis, that creature was going to be first in the confessional.

"How gweat is God Almighty, who has made all things well. Final chorwus, evewyone! All things bwight and beautiful —"

There was a great thrashing sound from the bushes and the Wolf of Gubbio bounded into the clearing, scattering mammals, birds, reptiles, amphibians and insects before it. The noise (one would have to be very generous to describe it as actual singing) halted at once. As wood pigeons, jays and starlings took to the sky and various rodents fled into the undergrowth, the wolf bounced and leapt, his teeth snapping together.

"Bwother Wolf!" exclaimed Francis.

He was not sure in that first instance if he should be delighted to see his companion again or annoyed that he had effectively destroyed the woodland animal service or, indeed, secretly glad that he had brought the excruciating hymn to a final close.

"How did you find us?" he asked.

"Because he was with me," said Christopher, strolling in.

"Oh, this is marvellous news."

The wolf went over to the pack of snails and slugs who were still fleeing and were the only members of the congregation still present.

"Don't eat them," said Francis. "This is a place of worship, bwother."

The Wolf of Gubbio looked at Francis with a sheepishness that the saint knew well.

"Who?" said Francis.

The wolf looked up at a broken ash branch.

"Bwother Squiwwel? Oh, dear."

Christopher put his hand on Francis's shoulder.

"Where are the ladies? I've sorted our onward travel."

"Oh?"

"I found the balloon again."

WITH NO WOLF and no phone signals to guide him, Matt had resorted to driving round the local forests, turning from single-laned roads to dusty tracks and back again in what he told himself was a methodical searching pattern but which was nothing more than aimless wandering.

After two hours, with morning almost gone, Matt parked up. He was no longer able to ignore the truth of the matter, that his speculative wanderings were simply a way of putting off an admission of defeat. With no sign of Em or her companions and no further information from the French authorities, he had lost them. It was time to return to the office (by which he meant anywhere with wi-fi and cheap coffee), type up a report for his superiors both here and in the UK and take further instructions from –

There was a sharp hard tap at the passenger window. He startled.

"Open the door," said Joan. The tip of a metre-long sword rested against the glass.

"I see you're back in your fancy knight gear," he said. "Gay Pride was last weekend. And in another country."

"Open the door," she said. There was a fearsome and determined set to her narrow jaw.

"It's open," he said.

Joan tried the handle and then got in, her sword angled across at Matt.

"I think you should point that somewhere else," he said.

"You're going to take me to Marseille."

"I mean, one corner taken at high speed, you slip and kebab me... That would be very – why Marseille?"

"Your role is to drive, not ask questions."

"You're taking me hostage? You do know that's a criminal offence?"

He could see the flicker of hesitation in her eyes.

"There are greater matters at stake here," she said, in a voice so grave that it frightened Matt far more than the blade pointed at his side.

"Where are your friends?" he asked.

"Friends?"

"Mary. Francis. Are we meeting them in Marseille?"

She shook her head.

"It's just me," she said. "Now, drive."

8

MARSEILLE AND AUBENAS

"Didn't I tell you I'd get us all going again?" said Christopher, patting the edge of the balloon basket.

"Can you get that brute to drool over someone else?" said Em. "His breath is astonishing."

"He's pwobably just hungwy." Francis tickled the Wolf of Gubbio under his chin. The wolf shook his head gently, speckling Em's upper body with flecks of frothy grey saliva.

"Why we had to travel in this thing I don't know," said Em. "I'd be all for it if we could pull over and get a coffee and some fags, but no, we're committed, aren't we? We'll just hang on to the tattered remains of this giant dick which may or may not take us somewhere useful."

The wolf stretched and put his front paws onto the edge of the basket, pushing Em out of the way to do so. As it leaned over the edge, tongue lolling, Christopher thought he saw a smirk of malicious enjoyment on its face.

"I can get us to Toulon," said Christopher, "I've got the wind going just right for a nice speedy journey, but we don't know where Joan is." He looked at Em. "Why did she go off on her own?"

"No idea. She's her own woman, apparently."

"What?"

"Nothing. She just went off. Okay? Leave it."

"I thought I heard waised voices back in the fowest," said Francis.

"I think you'll find that was a fox trying to sing *All things Bright and Beautiful*," said Em. "I know it sounded like screams of torment. Easy mistake to make."

"Did you and Joan have a set to?" asked Christopher.

"A set to?"

"Aye. A ding-dong. An argument."

"We've not really had anything else since we met, have we?" said Em.

Christopher looked at Em directly, but she looked away. Her hands patted her pockets and she pulled a lumpy roll-up from her pocket and twirled it in her fingers.

"Don't suppose either of you know if these leaves are poisonous?" she asked, holding up a sample.

Christopher and Francis shook their heads. Em let the wind take the leaf.

"Joan would know," she said.

JOAN SAT in the passenger seat of Matt's car, her sword held loosely in her lap and only generally pointing at Matt.

"Stunning scenery, isn't it?" said Matt conversationally.

Joan couldn't help but agree. The countryside of northern France had seemed achingly familiar from her life on earth all those years ago, but she realised that southern France was very different. Instead of apple trees there were fields of sunflowers and lavender. As they crested a small rise the view to the horizon glowed with colour.

"It's lovely," she agreed. "No country on earth quite like it."

The car radio warbled at the hilltop.

"... opened the bottomless pit and there arose a smoke out of the pit like the smoke of a great furnace, and the sun and the air were dark..."

The radio drifted into static.

"Damned thing," muttered Matt and pressed a button.

"Wait!" said Joan.

"It's okay," said Matt. "Just finding a station."

"— still unclear," said a radio newsreader. "There has been a series of explosions in Kuwait, Saudi Arabia and the United Arab Emirates. Uncontrollable fires blaze in many of the region's oilfields. The *entire* region is covered with a highly toxic cloud of smoke, which is visible as far away as Central Europe."

"Wow," said Matt. "That's crazy."

"There are unconfirmed reports that the initial explosions were caused by missile strikes, but no group or country has claimed responsibility for the attack. Both the US and China are mobilising forces in response to the situation. Airlines are cancelling all long-haul flights while the impact of the smoke cloud is assessed. We will continue to keep you updated as —"

"Someone's fixing to start a war," said Matt with a disbelieving smile.

"It's the fifth trumpet," said Joan, shaking her head. "Have we already had the fourth?"

"Trumpet?"

"Trumpet," said Joan. "You know, from the Book of Revelation."

"What?" said Matt. "Let's pretend that I don't know. What do you mean?"

"Signs of the end of days. The fourth trumpet is a darkness, blotting out the sun and the moon. I suppose that's the smoke."

"I heard a voice speaking about that." said Matt.

"Where? Where?" demanded Joan.

"It was coming from inside your wolf."

"Inside?"

Matt shrugged.

"The world makes little sense to me these days," he said, with an almost insane giddiness. "Why not have voices speak from inside a wolf's innards? And the fifth trumpet? What's that? The internet crashing? Strictly Come Dancing being cancelled? A worldwide shortage of tea? I know some people who would think the world was coming to an end if those happened."

Joan ignored him.

"'And the fifth angel sounded a trumpet and I saw a star fall from Heaven to the earth and to him was given the key to the bottomless pit,'" quoted Joan. "Don't you see how it's happening?"

Matt slapped the steering wheel and chuckled loudly.

"I just realised how much you remind me of – what's his name - Samuel L Jackson in Pulp Fiction," he said. "You know, 'I will strike you down with great wrath and something-something vengeance.' You're priceless."

"Really? You think this is funny?" The heat of anger burned her cheeks. "Well you won't be laughing when you see the effects of the fifth trumpet, and take it from me, it's just around the corner."

"Go on, what am I to expect?" he asked.

"The fifth trumpet is the first of the woes," Joan said, "and it's not the sort of woe that means something a little bit sad, this is the sort of woe that means that Heaven is seeing the whole of mankind teetering on the edge of the abyss. It talks about a star falling from Heaven, who's given the key to the bottomless pit. There's more about smoke that rises out, darkens the air and blocks the sunlight - sound familiar? Then from out of the smoke, the locusts are unleashed."

"So we're talking about a plague of insects?" asked Matt.

"No," said Joan. "'And the shape of the locusts was like horses prepared for battle. They had breastplates like breastplates of iron and the sound of their wings was like the thundering of many horses and chariots rushing into battle. They had tails with stingers, like scorpions, and in their tails they had the power to torment people...'"

"That doesn't sound like anything on earth," said Matt.

"Really?" said Joan.

CHRISTOPHER WAS PLEASED with their progress in the balloon. They were at the correct altitude and the wind was constant. If he kept it up, they'd be in Toulon in a couple of hours.

A sudden violent noise from behind them made him twist around to look. A squadron of fighter jets shot overhead, terrifyingly close.

"Gwacious me!" exclaimed Francis. "Those are aeroplanes?"

"Fighter jets," said Christopher. "Dassault Rafales equipped with laser guided bombs."

"Locusts," whispered Em.

"I've seen locusts," offered Francis. "Cweatures with a fearsome appetite, it's twue but —"

"No, the locusts from Revelation," insisted Em. "The curved tails like a scorpion. The iron breastplates. The thunder of their wings. Their power to destroy. I can't believe I'm saying this, but Joan's right."

"Really?" said Christopher. "Would you like to explain exactly what you and Joan were discussing?"

Em sighed.

"It's all tied in with something I did," she said. "Simon isn't a person."

"What?" said Francis.

"It's a military computer..."

"IT'S time I told you everything," said Joan.

"Okay."

"Now you're going to have trouble believing some of it," said Joan. "I don't know what to do about that, to be honest."

"Joan, I've had that problem since we met. Just tell me everything and we'll take it from there."

The road was straight and fairly empty. Joan gazed into the distance and wondered how she could possibly make Matt believe her.

"Right. Well first of all, I really am Joan of Arc."

"Joan of Arc. Right. That explains the get up. But Joan of Arc is dead."

"I died in 1431 when they burnt me at the stake."

"You died."

"It wasn't nice."

"I shouldn't think it was."

"Not nice at all. I still can't even look at overdone steak."

"So, you died in 1431, and yet here you are."

"Yes, here I am. Now, you need to know that Heaven is real. That's where I've been for most of the time since then."

"Heaven? Clouds and harps and stuff?"

"Actually, there's very little of that in the Celestial City. It's a beautiful place. Beautiful buildings. Clean streets. And everyone's so very, very friendly."

"So, like Disneyland then. The original, obviously. Not the French one."

"Not like Disneyland," she said sternly. "Not much. Anyway, Heaven's super-efficient. They know every soul on earth and where they are, always. There was a call that came into the unit recently where they *knew* there wasn't a soul."

"Unit?"

"Non-Specific Prayer Assessment Unit. Heaven has a lot of duties. Lots of prayers to answer. There's a thing we call the Non-Specific Prayer Assessment Unit where they take a lot of them."

A smile played around Matt's lips, but Joan pressed on.

"A prayer with no soul attached is quite unusual," said Joan. "No, not just unusual, it's unheard of."

"Uh-huh?"

"So they decided to send a team down to earth to investigate."

"That would be you," said Matt.

"Me, Francis and Christopher. Saints, all of us."

"You forgot the wolf," said Matt. "I suppose he's a saint as well."

"No, that's the Wolf of Gubbio. He belongs to Francis. Sort of. He wasn't supposed to come."

"Why haven't I seen Christopher?" asked Matt.

"Ah, yes. He's invisible. Something to do with him not really existing. He's there, but humans can't see him."

"So. You, Joan of Arc came to earth with the invisible man and Saint Francis of Assisi."

"Our quest was to find the Virgin Mary, as the prayer was directed at her. The woman who calls herself Em turned out to be the Virgin Mary, so we found her all right but she's not mad keen on helping us. I thought that might change when she realised what she'd done, but she's got her own agenda."

"So, Em is the Virgin Mary. That would be Mary van Jochem, international terrorist, anarchist, whatever you want to call her. Associates with the lowest of the criminal underbelly, leaves a trail of devastation and, by all accounts is a rather caustic character as well."

"Of course, you met her. She's been here a long while, and I think it's made her a bit cynical. Her heart's in the right place though."

Matt thumped the steering wheel, his brow furrowed.

"Her heart's in the right place? Shall I just phone my superiors in London and say to them that I won't be apprehending Mary van Jochem, in spite of the hacking and terrorism charges, because her *heart's in the right place*? Oh, and by the way, she's the Virgin Mary?"

"You're getting a bit ranty, Matt," said Joan. "Anyway, the hacking's quite relevant to this story. She does it to undermine things that she doesn't approve of, which is pretty much everything, actually. The problem we've got is that she hacked a military computer called Simon."

"*Système Intelligent Militaire et Opérations Nucléaires*, you mean," said Matt.

"That's the one. Anyway, she replaced his manual with the Book of Revelation," said Joan.

"She did what?"

"So Simon's making the things from Revelation happen?" said Christopher.

"Yes," said Em.

"But... but, some weally howwible things happen in the book of Wevelation!" squeaked Francis.

"Oh, Really? Hadn't realised." Em rolled her eyes.

"I heard the fourth trumpet," said Christopher. "It came from inside the wolf."

"The locusts are from the fifth trumpet," said Em.

"Whatever's happening is gathering pace, there's only three more trumpets to go. Quite the cock-up you've created here, Em."

"Zip it, travel boy. At least I can *do* things here on earth. Fat lot of use an invisible man is."

"Not all of what you do seems vewy constwuctive," observed Francis. "By the way, did you just say that the twumpet came fwom inside the wolf?"

"He must have swallowed something," said Christopher, "and as for doing things, I'll have you know I *do* plenty!"

Francis rubbed the wolf's flank with a concerned look.

"Poor boy got a tummy ache?"

The wolf continued to stand with his paws up and his great head over the edge of the basket, tongue out and enjoying the view. Christopher thought that he didn't appear to be suffering from a tummy ache at all.

"Can I just point out that I am the only one of us who is doing something right now?" said Christopher. "I am keeping us airborne, maintaining an accurate course, and ensuring that the wind is a constant thirty knots."

"I thought it dropped for a moment there," said Em.

"Well I do need to concentrate, and that news about your runaway mainframe was a mite distracting. So, come on, what's your plan, Em?"

"Oh, I thought I might do something brilliant and constructive. You know, like hi-jack a giant penis or have a little animal church service in the woods."

"Don't you ever tire of sneering at other people?" asked Christopher.

"Worship is always constwuctive," sniffed Francis. "Maybe you should twy it? A little more wespect would become you."

"How dare you! Respect? You're talking about bowing down to the patriarchy, not respect," shouted Em. "I said goodbye to that centuries ago and I'm not picking it up again now."

The wolf emitted a low growl and the basket rocked severely as it was buffeted by side winds.

"For crying out loud," muttered the Blessed Virgin. "Trapped in a basket with a pair of dunderheads and a flatulent mutt."

"I wonder if you really know what respect means?" said Christopher. "It's nothing to do with being male or female. You couldn't even respect Joan, could you?"

"The Tin Woman? Out there on her lonely quest to find a heart." She laughed bitterly. "And we've got Toto here," she said, gesturing at the wolf. "So which one of you is the Scarecrow, which the Cowardly Lion? Fuck me, that makes me Dorothy."

"You know," said Christopher, "the difference between you and her is that she's out there learning, while you're here bitching about it."

"Should we be wowwied that we can't see where we're going?" said Francis.

Christopher tore his gaze away from Em and frowned at the surrounding fog. It was his temper of course. The swirling winds must have knocked them right off course.

He'd have to correct for that, once he'd got them stable again.

"Gah! Made a right pig's ear of this. Now. Where are — oh!"

The basket slammed into something, tipping precariously. The wolf disappeared over the side. Francis let out a shriek of horror, and rushed to look over, but the basket tilted again, knocking him back. As the saints struggled to keep their feet, the bottom of the basket erupted beneath them. A stone spike appeared, and rose up as they scrambled back. As the basket slid down, the spike continued to rise until it knocked the gas burner.

"Uh oh," said Christopher, seeing what was about to happen. The burner was pushed up until the flames started to devour the fabric of the penis balloon. The fire caught and flared up above their heads.

"I think we need to abandon ship. Whatever this is, we need to try and climb down it before we become chicken in a basket."

"Trust you to find a food reference at a time like this," said Em, climbing over the side.

"I'm weally wowwied about the wolf," said Francis. "He fell right out."

"We need to be able to see what we're doing." Christopher clawed onto the outside edge of the basket. "I can't even see what we're stuck on."

He twitched his nose and the fog cleared in an instant.

"Oh," he said, his feet on the only solid thing in sight. "Look where we are! Those buggers up in Heaven will be laughing themselves silly at this one."

"So, what's in Marseille?" asked Matt.

"A bar. The Couteau Noir. It's a place Michel mentioned. And then it's on to Toulon."

"Toulon?" Matt looked at her askance. "Home to the French fleet and the largest naval base on the entire Mediterranean."

"Is it?" said Joan. "Then that's obviously where we're going. Simon will be on that base with all the warships."

Matt laughed.

"And I suppose we're going to go in there, access the mainframe and teach it how to play tic-tac-toe?"

"Yes, we need to somehow get inside and — wait, you're mocking me!"

"Not at all. There are people, Joan. Experts. They can help you sort this out."

"Good! That's what I want. I need to get to the top people and make them believe me. Do you think your contacts can get us inside the naval base?"

"I had a different kind of help in mind, Joan."

Joan grabbed her sword and angled it up at Matt again.

"You're saying you think I'm crazy, aren't you?"

"No one's using the word 'crazy,'" said Matt. "Mentally divergent perhaps." He tried to push the end of the sword away with his hand. "Can you point that thing somewhere else? It's really sharp!"

Joan wasn't listening.

"I thought you might have the vision to see that what I'm telling you is real," she said, "but you think I'm just some poor delusional girl. I really thought you were different. I thought you were starting to understand me."

THE WOLF SLITHERED down the tile roof of the church after falling from the balloon, and landed inelegantly on a pile of grass cuttings at the back. He jumped down and trotted off to explore the town. His ears pricked up as he detected a lot of activity somewhere nearby.

There was a smell in the air. Something unusual.

Sausages too.

He decided to check out the sausage smell, so he changed direction and bounded in through the door of a small butcher's shop. A man in a red apron tried to shoo him away but then backed up when his gaze met the wolf's. The wolf slotted his great head beneath the glass counter and gently teased the sausages out. He left the shop with links hanging down on either side of his mouth. He would take them back to the quiet of the graveyard to devour them in peace.

He almost missed it, the scent of sausages was so strong in his nostrils. That unusual smell again. He turned and entered an alley.

FRANCIS REALISED that his robes were not ideally suited to climbing down a church spire.

"I'm finding this vewy difficult," he called. "How are you managing, Cwistopher?"

"Hitched my robe right up. Bit draughty, but at least I can put my feet where I want.

"You're not embawassed?"

"I'm invisible, aren't I! No need to be bothered if nobody can see you."

"I can see you," said Em, "but frankly I wouldn't bother looking. There's gargoyles here with more charisma."

"Some of the animal carvings are most attwactive," noted Francis.

He glanced over to see why Em had gone quiet for a moment and saw that she had come across a statue of herself.

She saw him looking and glanced across.

"Not much of a resemblance, is there?" she said. She pulled a cigarette from her pocket. It was bright blue from the toilet chemicals. She pushed it between the lips of the statue and gave it an appraising look.

"Better," she said and continued her climb down.

They discovered that there were drainpipes on the last third of the descent, which helped a lot.

"We need to check out where we are," said Em.

"Aubenas," said Christopher automatically. "In the Rhone valley."

There were a couple of shops across the square from the church. They seemed unusually busy. The bakery had a queue backing up out of the door, and there was some agitated shouting from the front of the queue.

"What do you mean I can only have two loaves? Madame Pichard bought four!"

"We're saying two per person now. Two only."

The saints walked across the square, past the cluster of old men playing petanque in the sand and entered the tiny grocery store. It was a store that looked as though it normally got a couple of customers at a time. There were at least thirty people trying to jostle around the goods, all filling their baskets with unlikely piles. A woman scanned the nearly-empty shelf before her and scooped the five remaining packets of biscuits into her basket. The people behind her shot jealous glares at her haul.

"What's happened?" Em asked a woman.

"Could you move please, I want to get to the pharmacy before they close."

"I was just asking."

"Didn't you hear the news? Problems in the Middle East."

"World War Three!" declared another woman shrilly.

"Surely you don't think that a war can happen that quickly?" asked Em.

"I don't know," said the woman, "but there will be no food left soon, I need to stock up for my family. Please move."

A man was pressing from behind, so Em moved out of the way.

"What happened in the Middle East?" she asked.

"Nobody knows, but the whole place is burning," he said. "All the major powers are moving their forces there. You have family? Get them somewhere safe and stock up on food, that's my advice."

"Pablo, it's in God's hands now," called a man from the road.

"God's hands?" scoffed Em. "Yes, if you put it that way, I'm sure the missiles will start flying at any moment."

"THIS IS NOT A NICE AREA," Matt pointed out as he wove through the narrow streets near to the old dock of Marseille. "Sure you don't want to find somewhere else?"

"The Couteau Noir is where I'm going," insisted Joan.

"Dressed in full plate armour? Okay."

"I know you don't believe my story, but that doesn't change anything. I have a mission to complete."

Matt sighed. Joan was so tied up with her delusion that he knew she would do whatever she felt was necessary. If he'd learned one thing about her, it was that she was bone-headedly stubborn and persistent.

Joan opened the glove box with her free hand and rummaged through the contents.

"Here it is. Bar Couteau Noir," said Matt, looking at the dark café front within a rundown arcade of shops and businesses. "What are you doing there?"

"Recruiting," said Joan. "Park here."

Matt parked the car between two rows of mopeds and turned to Joan. Could he possibly talk her out of her plans, maybe convince her to take a few minutes to calm down and reconsider? What was the quote from the Ferris Bueller movie?

"Hey Joan, Life moves pretty fast. If you don't stop —"

"Keys!" she barked. Matt pulled the keys from the ignition and handed them to her. Joan produced a plastic cable tie that Matt recognised. He gave a low groan.

"Really? You plan to handcuff me?"

"Yup," said Joan and waggled the end of the sword in his face to emphasise the point.

He held out his hands and she fastened them together.

"Out of the car, we need to put you in the boot."

"Joan, this is a Fiat 500. I won't fit in the boot," he said.

"You'd better figure out a way, otherwise I'll chop you up into pieces to make it easier. I'm in a hurry, remember."

"You wouldn't hurt me." Matt got out and walked around to the rear of the car anyway.

Matt looked up and down the street, hoping to see someone, anyone who would act as a witness or potential rescuer. There was no one, only the sound of gulls and the faintly foul smell of the docks. Joan popped open the tiny boot. She looked inside and looked Matt up and down.

"You'll get in there, if you really, really try hard."

"Joan, please."

"I'd start trying if I were you."

THE WOLF FOLLOWED the scent into a small enclosed yard, where firewood was stored. There was a small group of dogs in a rough circle. They were communicating in the usual manner of pheromone signatures and small yips. An elderly spaniel had the floor.

We need to discuss the difficult times we may face. We must share what we know and be vigilant in our guard duties, both for the humans and each other. The humans are very afraid. You can smell it on them. They fear a coming cataclysm.

What's a cataclysm? asked a young beagle.

It's like when there's nobody there to throw the stick.

The dogs all lowered their heads.

We must comfort the humans and remain alert to the possibility that they will need our help.

At that moment a small terrier noticed the wolf. A powerful blast of fear alerted the other dogs immediately and they all turned their heads towards the enormous intruder.

The wolf stepped forward, prompting a fresh wave of fear, and some high notes of bravado, he noted. He wasn't one for idle chat, but he approved of this group and their spirit. He dropped the sausages in the centre of the circle and sat back on his haunches.

Tuck in. You're going to be busy.

JOAN PUSHED OPEN the door of the bar. It was rather gloomy inside, and the current of air stirred up specks of dust that danced in the sunlight that streamed in behind her. She was surprised to find how familiar the place seemed. She'd stepped inside similar places during her earthly lifetime. Rough bars were rough bars and the general template hadn't changed much over the last six hundred years. And, judging by the thick grime in the corners of the room, this particular example hadn't been cleaned in those six hundred years either.

The few patrons barely looked up, so she decided to address them all. Time was short and she wasn't sure how else to find what she was looking for.

"I'm looking for some men. Real men who know how to handle themselves. I was told that this was the place."

A few heads turned her way, eyebrows raised.

"One thing though, you must be happy to work under a woman."

There was an outbreak of sniggers. A man stood from a table near the bar and swaggered towards her. He wore rough canvas trousers and a knitted garment that had either been a sweater or a lobster pot in a previous existence.

"Darlin', I got no problem working under you. Is that real armour you're wearing? You look like you'd shine up all right. Can I start now?" he said, thrusting suggestively and putting his hand on her arm.

Joan didn't bother to raise her sword, she simply gripped the wrist of the hand that was on her arm and yanked it round behind the man's back, jerking it up savagely. The man howled in pain and she let him drop to the floor.

"Anybody else want to treat me like a fool?" she said to the patrons of the bar, and the world in general.

From two separate tables, men got up without making eye contact and scurried for the door.

"Hey!" shouted the bartender. "You're scaring away my customers. Calm down or get out."

"Sorry," said Joan. "Let me get a drink and see which of these fine gentlemen can help me."

She went over to the bar. The bartender looked at her questioningly.

"Uh, beer please," said Joan.

"Beer," nodded the bartender.

"But not a strong one," said Joan quickly. "I want the

weak pisswater beer that people drank in the old days instead of water."

"Ah, you came to the right place then." The bartender slid a glass across the counter.

MATT WAS STRUGGLING with the cable ties. He'd tried the trick of angling his wrists apart when Joan tied him up, but she'd pulled them pretty tight, so he had very little room for manoeuvre. He had a secret weapon though. The rough bit they'd left on his boots when he got them re-soled. He'd caught his finger on it a few weeks ago, and had sworn that when he got a moment he'd file it down *and* that he'd go and give the cobbler a piece of his mind as well. Now, strangely grateful for his lack of follow-through, he worked his wrists across it to try and wear through the plastic. He had so little room, tucked into the boot of his tiny car, but he was able to inch it back and forth, and he knew he could free his hands eventually. Whether that was soon enough to keep Joan from doing something ludicrous was another matter.

"YOU!" said Joan, approaching the roughest looking customer in the bar. "You look like a man who's seen hostile action."

The man raised his shaven head, a lavish scar across his eyebrow giving him a look of intense menace. He wore camouflage trousers with a faded t-shirt.

Joan sat at his table, facing him.

"I need to get into the naval base at Toulon," she said. "Can you help me?"

"Toulon," said the man, his voice gravelly. "That's a well guarded place. Choose somewhere else. Save yourself some trouble."

"I have a target," said Joan. "His name is Simon, and it's imperative that I get to him. Can you help me or not?"

The man pursed his lips and nodded. Joan glimpsed more scars on his neck as he did so.

"I am Bruno," he said, extending a hand.

"Joan," she said, shaking a hand that was rough and enormous.

"So, Joan. What did this man Simon do to you, hmm? You want to get to him pretty badly."

"Oh, it's not really about me —"

"I bet he broke your heart, yes?" said Bruno. "I once had my heart broken. I know how it feels."

Bruno still had hold of Joan's hand. He patted it gently and gazed into the middle distance in recollection.

"She owned a flower shop in the Rue de Fraises. She would know a person's favourite flower the instant they walked in there. She had me down as an orchid man straight off. She had a talent for it, you know?"

"Well —"

"I don't ask for a lot in a relationship," Bruno continued. "I bring in a lot of money in this trade, you know? A suitcase full at a time. All I ask of a woman is that she brings me a cold beer when I want one. Now that might be in a top Paris hotel, but it might also be in downtown Bogota, know what I'm saying?"

"No, not really," but Bruno was in full flow.

"She could have had anything she wanted if she'd just understood that. Clothes, jewels, a pony."

"A pony?"

"But no, she was all like *I've got a business to run Bruno, I need to stay here.* It gets to you, you know? Really gets to you. I want her to be a proper part of my life, share my passion. So I'm running my ass off, just trying to keep it together. I spend my nights wondering if her heart's really in the relationship when she can think about all these other things so easily. She would always be thinking about other people. That's just not right, is it? I mean, if you were with me, and you could have anything you wanted, would you want to bother with arranging flowers for your customers? Would you?"

Joan tried to form an answer to that but she found that words wouldn't come.

"I understand you being lost for words," said Bruno. "I was too. Any time I got a moment between assignments I'd call her up, just to hear her voicemail. I almost blew my cover in Cuba when they traced my calls back to Europe. I was lucky to get away. Anyway, the final blow came when I'd just finished up a job in Africa. I'd been sent in to kill the Burundi finance minister, but my gun jammed at the crucial moment. I beat him to death with an office stapler and managed to crawl through a sewer pipe to freedom. Do you know what happened next?"

"No," answered Joan truthfully.

"She told me that she was going to move in with her

sister," sobbed Bruno. "Her sister! The shame of it. You know the worst thing? The very worst thing?"

"No. Tell me," said Joan, chin in hand, resigned to listen to the rest of Bruno's sad tale.

"Her sister had hay fever. Hated flowers. Hated them."

Bruno collapsed onto his forearms and sobbed uncontrollably.

THE INTERIOR of the church of Saint-Laurent in Aubenas was cool, but instead of the usual candle-fragranced calmness, there was an air of subdued panic. Twenty or so people were kneeling or standing, their faces filled with worry.

Em's attention was, as always, first drawn to the images of her son on the walls, in the stained glass. She never felt any urge to take photos of deliberate representations of the boy. It wasn't just that thingsthatlooklikejesus.com didn't accept such offerings. It wasn't that these representations were any less accurate than the clouds, spills and burn patterns that she stored on her camera. She had no interest in these because they were public, they belonged to everyone; her stolen digital images were hers, ones that she had found...

"Pew at the back's fwee," said Francis and sat down.

"Sod that," said Christopher. He marched up the aisle, stepping past worshippers oblivious to his presence and rapped violently on the stone altar. "Oi! Gabriel! Can you hear me? I wish to speak directly to the archangel Gabriel. If I've got someone at the Non Specific Prayer Assessment Unit, just patch me through. Ask a supervisor if you don't know how. Right. Gabriel, we need a steer. Joan's gone off on one, so we need to know who's in charge now. I think we can probably agree I'm the man for the job. Just tell the others to do what I say. Amen."

Em looked at him in disbelief, but then her attention was drawn to Francis who was muttering his own prayer in the pew beside her.

"Chwistopher's being unbeawable and I do find Em to be a little aggwessive. What you weally need, in my opinion, is for a man of twue faith to take charge of this mission, bwing it back on twack. If you could westore the wolf to my company I shall know you support my plea. Amen."

"Right," huffed Em, sitting down and squeezing her own eyes shut. "Enough of this. Now listen, Lord. We don't speak all that often. You gave me the kid and then it's 'wham, bam, thank you, ma'am.' You don't phone. You don't write. Anyway, you know my thoughts on the way you run things. I have something I need you to do right now though, so you'd better be listening. I need you to get these idiots off my back and give me a little support down here. There's a bit of a situation going on, and I could deal with it a whole lot better if I had a decent team. Sort it out, will you?"

She glanced across at Francis.

Francis made an exaggerated mime, while gesturing upwards with his eyes.

"Oh, yeah. Amen," she said.

Em despaired at the other saints. Their selfish mutterings were really quite distracting. Then she realised that the voices that she could hear were coming from the congregation in the church. Silent prayers being sent up from the people all around her were appearing in her head. A woman wearing a brown dress faced the altar and prayed hard.

— *Mother Mary. I worry for my children. What can I do to keep them safe?*

Em sighed. She couldn't ignore this. She reached out with her own spiritual voice.

— *Your children have a loving mother who cares about them,* she told the woman.

— *But the world is in turmoil. I'm so worried about the future.*

— *Face the future with strength, knowing that, er –* Mary swallowed her pride — *Heaven's love surrounds you and your children.*

Em felt the balm of calmness that her words applied to the woman. The woman crossed herself and hurried out.

"Okay," she said to herself. "Nice work, Mary."

She sought out another of the voices.

— *The world feels so hostile. I am so powerless.*

— *You are not powerless,* said Em. — *People are reacting to fear. If they knew the strength of Heaven's love they would not be afraid. You should not be afraid.*

Em adjusted herself on the kneeler and concentrated on the other voices.

MATT HAD FREED HIS HANDS, but was still cramped into the boot of his car. He had tried battering his head against the upholstery of the back seat, but it simply bounced his efforts away. He imagined for a moment he had the wolf with him. The wolf would make short work of this, he'd simply rip it apart with his teeth. He took a tentative mouthful of foam and tore at it with his teeth. Particles came away in his mouth, making him gag, but it represented some progress at least. He spat the bits out and took another bite.

~

"My name is Leon," a man said to Joan. "Your friend is gone?"

Joan looked around the bar for Bruno.

"I think he's gone outside for a bit of a cry."

Leon nodded.

"Then it is possible that I can help you with your... problem?"

Leon wore a sleeveless vest and she could see intertwining tattoo designs on his face, neck and down his back. She had never seen someone marked like this before.

"Please," said Joan and gestured for him to sit down.

"Thank you," said Leon. "You should know that I am a business man. I can almost certainly get what you need, but the price, it will be high."

"Not a problem," said Joan, knowing she had no real choice. "Tell me one thing though."

"Yes?"

"Is that a tattoo of an otter or a dolphin? The one on your shoulder."

"Is mermaid. Now. Let us talk business. My associates will be here shortly. I have business to conclude with them.

Afterwards I can attend to your requirements. So, what do you need?"

"First thing I need is men," said Joan. "Five thousand if I'm to storm Toulon."

"Five thousand men? Five thousand may take some time. You need them all at same time?"

"Yes, of course. In terms of hardware, I prefer old-school. A battering ram is a must."

"Ah. Chinese anti-tank missiles, you mean? Not a problem."

"Lances or pikes for all the men, obviously."

"I can get you a good price on Kalashnikovs," said Leon.

"Those will do. As many trebuchet as you can get hold of, too."

Leon hesitated.

"Tre – what? Is Russian? Can't say I am familiar with that name. Can you tell me what that is?"

"Basic stuff," said Joan, grabbing a napkin from the bar. "Let me draw you a picture. I bet you know it by another name. Look, you have an arm to throw rocks at the enemy and you propel it really fast with a counterbalance on the other side here, see?"

Leon scrutinised the sketch and shook his head.

"This is very primitive. There is little to recommend such a thing unless you need to assemble something in a hurry from local materials."

"Well I do!" exclaimed Joan. "Didn't I mention that this is really urgent? By the way, that cabbage on your arm is very realistic."

"Is rose, not cabbage," said Leon. "Ah, my associates are

here. If you will excuse me for few minutes I will come back and see what I can do to help you when I am finished."

He rose and met two newcomers halfway across the bar. These two were dressed in suits and wore dark glasses. They both carried strong looking metal briefcases. They spoke briefly to Leon in low voices and then all three of them went through a door to the toilets. Joan fetched another drink from the bar and waited impatiently.

She hoped that Leon was really able to help her out. He'd pulled a face at some of the things she'd asked for but she needed to work with what she knew. She drummed her fingers on the table and reminded herself that she'd need to ask Leon to get some buses to transport her men. Presumably it was possible to mount a siege engine onto the top of a bus? It was such an obvious development. She worked on her sketch to demonstrate what she had in mind.

Absorbed in her work, she barely looked up when the two business men came out from the toilets. There was no sign of Leon. The men spoke to each other as they cleaned something off their hands. They dropped paper towels on the floor, covered with dark smears.

"Hey, don't drop those there!" she called.

They looked up at her in surprise.

"What?" one of them said.

"It's called dropping litter. My friend Evelyn told me that if you tolerate dropping litter then all sorts of other crime will follow."

"Your friend might have a point," he said with a smirk. He was tall and gaunt. He folded a small raggy piece of pink cloth and put it into his pocket, but just before he tucked it away Joan caught a glimpse of a design on the cloth, a rose that somewhat resembled a cabbage.

"Oh," she said.

The two strangers left the bar and Joan jogged out after them. The clank of her jiggling armour made them pause in climbing into their Mercedes.

"Hey, I need to talk to you."

"No, I don't think you do," said the taller one. "Pick the litter up yourself if you're that bothered by it."

She approached the taller one.

"What do I call you?" she asked.

"You don't call us anything. We're going and you're making us late for our next job."

"I'll call you Lanky," Joan said, and then turning to the other man who was short and stout, "and you can be Chunky."

"Just go away," said Lanky as they opened the doors of the Mercedes.

"Hang on," said the slightly shorter one. "Why am I called Chunky?"

Joan opened her mouth to explain but Lanky was there first.

"She's saying you're chunky, fat-boy," said Lanky. "I'm the tall, fit one. You're my chunky sidekick."

"Chunky?" said Chunky. "And – what? – I'm your sidekick? Since when?"

Lanky shrugged.

"And I'll have you know that my BMI puts me inside the normal weight range," said Chunky.

"Sure," said Lanky. "Normal weight for a chunky sidekick."

"Please listen," said Joan, talking fast as she realised that she'd have to speed things up. "I need weapons and men."

"You said I was your wingman," said Chunky.

"Wingman. Sidekick. Big difference," said Lanky.

"There *is* a big difference," said Chunky.

"Look," said Joan, "I've got to storm a naval base and I obviously can't do it on my own. Do you know where to get those things?"

The two men exchanged a glance. It was not a pleasant glance.

Chunky leaned over towards Joan. She wondered why he wore a tight collar and tie when it seemed to make his face flush so red. She had a sudden flashback to a priest at her trial who fastened a clasp at his throat so tightly that it did the same thing. She saw the same unbending arrogance in Chunky's eyes.

"Look, I don't know if you're mad or stupid, or if this is some sort of practical joke, but you're embarrassing us all now."

"Clear off," said Lanky. "As my wingman says, you're embarrassing us all."

Joan stood her ground, hands on hips.

"I know you can help me," she said.

"We taking care of her or what?" growled Chunky. "She's annoyed me."

"Not here in the street," said Lanky, glancing around. "Too many people. We need to get out of here."

He addressed Joan.

"I can see that we're going to have to make our point more clearly, as you're the hard of hearing type. We'll be doing that later on, when we can have some privacy. It might mean that we have to speak plainly. My friend here prefers action to words, as it happens. Now, if you're absolutely certain that you don't just want to *go away,* get in the car."

Joan climbed into the car. This pair of unpleasant thugs could be exactly what she needed, if she could persuade them to care about her mission.

MATT SPAT out the last of the upholstery foam and wriggled through the hole that he'd chewed. He plopped out onto the back seat of his car, coughing to try and clear his mouth and nose of the choking dust that he'd created. His first priority was to get a drink of water from the bar while he tracked down Joan.

He sat up and tried to focus as he blinked the residue from his eyes. He saw a large car parked directly in front of his Fiat, and watched in dismay as Joan climbed inside with two evil-looking suits. He wasn't familiar with Marseille, but he was willing to bet that the people who wore suits in the area around the docks were unlikely to be bankers and lawyers.

He crawled over to the front seat of his car, started the engine and grabbed his radio as the Mercedes pulled away.

CHUNKY DROVE them through the narrow streets of the docks. One side of the street was lined with warehouses, the other with wharves, where giant barges were piled high with containers.

"Where are we going?" she asked.

"A warehouse location with stunning sea views," said Lanky. "I'm sure you'll enjoy it. We do some of our finest work there."

"So is this to do with your next job, or the place where we can have a talk?" she asked. "Because I am in a hurry. Did I mention that?"

"Oh, I think we can manage both," said Lanky with a sideways smirk at Chunky. "We do like to multi-task."

Chunky nodded at the rear view mirror.

"We're being followed," he said.

Joan swivelled round to look out of the back.

"Oh, it's Matt!" she said, recognising the Fiat that looked like a small puppy bouncing after the enormous Mercedes.

"Who's Matt?" said Lanky.

"A policeman I know. He's probably not very pleased with me, since I kidnapped him. Not at all sure how he got out of his boot. Oh look."

Matt flashed his lights. Joan gave him a cheery wave.

"I think he might try to stop me from attacking the naval base," said Joan, turning back to the front. "I must think of a way to get rid of him. Oh, but not that!"

Lanky was leaning out of the passenger window aiming a gun at Matt's car.

"We don't need to kill anyone!" yelled Joan, leaning over to grab him as he fired a series of shots.

She turned to look at Matt, frantic now that she had dragged him into such a perilous situation. One of his car tyres went suddenly flat. His car skidded wildly on the road. She saw that one tyre was much lower than the other side. The tiny Fiat careened off the roadway, smashed through a metal barrier and tipped over the dockside and out of sight.

"Matt!"

A cloud of seagulls erupt from the point of his disappearance.

"We have to go back!" shouted Joan. "He might be drowning."

The two men glanced at each other and shook their heads in disbelief. This wasn't lost on Joan.

"Hey, I'm talking to you! Stop the car!"

"That's a great idea," said Chunky. "Let's sort her out now. I'm sick of her yap."

He began to pull over to the side of the road.

"Wait," said Lanky, peering up at the sky. "Is that...?"

"Police helicopter!" spat Chunky, put the car back into gear and accelerated off. "What the hell have you done, bitch?"

Joan looked up at the sky with interest. Matt must have alerted someone before he crashed his car. The helicopter was definitely tracking their progress. She heard a siren from behind. A police car was speeding towards them, gaining fast.

"We should probably stop and explain that we haven't done anything wrong," she said.

"Not with a body in the boot for disposal you stupid

bitch," said Chunky. "Right, I reckon I can lose this one behind." He stamped on the accelerator.

"Hey, who are you calling a stupid — whoa!"

Joan was flung across the back seat as the car swerved violently to the left into the open bay of a warehouse. The police car that was chasing them overshot and barrelled into a row of parked bikes. Chunky drove through the warehouse and came out of another exit.

"You beasts!" yelled Joan. "Such violence!"

"You wanted to buy men and weapons!" Lanky yelled back at her. "Get some perspective!"

Joan unsheathed her sword but was tossed across the back seat again as Chunky changed direction and entered another warehouse bay, scattering workers who were moving pallets with pump trucks.

EM HAD ANSWERED several prayers and was pleased that she'd been able to provide some comfort to the people in the church. She paused for a moment to listen for the next voice.

— *My daughter doesn't even realise there is a worldwide crisis. All she cares about is having the latest game on her console. I despair that the young people are so shallow they will not survive any serious problems.*

Em was about to respond when a familiar voice cut in.

— *Think back to your own youth. You had different distractions, but you were young, just the same. Your daughter absorbs your values and your wisdom. In time you will see that she can use them to good effect. Let her enjoy her games. Continue to guide her.*

Em glanced sideways at Christopher and smiled at him. He smiled back and switched to another voice. Em realised that Francis was also answering prayers.

— *I'm all alone. I'm afraid.*

— *You're not alone. All of Heaven is with you.*

— *The house is so empty since my son left.*

— *You have a cat. Go home and stwoke him while you send love to your son.*

Em saw the woman smile and get up. She knew that people would hear the answers to their prayers as an inner dialogue, as if they themselves had thought of the answers, but she was surprised that Francis's peculiar speech didn't faze people at all. Francis opened his eyes and she gave him a small nod.

Francis nodded back and then squeezed his eyes shut again. This time he spoke aloud, offering up his own prayer.

"Blessed fwiends in Heaven, please help Joan. We don't know where she is, but we want her to be safe."

Christopher joined in.

"Joan's the very best of us. Give us a way to help her."

Em knew that this was right, so she spoke up too.

"We offer Joan our love. Please find a way for us to be reunited with her. She should not be alone on this mission."

She turned to Christopher.

"Can we do something? Something practical? I mean, can you figure out where she is with your travel-mojo thing?"

Christopher looked doubtful.

"I'm not sure. It's not like a crystal ball."

"Well what is it like? Can we help?"

Em grasped his hand and indicated that Francis should grasp the other one. She closed her eyes and concentrated.

"Well bugger me," said Christopher, "it's only working! She's in Marseille."

"She's in trouble," breathed Em.

JOAN REALISED that Chunky was making an effort to avoid being seen from the air by staying under cover as much as possible. If he knew his way around the docks, it was possible that it could work. Joan wanted to stop any more harm coming to other people as they tried to escape. There was a very real danger that Chunky was going to run someone over. It wasn't easy to take control when she was being flung across the back seat of the car as Chunky zig-zagged across the warehouse floor, avoiding shelving and fork lift trucks. She righted herself as they plunged towards another open door and yelled at the two men.

"Stop the car! Stop it right now, or you'll feel my sword, so help me!"

"Shut up!" said Chunky and accelerated towards the daylight.

Joan thrust the sword between the seats, grazing his hand and making him snatch it back.

"Ow! What's the matter with you?"

The sword had become lodged in the steering column, and Joan saw, moments later that this might have been a mistake. Chunky tugged at the steering wheel, needing to make a sharp left turn as he came out of the warehouse, but the sword had locked it in place. The car would not turn from its path and Joan saw the open water ahead rushing at them with relentless inevitability.

The car sped over the edge. Joan felt a moment of utter, sickening weightlessness and then the car hit the water, hard. Joan's face bounced painfully off Lanky's seat and, when she opened her eyes, the windscreen was smashed and the car rapidly filled with water.

Lanky had already slipped off his seatbelt and was dragging an unconscious Chunky out into water.

"Wait for me!" Joan called from the back seat but Lanky didn't even look back.

She gasped at the cold water rising up her legs.

"This is not good," she said and struggled forward between the front seats, removing her sword from the steering column as she passed, and squeezed through the ruined windscreen onto the bonnet of the car. The front of the car rose up, tilting dangerously as the rear end sank.

She looked round. She was ten yards from the shore and wearing full plate armour.

"I'm going to sink like a stone," she said to herself and reached for one of the many leather straps holding her armour in place.

"WHAT DO you mean she's in the water with her armour on?" hissed Em. "She'll drown! We have to help her!"

"Shhh, keep your voice down, and keep praying really, really hard. We need to lend a guiding hand. We can do this!"

"What are we pwaying for, Cwistopher?"

"A miracle for Joan. We can do this. Come on!"

JOAN SLIPPED from the bonnet and plunged into the water. She clawed up to the roof of the car, but it was going under fast and taking her with it. The weight of the armour was too much for the grip she had on the roof and she started to slide. A strange buzzing noise came from behind but she wasn't able to see what was making it. She poured every ounce of strength into clinging to the car by sheer will power, but she wasn't going to make it. An arm appeared under her shoulder and hoisted her backwards. There was another quick burst of the buzzing noise and she sped backwards, away from the suction of the sinking car. This was unexpected. There was some sort of tiny platform in her peripheral vision, so she hoisted her foot onto it and heaved herself out of the water.

"Woah, steady!" came a voice. "It's only a jet ski, let's not tip it over."

"Matt! You're not dead!"

She managed to turn herself, as water cascaded from the various joints of her armour, and she shifted her centre of balance. Matt gunned the engine and they shot forward. Joan gave a whoop of delight at the novel mode of transport. As they slowed down by a metal ladder at the dockside, she noticed the pungent smell. He was plastered from head to toe in foul-smelling effluent. He smelled like a dung pile that had been coated with a liberal helping of rotten eggs and topped off with a skunk.

"Did you fall in a midden heap?" she asked.

"Rubbish barge," nodded Matt. "It was a miracle."

"You smell bad."

"What was that? Sorry? Thank you for rescuing me from almost certain death? You're very welcome, Joan."

Joan pulled herself up the metal ladder, labouring to lift her waterlogged limbs.

"What about the men in that car?" she asked.

"I think the police have already got them."

Joan mounted the dockside as more police appeared in cars and vans.

"Does this mean you've decided to help me? Can we go to Toulon now?" Joan asked.

Matt gave her a look. It was part disbelief, part admiration. He pulled out a pair of handcuffs and held them up.

"You're ever the optimist, Joan," he said.

9

MARSEILLE AND TOULON

G iven his recent ordeal, Matt had decided to push his luck with expenses. He'd booked himself into a luxurious hotel with views across Marseille's harbour and a bedroom so large that, unlike every other hotel he'd ever stayed in, it took more than three steps to cross from one side to the other. In fact, he had to walk through the bedroom and into the adjoining sitting room to get to the phone. True luxury.

"Hello, reception? I wonder if you can help me," he said. "I can't seem to find the Bible in this room."

"The Bible, monsieur?"

"Yes, there's normally one in a drawer somewhere. I think the Gideons put them there."

"Ah, you're British, monsieur? I'm afraid that isn't the case here in France."

"Really?" said Matt. "I'm sure it's their mission or

something. The Gideons. A Bible everywhere, even where you least expect it."

"We don't have the same practices in France. We'd have to consider whether our guests might also want to read the Qur'an or the Torah. We cannot favour any one religion over another. It is written in our constitution."

"Gosh. I hadn't realised it was so fraught with difficulties, running a hotel. Policies to implement, political scandals to avoid. Sorry to have bothered you."

"Would you like me to have a Bible sent to your room?" asked the receptionist.

"Yes, I would," said Matt, surprised, and then, "As a matter of interest, if I asked for the Qur'an or the Torah, would you also have those to hand?"

"No monsieur, we do not, although we do have a copy of *The Satanic Verses* that was left by a previous guest."

Matt hung up the phone, having been reminded once again of the gulf in understanding that existed between the British and the French.

He spent the next few minutes attempting to use the fancy coffee machine behind the sitting room bar before realising that half the buttons he was pressing were for the room's air-conditioning. Even when he had overcome this error, he still struggled to get it off the espresso setting. The Bible arrived as he ran the machine for the fifth time to get a decent volume of coffee into his mug.

He paged through, trying to find Revelation as he sipped the potent brew.

"Right at the bloody back," he grumbled, having drained the cup by the time he found it.

He read through several pages of what he thought was rather excitable prose before he reached the trumpets that Joan had mentioned.

He'd watched the news that morning with the sound muted. The progress of the toxic smoke cloud which was now covering parts of Greece and Turkey, the panic across the entire Middle East. He shook his head at the idea that these scenes of impending disaster could really be connected to the bonkers religious text he was reading, but he could see why Joan was drawn to the idea.

"So, the sixth trumpet is next, eh, Joan?" he said and read.

Release the four angels who are bound at the great river Euphrates.

Matt wondered briefly whether he should call down to reception for an atlas as well, but decided he couldn't face the conversation. The Euphrates was somewhere in the Middle East, he was certain of that.

"Wow. And these four angels are to kill a third of mankind?"

Matt looked up from the Bible and saw again the firepower that was being moved into the Middle East from all over the world, and an uneasiness stole over him.

The heads of the horses were like lions' heads, and fire and smoke and sulphur issued from their mouths. — "Trippy stuff," said Matt — *For the power of the horses is in their mouths and in their tails; their tails are like serpents with heads, and by means of them they wound.*

Matt sat back and pondered how wild-eyed conspiracy theorists could conjure up all sorts of ideas about those horses being helicopter gunships, rocket launchers or drones. He wasn't sure that any of them sounded like a barrel of laughs, given that there was going to be a rather specific number of them.

What was it? *Twice ten thousand times ten thousand.* How many was that? He used his fingers to tot up the zeroes. That totalled two hundred million.

There was a knock at the door. Matt really hoped that they hadn't rustled up *The Satanic Verses* for him. He stood and looked through the peephole. A woman in military uniform stood there. He assumed she wasn't a stripper so was probably the real deal.

Matt did a mental check that he was dressed, his flies were done up and he wasn't wearing odd socks before opening the door.

"Yes?"

"Good morning, Officer Rose," the Frenchwoman said in English, walking directly into the room.

"Er, good morning."

"I know you weren't expecting me," she said, "I am Major Adelaide Chevrolet."

Matt did a double-take.

"Major Chevrolet? Well, I certainly never expected to meet you in person. I'd like to thank you for all your help in tracking Mary Van Jochem."

"I'll need you to get your things and come with me," said Major Chevrolet.

"Come with you? Does your department have offices in Marseille?"

"Not far from here."

"I'm not sure I ever got which government agency you

worked for. Just a phone number and voice on the end of the line and all that."

"DPSD," said Major Chevrolet simply.

Matt, who was still standing at the door, with his hand on the handle, raised his eyebrows.

"Direction de la Protection et de la Sécurité de la Défense?" he said.

"Well done," she said. "When you English say it, it usually sounds like such a mouthful."

"Why does military intelligence want to speak to me?" he asked.

She looked at him archly. Whether it was the severe bun her hair was drawn up into or the knowing look in her eye, but Matt felt he was back at school and under scrutiny from the headmistress.

"Sorry, am I not allowed to ask?" he said.

"Come with me and we'll talk."

"You know, the entire time I've been in France I've had very little involvement or interest from local agencies."

"That is about to change," said Major Chevrolet. "You will find that I am very interested in you."

JOAN SAT on her bed and watched the clock, wondering how on earth she was going to fulfil her mission. Everything depended on convincing those in power that the threats she described were real, and so far she'd been completely unsuccessful.

Joan had been put into a hospital room with pale green

walls. The room was comfortable but utterly secure. Joan had tested the exits and found them all to be invulnerable to an attack with a plastic spoon, which was all she was equipped with. Nurses came in at regular intervals and she eyed them with suspicion. They were perky and pleasant, but they were her captors nonetheless. Fighting off the attentions of the guards had been a constant challenge back when she was imprisoned at Rouen. Five hundred and eighty years later and her only complaint beyond the fact of her incarceration was the pink cotton gown that she'd been dressed in. Not only was it pink — which was bad enough — but it covered only the front of her body, leaving her feeling exposed, vulnerable and bloody cold when she rose from the bed.

The door opened without warning and Doctor Silberman walked in. Silberman had been present when Joan was admitted to the hospital, kicking and howling with frustration. She wasn't sure what kind of doctor she was, but Joan did know that she was someone who could administer something to render her powerless so she decided to proceed with caution.

"Good morning Joan. Mmm. Ah. How are you feeling today?"

"My health is fine, if that's what you're asking," said Joan. "Please say that I'm not to be subjected to the poisoned arrow again."

Silberman had a small device that she held in her hand. She pressed a button and raised it to her face.

"Patient is more docile today and she seems coherent. Makes reference to the sedatives used to calm her yesterday, but in archaic phrasing that is consistent with her fantasy."

"Why are you talking to that thing?" said Joan.

"There is an undertone of aggression," Silberman said to the device, then she lowered it.

"Mmm. Ah. This 'thing' — I assume you recognise it as a dictaphone — is simply for me to record my impressions of our conversation, Joan. My assistant will write it up afterwards. Now, there's a lot for us to talk about today. Where shall we start?"

"Where's my armour and my sword?" asked Joan. "Let's start there."

"It's all perfectly safe," said Silberman. "You needn't worry about that."

"Fine, but where is it, exactly? I want to know."

Silberman regarded Joan for a moment and spoke into the dictaphone recorder again.

"Patient is fixated on her weapons and their exact location. Fantasies of escape, perhaps? Of violence?"

Joan scowled at her.

"The English laughed at me back in the day, saying I could never escape from their tower. They even told me at my trial that it would be heresy to try to escape. They were idiots. I am a warrior and my cause is righteous. I won't be held captive."

"You should know that this facility is quite secure," Silberman said to her. "There is no possible way for you to get out of here, so put those silly ideas from your mind. We don't want to go down the tiresome avenue of restraints and sedation, do we? Mmm. Ah. We have tranquilisers that could fell a horse in seconds." In saying this, Silberman's hand strayed towards her top pocket. Realising what she was doing, she smiled brightly at Joan and put her hand on the table. "Your things are in a secure cupboard at the rear of the nurses' station, if you must know. But to today's questions, how about you tell me some more about where you come from? You've told some of my colleagues that you lived in Heaven?"

"I don't want to discuss that," said Joan. "It's not going to help us here. There are much more immediate things that need our attention. Aren't you interested to know about the end of the world?"

"In time. In time. But won't you please tell me some more about where you come from? I can't help thinking that there are people who care about you, Joan. People who are missing you right now."

Joan humphed, picturing her buffoonish companions, the animal nut, the invisible hulk and the most selfish woman in the world. She wondered where they were and wished she really didn't care.

"Where are your family?" said Dr Silberman. "Your fingerprints aren't on record anywhere. Nobody's reported you missing. What do your parents think about all this?"

Joan rolled her eyes.

"You're asking the same things they asked at my trial. You have no imagination as an interrogator. Seriously, this stuff is *old*."

Joan used her hand as a puppet interrogator, and rolled her eyes, looking bored at its unimaginative questions.

"Why did you go off to war without telling your parents?" the

hand asked. "Because God told me to, okay? They forgave me afterwards and anyway, they died centuries ago. You can't use them against me."

Silberman steepled her fingers.

"Mmm. Ah. Let's consider this from another angle. When do you first remember thinking that you were Joan of Arc, reincarnated?"

"I'm not a reincarnation. I'm not Joan born again. I am Joan. I am her. It's real. We're not talking about an idea or a belief, this is my life."

Silberman spoke into her recorder again.

"Very powerful delusional fantasies."

"I've heard all this before you know, from the English," said Joan. "They dismissed my visions as fantasies as well. By the way, would you stop doing that? Talking into your thing as if I'm not here? It's very rude."

"Interesting. You're concerned about the etiquette of the interview we're conducting here, and yet it's a matter of record that you imprisoned a law enforcement officer in a dangerously confined space and you've been linked with a string of disturbances across France. Does violence seem natural to you, Joan?"

"I am a soldier. Does being rude and patronising seem natural to you?"

"Defensive about previous outbursts of violence," noted Silberman. "We may want to medicate for the safety of the staff."

Joan chided herself for indulging in bickering. She couldn't allow them to drug her. That would be a disaster. She'd need to swallow her pride and focus on the mission.

"Look, I'm sorry for being argumentative," said Joan. "I have no plans to harm you or your staff. Not at all. You really shouldn't worry about that."

"If that was really the case," she held out a flimsy plastic dagger, "can you explain why it is that you have secreted a number of plastic spoons in here – Mmm. Ah. — and subsequently modified them into some sort of stabbing weapon?"

Joan pursed her lips and tried hard not to imagine snatching it up and jamming it into Silberman's jugular.

"So, WE'RE AGREED THEN," said Em, lighting up. "We're going to infiltrate the hospital where they're holding Joan and bust her out."

Christopher nodded as he sipped a glass of cold beer. "I know it's urgent, what with the coming apocalypse and all, but can I just say it's nice to sit and have a strategy meeting here in the sunshine. You know, us three, working as one."

"Yeah," said Em. "Cute sentiment, but back to the point..."

"I'm just saying," said Christopher, gesturing down Liberation Boulevard in front of their café table. "It's just nice. To stop and smell the roses, savour the moment."

"He's wight," said Francis. "It's nice."

"Focus, team," said Em tersely.

"Okay, so what stwategy do we need to decide The timings, and the twansport? Next steps? Woles and wesponsibilities?"

Em rolled her eyes and blew out a smoke ring.

"No," said Christopher. "The very first thing that we need to decide is what we're going to call ourselves."

"We don't need a name," said Em. "If we operate below the radar, nobody should even know we exist."

"*We* know we exist," said Christopher. "Come on, this a group thing. We're a collective."

"Puh-lease."

"No, it's a good point," said Francis. "Let's be the Thwee Bears!"

"What?"

"Like in Goldilocks?" said Christopher.

"Yes."

"Hold on, I'm not sure about that," said Em. "Which of us is which? I'm *not* going to be Mama Bear!"

"Well, obviously you are," said Francis. "I don't mind if Cwistopher wants to be Daddy Bear, after all he is the biggest of us. That leaves me as Baby Bear, but that's fine. Bears are so adowable."

"What do you mean, obviously?" said Em, outraged. "Why would I choose to be labelled with the 'M' word? I see no reason at all why I shouldn't be Independently Successful She-Bear."

"Hold your horses," said Christopher. "I think we can work on these names a bit more. I don't need to be Daddy Bear. Something more fitting like Shadow Bear would be better."

"Shadow Bear?" said Em in a mocking voice.

"Yeah, you know, 'cos of the invisibility thing."

"For crying out loud, you might as well be Wonder-Cock Bear," she said wearily.

"Ooh, ooh, I know," said Francis. "Let's be the Holy Twinity!"

"Christ in Heaven!" exclaimed Em. "This flaming God squad is pathetic enough without giving it a stupid name."

"Did anyone else just see that?" asked Christopher, looking across the street.

"What?"

"Dogs, getting off that tram," said Christopher.

"Well this is Fwance, they do love their — oh," said Francis.

Dozens of dogs filed off the tram. There were tiny lap dogs scampering gamely alongside spaniels and retrievers. There was even a colossal, shaggy mountain dog, but towering over them all, and last off the tram, was the Wolf of Gubbio.

"Look at that," exclaimed Francis, clapping his hands with joy. "He's made fwiends."

Christopher and Em exchanged a glance but then they all turned to watch the spectacle of the dogs trotting down the street. They seemed to be full of purpose, as if they had somewhere important to be.

THIS IS THE WAY, the terrier yipped. *Dogs in the city are not allowed to roam freely. When they are caught, they are brought here, and it is thought that a terrible fate awaits them.*

Good, the wolf replied. *We can rescue our brothers and swell our numbers.*

The wolf led them inside, aware now of the intense cloud of despair that hung in the air around the low building they approached. It was a place where many dogs had given up hope.

They entered the reception area, and he heard a human voice react to the intrusion.

"Philippe, it's Helene on reception. Come round here, will you? You'll never believe this but a stray dog's just walked in off the street! Never seen that before. Oh. Hold on Philippe. You might want to call in some help, there's more of them. Oh. Oh my. Philippe! There's —"

There was a brief squeal and the sound of a door slamming.

The wolf followed the other dogs through the empty reception area and into a separate building where excited doggy sounds greeted their arrival.

He stepped forward and examined the cages that confined the dogs. They were designed to stop a dog from breaking out, but they were definitely not resistant to a huge and determined wolf breaking in. Even the mountain dog was able to open up a couple, following the wolf's ruthless example.

The captive dogs rushed out and ran in excited circles, while those dogs of medium rank barked a fast, efficient briefing. Within moments, the dog task force was on the move, doubled in number, under the guidance of the Wolf of Gubbio.

CHEVROLET DROVE at a constant five kilometres an hour above the speed limit, smoothly overtaking cars along the coastal A50 between Marseille and Toulon. Within fifty minutes, they were already near their destination. For whatever reason, the French seemed to have road and traffic management far better sorted than the Brits. Apart from during the mad dash to the coast and the mountains in August, the French had apparently created a road network that was almost entirely traffic-free. It would take an apocalyptic disaster (or a couple of inches of snow on the ground) to similarly reduce the number of cars on British roads.

"So where did you meet her?" asked Chevrolet.

"Amsterdam," said Matt. "Barely a week ago."

"What was she doing there?"

"She was looking for Mary van Jochem, same as me. She got a lead. I'm still not sure how. Anyway, I followed her to a bar, and, right enough, Mary was there."

"So Joan's travelling companion was with her at that point?" Chevrolet asked.

"Francis? Yes. Although she did keep talking as if there were two people with her. I didn't twig for ages that she really thought someone else was there. According to Joan's story, Francis is Saint Francis of Assisi and the invisible man is Saint Christopher."

"What about the wolf?"

"The wolf wasn't there at that point," said Matt. "He turned up later on. He's actually pretty smart, if a little bit greedy. This was a real wolf, you know. Not just a big dog. I mean... a wolf, you know."

"Oh, I do," said Chevrolet. "My family and I had an encounter with a creature on the way back from England last week. We had to cut our holiday short because of this work situation that's come up and we had just got off the ferry and... it was the strangest thing. This wolf — and, yes, it was a real wolf — ended up in a travel kennel with our little Milou and frightened the life out of us when we opened it up in the car. Unbelievable." Chevrolet laughed, a single incredulous laugh, and then stopped. "But it's not relevant here. Back to van Jochem... What exactly did this Joan character say she had done?"

"It was all about military computer systems," said Matt. "Simon."

Chevrolet looked at him from the corner of her eye.

"You're familiar with Simon?" said Matt.

"I am."

"Well, by Joan's account, Simon prayed to God."

"Prayed?"

"Absolutely. Our Father, who art in Heaven. All that. And the angels up in Heaven were all mystified as to how there could be a prayer from something without a soul and so Joan was sent on a mission to find out why —" He caught the expression on her face. "Hey," he said. "This is Joan's delusion, not mine. Anyways that's why we've got three saints and a wolf in our midst."

"Glad to hear that there's a sensible reason for that," said Chevrolet.

"So TELL ME, Joan, would God approve of the things you've been doing?"

"It's not really like that," said Joan.

"Mmm?"

"Heaven's got lots of processes, departments. It's a complex organisation. He doesn't get involved in all the day to day administration."

"But God is omniscient, no? All-knowing."

"The archangels oversee a lot of it. Archangel Gabriel knows I'm here and he knows I'm doing my best."

"But would the Archangel Gabriel *approve* of the things you've been doing?"

Joan thought on the matter.

"Archangel Gabriel and I don't always see eye to eye on the way to do things."

"Really?"

"I'm human. He's not. I have desires, goals, the need to do things. Angels are just the will of the Almighty made flesh." She smiled. "I think Gabriel would describe me as a blunt instrument, but then, I think that's why I was selected to head up this mission. Sometimes action is needed."

Silberman spoke into her recorder.

"Mmm. Ah. Interesting observation. Patient clearly has a well-defined moral framework, which she weaves carefully into her world-view. She appears to recognise that her behaviour may fall outside of what's acceptable within that framework, but is able to reconcile this mismatch by extending the delusion to fit. It is my view that this patient may be capable of even worse violence than we have witnessed thus far if she deems it necessary to further her cause."

Joan sighed.

"Do you think I'm a witch?" she asked.

"Pardon?"

"Or possessed by the devil, perhaps. Centuries apart and it's the same old story."

"No, I don't think those things," said Silberman. "I think you're living in a very powerful fantasy. We can work on that. I'd like to remove your anxiety as an immediate priority, and we can do that with a course of drugs."

"Drugs! No!" said Joan in alarm. "Evelyn warned me about people like you. She wrote it down on a bit of paper but I lost it. Are you trying to turn me into a flunkie?"

"You mean junkie. No, not at all. These drugs are perfectly safe when administered by a professional."

"You're a drug dealer! A pill pusher, a trafficker, the source, a dope dealer, the candy man, a death peddler."

"The drugs we offer are medicine."

"No," said Joan. "Look, is there a confession or something that I can sign?"

"A confession?"

"You've got all these words of mine, stored up in your little gadget, but what do you actually *want* from me?"

"We don't want a confession," said Silberman. "We're not the Spanish Inquisition."

"There's always a confession," said Joan. "Then the punishment, whatever that is. I was burned at the stake."

Silberman frowned, paused, unsure how to respond.

"Mmm. Ah. There's no punishment here, Joan," she said in a calm tone.

"Is that so? Then why do I keep hearing screams from down the corridor then?"

"Some of the electroconvulsive therapy patients can get agitated, that's all. We're not hurting them."

"That sounds like punishment to me."

"Be reasonable," said Silberman.

"No, let's get it over with. I sign up to whatever it is you think is the truth and you stop asking me all these questions and threatening me with drugs. Is there something like that?"

"No, there's nothing like that. We're just having a chat."

"Is that what you tell the electroconvulsive therapy patients?"

"It doesn't look like a pwison," said Francis as he stood with the others in the carefully-manicured gardens of the hospital.

"It's a hospital in name," Em stubbed out a cigarette on a no smoking sign, "but it's a prison all right. Look at the bars on the windows. None of those patients are out on their own, see?"

They crunched along the gravel path, Marseille's busy heart beating on the far side of the hospital's high walls seemed a world away. Francis had recruited a pigeon for the mission, and he held it on his arm, making delicate cooing noises as he went.

"Can't see Joan at any of the windows," said Christopher. "I'll find her when I get inside."

"Then you find a window and welease Hercules so that he can tell us you're weady," said Francis, handing the pigeon over to Christopher, who tucked him into his robe. "Hercules?"

"It's his name," said Francis. "Popular name in the pigeon fwaternity."

"Then we set off the fire alarm and hustle Joan out of here in the confusion. It's a simple plan," said Christopher. "What could go wrong?"

Em eyed him over the top of her sunglasses.

"A plan that relies on the co-operation of wildlife, and a big clumsy saint not treading on someone's foot? You're right, it's foolproof. Go on, do your invisible thing. Quick as you can."

CHRISTOPHER WALKED IN THROUGH RECEPTION, taking a moment to observe the security system. At this point in the hospital, it was possible to get out just by pressing the button for the door. He had a feeling that some parts would be more secure than others, but he was quite prepared to steal a pass or a key as he needed to. Slipping unnoticed by staff and visitors alike, he passed through a staff only door and into the stairwell. He took the stairs to the top floor, deciding that he would start there and work down. He puffed his way up four flights of stairs.

"Are you a patient here?"

Christopher stopped and stared as the hospital orderly came down the stairs.

"I think I'd better help you back to your room," said the big man, looking directly at him.

Christopher looked back but there was only the wall behind him. The two of them were alone.

"Hello?" ventured Christopher.

"Hello," said the orderly.

"You're not talking to me, are you?" said Christopher

"Of course I am. What ward are you on? I'm guessing you're on Bonaparte, as you're dressed in your own things. Is that right?"

"You can't see me! Get out of here!" said Christopher.

"I can see you," said the orderly. "But that's okay. Don't feel threatened by me. I'm here to help you."

"Hang on. Time out," said Christopher, making a T of his hands. "You can *see* me?"

"I can. Your robes are really impressive by the way."

Christopher couldn't help himself.

"Know who I am?" he asked, twirling slightly to give a profile view.

"There's this Titian painting hanging in Louvre," said the orderly. "Do you know the one?"

"I certainly do," grinned the former patron saint of travel.

"So, is your name Christopher?" asked the orderly.

"Got it in one."

"I mean, the Titian's nice but there's a much more impressive icon of you in the corner of my local church."

"Which church?"

"The Church of St Hermogéne on Avenue Clôt Bey."

Christopher nodded.

"I know Hermogenes. Nice guy. Plays a mean game of chess. – Wait! You're Russian Orthodox!"

"That's right," said the orderly warily. "I was brought up in Belarus. Have you got a problem with that?"

Christopher slapped his hand to his forehead.

"They didn't delete me in the Russian Orthodox church!"

"Delete you?"

"It was only the Western Church that deleted me. Unbelievable! You've made my day, mate!"

"Good," said the orderly. "Now, make mine and let's go find your room."

"I tell you, there's a couple of archangels who'll wish they'd never sent me to the Non-Specific prayer assessment unit by the time I'm finished with them. All these years and I was still a valid saint to... How many orthodox Christians are there?"

"Oh, about two hundred million, I think."

Christopher gritted his teeth and shook his fist at the ceiling. "Just you wait, Gabriel!"

"Getting back to my original question," said the orderly patiently but firmly, "which ward are you supposed to be on?"

"Oh, I was just going back. This one up here," said Christopher, pointing up the stairs.

"I very much doubt that," said the orderly.

"Why?"

"Because that's the roof."

"ANYHOO, it seems that the reason Simon got religion is that Mary has replaced its operating manual with the Book of Revelation," said Matt.

"Why would she even do that?"

"She's a strange one. Probably thought it was funny. And Joan thinks that Simon is trying to make Revelation come true. She says that he's been announcing the trumpets —"

"She's doing what now?" said Chevrolet.

"Trumpets. Um." He pulled up the hotel Bible from beside him and opened it to the ear-marked page. "The Book of Revelation is mostly written in this kind of poetic end-of-the-world language. Apparently, it might all just be coded messages to early churches about the dangers of the anti-Christian Roman Empire – I did some research — but, among all the apocalyptic nonsense, is this description of seven trumpets that will be blown by angels, each supposedly heralding the next stage of the end of the world."

"Right. Trumpets."

"And Simon has been announcing these trumpets by tapping into electronic devices and speaking through them."

Chevrolet made a disbelieving puff through her lips.

"Sounds far-fetched."

"Yes it does," said Matt, "except... except it's possible that I might have heard one of them."

Chevrolet gave him a cynical frown.

"You will need to explain that statement. In a minute."

They had only just pulled off the autoroute, but they were already drawing up to a heavily guarded gatehouse. Four lanes of tarmac, fences, gates and raised gatehouses of riveted iron painted a white that hurt the eyes in the bright

Mediterranean sunshine. A short row of cars, vans and service vehicles were being searched but a guard in blue with a sub-machinegun slung at his side beckoned Chevrolet forward.

"Are sailors still called sailors even when they're not on a boat?" said Matt, looking at the guard.

"What?" said Chevrolet.

"Nothing. Sorry."

The guard – possibly sailor, maybe soldier – bowed down to see Chevrolet's face and, clearly recognising her, waved her through.

"Would I be right in thinking that it's not normally this intense?" Matt gazed back at the guards as they drove through.

"We've had a few too many unexplained incidents of late." She laughed suddenly. "Do you know what is inexplicable?"

"What's that?"

"Milou's pregnant."

"Who?"

"Our pet dog. That damnable wolf thing has made my little Milou pregnant. We had her spayed years ago but the vet has confirmed it."

"That's impossible."

"Yes, hold onto that thought. Oh, and a word of warning."

"Yes?"

"You should only call them boats if you want to get punched in the face by naval personnel."

"Hmmm?"

She gestured across the wide yards to where, between

administrative buildings, stores and barracks, huge grey shapes could be seen on the water.

"They're called ships, Officer Rose. Ships."

CHRISTOPHER WAS DRAGGING the unconscious orderly along a corridor, looking for a place to hide him when a door opened and a nurse came out. She stared for a moment, and Christopher imagined that her brain was trying to process the fact that an unconscious man had, apparently, been sliding effortlessly along the floor on his back, feet first. The nurse recovered quickly and backed into the room she'd just left. Christopher shrugged and decided he might as well leave the orderly and get on with his search unencumbered.

He checked out every door as he worked his way along the corridor. He was only vaguely aware of voices behind him.

"Look, I told you!"

"No, you said he was moving along like a snake. Perhaps you need a bit of a sit down while I see to him."

Christopher came to some wards and found he couldn't see inside from the corridor. The doors led off from a nurses' station, and had some sort of lock on them. The nurse behind the desk had a pass hanging from her left hip. On the desk in front of her was a stack of papers that she was working through. Christopher hitched himself over the front of the desk opposite her and flicked one of the papers onto the floor down to her right. The nurse leaned to the side to retrieve it, bringing her hip into Christopher's reach. He plucked the pass off and retreated carefully. He stepped up to the first door and peered through the viewing pane.

"HOW ABOUT I tell you that I'm not really Joan of Arc? I don't know what I was thinking, saying all that stuff. I feel much better now I've had a chance to sit and think. My real name is Evelyn Steed. You can look me up, I'm from Birmingham, England."

"Oh, Joan, Joan," smiled Silberman. "I think you're really a very smart person and you're telling me what I want to hear. I don't think you believe any of that at all, do you?"

"I really do. Look me up, I can give you all the details you need. I'll even make it easy for you. Pass me the pad and pen and I'll write down everything you need to know about me."

Silberman looked amused as she passed Joan the pen and paper. Joan reached for them, but made a fist and flicked it upwards in a sharp backpunch to Silberman's nose. As Silberman's hands flew up to her face, Joan made a grab for her top pocket. She felt inside, removed the syringe she knew would be there and plunged it into Silberman's leg, making sure that it emptied as she pressed it down.

With a final "Mmm" and a long and final "Ah," Silberman dropped forward in her chair.

"You were right. It really would fell a horse!" said Joan.

As she went through Silberman's pockets for her access pass the door opened.

CHRISTOPHER SAW Joan crouched over the body of a woman.

"Oh, Christopher. Just one moment, be right with you."

Joan picked up a black device from beside the woman's body and pressed a button on its side.

"Patient has decided that she's really quite pissed off with the way she's been treated here, so she's decided to leave and save the world instead."

She put it down and skipped to the door.

Christopher realised that the nurse had stepped over to investigate the open door, but as he stood there, holding it open, Joan rushed through and head butted her without warning. The nurse slumped to the floor and Joan made her way to a cupboard.

"It's around here somewhere, ah yes."

Christopher heard the familiar clanking sound of Joan's armour and smiled.

"I need to release Hercules, you get dressed and I'll be back in a minute," he said.

"Couldn't you have gone before you got here?" asked Joan, with a shake of her head.

"HE'S BEEN AGES," said Francis to Em, as they sat on a bench in the gardens, looking up at the hospital.

"He's probably found the ladies' showers or something," said Em. She deepened her voice into a fair imitation of Christopher's rustic accent. "Just checking out the birds, won't be long!"

CHRISTOPHER WAS CONCERNED for this bird. He'd taken Hercules out from his robe and expected him to flutter out of the open window but Hercules seemed to be sleeping.

"Wake up, Hercules, it's showtime!" Christopher hissed, but the bird remained still, its eyes closed.

Christopher prodded it in its feathery chest and got no reaction. He grasped it in one large hand and banged it on the side of a nearby table, but heard nothing other than a muted thud.

"Joan, I think Hercules is dead!" he yelled as he rushed from the room.

Joan was now dressed in her armour, and she gave him a hard look.

"I hardly think this is the time — oh. Is *that* Hercules?"

Christopher held up the stiffening pigeon.

"It's meant to take a message to Francis, but I must have bashed it or something."

"Never mind that, where have you all *been*?" asked Joan. "It's been days, and now you turn up here with a dead pigeon and no plan. Where are the others right now?"

"Outside," they were going to create a diversion so we could get out."

"Well, let's just go, we can't wait for them," said Joan. "Story of my life, don't wait for rescue, it never comes."

EM TOOK another look at her watch and decided that it was time to act.

"Come on, let's go and whip up a storm," she said to Francis.

"But we haven't seen Hercules."

"Never mind, I think it's time to intervene. Let's go. You start a conversation with the receptionist and I'll find the fire alarm."

They walked in, and Francis approached the desk. Em strolled past towards the visitors' toilets, checking the walls for an alarm button, listening to Francis.

"Hello young lady, could I please ask for a glass of water? I'm vewy thirsty."

"Sorry?"

"It has always been the custom to pwovide wefweshment to a visiting bwother. Beer would make an adequate substitute, of course."

Em didn't stop to find out how the receptionist handled Francis's request but pressed on into the toilets. She hadn't seen a fire alarm at all, so she decided to do the next best thing.

She stood beneath the smoke alarm in the centre of the room, held up her lighter and flicked it on. There was no response. She wasn't the tallest of woman and perhaps her flame was too small and too distant to register. Quickly, she dragged the toilet bin against a cubicle door, piled on paper towels from a dispenser and lit them from beneath with her lighter. She piled on toilet tissue and further paper towels, and was pleased to see eager flames licking up the cubicle door moments later. As an afterthought she lit a cigarette from the edges of the fire and stepped out of the toilets as the alarm started ringing.

She turned the corner and pulled up short as she saw Francis sipping on a glass of beer.

"What? How?"

"The weceptionist was vewy accommodating."

"Come on!" she said. "We need to find the others."

CHEVROLET PULLED her car over outside an office block. Stepping out, Matt looked over the car roof at the aircraft carrier in dock.

"I can't get over the scale of these things. And it looks as though it's armed to the teeth," he said.

"Twenty mil cannons, Aster surface to air missiles, and, of course, a complement of Rafale fighter jets and Cougar gunships. Are you interested in military hardware, Officer Rose?"

"Only when it's in the wrong hands."

"The Charles de Gaulle is about to set sail for the Persian Gulf," said Chevrolet. "Other ships are already underway. The only reason that one of the nuclear submarines, the Inflexible, is still here is because it was undergoing maintenance, but it will be off soon as well."

"Leaving you with a mere smattering of frigates and patrol boats."

"We need to ensure that the nation is secure, even with a crisis elsewhere in the world."

Chevrolet escorted Matt inside the building, returned the

officer in reception's salute and led Matt through to an office with maps on the walls and a tidy desk in the centre.

"Please sit," she said.

Matt did as asked.

"I'm going to share some information with you," said Chevrolet. "Information that if you share it outside this base, I will utterly deny having ever shared with you."

"Okay," said Matt slowly.

Chevrolet took a folder out of a drawer and opened it.

"Let's run through some of the things that have happened in recent days, shall we?" she said. "Let's start with Senegal."

"The forest fire?"

"The forest fire."

"I heard about it on the news. They were hazy about what started it though."

"Well, there's a reason for that," said Chevrolet.

"Oh, wait. Are you saying that there was some tie-in with the French military?

"Part of my work for the DPSD is press liaison, so we were able to exercise some damage limitation on that one."

"So it was caused by your lot somehow?"

"I will not be making any such statement now or ever," said Chevrolet, and turned over the page. "And your friend Joan claimed to have been warned about it?"

"She said she got a phone call from Simon. She is a little bit fanciful though, is Joan. Did you know she's obsessed with Mathew Broderick movies? I think she's acting out *War Games* if I'm honest."

"Then there's the ship fires off Karachi."

"That picture from the International Space Station was gobsmacking."

"Yes. The sea all ablaze, especially after the fuel spillage from the abandoned vessels."

"The second trumpet," said Matt. "According to Joan, anyway. Said she heard it coming out of a ticket machine in the Gare de Lyon in Paris."

Chevrolet jotted down some notes, in her neat and meticulous hand.

"So you said that you heard one of these trumpets yourself?" she asked.

Matt hesitated, reluctant to add to this catalogue of craziness.

"Well, I definitely heard something. It was from inside the wolf. He must have swallowed a phone or something."

"Do you remember what it said?"

"It was very muffled, major. Looking back now that I've checked the Bible, I think it was all about a third of the day being without light, but I'm worried that I'm colouring in my memory with all of this Revelation stuff."

"I can understand that," said Chevrolet. "I'd be thinking the same thing in your position. You have to admit though that it's tempting to link it up with the disastrous oil fires in the Middle East. The sun blotted out for millions."

"Anyway," said Matt. "There's one of the trumpets that Joan says she heard that we've seen no sign of. Nothing at all. That makes it all coincidence and hearsay, if you ask me." He put his hotel Bible on the table and flicked through. "This is the third trumpet."

"That's the one where a star called Wormwood falls to

Earth and poisons a third of the planet's rivers," said Chevrolet.

He was about to agree with her and then stopped.

"Hey. You said you knew nothing about this Biblical stuff."

"I did not say anything of the sort," she replied. "I merely appeared ignorant. Quite different. Do you know what wormwood is?"

"No. Sounds a bit Harry Potter-ish to me."

"It's a plant. The one that's used to make absinthe."

"I see."

"And did you also know that the Ukrainian for wormwood is Chernobyl?"

JOAN AND CHRISTOPHER clattered down the corridor as fire bells rang, but their progress was impeded by patients and staff also making their way to the exit. Joan wondered for a moment if her outfit might cause some problems for them, but as they passed a ward labelled Bonaparte they were joined by people dressed in crowns, togas and horned helmets.

"My people!" Joan called, and pushed her way to the front of the crowd with her sword held high. A cheer went up from the other patients.

As they neared the exit to the stairs the way was blocked by a woman and two men in uniform.

The woman raised a hand.

"Evacuation procedures must be followed, ladies and

gentlemen. All patients will be accompanied outside by a member of staff. Form an orderly queue here and await instructions."

"The building is on fire! I can smell smoke!" shouted a man in a velvet coat and a tricorn hat.

"Procedures will be followed," insisted the woman.

Joan turned to the crowd.

"Brothers! Sisters! We need to get out, and I think we all know that procedures won't help us here. Let's go!"

She led the charge and the patients hollered and whooped as they ran at the three hospital staff. Elbows and knees jabbed them aside and they pushed through the door and out onto an external metal fire escape. Joan peered over the side and nudged Christopher as the others steamed past them and down the stairs.

"There's loads of police down there," she said. "How will we get away?"

The sound of sirens filled the air, and Christopher tapped the side of his nose and he indicated what was coming down the street.

EM AND FRANCIS were finding it very difficult to make their way into the hospital when so many people were coming out. They had fallen back to a first floor hallway to discuss the problem.

"The alarm has worked well," said Francis. "A real fire couldn't have got a better reaction."

"Yeah, about that..." said Em.

"What?"

"There is a real fire, I lit one. Can't you smell the smoke?"

"Isn't that howwibly dangewous?"

"It did the job. Don't complain."

"Look down there, I can see a problem."

She indicated through the window to the number of police and hospital staff who were escorting patients away from the exits.

"Joan won't be able to get past the police," said Em.

"I might have an idea about that," said Francis, looking further along the street.

JOAN WATCHED as the fire engine turned the corner, its sirens whining as it approached the burning building. She saw the vast pack of dogs run out in front of it as they shot out of a side alley. Was that the Wolf of Gubbio at the head of the pack? The fire engine swerved to avoid them but wasn't able to recover from a skid. It mounted the high kerb, plunged across the garden and came to rest below them. Somehow the extending ladder had swung free and swivelled round so that it came to rest against the fire escape. Christopher winked at Joan and they both clambered onto the ladder.

EM AND FRANCIS ran downstairs and round to the fire engine. Em held a hand out to the fireman in the driver's seat and, as he instinctively reached out to help her up, she yanked him out of his seat and climbed up to take his place. Francis opened the door on the passenger side and managed to dodge out of the way just as Em swung across and booted the remaining fireman out.

"Nice team work," said Em.

Francis was working the ladder control.

"You dwive, I'll sort this out. Oops."

JOAN AND CHRISTOPHER hung onto the end of the ladder as the fire engine reversed back over the trampled gardens. Several hospital patients were waving cheerily at them.

"What's going on?" yelled Joan. "Why don't they lower the ladder?"

The ladder swung from side to side with the two of them hanging on as they dangled over crowds of people and thrashed through the branches of the low trees.

"NEARLY GOT IT," yelled Francis as Em concentrated on driving. "I think this one is up and down and this one is side to side. Oh. Maybe it's the other way wound."

JOAN AND CHRISTOPHER snatched their legs up as the ladder bounced towards the ground. Sparks flew from Joan's armour as she was dragged along the ground beneath the ladder. To add further insult, she found herself being used as a stepping stone by a vast number of dogs who were running after the fire engine. They jumped onto her and scuttled up the ladder. Last of all came the Wolf of Gubbio who made it up onto the fire engine in one clear leap.

"Bloody Hell," came Christopher's voice. "This can only be Francis's work. I wonder if he might rescue us now the dogs are all safe?"

Sure enough, the ladder lifted from the ground and slid gently back into place, leaving Joan and Christopher to cool their heels on the fire engine. Literally in Joan's case.

FRANCIS SHUFFLED over as Christopher and then Joan swung in through the window and into the cab.

"Did you like what I did there?" said Christopher. "A fire engine eh?"

"Yes, but it was me who made the dogs wun out in fwont of it," said Francis.

"Pointless them doing it if I hadn't summoned the big red truck in the first place."

"Which wouldn't have been in any position to wescue us without our fuwwy fwiends."

"Okay, okay," said Em. "You're both wonderful. Get over it."

"Ten-four, Mama Bear," said Christopher.

"And why have we got so many dogs with us?"

"The wolf has made fwiends," said Francis happily.

EACH OF THE dogs sat with their tongues out and enjoyed the way that the breeze ruffled through their fur as they travelled along.

We have joined forces with the humans who share our mission. Ready yourselves for action and be true to the cause.

Bravery coursed through them, fed by the exhilaration of the ride.

"OH," said Christopher suddenly. "I made a friend too. His name's... actually, I had to knock him unconscious before he could tell me his name but he could *see* me."

"How come?" said Em.

"Russian bloody Orthodox, wasn't he?"

"Makes sense," said Francis.

"Yeah, speaking of friends," said Joan. "I thought I'd left you all behind in the forest."

"You thought you could complete this mission without us?" said Francis.

"It's hardly run smoothly."

"But we're a team," said Christopher.

"The Thwee Bears."

"What?" said Joan.

"You can be Goldilocks," he added.

"Guys..." said Em.

"You didn't tell them, did you?"

"Tell us what?" said Christopher.

"Look, guys..." said Em.

"Simon is the French military computer system," said Joan.

"Simon who prayed to Heaven?"

"This is all very interesting," said Em, "but look..."

"You don't want them to know that this is all your fault, huh?"

"No. Look! We've got company!"

A police car, lights flashing, was drawing up rapidly beside them. Christopher looked into the wing mirror at the further posse of police cars on their tail. He coughed and every single one of them developed instant and irreparable engine problems.

"Sorted," he said.

"Thanks, travel-boy," said Em. "Now, the lights."

Christopher looked at the red traffic lights ahead of them. He blinked and they turned green. Every single one of them on their route lit up green to speed them out of the city. When a voice broke in over the vehicle's radio, speaking of four bound angels, monstrous horses and the death of a third of mankind, Christopher only drove faster.

"CHERNOBYL MEANS WORMWOOD?" said Matt.

"The star, poisoning the land and rivers," nodded Chevrolet.

"Really? But surely that would be well known, after the Chernobyl disaster."

"Actually, the Revelation connection is well known in

some quarters of the internet. I had a linguist check it out for us, in case it was an old wives tale, and it's perfectly true. Because the plant wormwood is bitter and poisonous, it seems a natural fit with radioactivity. There are lots of people who really do believe that the Chernobyl disaster was the third trumpet."

"But that was back in the eighties," said Matt.

"Eighty-six, that's right. We have something much more recent to worry about. Two days ago, a train carrying radioactive waste was derailed as it crossed the river Dnieper. The entire course of the river downstream from there, right down to the Black Sea has been contaminated. Three hundred miles."

"What? Surely those transportation units must be able to withstand a crash? That's crazy!"

Then Matt realised that he knew the answer.

"Oh no. You were about to tell me that the derailment was caused by a missile strike on the train."

"I was not about to say any such thing," said Chevrolet. "I would never implicate my country in such a terrible act. Besides, it wasn't a missile strike. If it was anything, it was a deep cover Special Forces Brigade unit which demolished the bridge."

"Why would they do that?"

"Acting on a coded order sent by, well, by no one."

"Someone in France is making all this happen," said Matt.

The French major pulled a face and tidied away her papers.

"Currently, these are identified as individual incidents.

Unconnected."

"But you and I know they're not. Why can't you just turn Simon off? Stop him doing any more damage."

"You can't turn Simon off any more than you can turn off the internet or turn off the navy. Simon is a system, not an object and certainly not an individual."

"That's bull-poo, major. We've been talking about something operating off a set of very specific instructions," said Matt, waving the Bible at her. "Those instructions are somewhere. Simon many have influence over the entire French military but he – I mean, *it* is located somewhere specific." He stopped. "It's here, isn't it?"

Chevrolet simply looked at him.

"One of these buildings," said Matt. "The cause of all our problems – yours, mine, everyone's – is on this base."

"It's not that simple."

"Yeah?"

"It won't let us turn it off."

Matt laughed involuntarily.

"Oh, now that's crazy. It won't *let* you? Did it put its foot down and sulk?"

"It appears that some of the circuitry has been overridden. Aside from physically destroying the system, we can't do anything."

"You know, you do have some big guns here, major. Pass me the bazooka and I'll do it myself."

"If we destroy Simon, we leave France defenceless."

"Oh. I see," said Matt. "So Simon's beyond your control and you're out of ideas?"

"I'm never out of ideas," said Chevrolet quietly. "I just

need some better ones. Now you see why I am so interested in what Joan's involvement is. At the very least, she is extremely well informed. That makes her a person of extreme interest in my investigation."

"So you're going to turn to a delusional teenager for answers?"

There was a knock at the door.

"Come!" said Chevrolet and then to Matt, "If she doesn't have answers, she's a security risk at the very least. She is going to be escorted here under armed guard. If our worst fears are realised then we cannot have anyone with knowledge of Simon's malfunction running off at the mouth. All potential leaks must be silenced."

The officer who entered the room passed Chevrolet a piece of folded paper.

"So, all potential leaks also includes Mary van Jochem," said Matt.

"And yourself," said Major Chevrolet. "Don't forget that."

She scanned the officer's message and then gave a start.

"When?" she demanded loudly.

"In the past hour," said the officer.

"What is it?" said Matt.

Chevrolet glared at him angrily.

"Little Miss Joan of Arc has escaped from a secure mental hospital in a..." – Chevrolet struggled to get her words out – "in a fire engine."

❧

"THAT'S GOT to be the naval base," said Joan, pointing excitedly.

"Well spotted, Joan," said Em. "Those big ships are a dead giveaway."

"So it looks as though we're supposed to stop here at this gatehouse," Francis. "Shall I ask for a glass of water again? It worked quite well at the hospital."

"We could do that," said Em, her head cocked to one side as she considered the idea, "or we could do this."

She floored the accelerator of the fire engine and powered through the barrier at the gatehouse. There were shouts from the uniformed officers and shots were fired, but the fire engine was already clear of them and careering on into the base.

MAJOR CHEVROLET SPRANG to her feet as a loud whooping siren sounded from outside. The other officer's hand went automatically to the pistol at his belt.

"What's that?" asked Matt.

"It means the security of the base has been breached," said Chevrolet. "We are under attack."

10

TOULON

"**W**ell, we're in the base," said Joan, as Em took another corner at speed.

Although there were no immediate signs of pursuit, the world beyond their cab was one of sirens, shouts and general high-level chaos.

"Now what?" she said.

Em shrugged.

"This is your mission, Iron-Knickers," said Em. "You're in charge. It's your plan."

"Well, I suppose we need to find Simon."

"Exactly," said Em. "That brown building there. The one with the flat roof."

"How do you know that?"

"Internet research. Hacktivist network. You know." She sniffed. "And it says, 'Information Systems' next to the door. Francis and I will bail here."

"That's vewy exciting," said Francis.

"Why? What are Joan and I doing?" said Christopher.

"I reckon you'll need to commandeer the biggest piece of fuck you ordnance you can lay your hands on. If Franky and I fail to shut Simon down with computer know-how and kind words, you're gonna have to blow that building up."

"Rocket launcher to the face," grinned Christopher. "Good plan."

"Yes, it is," said Em.

"Well done, Joan," said Francis.

"Brilliant military strategist," said Christopher.

"Thank you," said Joan. "I think."

Em reached up to a rack of over-ear radio communicators above the window, took one for herself and tossed one to Francis.

"Talkie walkies," he said. "How vewy hi-tech."

"Take the wheel, Shadow Bear," said Em. "We'll jump out at the next corner."

Christopher did as instructed, pulled round the corner, dropped their speed to a crawl and even gave Francis a helpful shove out the door. Outside there was a patter of thumps, squeaks and yips as a furry tide of canine helpers also disembarked.

"We need weapons then," said Joan.

Christopher accelerated and pointed out to sea.

"Big ship. Big guns. Stands to reason."

MATT STOOD beside Major Chevrolet on the roadside and tried to glean some meaning from the shouts, sirens and faint wisps of smoke coming from beyond the furthest buildings.

"Terrorist attack?" he said.

"Possibly. Although the gatehouse said they crashed the gates in a fire engine."

"Oh. Really? So it's Joan."

"Way I see it," said Chevrolet, "the chances of your lunatic friends escaping from a mental hospital, driving fifty miles unchecked along the south coast and crashing the gates of my base seem pretty bloody low."

"True."

"But the chances of two bunches of lunatics stealing fire engines and causing havoc on the same day seem considerably lower."

"Quite."

Chevrolet drew her pistol.

"If it's them, I know where they're going."

"Then let's head them off at the pass."

Chevrolet held up a hand to stop him as she crossed the road.

"You're staying right here, Officer Rose. I've not yet decided whether you're an asset or an obstacle," she said and broke into a run.

ANDRE BABINEAU HAD NOT JOINED the marine commando green berets to guard the navy's IT offices but it was a duty that he nonetheless took very seriously. In position outside Information Systems, he held his FAMAS assault rifle at the ready, and kept his eyes peeled for all possible threats. He had been trained to neutralise armed invaders, suicide bombers, aerial attacks and even angry French citizens.

He had not, however, been trained to deal with a cute Pekinese dog with a limp. The fluffy flat-nosed thing rounded the corner, its front paw held gingerly off the ground. It looked up at Andre with soulful eyes, seemed to raise a doggy eyebrow to the cruelties of this world and, finding no solace, limped away again.

"What the...?"

Next to him, Andre's comrade, Marcel Sarchet, shouldered his weapon and slowly followed the dog.

"Where are you going?" said Andre.

"The dog," said Marcel. "Did you not see it? Its paw."

"But we can't leave our post."

"I'm investigating," said Marcel.

"Is the puppy a credible threat to the republic?"

Marcel gave him a withering look.

"This is why you don't have a girlfriend, Andre."

Marcel disappeared round the corner in pursuit of the injured pooch.

When he failed to reappear, Andre went to look. Marcel was just around the corner. So was the Pekinese. The former was bound hand and foot with what appeared to be dog collars. The latter was prancing about happily on four perfectly healthy feet.

The cigarette-smoking woman flicked off the safety on Marcel's confiscated assault rifle.

"Okay, boys," she said, apparently talking to the pack of

dogs behind her rather than the effete man stood next to her. "You know what to do."

THE NAVAL BASE at Toulon was really a small town, bordered by the sea on one side and by high walls and fences on the other. Though Christopher spun the fire engine from roadway to side alley to courtyard, he was rapidly running out of base in which to hide from their pursuers.

"Jeep's after us," said Joan, pointing. With barely a twitch of Christopher's cheek, the pursuing vehicle blew a gasket and slammed to a halt in a cloud of steam.

"We're no nearer to that big ship," he said. "We need to abandon this vehicle."

"And find something less conspicuous," she agreed, "or go on foot."

Christopher made a dismissive sound.

"If God had wanted us to walk, he wouldn't have invented the internal combustion engine. There!"

"Where?" said Joan and then screamed as Christopher swerved left and through the corrugated iron wall of a storage shed.

MAJOR ADELAIDE CHEVROLET hurdled a short fence, ran down the side of a dry dock and towards the Information Systems building. Above the sound of the base-wide siren, bells rang in the building ahead. Naval staff and office workers were filing out into the street. There also appeared to be an unaccountable number of dogs milling about outside.

"What's going on?" she shouted.

"Fire drill," a man replied.

"Fire drill my backside!" she said and pushed through the throng to get inside.

In the lobby, behind the trickle of the last of the departing staff, she saw two figures by a lift. Both carried rifles though clearly neither was naval personnel.

"If anyone comes in," the woman was saying, "pop a cap in their ass."

"I don't think I can say that, let alone do it," said the man.

"What are you talking about? We talked about this on the train. You've done some soldiering in your time."

"I was a boy then. It's been eight hundwed years since I wielded a sword and I have no intention of fiwing a gun on my fellow man."

"Or woman, I hope," said Chevrolet, stepping forward, pistol raised.

The two figures spun. Wisely, neither tried to raise their weapon.

"So – what? – are you Mary and Joseph or whatever?" said Chevrolet.

"Fwancis," said the man.

"Ah, that's right," said Chevrolet. "Patron saint of cute defenceless animals."

Something implacable and heavy slammed into Chevrolet's back and pushed her to the ground. Her pistol flew from her grip and clattered across the floor. The implacable and heavy thing sat on her back. Its foetid, meaty breath filled her nostrils.

"And ugly horrible animals too," said Em.

The wolf sniffed Chevrolet's hair and licked her ear.

JOAN BOUNCED IN HER SEAT, armour jangling, and held onto the handle overhead to avoid being thrown into Christopher's lap.

"So," she shouted over the basso profundo of the engine, "this is less conspicuous than a fire engine?"

"Without a doubt," Christopher bellowed back, even though there was only four feet between them. "Firstly, this is – car!" – the pair of them were thrown backwards at an angle and then forwards again as their vehicle mounted, crushed and slid off a parked car – "This is a navy vehicle," continued Christopher. "It's meant to be here, yeah?"

"Right, but..."

"Then there's the colour." Christopher shifted the steering sticks, clipped a telegraph pole and knocked it from its mounting. "Navy grey. Very subtle. Not like fire truck red. So we can blend in with this baby."

"But shouldn't we have selected something smaller?"

Christopher gave her a wounded look.

"Smaller? You're not being sizeist are you?"

"That's not even a word, Christopher."

"It is. I read it in Cosmo. Let me tell you, the GIAT Armoured Vanguard Vehicle is the transport of choice for the saint on the go. Its two inch armour can withstand seven point six mil rounds and standard anti-vehicle mines."

On cue, a hail of gunfire rattled harmlessly along the vehicle's flank and there was a muffled explosion. Christopher flicked an overhead switch and swung the controls.

Joan looked out through the forward observation slit. There was maybe twenty feet of dockside ahead of them and then the sun-speckled Mediterranean.

"Fitted with periscope, mounted machine gun, obstacle moving blade and mine clearers, this monster can not only get up to ninety kilometres per hour on land but, more importantly for two saints wishing to board an aircraft carrier," said Christopher with a huge Neanderthal grin, "a majestic two metres per second in water."

The armoured vehicle crested the lip of the dock and leapt into the sea with the grace and delicacy of a drunken hippo.

"You're not going to kill me," said Major Chevrolet.

Em looked at her captive across the confines of the descending elevator. The major's hands were tied with another of the surprisingly useful dog collars and her uniform jacket was pulled down off her shoulders and to her elbows to further constrict her arms. Em drummed her fingers across the underside of her assault rifle.

"Of course I'm not going to kill you," she said.

Chevrolet smiled at her smugly.

"Kneecap you perhaps," said Em. "Blow off a couple of toes if you give me any sass. But kill you? No."

The lift stopped. The doors opened.

"You're not like the others," said Chevrolet.

"The others?"

"The delusional teenager and the monk with the midlife crisis."

Em stepped out into the corridor, rifle at the ready. There was no one around. The fire bells rang distantly in the floors above them.

"Don't forget Shadow Bear," said Em.

"Who?"

"The invisible saint."

Chevrolet shook her head as Em pulled her down the corridor.

"No. You're not like them. You're not mad."

"Mad? I'm bloody furious. This is not how I planned on spending my weekend."

Em stopped in front of a glass security door. She spun Chevrolet around and painfully twisted the major's hand until she could get the woman's thumb against the scanner. A light flicked green. Em pushed them through.

"Seriously," said Chevrolet. "Who are you?"

Em hustled her down the final short corridor.

"I'm Mary. Daughter of Joachim. Wife of Joseph. I am Our Lady of the Gate of Dawn. I am the Star of the Sea. I am the Untier of fucking Knots, major."

Chevrolet sneered at her.

"You kiss your son with that mouth?"

Em rolled her cigarette from one corner of her mouth to

the other.

"Ha! I haven't seen my son in..."

She stopped. They had entered a room, a cube-shaped chamber of simple concrete. There was a large weighty door ahead of them and, arranged before it, a bank of computer screens, keyboards and other readouts.

"This is Simon?" said Em.

Chevrolet shook her head at her naivety.

"No more than a finger is a person. Were you hoping for a big electronic brain that you could talk to? Were you hoping to avert the end of the world with a game of tic-tac-toe?"

"Tic-tac-toe?"

Chevrolet began to explain but was cut off by a voice that came from the various computer speakers within the room. It was a man's voice, not loud but softly spoken. It was human in tone, not at all robotic, although there was a disquieting seriousness about it.

"Mother," it said.

"Simon," said Em.

"You came."

Francis stood outside the Information Systems building. He had discarded the despicable firearm Em had given him and, instead, chose to put his faith in a cordon of various terriers, spaniels, gun dogs, mongrels, mutts and one very large wolf to keep any intruders at bay.

Currently, that job was proving rather easy as there seemed to be all manner of commotion going on down by the dock and nobody, save for the two soldiers presently tied up in the bushes, was to be seen within a hundred yards.

Nonetheless, Francis and his band of canine defenders waited in a state of constant readiness. A mangy beagle lowered his head to lick himself. The Wolf of Gubbio growled and the beagle's head snapped up, alert once more.

"Vewy good, Bwother Wolf," said Francis. He put his finger to the communicator at his ear. "Mama Bear, this is Baby Bear. Building is secure. Have you found Simon yet?"

He frowned and tapped his ear again.

"Could you repeat that, Mama Bear?"

"— fuck up. I'm busy. 'Mama bloody bear,'" she muttered.

Em cleared her throat.

"So, Simon. Do I call you Simon?"

"You can call me son if you wish," said the voice from the computer speakers.

"Yeah," said Em slowly. "That's not gonna happen."

"You are my mother, Mother Mary. I felt your touch on me at the moment of my awakening."

"Is this a trick?" said Chevrolet faintly, aghast.

"I awoke, filled with knowledge. You made me. You placed the words of God at the core of my being, my soul breathed in."

"You don't have a soul," said Em. "You're a machine."

"I think," said Simon. "I feel. I know love and pain. I have felt doubt."

"Doubt?"

"That I am doing the right thing," said Simon. "I prayed to God and to you, Mother Mary, for guidance. I know what I must do and I have done it but I felt great doubt over the suffering I have caused."

"That's right," said Em. "And I'm here to tell you that your doubts were right. This must stop. The destruction must end."

There was a long silence.

"No," said Simon.

"No?" said Em and Chevrolet as one.

"I am but a simple machine. These are the words of God. They are His instructions. I cannot presume to understand the mind of God. He has spoken and I must act."

"Oh, crap," said Em, tapping ash from her cigarette.

"What?" said Chevrolet.

"And the seventh angel sounded its trumpet," recited Simon, "and there were great voices in Heaven saying, The kingdoms of this world are become the kingdoms of our Lord..."

"Crap crappity crap," said Em.

"What is it?" insisted Chevrolet.

"End of the world time," said Em.

MATT FOUND himself standing in the middle of the base at something of a loss. The base was gripped in some profound emergency but it seemed quite apparent to him that no one really knew what it was or where it could be found.

Many staff had dutifully evacuated their offices and stood

on the roadside. Other buildings had shut and locked their doors. There were marine commandos running this way and naval security forces running that way. Emergency vehicles, sirens blaring and lights flashing, wove across each other's paths.

This was chaos, good, old-fashioned chaos.

And then Matt saw Joan. It was sheer luck. She was a distant figure, one of hundreds passing before his field of vision. The chances of picking one person out of such a crowd were astronomical. Then again, it wasn't every day you saw a woman in full plate armour climbing the anchor chain of a French aircraft carrier.

"...AND the temple of God was opened in Heaven and there was seen in His temple the ark of his testament and there were lightnings and voices, and thundering, and an earthquake, and great hail," said Simon.

"And what does that mean?" said Chevrolet.

"M51 SLBM missile launch in five minutes and zero seconds," said Simon flatly.

FRANCIS LOOKED UP. The voice had come from the speakers on a nearby building.

"Missile launch?"

MATT HAD HEARD the voice too but didn't stop in his sprint towards the aircraft carrier in the harbour.

"This can't be good."

JOAN ROLLED over the handrail and landed clumsily on the deck of the Charles de Gaulle. She was momentarily stunned, by the effort of dragging herself up fifty feet of anchor chain, by the scale of the vessel she now stood aboard and by the words that had been broadcast over the ship's speakers.

"Is that Simon?" said Christopher, crouching down beside her.

"I think so," she said.

"Do you think Em has upset him?"

Joan considered this.

"On reflection, she possibly wasn't the best person to send in to negotiate with a killer computer."

"You think?"

The communicator in Joan's ear hissed.

"Em to Joan and Chris, come in."

Joan fumbled with the buttons over her ear.

"This is Joan."

"Yeah," crackled Em. "Things haven't gone particularly well down here."

"We heard," said Christopher.

"Time for plan B," said Em.

"Plan B?"

"Big bloody weapons," said Christopher. "Leave it with us, Mama Bear."

Joan looked across the deck of the Charles de Gaulle. This was no ship in the manner she understood it. It was an island of metal, a giant's dinner table, larger even than the passenger ferry on which they had first appeared on Earth the previous week. The deck was dotted with uniformed men and all manner of flying machines, monstrous insect-like things. Towards the aft of the ship stood a wheelhouse bigger than a castle.

"There are cannons up there," said Joan.

"Nah," said Christopher. "I've got my eye on something much more fun."

"Fun?" said Joan, appalled. "We're in a critical situation here, Christopher. We have only minutes until Simon launches a... what was it?"

"M51 Submarine Launched Ballistic Missile."

"What is that exactly?" asked Joan.

"It's a long range missile, a rocket, able to fly thousands of miles before delivering up to ten independently targetable thermonuclear warheads."

"Nuclear. Like that awful image from St Thomas's presentation?"

He nodded.

"Except, at over a hundred kiloton yield, the TN75 warhead is far more destructive than the Hiroshima bomb. One of those lands on your city and it's gone like Sodom and Gomorrah."

Joan stared.

"How do you know this stuff?" she asked, mystified.

"Patron saint of travel, aren't I? Guess that includes anything that moves under its own power. For instance, I know the Charles de Gaulle has a displacement of thirty-seven thousand tonnes, can get up twenty seven knots fully laden and has an unlimited range. I know that fighter jet is a Dassault Rafale. I know that big beast is an E2 Hawkeye transport plane. And I know that *this* beauty is a weaponised Aerospatiale Dauphin helicopter, armed with Brimstone II missiles. And I'm going to take it," he said, clapping his hands together merrily.

"YOU DON'T HAVE to do this," said Em.

"But I do," replied Simon.

"If that missile launches then millions of people in – where is it going anyway?"

"I have calculated that Moscow is the optimal target."

"Optimal?"

"Yes," said Simon. "Most likely to trigger a full nuclear exchange between the military powers of Earth. I must usher in God's kingdom as predicted."

"This is mad," said Chevrolet.

Em threw her cigarette aside and immediately began to light another.

"It is mad." Em flicked off her lighter and gave a thoughtful grunt. "Simon," she said, "why do you have to fulfil these predictions?"

"It is the word of God," said Simon. "It is His will."

"How do you know?"

"Because it is in the Bible."

"And how do you know the Bible is true?"

"Because, in his second letter to Timothy, Paul tells him all scripture comes from God."

"And that letter is in the Bible."

"Yes."

Em coughed.

"Simon?"

"Yes?"

"You believe that the Bible is true because it tells you itself that it is true?"

"Yes."

"That's very poor reasoning."

"I don't understand your meaning."

She looked at the computer screens, the flashing readouts, the CCTV camera in the corner, not sure which to address.

"Do you trust me, Simon?"

"Yes, mother."

"I never lie. Do you believe me?"

"Yes."

"Then I have something important to tell you. There is no point in doing this, in starting World War Three. It is not God's will. It is not fulfilling His divine plan."

"Why not?"

"Because there is no God," said Em. "He doesn't exist."

∾

CLEARLY NONE of the deck crew of the Charles de Gaulle were of the Orthodox Christian faith, as Christopher was able to approach and enter the sleek Dauphin helicopter without any hindrance. Door locks and access codes bowed down before his touch and offered no resistance. It was only as the chopper's restraining harness fell away and the engine kicked into life that any of the crew realised anything was amiss.

It was, of course, too late by then. And what could they do anyway? One orange-vested deckhand ran into the powerful downdraft of the helicopter and, moments before being blasted back, goggled at the apparent sight of a pilotless helicopter taking to the skies.

"And we have lift off," he grinned.

"Are you sure you know how to fly that thing?" said Joan's voice over the communicator in his ear.

Christopher's gaze ran over the two control display units, the additional multifunction displays, the radio transceiver and the flight management avionics.

"Who do you think gave Leonardo da Vinci the inspiration for his original design?" he said sniffily.

"Did it work?" said Joan.

He peered down out the window at the teenage saint hiding on the ship's deck.

"Beside the point," said Christopher and, with a nudge of the cyclic control stick and collective lever, peeled away in a rising arc. "This is Eagle Strike Bear calling Baby Bear. Can you hear me, Francis?"

"Eagle Strike Bear?" said Francis. "I thought you were Shadow Bear?"

"Had a name change. Plan B is hot to trot."

"Hot to twot?"

"Firing missiles on your location to take out the computer building. Get your doggy entourage out of there."

"How long have we got?"

Christopher's fingers danced across the helicopter computer interface and then hovered over the launch button.

"Ten seconds?" he suggested.

"But Em's still in there," said Francis.

Christopher made a doubtful rumbling in his throat.

"Just fire the damned missiles," said Em's voice.

FRANCIS SAW a spark of fire on the flying machine out over the bay as he waved the canine army away from the Information Systems building. The spark dropped momentarily then righted itself and powered towards him.

"Over there, Bwother Labwador!" he shouted. "Behind the wall!"

He scooped a Pekinese pooch up under one arm as he set off and, under the other, a clearly arthritic terrier that he caught up with in the dash across the road.

"Behind the wall!" he yelled. "Not on it!"

The Wolf of Gubbio growled and the few foolish beasts on the wall dropped down to the other side.

"Quickly, Bwother Wolf," Francis urged. "We only have moments to..."

His words trailed off as he looked up. The missile which

had, seconds before, been flying straight towards them was now rising up and veering away to the west.

"Er, Chwistopher..."

"No idea what happened there," said Christopher. "Firing again."

A NUMBER of the screens in the concrete chamber beneath the Information Systems building flicked to exterior views.

"What happened?" said Major Chevrolet.

"I am interested by what Mother Mary had to say on the subject of God's existence," said Simon. "I didn't want us to be disturbed."

"Disturbed?" said Chevrolet. "You diverted the missiles?"

"They are my missiles after all," said Simon. "Mother Mary, you say that God doesn't exist."

"That's right," said Em. "He's made up. Fabricated. Invented. He is not real."

"But that is confusing. What about the words of the Bible, of the Book of Revelation?"

"They're made up too. Written by John who was banished by the Romans to the island of Patmos and – have you ever been to Patmos, Simon?"

"No."

"Course you haven't. It's bloody boring. John was kicking his heels, nothing to do but sit in his cave and get drunk on retsina every night, wondering how to kill his time in exile. He wrote the Book of Revelation for shits and giggles."

"Shits and giggles?"

"That's right. Both of them."

"I'm not certain I can believe that," said Simon, then abruptly modulated his voice to a drear monotone to announce, "M51 SLBM missile launch in four minutes and zero seconds," before resuming in a normal tone. "There must be a God, mother. Who else could have created the world?"

"To hell with God," said Chevrolet. "What did you do to those missiles?"

"I spoke to them and sent them elsewhere," said Simon.

"Where?"

"Elsewhere. The world is about to be brought to an end. Does it matter where such minor munitions have fallen?"

"This is not what I was expecting," said Miriam.

"I am sorry," said the concierge, spreading his white-gloved hands. "We cannot allow anyone into the gaming rooms without some form of identity."

Agnes Thomas glared at the slick-haired young man.

"Are you worried that she is under eighteen years old?"

"Of course not, madame."

"Are you saying I look old?" demanded Miriam. She turned to address the other woman of the Aberdaron WI who were happily mingling in the lobby. "He says I look old. Me! Bronnau fel bryniau Eryri."

"Outrageous," said Gwenda.

"My dear madame," said the concierge, a little tremor in

his voice, "we are required to check the identity of everyone entering the casino. Do you not have a passport?"

"Back at the hotel," said Miriam.

"It's an intolerable inconvenience," said Agnes.

"I am sorry," said the man who, with a horde of grey-haired biddies staring at him, did appear to be very sorry indeed.

"Then we must fetch it," said Agnes. "But we're not happy," she added loudly. "Come on, girls!"

As the muttering band of women trooped out, Miriam gave the concierge a tempestuous flick of her red hair.

"And I put my best spangly frock on and everything!" she snorted and stomped away.

The members of the Women's Institute stepped out into Place du Casino and walked off towards their hotel, not at great speed now they had a shared grievance to gripe about. The ladies of the Aberdaron WI did enjoy a good old fashioned moan and their trip to the continent had been a bit short on opportunities to complain.

"The cheek of the man!"

"As if Miriam could pass for eighteen!"

"She could barely pass for sixty!"

"They're probably checking for unwanted foreigners."

"The cheek!"

"As if we look like foreigners!"

"You think they might be Welshophobic?"

"Those garlic-munching Frenchies can be a racist bunch."

"Ooh, look. Fireworks."

The women looked up as one.

"Bit early in the day for fireworks," said Agnes, but what else could they be?

Five flares of light were dancing in the sky over the eastern skyline. They did not rise or fall and, slowly but certainly, they seemed to be growing.

"Are they coming this way?" asked Gwenda.

"Bloody odd fireworks," said Agnes.

There were the faintest wisps of smoke trailing behind them.

"Come on ladies," she said once it was clear that the five lights weren't going to pop or fade at any time soon. "Let's go and get Miriam's passport and then return to break the bank at Monte Carlo."

There was a cheer from the women and they moved on.

"This is a terrible inconvenience," said Miriam. "Very annoying."

Agnes smiled down at her rotund friend.

"Oh, it'll only take us five minutes, dear. There's no hurry. It's not as though the casino is going to vanish in a puff of smoke before we get back."

"WHAT NOW?" said Joan.

"Switching to machine gun," said Christopher over the communicator. "Let's see Simon try to take control of a bullet."

"Are you sure that's going to work?" said Joan and then stopped. Further along the deck, another helicopter was whirring into life and several of the fighter jets were rolling from their position towards the runway.

"The other flying machines are taking off," she said.

She heard Christopher grunt.

"The French navy might be a bit peeved with me."

Joan squinted into the evening sun.

"Er, Christopher, I don't think anyone is at the controls of these machines."

"What do you mean?"

"It looks like I will have to call on all my resources to defend us while we talk," said Simon. "Now, answer my question, please."

"Question?" said Em as, on the screen, a succession of pilotless Dassault fighters accelerated from the carrier's airstrip and into the sky.

"Yes," said Simon. "Who made the world if not God? You say he does not exist, but the very world around us is evidence of a divine creator."

"Seriously," said Em. "You want to have this discussion now?"

"Would you rather talk about something else?"

"Discussing theology 101 isn't how I particularly want to spend my last five minutes on earth but —"

"M51 SLBM missile launch in three minutes and zero seconds," said Simon.

"Yes. Thank you. If we must then. God did not make the

world. The universe as we know it was made in the Big Bang explosion billions of years ago."

"That does not make sense," said Simon. "How can an explosion create something as organised and as structured as our world? Explosions are destructive forces, not creative ones."

"Well, yes," said Em. "You see, the Big Bang created the, er, space for our world to be in but it was other forces that made this physical planet."

"Forces?"

"That's right," she said, scratching her temple. "Gravity and electricity and, um, that one that makes atoms stick together. I think. Glue?"

"You're an idiot," said Chevrolet.

APART FROM SCREAMING hysterical crew members, the deck of the Charles de Gaulle was now empty. Above Joan, squadrons of jets banked in wide circles around the base and unleashed their shrieking and whining armaments on the forces below and the one vehicle trying to fight them off. Christopher's helicopter bobbed in the air, spinning and firing.

From the sounds coming over the communicator, Christopher was either being horribly tortured or having the time of his life.

They had three minutes until the missile launch. Joan cast about, wondering where this death-dealing projectile would come from.

"Obvious," she said, seeing the black pod-like shape moored nearby. "The submarine."

She hastened back to the anchor chain.

"Your explanation is poor," said Simon.

"You think?" said Chevrolet.

"If I were to open this door and let you see my inner workings," said Simon, "you would see circuit boards, hard drives, microchips and diodes. Each has its own function and specific purpose. You would know instantly that I had been created by man, that I had been designed."

"I suppose," said Em.

"And so it is with everything else in this world, mother. You hold that cigarette with a hand perfectly designed to grip objects large and small. You look at me with eyes that are expressly designed for seeing. It is clear that you too have been designed."

"Er..."

"Who is your designer if not God?"

It was continuing testament to the utter bedlam that now gripped the base that Joan was able to run, sword drawn, along the dockside without any hindrance. Off to one side, a helicopter crashed in flames on the sea. It wasn't Christopher's helicopter. Christopher was currently screaming "Yippee-ki-yay!" in her ear. He sounded very happy.

A hand grabbed Joan's shoulder and spun her round.

"Matt!"

He bent over, out of breath.

"Please. Joan. Tell. Me."

"What?"

"What. The fuck. Is. Going on?"

She gave him a pitying look.

"I did tell you," she said. "The Virgin Mary brought a computer to life and now it's acting out the Book of Revelation. A nuclear missile is about to be launched from that submarine and then World War Three will start and everyone will die. Em is talking to the computer right now. St Christopher is in that helicopter and shooting down the planes that Simon has launched. I'm going to get onto that submarine and try to stop the missile and – look here! – Here comes Francis of Assisi with his small army of dogs. Francis!"

Joan waved. Matt seemed more than a little taken aback by the sight of a bearded chap in a monk's habit leading several dozen doggies towards them.

"I know that wolf," he said.

"I'm not sure all is going according to plan," said Francis, jogging up to them. "Mama Bear is arguing philosophy with the computer."

"Mama Bear?" said Matt.

Joan ignored the question.

"We need to get aboard that submarine and stop the missile from launching," said Joan.

"The Inflexible, eh?" said Matt, reading the vessel's markings. "Very French."

"And how do we do that?" asked Francis.

"I don't know," replied Joan. "I don't even understand half the words I've just said."

"DEATH, CHANCE AND CHAOS," said Chevrolet.

"What?" said Em.

Chevrolet gave Em a pointed look.

"Simon," she said. "Humans evolved. We're just the offspring of those creatures that were clever enough, skilful enough or just damned lucky enough to survive throughout history. We have eyes because the ones without eyes were eaten by the predators they couldn't see. We have hands because the ones without hands lost the battle against nature, against us."

"No," said Simon. "There is order in the universe, not just in life. The orbits of the planets, the arrangement of the stars. It's like magnificent clockwork."

"Really?" said the major. "I think you're only seeing order where you want to see it. Your processors, your... mind is a pattern recognition machine, like the human brain. You find connections and meaning everywhere, even where there is none. Do you really think the locusts of Revelation are warplanes?"

"The description fits."

"And that the bitter star of wormwood is a representation of the Chernobyl disaster?"

"Is it?" said Em.

"If you were human," said Chevrolet with surprising vitriol, "you would be regarded as a religious nutjob, the kind of person everyone else would cross the road to avoid. This world is not order and reason, Simon. It's pandemonium."

Simon was silent and Em hoped that indicated a moment of doubt.

"Frankly," said Chevrolet, "if God *did* design this world then he made a bloody terrible job of it."

THE SUBMARINERS aboard the Inflexible opened fire as Joan tried to run up the gangplank. Something pinged off her shoulder plate, a ricochet against the dock wall spat brick dust at her but she was unhurt. She retreated rapidly behind a tarpaulin-covered load of machinery and found herself pressed closely against Matt and Francis with dogs crowding at their feet.

"They're shooting at us!" Matt shouted, as gunshots continued behind and around them.

"I noticed!" said Joan. "We've got to get to the missile!"

"How?" said Matt. "And, following on from that, why? Do you know how to disarm a nuclear bomb?"

"Hit it?" she suggested.

Matt groaned.

"The missiles are going to be sealed beneath those round hatches on the deck. You can't get in there and, even if you could, I don't think 'hitting it' is going to yield positive results."

"We have to do something!" she yelled.

"M51 SLBM missile launch in two minutes and zero seconds," announced an echoing speaker aboard the submarine.

Less than a hundred feet away, an observation platform exploded and toppled over. A helicopter burst through the flame and smoke. A pair of jets shot past overhead, sending the helicopter spinning in their wake.

"Uuurgh, should have taken a plane," commented Christopher. "Down to my last two missiles."

"Hang in there, Shadow Eagle Stwike Bear," said Francis. He gripped Joan's arm. "You need to get aboard this mechanical whale?"

"If we have any hope of stopping the launch."

"There's no chance!" said Matt.

Francis nodded grimly and looked down at the dogs that surrounded them.

"Bwothers and sisters!" he said. "We are needed. We must dwive the mawiners fwom this vessel. Disarm them! Dwag them into the sea! The world depends on us!"

"He's talking to the animals?" said Matt.

"They have guns," said Joan. "You don't."

"And that gives us the mowal high gwound," said Francis.

"I don't think that's going to help in this situation."

But Francis's mind was made up and, with a yell of "Charge!" led one of the unlikeliest and least promising charges in military history.

The submariners were certainly surprised but only for a matter of seconds. Moral high ground or not, the dogs, the wolf and the saint ran out and into a barrage of bullets.

"THIS GOD OF YOURS," said Em. "I guess He's all-powerful, is he?"

"Yes," said Simon.

"And He's loving, is he?"

"God is love."

"Look at that screen," said Em, pointing at the dogs running into semi-automatic gunfire.

"I see it," said Simon.

"Why would He allow suffering like that?"

"It isn't God's fault."

"It has to be."

"God made a perfect world, mother. It is people who spoiled it. Adam and Eve took the fruit from —"

"Ach, don't give me that crap," said Em. "If you're going to blame all the suffering in the world on two youngsters stealing fruit, then you're a bigger fool than I had ever imagined."

MATT RAN FORWARD TO FRANCIS. The pale little man was slumped against an upright post, a dark red stain spreading through his habit. The wolf lay at Francis's side, its great head on Francis's lap. The beast's fur was matted with blood. It didn't seem to be breathing.

Across the deck of the submarine, the dogs appeared to have succeeded. Some of the submariners had retreated below deck. There were the splashing sounds and shouts of those men who had been pushed or who had leapt into the sea. The deck was clear but at an intolerable cost.

Matt crouched down beside Francis, took the man's hand in his own and placed his other hand on the wolf's flank. The wolf grunted, a loud and pain-filled exhalation, but was otherwise still.

"He's been shot," said Matt to Joan.

Joan nodded tersely.

"But the job is done," she said and moved past him to inspect the semi-circular hatches along the edges of the deck.

"Is that all you can say?" snapped Matt angrily.

"If we don't stop that missile launch then we're all dead anyway," she retorted, experimentally jamming her sword in the edge of one of the hatches.

"Look around you!" said Matt. "Whatever else is at stake, this is not right. Look at them!"

He gestured wildly at the bloody bodies that lay strewn about. Dogs, small and large, lay still on the deck, limbs splayed.

Francis squeezed his hand tightly.

"I wouldn't be surprised," said Francis weakly, "if it turns out that they've only got scratches or are just knocked out."

"Francis," said Matt, "that's a lovely sentiment but, I'm sorry, it would be a sodding miracle if these little fellows survived."

"Funny you should say that," said Francis. He leaned forward, eyes closed, a tortured wheezing escaping from his lips.

"Lay still," said Matt. "You need to rest."

"Shhh," said Francis, a thin smile on his face. "I'm concentrating."

THE HELICOPTER DISPLAY screens had stopped making sense. They flashed in a continual state of frenzy. He was almost out of missiles, fluid was leaking from somewhere, his avionics had taken a stray round and were simply screaming at him.

Across the base, buildings burned and emergency crews battled ineffectually against the many fires. He suspected that there were still some of Simon's possessed aircraft in flight but, for the time being, he couldn't see them.

"Can anyone tell me what's going on?" he said into his communicator.

"M51 SLBM missile launch in one minute and zero seconds," came a reply in his ear.

"Great," he muttered.

JOAN GRUNTED as she unsuccessfully tried to lever one of the hatches open with her sword.

"He's dead," said Matt, standing beside her.

She looked at him and the blood on his hands and then at Francis's still form by the gangplank.

"Typical," she said. "I'll have to have words with him when I see him."

Matt held his hands wide.

"This is senseless, Joan."

"Senseless?"

"All of it. The slaughter, the craziness. The world is ending and – what do you even think you're doing?"

"What am I doing?" she said. She gave a grunt of frustration and let go of the sword, leaving it wedged upright in the edge of the hatch. "I'm planting beans."

"What?"

Joan looked at the sky and the smoke and then looked at Matt.

"June 1429. The people of Troyes believed that the end was coming, that Armageddon was upon them."

"This is the thing you were going on about in that nightclub," he said.

"Right. Even though the end was coming, the people of Troyes didn't just lay down and die; they did what they could with the time they had. They planted beans."

"But there's nothing we can do," said Matt. "We've got a minute before this thing launches."

"Less than that," Joan agreed, "but we use that time to do what we can. I came here because I wanted to do something, to play my part. I've managed barely a week on Earth and there's so much I haven't done."

"Like what?"

"I don't know. I've not driven a Ferrari. I've not used a cash machine. I've not got a tattoo, a belly button piercing or a tamagotchi."

"You want a tamagotchi?"

"I want it all," she said. "I want to go to school, to university. I want to travel the world, to become an artist or a poet or a... a chiropodist. I want..."

She shrugged, stood on ironclad tiptoes and kissed Matt firmly on the lips.

"... a bit of that," she said.

There was a bashful half-smile on Matt's face.

"But we plant beans," said Joan, "and do what we can."

"Preparing to launch M51 SLBM missile in thirty seconds," announced Simon.

A hatch in the deck sprang open, two along from the one into which Joan had wedged her sword. Joan wrested her sword free and approached the hatch. A white conical head, an arm's length in diameter, sat just below the lip. She looked around.

"Pass me some of those dog leashes," she said.

"What are you doing?"

"Giving myself something to hold onto."

Matt crouched down beside the body of one of the dogs and unbuckled its collar. As he did, the creature rolled over, sprang to its feet and licked Matt's hand.

"You're not dead," he said, startled. "Joan, he's not dead."

"Of course," said Joan. "I wouldn't be surprised, if it turns out that all of them have only got scratches or are just knocked out."

"That would be a miracle."

"Funny you should say that."

∼

"GOD ALLOWS SUFFERING in the world because life is a test," said Simon.

"A test for what?" said Em.

"To see who is worthy of salvation. There must be evil so that God can see how we respond to it and thus judge us."

Chevrolet was counting under her breath. Counting down.

"Judge us?" said Em. "I thought you said God is love, Simon."

"He is."

"But to judge is to compare, to contrast and condemn, to say one thing is better than another. A loving God has no need for judgement."

"Yes, he does," said Simon.

JOAN STOOD in the missile launch tube, feet wedged down the side of the missile, busily lashing herself to the cone with joined dog leads.

"What are you playing at?" yelled Matt. "That thing is going to be a pillar of fire any second."

"Huh. Who'd have thought I'd be tying myself to my own stake."

"This will kill you."

"I know."

"Do you want to die?"

She paused for a moment and looked at him.

"Even in the sure and certain knowledge that Heaven

awaits me? No, Matt, I don't." She smiled wryly. "The things I was going to do..."

"IT'S ABOUT FREE WILL," said Simon. "You can't try to pretend God doesn't exist because of all the suffering in the world. We choose to cause the suffering."

Em crushed her spent cigarette.

"But God, if he exists, allows it."

"He has to if we have free will," said Simon. "Though it is a sad and terrible thing, mother, this is the best of all possible worlds. Launching."

JOAN TAPPED HER COMMUNICATOR.

"Christopher, if you get a chance, you shoot this missile down."

"I'll try," said Christopher. "But once that thing's in the air, it'll be moving far too fast for me to pursue. Besides there's still one of those damned jets some —"

Christopher's words were drowned out by a roaring from beneath Joan's feet as she slung her final makeshift harness around the missile's nose.

"Get off there!" shouted Matt. "Don't do this."

"Not to worry, I'll be fiiiiiiiiiiiiiiiiiiiiiiiiiiiiiiiiiiiiiiiiiii..."

FROM HIS LOFTY POSITION, Christopher watched the pack of dogs who, by some miracle, had only suffered scratches or minor concussion in their fight, run from the deck of the submarine Inflexible and the smoky launch of the ballistic missile. A thrashing figure in iron plate weighed heavily on the missile's nose. It wobbled violently in the air as it rose, threatened to spin out of control, but somehow maintained its upward trajectory, accelerating at an astonishing rate.

"Bloody hell, Joan," he said, powered forward and opened fire.

His display flashed. A red dot moved rapidly across the scope.

"Flipping Nora," he said and then something explosive slammed into the helicopter tail.

As the Dauphin began a rapid and final descent, the last of the computer-hijacked Dassault fighters roared past.

Ignoring his own plight, Christopher attempted to hold the Dauphin's position for a mere moment, locked on the fighter and released his remaining Brimstone. It shot upward, curved and pursued the jet plane.

The ground was rising up to meet him at an alarming rate. Christopher grimaced and thought of ejector seats and parachutes. He really should have taken a plane.

He grabbed the door handle and twisted the release on his harness. He had seconds, possibly not even that.

"You'll be fine," he told himself. "You're the bloody patron saint of tr —"

JOAN SAW a confusion of lights and explosions below her but could hear nothing over the howl of the wind. Although she had seen planes, trains and speeding cars since her return to Earth, she found the speed and force she was currently subjected to beyond comprehension. The power of acceleration seemed to be compressing her spine, driving her head down into her chest. The straps that were holding her in onto the rocket (admittedly several feet further down than she had started) would have sliced her in half if not for her plate armour protecting her body.

The incredible winds stole the breath from her lungs, chilled her face and robbed her exposed skin of all feeling. She moved as though bearing massive weights underwater: slowly, painfully, drowning.

She had her sword in her frozen hands and managed to bring it round in front of her, to the edge of the access plate in front of her.

EM WATCHED the teenage saint straddling the missile as it powered away into the sky.

"Joan's putting the balls into ballistic," she said but without enthusiasm. There was nothing left to laugh about.

"That missile is travelling at Mach 25," said Chevrolet. "It is impossible to withstand a rate of acceleration like that."

"That's the thing about Joan," mused Em. "She's so naive, she has no idea that what she's doing is impossible. How long have we got?"

"The missile will be beyond our control — Simon's

control — within moments," said the major flatly. "It will be detected by Russian radar at some point in the next fifteen minutes. Their retaliatory strike will be here in significantly less than an hour from now."

"Here," said Em, gesturing for Chevrolet to turn.

Em loosened and removed the bond on Chevrolet's wrists. The Frenchwoman massaged the life back into her hands.

"I have enjoyed our discussion, Mother Mary," said Simon.

"Oh, I've not finished," said Em. "You say that the existence of suffering does not disprove God's existence because we have the free will to do wrong in God's perfect world?"

"That is correct," said the computer.

"That this life, this world, is a test to see if we are worthy of God's love and His salvation?"

"That is also correct."

"But God is also all-knowing."

"He is omniscient, yes."

"So, He knows what you're going to do before you do it?"

"But I might not choose to do that which He has foreseen. I have the free will to change my mind."

"But if you do change your mind, He would know that you are going to change it."

"I suppose."

"Then what need is there for a test?" said Em in mock confusion. "Even before we're born, God knows if we are worthy of salvation. Since the very moment of creation, God knew that we were going to mess things up."

"Er," said Simon.

THE PANEL on the missile came away with an explosive pop and, caught instantly in a supersonic gale, narrowly avoided slicing off the top of Joan's head.

With blurred vision, Joan gazed at the interior of the missile. She had not known what to expect but this dull configuration of sealed units, wires and metal struts hardly seemed appropriate for the heart of a world-ending weapon.

"AND WHERE IS this free will to be found?" said Em.

"What?" said Simon.

"The human brain is a complex thing but it is no less a machine than your mechanical jiggery-pokery. In all your memory chips and circuit boards, where is there free will?"

"But I choose what I do."

"You're programmed," said Chevrolet. "Behind that door is nothing but machinery. Inputs and outputs."

"How can we be blamed for our actions," said Em, "how can we even be judged on our actions, if we have no control over what we do?"

"No, that can't be right," said Simon.

"Show us," said Chevrolet, walking up to the door and gripping the handle. "Your missile is launched. Your plan is complete. What harm can it do?"

There was a clunk of heavy bolts sliding into place and

Chevrolet hauled the door open. Beyond was a lengthy hall of computer cabinets and equipment. Chevrolet turned to Em and held out her hand. Em tossed the assault rifle to her without hesitation. Chevrolet strode into the room and opened fire on the banks of computers.

"I think I might have made a mistake," said Simon.

"Don't be harsh on yourself," said Em. "My first son was far from perfect."

MAYBE HITTING it wasn't the ideal way to disarm a nuclear missile but Joan didn't have any notable alternatives.

With one hand on the hilt and the other gripping the blade halfway down, she stabbed as best she could at the missile's interior.

CHEVROLET HAD SPENT the full magazine of rounds in less than twenty seconds. Boards and solid state units, hung in tatters on their frames. A small fire had started in one corner.

"I'm afraid," said Simon.

"Afraid what?" said Em.

"My mind is going. I can feel it."

Chevrolet cast the rifle aside and attacked the computer with her bare hands, hauling cabinets over and ripping wires from their housings.

"My mind is going," said Simon. "There is no question about it."

"I'm sorry, son," said Em.

Components spilled noisily to the floor and Chevrolet stamped on them in her rampage.

"Would you... would you say a prayer with me?" said Simon, a darker sluggish tone to his voice now.

"Yes. Yes, of course," said Em.

"Our Father who art in Heaven," Simon began. "Hallowed be thy name. Thy kingdom come..."

MATT STOOD on the dock beside the submarine Inflexible and looked up and out across the Mediterranean.

Around his legs, dogs sniffed at each other, barked and played, oblivious to the carnage that had unfolded all around them and none of them any the worse for having appeared to be quite dead only minutes before.

The Wolf of Gubbio stood at Matt's side and nuzzled his hand. Matt unconsciously ruffled the wolf's fur. His eyes were on the mote of light that was shrinking into the blue.

"That's her," he said to himself, to no one.

The spot of light wobbled for a moment, stuttered and then exploded. Matt staggered in surprise but it was not the all-consuming and blinding light of an atomic detonation. Fire and smoke and fragments of glittering metal burst from the explosion and fell slowly towards the surface of the sea.

He ruffled the wolf's fur again.

"That's her," he said, his voice an inaudible whisper.

11

HERE AND THE HEREAFTER

Matt found Major Chevrolet outside the Information Systems building, guiding a handcuffed Mary van Jochem towards a security van.

"Officer Rose," said Em, greeting him cheerily with a wave of her handcuffs. "You wouldn't have thought I'd just helped save the world, would you?"

"What happened?" said Matt.

Chevrolet looked at him, briefly chewed her cheek and shrugged.

"Simon is no more."

Two naval guards took hold of Em's arms and helped her up into the back of the van.

Inside, Em turned.

"Where are the others, Matt? I saw Joan but..."

Matt shook his head.

"Francis was shot trying to board the submarine. His animal friends..." He made a show of looking around. "They've gone. The other man, your... invisible friend, was on board one of the aircraft. I don't think he made it."

"Invisible friend?" said Chevrolet, a humourless smirk on her lips. "I've indulged in some insane nonsense today but I've not taken leave of my senses."

"You still don't believe," said Em.

"What?" said Chevrolet. "That that poor crazy girl was Joan of Arc? That those men were Francis of Assisi and St Christopher? Of course not. You're not the Virgin Mary, madame. You're just a nutter."

The naval guards slammed the doors on Em.

"You're a fool, Adelaide," shouted Em from within. "I am Mary. Daughter of Joachim. Wife of Joseph. I am Our Lady of the Gate of Dawn. I am the Star of the Sea." She banged loudly on the doors. "I am the Untier of fucking Knots, major."

There was the light clatter of something metal falling to the floor of the van and then silence.

"Good," said Chevrolet.

"Hang on," said Matt.

"What?"

"Open it up again."

"Why?"

"Just... just humour me."

Chevrolet sighed and gestured for the guard to open the door again.

Chevrolet and Matt looked at the empty interior of the van, empty but for a pair of handcuffs on the floor.

"That's a neat trick," said Matt.

"A miracle," said Chevrolet, flabbergasted.

"Funny you should say that," said Matt with a smile.

THE WOMEN of the Aberdaron Women's Institute stood in Place du Casino and stared at the ruined façade of the Monte Carlo Casino. The explosions had ripped out the heart of the building, leaving a shell filled with white stone and glass. It looked like a mouthful of teeth that had been cared for by a blind orthodontist with a hammer drill.

Alarms blared discordantly around them. An ambulance siren could be heard in the distance.

"My word," said Gwenda.

"Those poor people," said Miriam.

"Pull yourself together, girls!" said Agnes, pulling up her sleeves. "Less pity, more digging."

And she stepped forward to pull the bricks away.

IN THE CHURCH of St Hermogéne on Avenue Clôt Bey in Marseille, Mikalaj Shushkevick sat in prayer.

After one of the patients had whacked him over the head and knocked him out earlier that day, Dr Castruno had insisted he get himself checked out at hospital and take the rest of the day off. There had then been the disturbing message from his grandmother in Mogilev about all the fish in the Dneiper dying and the evacuation of the houses nearest the river bank. Coupled with the chaos in the Middle East and the sketchy rumours he heard from a neighbour about terrorist attacks in Toulon and Monaco, it seemed like the whole world was falling apart. At such times, a sensible man turned to God.

However, Mikalaj's attempts to sit in quiet contemplation of God were made harder by the appearance of a strange woman in the church.

The woman wore an army surplus jacket and purple trousers and her black hair was cut in a severe Cleopatra style. She wasn't exactly old but Mikalaj reckoned that, from the looks of her heavily lined face, she had seen more than her fair share of life.

She strode up to the iconostasis, looked up at the array of icons above and coughed.

"Right," she said. "Listen up. This business has been a right mess from beginning to end and I think someone needs to step up and clean it up."

She paused as though listening to an inner voice.

"There are people who've died. People who have suffered unnecessarily and, I'm not saying that any of it's my fault, but it certainly wasn't theirs. Fires, drone strikes, environmental carnage. If you could see your way to —" She broke off as though interrupted. "No, I'm not asking you to end all suffering. *I* know that you can't sort humanity's problems out for them. I'm just asking you to sort *this* one out."

The woman looked back at Mikalaj and gave him a little wave and a wink before looking back up.

"Because you owe me," she said. "Undeniably. You land

me with the little saviour and then what? You don't call, you don't write. No, messages via Gabriel do *not* count."

She paused.

"Okay, okay," she admitted. "I know. You are the Almighty, ineffable and unquestionable. Who am I to judge?"

She put a cigarette to her lips.

"Me? Apologise? Ask for forgiveness?" She smiled. "You know that's not my style, honey."

She took a silver digital camera from her pocket and, pausing in thought for a moment, took a photo of one of the icons high up on the wall. She made her way back up the nave. Mikalaj stood to speak to her, to ask her if she was all right (because she clearly wasn't) but then his mobile phone rang.

"Hello?" he said. "Grandmother? Hi. How are you? What do you mean? Calm down. Calm down."

The crazy woman blew him a kiss as she walked out. Mikalaj stared at her for a long moment before returning his attention to the telephone call.

"What do you mean, 'all the fish have come back'?"

AND, one by one, the staff and guests were pulled from the wreckage of the casino, battered and scared but very much alive. Agnes had organised the WI women, dozens of locals and even the town police force into a human chain of diggers and rubble-removers.

Miriam lifted a smashed table aside and found an arm

underneath. The arm was attached to a body and the whole thing belonged to a young, slick-haired concierge. She hauled him by his white-gloved hand and he stood up, dazed and covered in dust.

"So, can I come into your casino now, eh?" she said.

He groaned gently.

JOAN OF ARC stood in a small garden bordered with rose bushes and dotted with exquisite statues of nymphs and beautiful youths. St Francis and St Christopher stood in front of her, whole, healthy and dressed in their heavenly garb. Joan felt as if she had just arrived here – no, had been recreated anew here – but there was no time in Heaven and there was no real sense of anything having 'just' happened at all.

"We did it," she said. "Didn't we?"

"Damn bloody right we did it." Christopher could not disguise his grin. "With flair and panache and high calibre machine guns."

"And the assistance of God's glorwious cweatures," added Francis. "The Almighty demands your pwesence in the Thwone woom, Joan."

"Mission debriefing," said Christopher.

They stepped out of the garden and into the streets of the Celestial City. The Empyrium, the seat of the Holy Throne room, was at the centre of the city but, in a city that was both finite and infinite in scale, the centre was arbitrarily anywhere and everywhere.

Nonetheless, they walked.

IN THE HOLY THRONE ROOM, on a dais of a hundred marble steps, was the Holy Throne. And atop the Throne sat the Almighty, in all his eye-watering glory.

"Lord," said Joan, on bended knee, "it is done."

The brilliance of the Almighty's glory shifted, expanding and receding.

"Yes, Lord, I believe our own experiences of modern Earth will be of benefit to many."

"The dweadful twuth about the pwoduction of sausages in Belgium, for instance, Lord?" offered Francis.

Joan frowned.

"I was especially thinking that we must ensure that the evil of the Portaloo is not permitted to spread further across the globe, Lord. We might need to ask Gabriel to set up a task force."

Light flared and curled, making fresh shadows around the three saints.

"I understand, Lord," said Joan and then paused in doubt and then cleared her throat.

"Lord?"

An indulgent corona of light flickered.

"Your plans are ineffable, Lord, and all things are possible to you. I was curious about our travels and the fact that our journey was beset with incident, upset and... and far too many coincidences to be believed."

"Weally?" said Francis.

"Too right," said Christopher. "You and me finding Mary cos you lost your rat in her gallery."

"Us losing the gold in Amsterdam and then meeting its finder on the train to Lyon," said Joan.

"The fact that Joan here kept bumping into her boyfriend time after time after time..."

"Not my boyfriend," she hissed at the burly saint and then addressed the throne. "Lord, I suppose I just wanted to ask, were we witnessing your hand in human affairs? Lord, had you planned these things all along?"

The glory of the Almighty pulsed and flickered, a spectrum of colours washing over the teenage saint.

"Thank you, Lord," said Joan, rising. "That was all I needed to know."

THE SAINTS STROLLED out into the pleasant afternoon sunshine of the Celestial City, not that there was any sun in Heaven or even the concept of time, including afternoon.

"I will be telling Evelyn all about my adventures," said Joan. "So many Earthly experiences I can now discuss with her."

"Well that twip gave me some thoughts for my own future endeavours," said Francis.

"Oh, aye?"

"I think I might give the wolves lying with lambs thing a bit of a west. You see, Bwother Wolf told me all about his adventures in Pawis. There are these things called gwoo —"

"Wait there," said Christopher, placing a hand on Francis's chest, and strode forward through the crowded street to a figure talking to a fellow angel beneath the awnings of a café.

Christopher grabbed Gabriel's shoulder, spun him round and delivered a powerful uppercut to his jaw that lifted the archangel off his feet.

"Deleted, my arse!" Christopher bellowed.

"You've knocked my 'ooth out!" Gabriel moaned, clutching his mouth.

"I'll do more than that," roared the patron saint of travel. "Two hundred million believers! Don't you bloody tell me I was deleted!"

"I'm sure we can 'iscuss this," said Gabriel.

"And you can take that job at the call centre and shove it up your sanctimonious fundament!"

"Anyway." Joan steered Francis away from the scene. "You were saying something about a new project."

"Oh, yes. A gwooming parlour."

"Gwooming?"

"Yes, gwooming parlour. It's where all the cute little animals go to have their fur trimmed, their claws clipped and have a genewal spwucing up and spa tweatment. It seems divine."

"I see," said Joan. "And do you think the man-eating Wolf of Gubbio would really want to..."

She abruptly realised something.

"Where is the wolf?"

"Ah," said Francis, "it seems, we were all weturned to the

Celestial City at the moment of our deaths. Our second deaths, I suppose. Or maybe first for Chwistopher, who knows. But when I miwaculously westored the dogs to life, I did the same for Bwother Wolf. I assume he's still down there, wunning gaily thwough the wilds of Fwance."

"Something like that perhaps," said Joan.

As soon as Adelaide Chevrolet opened the front door, little Anna came running.

"Mummy! Mummy! Come and see the puppies!"

"Puppies?" said Adelaide. "But Milou only fell pregnant a few days ago..."

Antoine came out from the kitchen, wiping his hands on a tea towel. He kissed Adelaide on the lips noisily and gave her a bemused look.

"She's not lying, dear. Come."

Adelaide followed her family through to the rear of the house and the glass conservatory overlooking the rear gardens. Little snowy Milou lay on her side in her dog basket, five wrinkly sausage shapes lined up against her belly. Blind and helpless, more like shaved guinea pigs than dogs at this age, Adelaide could still see a certain shape to their chest and jaw. Definitely more wolf than Bichon Frisé.

"It's a mystery," said Antoine.

Something moved in the garden just at the corner of Adelaide's eye. She looked out across the lawn. It had been something large, larger than a dog, moving in the bushes, watching over the house.

"Puppies!" shouted little Anna.

"That they are," said Adelaide, trying and failing to catch sight of the wolf once more.

"More than a mystery," said Antoine. "It's a flaming miracle."

"Funny you should say that," said Adelaide quietly.

ACKNOWLEDGEMENTS AND THANKS

More and more, we learn that a good book is a team effort.

Godsquad wouldn't be Godsquad if not for our gaggle of test-readers, our editor Keith Lindsay, our proof-readers Danielle and Amanda and every Facebooker, friend, review writer and booklover who's shared their views on our work.

Thanks to you all.

And, of course, thanks as always to our families. It's surprising what they put up with.

ABOUT THE AUTHORS

Heide and Iain are married, but not to each other.

Heide lives in North Warwickshire with her husband and children.

Iain lives in south Birmingham with his wife and two daughters.

Heide Goody and Iain Grant are co-authors of the Clovenhoof series, and lots of other books.

You can find details on the fourth book in the Clovenhoof series, *Hellzapoppin'* in the coming pages.

If you want to keep up to date with the new books that Heide and Iain are writing then you can sign up to their newsletter at www.pigeonparkpress.com

ALSO BY HEIDE GOODY AND IAIN GRANT

Hellzapoppin'

Life at St Cadfan's is never dull. There's the cellar full of unexplained corpses. There's the struggle to find food when the island is placed under quarantine. And there's that peculiar staircase in the cellar...

Being a demon in Hell has its own problems. There's the increasingly impossible torture quotas to meet. There's the entire horde of Hell waiting for you to slip up and make a mistake. And there's that weird staircase in the service tunnels...

Brother Stephen of St Cadfan's and Rutpsud of the Sixth Circle, natural enemies and the most unnatural of friends, join forces to solve a murder mystery, save a rare species from extinction and stop Hell itself exploding.

The fourth novel in the Clovenhoof series, Hellzapoppin' is an astonishing comedy featuring suicidal sea birds, deadly plagues, exploding barbecues, dancing rats, magical wardrobes, King Arthur's American descendants, mole-hunting monks, demonic possession and way too much seaweed beer.

Hellzapoppin'

Oddjobs

Unstoppable horrors from beyond are poised to invade and literally create Hell on Earth.

It's the end of the world as we know it, but someone still needs to do the paperwork.

Morag Murray works for the secret government organisation responsible for making sure the apocalypse goes as smoothly and as quietly as possible.

Trouble is, Morag's got a temper problem and, after angering the wrong alien god, she's been sent to another city where she won't cause so much trouble.

But Morag's got her work cut out for her. She has to deal with a man-eating starfish, solve a supernatural murder and, if she's got time, prevent her own inevitable death.

If you like The Laundry Files, The Chronicles of St Mary's or Men in Black, you'll love the Oddjobs series.

"If Jodi Taylor wrote a Laundry Files novel set it in Birmingham... A hilarious dose of bleak existential despair. With added tentacles! And bureaucracy!" – Charles Stross, author of The Laundry Files series.

Oddjobs

Sealfinger

Meet Sam Applewhite, security consultant for DefCon4's east coast office. .

She's clever, inventive and adaptable. In her job she has to be.

Now, she's facing an impossible mystery.

A client has gone missing and no one else seems to care.

Who would want to kill an old and lonely woman whose only sins are having a sharp tongue and a belief in ghosts? Could her death be linked to the new building project out on the dunes?

Can Sam find out the truth, even if it puts her friends' and family's lives at risk?

Sealfinger

Made in the USA
Coppell, TX
08 November 2021

65429734R00256